Sufi in Spain

By

G. G. Lewis

By the same author:
Andean Adventures
Kingdom in the Clouds
The forgotten paths of India

Spread a map of Spain on a table and you will soon find Madrid and Barcelona. If it is a good map it won't be difficult to locate Cadiz and Cordoba, with a modicum of persistence Oviedo or Osuna. But no matter how detailed your map, even with a hand glass, you will never find Purusha and Champa or a host of other villages mentioned in this book. The reason is simple. They, like the cast of characters in this novel, don't exist. A Sufi in Spain is a work of fiction and should be read as such. This is not to say that there aren't pages with tints and hints from a life lived, for how else can a writer authenticate what he writes, colour the words he uses other than from the palette of his experience.

In memory of Joe Cole

1

IN THE AGE OF CLASSICAL ANTIQUITY AN EMINENT THINKER WROTE THAT man was the measure of all things. In my time there was another philosopher, a gardener who cut his neighbours´ lawns once a month, a thoughtful fellow who believed that men were like trees. 'Best to let them grow up where they will,' he told me. 'Once they've put out roots, never move them. If you do, you're asking for trouble.' He made an exception with root balls, but that was it. I was fourteen at the time, and that an adult, any adult, might share their golden words of wisdom with me was a delightful honour. He even told me about a mysterious philosophy called Taoism in which a sage could be born in a village, never leave it and yet understand all that needed to be known. His words made sense of the lyrics of '*The Inner light,*' one of my favourite Beatles songs. This was confirmed a few years later, when in the tempestuous height of adolescence, I discovered that the words were directly inspired by the 'Tao Te Ching', the Taoist classic. But somehow something wasn't right. The idea of staying put didn't rest easy with me. In my geography classroom there was a globe of the world that I often spun with my eyes closed. The idea was to stop its rotation with my finger, to see where I landed and then embark on a quest to uncover in the school library as much as I could about the region my blind choice had made. More often than not my finger found a vast ocean, but not always. In this way I discovered the Kikuyu and Maasai tribes of Kenya, the whereabouts of Bhutan, a Buddhist kingdom in the Himalayas, and that Haiti was and remains the only independent state in the world that was founded by slaves. Three exotic soils upon which my adult feet would tread. At such a tender age, it was difficult to know if the game fired an appetite for faraway adventures or if the appetite prompted the game, but the globe spun in me a question I would ask myself a thousand times in the years ahead – who would I have been if I had known birth on another continent?

I respected my Sophist gardener as I respected no other adult in my fourteenth year. He wasn't alone in what he thought. I knew a handful of elderly neighbours who were comfortable knowing they would die where they had been born. A year earlier, on a school field trip to a hop farm in Kent, I had met a seventy-three-year-old farmer who had never been to London, boasted that he had never seen the sea, and in the years to come would meet many like-minded people in the Andalusian village which was to provide my *pied-a-terre* for nigh a decade. But in my heart there was no song of a homebird. To die where I was born was anathema to me. In my twenties I even told friends that I travelled to avoid such a dreadful fate. I was the son of two migrants who had met in London. I was destined to travel, wanderlust coursed through my veins. If, in respect to my thinking gardener, I was akin to a tree, then my roots went deep and straddled the world.

But that's not the reason I give when I'm asked why I left my homeland and chose to live in a small Andalusian village. Nor do I ever mention the irony in knowing that the more I travel, the more deeply I understand the words of my boyhood friend. No, nothing of that sort passes my lips. Instead I talk about a postcard.

2

A TYPICAL SPRING MORNING IN LONDON. RAIN CLOUDS OF SLATE GREY complexion – a lowering sky. I make a coffee and take it to the conservatory to see how the daffodils are holding up. It has been raining all night, the daffodils are wilting, there are puddles on the lawn. I think of my father who died of a heart attack a few months earlier only to realise with the first cigarette of the day that I have three cards in my hand – three aces or peradventure a trio of jokers. I am parentless, childless and without wife. Toying with the image of an open door a poignant flash of freedom sweeps over me. It leaves me with a faint sense of restive impatience. At the very least a break I need. I think of Spain, my favourite haunt in Europe, somewhere I've been over a dozen times.

Almeria airport isn't exactly an international hub. The runway is practically on the beach. As airports go it's pretty relaxed, albeit not without rules. While I'm at a bureau de exchange there's an incident at the entrance to the departure lounge. Egged on by his friends, under the watchful eye of a security officer, a middle-aged English tourist is making a fool of himself by draining every drop of wine from a bottle he's not allowed to take on his flight back to Stanstead.

Outside the airport I'm greeted by palm trees under a piercing bright blue sky. Beneath the lee of a bus shelter I watch the antics of a gecko chasing flies, smoke a cigarette as I wait for the hourly bus to Almeria. If the bus is on time I will only have to wait a couple of hours for the connection to Almerimar. There will be time to have a coffee. I'm already in my beloved Spain, without need of hurry.

It's low season so it isn't difficult to find accommodation. In less than an hour I'm installed in a furnished apartment with a balcony overlooking the marina and the open sea. The town might have a smattering of ex-pats, an Irish pub, bars where Brits can read a tabloid, watch Sky TV, but Almerimar isn't a big resort, no Magaluf or Marbella. I opt for a local bar, order another coffee, *a café con leche* and a glass of brandy. I could have ordered a *carajillo* where the two are mixed, but I prefer to savour my brandy undiluted. Strangely, the Spanish call their brandy *coñac* after the French, even though, in my opinion, it's better than anything found in France. It's nearly two in the afternoon, lunchtime in Spain, but I'm not hungry. I finish my brandy, the equivalent of a triple in England, wander down to the beach, find an abandoned parasol where I can watch the waves. There is no one in the sea as the waves are awash with jellyfish. Nearby, an English family are roasting in the sun. Mancunians if I'm not mistaken. The colour of an uncooked prawn, the mother rolls on to her belly to grill her back as might St. Lawrence. I curl up and try to read a few lines from a novel by Turgenev. The words dance across the page; I'm not in the mood for Russian literature. I could ask myself why I'm here but the euphoria of the brandy doesn't allow me. *Later – there will be time,* my introspection stretches no further. A Senegalese hawker approaches with a tattered suitcase full of fake watches and replica Real Madrid shirts made in Malaysian sweatshops. I tell the perspiring pedlar I've got a watch, when I haven't, that I don't like football, when I do. Undeterred he trundles off to pester the northerners. I linger on the beach until the sun creeps under the parasol.

In my apartment I stretch out on a bed. It has been a long day; a day that began in the dark to catch a cheap chartered flight. I take a late afternoon siesta, my intention a short nap. It lasts until dawn.

A pleasant week passes. I walk up and down the marina, look at the yachts and sailing boats, feed the fish in the harbour too many times to count. 'Good morning Kim,' I'm greeted by my first name in the bar where I take my breakfast. It's all very friendly, in the town, like the bar, but everything is so new, too modern for my taste, a product of tourism, the sort of place where the town hall is planning to build a golf course. I'm told that the resort used to be a small fishing community, but its modest past is buried under hotel and apartment blocks. There are no old churches, no monuments. There's no central plaza where old men in black berets chew the cud; even the girls in the local supermarket speak English. Gabriel, the amiable barman, advises me to visit nearby El Ejido to sample something more Spanish. He tells me that I will find the town interesting, that it's famous for two things – the sea of plastic, the vast expanse of *invernaderos* or greenhouses that from the air look like the sea, and for a corrupt administration. 'Local corruption is rife in Spain, he informs me, 'nepotism a national sport.'

'Not only in Spain,' I respond.

'But the mayor of El Ejido takes the biscuit,' Gabriel pauses for me to admire his mastery of an English idiom. 'He paid over a hundred thousand to a family business to repair a street light. And it gets worse."

How exactly it gets worse I never discover as the talkative barman leaves me to serve a customer. When he returns he hands me a four-page leaflet, tells me I can read about the town, that if I'm quick I'll be able to catch the next bus to El Ejido which leaves in five minutes.

On the bus I read the leaflet, learn that the infamous mayor once brought Mick Jagger and his band to El Ejido, that the greenhouse revolution has turned the province of Almeria into a major exporter of fruit and vegetables, brought prosperity to a region that was once the poorest in Spain. What I don't read, but find out later, is that the wealth is driven by cheap labour, mostly from Africa, that the conditions under the plastic awnings are atrocious, for some, without official papers, bordering on modern-day slavery.

I don't spend much time in El Ejido, perchance an hour. The bus station is teeming with men from the Maghreb, women in hijabs, signs in Arabic. It reminds me of Tangiers. It's much the same in the town, or at least the parts in which I wander. On every street corner I encounter knots of Moroccan men. No one smiles, no one greets me, but I'm aware that I'm being watched. It's enough for me to conclude that the place isn't pretty, unique perhaps, but not particularly Spanish. I step into a bar for a *cana*, a small beer. I'm served by a Romanian woman. The woman is in black, in mourning she tells me. Her Spanish is good, surprisingly clear as she explains how her brother, a forty-eight-year-old plumber by trade, found work in a hothouse when he was down on his luck. Choking on her tears she struggles to tell me how he died of hyperthermia in a temperature that matched his age, that his wife and children were paid his weekly wage as compensation.

At the bus station I'm given the evil-eye from a ragged pair of unsavoury looking Moroccans. As a full-bloodied Londoner I return the unblinking glare, but am glad when the bus pulls out of the station and I'm back on my own patch.

The next day I decide to hire a car. After signing the rental agreement I'm given the keys to a two-door hatchback and a road map. The map will be useful once I know where I want to go. Not knowing where to go isn't an insurmountable problem, abroad I've faced it many times before. Determined to try a travellers' trick, another version of spinning the globe, I head for a shop that caters for tourists. The idea is to examine postcards as they invariably cover local sights. There are plenty of the Alhambra, the Moorish palace in Granada, but I've already seen the hilltop pile on two occasions. The shopkeeper, watching me thumb through endless sunset scenes that could be anywhere in the world, asks me what I'm looking for. When I explain what I'm about he looks at me as if I might be dangerous, but evidently my plan makes sense to a fellow customer, a tall, burly fellow in an ill-fitting poncho. Eyes hidden by sunglasses, his brow by a sombrero, 'Here,' the stranger says in English as he hands me a postcard. It's the postcard I've been looking for. Beneath the snowy peaks of the Sierra Nevada there's a chapel with a crenelated tower surrounded by pine trees, olive and almond groves. I turn the card over and read the word Purusha. I look up from the card to thank the stranger, but he's nowhere to be seen.

'Who was that?' I ask the shopkeeper as I pay for the card.

'I don't know,' he says. *'Un bicho raro.'* It isn't a compliment, for literally it means a rare insect, colloquially, a weirdo.

3

TWENTY YEARS AGO THERE WERE TEN THOUSAND PEOPLE LIVING IN Purusha; when I enter the village the population has dwindled to below two thousand. It's an ancient pueblo, predates Christianity, with extremely narrow streets. I'm held up in one narrow street by a daydreaming donkey. My city self is tempted to sound the horn, but it doesn't seem appropriate in a village that appears to be stuck in the past. Instead I turn off the engine, listen to church bells in the distance, the song of birds, the chirp of locust. At length the donkey moves on, and I'm able to drive up a steep hill, past a cluster of shops into the main village plaza. There's a stone fountain in the plaza around which a few locals sit on benches under shady trees. On one side of the plaza there are terraced houses with balconies bedecked with flowers, on the other side a columned passage in front of the white-washed town hall. Tucked away in a corner of the passageway, with a few tables outside, I descry a bar. And, of course, there's the Catholic church. Towering above all the other buildings the church has a thick, oak door, studded in *mudejar* style to speak of a chequered past. Much as I might wish to have a look inside the church that was once a mosque, there's nowhere to park. Thus in second gear I enter a narrow road off the plaza that takes me to the edge of the village, to a secondary road that leads to a highway that ends in Cadiz. Something persuades me to perform an illegal three-point turn; some might say my inner voice, but I prefer to think it's because I haven't seen the prospect on my postcard. This time I find a parking space in the road that wasn't there before. It's a tight fit, but I squeeze in without harm to paintwork or bumper. Fortuitously, I park outside an *immobilaria*, the office of an estate agent. I try the door, but it's locked with no sign of anyone inside. In London everyone is a film star, appearing on CCTV cameras around four hundred times a day. In Purusha there's are no security cameras, but there are plenty of curious eyes. A widow in black approaches to tell me to pop into Francisca's shop if I want someone to open the *immobilaria*. It seems strange to enter one shop to see another, but I do as I'm advised. Francisca, the middle-aged shopkeeper, seems to know why I'm in her shop. Without asking what I want she's on the phone to Puri, a girl of nineteen, who, I later learn, is engaged to her youngest son.

'Puri'll be here in twenty minutes,' I'm told even though I haven't said a word. 'She's got the key to the *immobilaria*.'

I sit in the bar in the plaza and order a coffee. It's a typical Spanish bar. There's a leg of ham on the counter, a stack of lottery tickets and a picture of a saint behind the bar, a couple of slot machines and a TV on a shelf near the ceiling that's so loud that it forces people to shout. There are about a dozen drinkers in the bar, all men. The only woman in the bar is the owner's wife. In and out of the kitchen, she cooks and serves tapas, small plates of food. No one pays me much attention, but I'm aware that my presence is noticed. I'm not put out, uncomfortable in any way. In small villages I know that any stranger stands out like a sore thumb. As I get up to pay I note a painting of the village on a wall and next to it a framed jigsaw puzzle of the Houses of Parliament reflected in the River Thames. Walking through the plaza I reflect on the curious juxtaposition.

I arrive at Francisca's store on the dot, but there's no sign of her son's fiancé. I'm told that Puri will arrive in a few minutes and soon discover that in Purusha a few minutes means at least thirty.

The house is situated in a steep, twisting alleyway not far from the plaza. There will never be a problem with the sound of traffic for the alleyway is too narrow for a car. 'Anywhere,' is Puri's reply when I ask her where the neighbours park their cars. Word travels like an Australian bushfire in the village – it's already in the alleyway before Puri and I arrive. Rosa and Rubin, a married couple who live a few doors away from the house for sale, are out and about, doing this and that, keen to get a glimpse of the newcomer. The house has so much character it looks like it might be haunted. Built over three floors, it's a labyrinthine collection of rooms, some interconnecting. There are Catholic saints on every wall, votive lights and framed black and white photographs of dead grandparents in stiff poses, wedding scenes, and young men in military uniforms. Every room is cluttered with heavy, old-fashioned Spanish furniture. I probably spend fifteen minutes in the house. I can't remember where the bathroom is, which of the bedrooms has a balcony, a day later, everything is a blur. The only thing that is clearly painted on my memory is the prospect from the belvedere on the rooftop terrace. It's not an exact photocopy of my postcard – there are tiled rooftops in the foreground. But the vista is breath-taking, expansive, panoramic, makes me realise that as much as I love the sea, I love mountains more.

Back at the office I sign a few papers. The owners, Eduardo and Asuncion, an elderly couple, watch nervously as my signature seals their fate as well as mine. It is obvious that the house has been on the market for some time; over a year I discover later, but I don't haggle over the price. Perhaps it's because I'm a foreigner and the owners think I'm rich, or perhaps they think I'm an idiot for not arguing over the price, but I'm offered the furniture in the house for a sum so inflated that I could furnish a small mansion in London for the same amount. Graciously, but with a wry smile I decline the offer. At this point the wife turns tearful. It's not because I don't want her furniture, Asuncion explains between hiccupping sobs. It's because she will have to leave the house where she has lived for fifty years if I buy it. 'It's where my children grew up,' she tells me with puffy, pink eyes. As I believe a house can absorb the impression of its inhabitants, have the wistful experience of passing a house where I once lived, a home of memories to which I can never return, I tell her that I will love her house and look after it and that she can visit anytime. My words seem to comfort her, but the deal is only clinched in her eyes when her husband reminds her that she can't cope with the steep alleyway anymore, that with the money from the sale they can finish and move into the single-storey villa they've been building for their retirement. A villa at the other end of the village – for Hercules barely a stone's throw away.

I'm elated, in a state of shock when I leave the village. *What have I done?* I ask myself with hoots of laughter as I turn my back on the coast and head into the hinterland of Andalusia. Later, when I'm comfortably ensconced in a cave apartment in the small city of Guadix, a place famous for having the highest concentration of troglodytes in the Western world, I have the answer to the question I wouldn't ask myself on the beach in Almerimar. I know why I am here. My heart is revealed by my deeds. I want a new challenge, to live in Spain, to give up my life in London. I'm aware that my decision will diminish the possibility of dying where I was born.

4

I WAKE UP IN A ROOM THAT'S FREEZING COLD, SO PITCH BLACK THAT I CAN'T see my hands. For a moment I wonder where I am; something familiar to a traveller, not unpleasant. And then it all floods back. The room is dark because the shutters are down, the door to the balcony hidden by William Morris curtains, heavy curtains to keep out the draught. It's the room I've slept in for nine months, the time it takes a woman to give birth.

I arrived in Spain at the end of spring when there were still patches of snow on the mountains and the almond trees had lost their blossom. Summer came and scorched the earth, on its heels an Andalusian autumn hotter than any summer I had known in England. Now, I lie under a duvet and three woollen blankets, my feet in socks, tucked under a hot water bottle that has turned cold. I shouldn't be surprised by the weather as I'm in a village perched on a plateau three thousand feet above sea level, flanked on either side by sierras covered in snow throughout the months of winter. In the summer, although it's difficult to believe in August, it's a lot cooler than the coast.

I switch on a bedside lamp, contemplate my steaming breath. I grab my mobile phone and dive underneath the covers to call Carlos, a neighbour, to ask him what's happened to the cement I ordered a week ago. Carlos is a heavy drinker, new to the world of mobile phones. It's no great mystery that it takes three attempts to get through. It's barely past nine, but the background cacophony informs me that he's in one of the sixteen bars in the village, his slurred speech that he has probably been drinking since dawn. I speak slowly, clearly, use my best Spanish, but to no avail. He doesn't understand what I'm trying to say, perhaps doesn't want to. Roaring with drunken laughter, he tells me to speak *Purushi*, the syllable-cutting village dialect. There's no point in continuing the call, so I bid him a good day, tell him I might join him later and then hang up. I'm tempted to stay where I am, but the urge for nicotine has me throw back the covers and head downstairs.

Unlike the modern brick on the first and second floor it's much warmer on the ground floor where the walls are ancient, made of rock, thick as a fortress. Coffee in hand, I repair to the front room, a windowless room, cosy, a bit like a cave. I drag a wooden table with a glass top across the floor tiles to rest by the sofa. It's a common piece of furniture in Spain, all my neighbours have one. A social table, a focal point where families gather to eat, to play cards, to watch TV, to share their thoughts. In Spanish the table is called *'La mesa camilla,'* meaning the little bed table. To me, as an outsider, it was a strange name at first, difficult to understand. But that was before I had fallen asleep at a little bed table in a neighbour's house, unable to resist the pull of somnolence after I'd drunk a jug of wine. After that, and similar social occasions, I realized the aptness of the table's name. By the end of autumn, I was convinced I needed my own *mesa camilla*, covered by a heavy tablecloth called a *mantel*, long enough to wrap around my thighs, and of course a *brasero*, a circular heater embedded in the table's legs, a vital line of defence against the bitter cold of arctic months. In houses with a hearth it's not unknown for villagers to place an old tin bucket under a table to warm their legs with the embers of an olive log. As I'm not blessed with an open fire, my brazier is electric, easier to clean, and I assume less of a fire hazard, especially when I remember to unplug the heater before I go to bed. It's an assumption I'm comfortable with, albeit not water tight, for I'm sure it happens from time to time, but since my arrival in the village I've never heard of a *brasero* setting a house on fire, perchance a tablecloth or a pair of trousers, whereas a local shop was recently burnt to the ground by faulty wiring after the shopkeeper installed a fancy, digitally-controlled central heating system. I know the owner of the shop, Roberto, a fine fellow, always smiling. We became friends when I asked him for a *bomba* instead of *a bombilla*, a bomb instead of a lightbulb. According to some he was gutted to discover the charred remains of his shop, whereas one family, denied credit, said it was dirty business, an insurance scam. In a village broken into clans, where families have lived for generations, such pernicious rumours aren't uncommon. Every villager I know seems to have at least one enemy, a bar or shop, he or she won't enter. Only an outsider is spared, a foreigner without history, a newcomer without family ties, a stranger who doesn't take sides. Much as I might wish that to remain my case, somewhere deep down I doubt if it will.

Under the *mantel* my legs thaw out as I settle back into the sofa to consider the day ahead. It's a Monday morning, a morning I used to dread in London. In Purusha it feels like the beginning of the weekend. I've no set timetable, no appointments to keep, no clients to meet, no one to tell me what to do, the only clock in the house is in a kitchen drawer, next to the cutlery, waiting for a new battery. I could join Carlos, have tapas for lunch and drink all day. I've been down that social road before, and not only with Carlos. It happened quite a bit when I first arrived in Purusha, trying to make friends, accepting invitations to be accepted. But those days are consigned to the past, part of the learning process, in my case the knowledge that a sunlit bacchanalia leads to a fruitless morrow, invariably under the cloud of a hangover. There are plenty of things to do in the house, the two most pressing, tasks incomplete – tiles in the kitchen or the wall on the terrace. That I have a choice is down to Carlos. Under his tutelage I acquired both skills and the confidence to change a tap. He might be a drinker, but he's a man of considerable ability. Like many men in the village there isn't much he doesn't know about building a house from scratch. Need, combined with a paucity of pesetas, is a great teacher. With barely half a sack of cement left I decide to tile, but before I can get started there's a knock on my door to change my options.

'Carlos told me you needed cement. I've brought you a sack,' Diego says without removing a hand-rolled cigarette from his mouth. I try to take the twenty kilo sack from him, but Diego insists on shouldering the weight like a cross to the terrace. 'I want to see the wall,' he tells me. There's no need to furnish Diego with directions, he knows the layout of the house as he was born in my front room – a third or fourth cousin of one of the previous owners. Trailing behind him on the *caracol*, the spiral staircase that leads from the first floor to the terrace, I'm appalled by a gust of foul wind that breaks out of his overalls. The faux pas isn't followed by an apology, for Diego, approaching his fifties, is a natural fellow, *'un nino del campo'*, a country lad who insists faeces is the best fertilizer so shits in the fields outside his mouldering caravan, uses a leaf to clean up rather than toilet paper. It's a belief I've encountered before, common in the Tibetan community of Ladakh. *Who am I to argue?*

'Hardly China's Great Wall,' Diego concludes after giving my knee-high work the once over. 'It's not even straight,' he adds, and then tells me I haven't been laying the bricks correctly and that Carlos is a bad teacher. I take the criticism lightly, for I know it's not personal, but directed at Carlos. They might be great friends, in some obscure way, like nearly everyone else in the village, interrelated, but they are also rivals. In their early years, before the devil of drink moved in, the pair of them were considered the best builders in the village. I've been told they were in such high demand that they had more work than they could handle. Sadly, their heydays are history, their off-the-cards careers, more so for Diego than Carlos, washed away in waves of wine. The final straw that broke Diego's reputation happened a few months before I arrived in the village when a neighbour asked him to hang a door to a storeroom at his *finca* or farmhouse. Not a difficult task for an experienced builder. But that night Diego didn't turn up at the agreed bar to collect his wage, no one knew where he was. It was a local mystery, but short-lived; solved the following day when the neighbour returned to his *finca* to find Diego fast asleep in the storeroom, his face and hair covered in flour. Apparently he had got so drunk on the job that he had put the door on the wrong way, and with no handle on the door had locked himself in. There was no window to the room, no lightbulb hanging from the ceiling. With nothing to eat or drink for twenty-four hours, he stumbled on a sack of flour, ate his fill, and then used the sack as a pillow, hence the ghostly appearance when he was found. An amusing story that would have reached a few ears, hadn't the neighbour taken a snap on his mobile of Diego's blanched face and then shown it to everyone he knew. According to Carlos, for a few weeks his friend was the laughing stock of the whole village, no one used his name, everyone called him *el fantasma*, the ghost.

'Tienes fuego?' Diego asks me for a light for the cigarette he grips with his teeth. But then he changes his mind, flicks the dead butt to the floor, tells me to fetch him a beer. 'I'll show you how to lay bricks.'

When I return from the kitchen with a cold beer Diego has already mixed a bucket of cement. He drinks the beer while the cement settles and then begins to work, laying half a row of bricks in the time it would take me to lay one. 'Don't listen to Carlos. That's the way to build a wall,' he says, throwing the trowel into the empty bucket. I thank him for his lesson, forbear mentioning that his method is exactly how my teacher taught me.

Relieving himself in the sink in the belvedere, he washes his hands before he shakes mine, tells me he has to go, that Carlos is waiting for him in a bar. At the front door he asks if I want to join them. I decline the offer, tell him that a glass of wine is too much for me, a bottle not enough, if I drink I won't lay a brick, that I come from a culture where people drink to get drunk. My confession elicits nothing but a puzzled look. It's only when he's at the twist in the narrow street, about to disappear, that he turns back with a reply. 'Why else would anyone drink?

I'm still on the ground floor when Diego returns a minute later. He tells me he forgot to ask, that he needs a loan, ten euros will do. Gladly I hand over the note, even though I know I'll never see it again. Diego may have his faults, but he's a generous soul. He has bought me several beers in the past; in fact, when his pockets are full he buys everyone a drink.

A friend who slept under my roof in the summer told me a story about the second world war. According to my friend a prominent member of the war cabinet often retreated to his country estate where he built walls to escape the terrible burden of office. I don't know if the story is true, but it makes sense, for I too have found a peaceful retreat in laying bricks.

Before the cement runs out I finish Diego's row, one of my own, a few bricks on top. It's no great return for over two hours' sweat, but when I stand back to admire my work I'm filled with immense satisfaction. It's something to do with the tangibility of a wall, an achievement made solid. The wall is just above my waist, but with another five or six rows I will have complete privacy on my terrace. In an old Moorish village where everyone looks over someone else, where the white-washed houses tumble into one another like giant stepping stones carved out of a mountain it's something I need. Most of the villagers have ancestral land on the fringe of the pueblo, somewhere to escape prying eyes. My terrace will be my land, my private sanctuary beneath the stars. It's where I will sit late at night to contemplate the milky way, look across the village rooftops to the snowy mountains and fall asleep with dreams of Moors and the Barbary coast.

A week later, I'm in my kitchen brewing tea in a pot, when Carlos turns up at my door. He's obviously drunk, but I'm pleased to see him.' This is for you,' he says as he puts an old two-litre plastic Coke Cola bottle full of *mosto* or new wine on the table in my front room. 'You helped make it,' he adds, as if I need reminding. How was I to know that the wooden wine press had arrived in the village ten years earlier than I had, that I needn't have removed my shoes and socks, rolled my trousers up to my knees to squelch grapes with my toes. 'No toes in my wine,' Carlos reads my thoughts as he takes a swig from the bottle. 'Want some?' he pushes the bottle in my direction. I shun the pleasure; tell him I've just made a pot of tea. Carlos takes another swig as he contemplates a man who prefers tea to wine – it's beyond his experience, something he can't make head or tail of. 'What have you been up to?' he asks, to change the subject.

'I've finished the tiles in the kitchen.'
'And the wall?'
'The last brick I laid was last week when I ran out of cement.'
'But Diego brought you cement!'
'One sack.'
'One!' Carlos explodes, 'I paid him for six.' He simmers for a silent moment, but another slug of *mosto* seems to calm him down. He tells me that he still wants to see the wall, adding with a sneer that he will deal with *el fantasma* later. Clutching the bottle of wine, he stands by the table to find his balance before zigzagging through the front room to the staircase. Outside, under the mid-afternoon sun it is still warm enough for me to sport a T-shirt, but Carlos has the shivers. My wall is given a cursory glance; I'm told I've done a good job. He asks what bricks Diego laid. When I point out the half row he gets on his knees to examine his rival's work. 'He didn't use a spirit-level, did he?'
'No.'
'I knew it.'
'Knew what?'
'His bricks aren't straight,' he smiles, shaking his head. *'Una chapuza!'* he uses a word that means slapdash, a botched job. They look straight enough to me, but arguing with a man who has an issue standing upright, who rocks on his feet as if on a boat isn't my strongest gift. I offer him a seat to secure his bearings. With the sun beating down on his pate he lifts the bottle to have another drop. Perhaps it's

the sun, but he has a problem finding his parched lips, pours the wine through his snowy-white beard on to his chest. He's as drunk as a lord, but still not as drunk as the first time he came to my house.

It was my first week in the village and I had a burst pipe. The plumber I had called failed to turn up ten days in a row, leaving me without running water, reliant on Rosa and Rubin to provide buckets of water so I could make tea, wash, flush the loo. What made matters worse was that I couldn't locate the leak as the pipe was hidden, embedded in a wall of concrete. I had a pickaxe a neighbour had lent me, but in truth I hadn't a clue. When Carlos arrived on the scene with a *disco,* an angle-grinder, I thought my prayers had been answered. But I was wrong, for what happened next in my kitchen, when I have the courage to look back, still sends shivers down my spine. Like a scene from '*The Texas chainsaw massacre,*' Carlos careened out of control with the lethal spinning top in his hand. Somehow, after mastering the paralysis of disbelief, I managed to unplug the *disco*. But like anyone who has witnessed a miracle I had to sit down after the experience to find composure. How the wall tiles weren't decorated with gory flesh, how there were no severed limbs scattered on the floor, no rivers of blood, I will never know. I'm convinced, had Bertram Russell been there, he would have become a believer.

'You want some wine?' Carlos, struggling to keep his eyes open, asks to break my morbid memory. I decline, point to my mug of tea.

'Carlos, you are falling asleep.' I touch him lightly on his shoulder.

'*Si,*' he replies sleepily.

I wonder if I should put a cap on his head to protect him from the sun, but then I hear his name called out in the street. It's his sister-in-law, summoning him to the midday meal which in the village can be as late as three. 'Carlos, Rosa's calling you,' I shake him by the arm.

'She is?' he asks with unwarranted surprise for he eats with his brother's family every day. It's the routine that saves him, for without their support he would probably live on tapas, without cause to leave the bar, drink until he dropped. 'How's Cassie? is she coming back? he asks, climbing to his feet.

'I don't know.'

'Oh,' he responds with a single syllable, seeing sadness in my eyes. 'Don't worry about the cement,' he says with a gentle slap on my arm.

Alone, I sip my stone-cold tea, linger on the terrace to enjoy what's left of the day. The sky is cloudless, the peaks of the sierra in sparkling splendour under the winter sun. An eagle glides into the valley below the village. I follow the hunter's flight of graceful circles, watch it dive like a kamikaze pilot, hover as a hummingbird, and then swoop to snatch a rabbit. Nature is beautiful, but brutal. I recall a time in Tanzania, on safari with Cassie, when we saw a pride of lions bring down a buffalo. A mature bull with magnificent horns, too dangerous to kill outright, the lions attacked from the rear, ate it alive. We witnessed the whole hour, the time it took for the animal to die with a lion's head buried in its back. We saw it all. Cassie cried, said it was murder. When the driver, our guide for the day, said it was nature, God's way, she snapped at him, said no, unless God was the Devil. She knew we had to stay, pay in nightmares for a memory we would never forget. At the lodge that night she refused dinner, said the need to eat was a curse. *Poor Cassie. So brave.* When she was in Spain, everyone, including Carlos, loved her. I miss her deeply, her insights, her humour, the warmth of her body in my bed. It hurts me to know that I hurt her at Granada airport when I said no when she offered to stay.

I'm still on the savannah, the leonine banquet banished, reliving other, more pleasant moments with Cassie, lost in maudlin thought, when my phone bursts into life, causing me to jump. '*Digame*', I answer, expecting a Spanish voice, but the call's international, from George Burroughs, my estate agent in London. He calls me Kim as if we're old friends, tells me he has had an offer, only five grand short of my asking price. He says the market's tough, it's a good offer, chain-free, trying to convince me his concern is for me not his commission. He doesn't know the deal is done, he can't see the smile plastered across my face. But I don't much care for his profession. I fall silent for a few moments, make him sweat, before I put him out of his misery. Relieved, he says he will be in touch as soon as he has got the papers sorted. I put the phone back in my shirt pocket, feel as light as a feather. That the sale will put bread on my table for years to come is a weight off my shoulders, but I'm moved more to know that when my house has gone I've really burned my bridges. I think of Bill, a great painter, a good friend over the years. He said I'd be a fool to sell up. Let the house out, he advised, in case it didn't work out in Spain. When I told him I'd fain tempt fate on a tightrope across the Grand Canyon rather than in a circus tent above a safety net, he grimaced, said that I was going through a mid-life crisis. His sage conclusion was that I was lost, until I convinced him I couldn't be, as I didn't know where I was going. I'm tempted to call him. My right index finger hovers over the keypad. I can imagine the consternation on his bearded face when I share the news, tell him that Dr Johnson was talking about himself when he told his friend Boswell, a man tired of London is tired of life itself. But, of course, it's Cassie I ought to call, of all my closest friends, the only one to really understand my quest for new pastures. When I apprised her of my plan, she laughed heartily, told me about a man who slipped from a mountain on a moonless night, how his hands turned bloodless clinging to a rock until the sun rose to reveal a terrace a foot below his feet. 'You are and aren't that man,' she said, 'you love risk, but if you slip you wouldn't hang on to a rock; you'd let go, trust life to land you on your feet.' I have the phone in my hand, but I hesitate, aware that we haven't spoken since the summer. We hardly spoke on the journey to Granada, and once there, at the airport, only a few sad words. Everything had been said the night before. 'It was now or never,' she said. Her time had come, at thirty-seven, she wanted a child, and me to be the father. After an intake of breath, I tap in a number I know by heart. The phone rings in Hampstead four times before I'm invited to speak after the bleep. I leave my message, one word, *shraddha*, a Sanskrit word Cassie taught me; a wonderful word that means faith, not in God but life, the sort you need to jump into the unknown.

The following day, I find five heavy sacks of cement stacked against my front door that weren't there when I went to the bank. It hadn't been my plan, but I'm flexible, can respond to the moment, have the energy to work. I drag the sacks into the reception, carry them one by one up to the terrace. While the first batch of cement settles, I prepare a flask of coffee, stuff a baguette with tomato and cheese. I drink and eat, smoke a cigarette, and then I lay bricks, one after another, row upon row. My mind, quietened by unwonted labour, pays little heed to the passing day. When I finish my hands are trembling, my clothes, my shoes splotched with cakes of cement, my hair, tied back, knotted by grit. With five new rows, two more than I've ever managed, the wall's complete. But I don't stand to admire my work. My tribute is to sit on my terrace under an open sky, for the first time know what it feels like to be on my rooftop without being seen. I light a cigarette, survey the sierras, watch the dipping sun break through a swirl of lenticular clouds to paint the peaks a golden hue. I find a new face in a crevice beneath a snow-tipped crag, the face of a giraffe in the shifting shadows. I'm happy to find the face, but then in a moment of unbidden sadness ponder the fate of a prisoner, the count in a nineteenth-century story who discovered solace in a little flower he found growing between flagstones in his prison cell. In need to share my fortune I phone a friend. 'Hello,' an unfamiliar voice comes on at the other end. I wonder if I've misdialled, but when I ask to speak to Cassie, the man says he'll call her. I can hear music, perchance Mozart, muffled voices in the background, but the reception's too poor to catch what's being said. When Cassie comes to the phone she congratulates me after I tell her I've accepted an offer on my house, and that I've built a wall. I have to ask her twice how she is, the second time after the first is followed by silence.

'I'm pregnant,' she says.

'Goodness!' is all I can manage.

'It doesn't show, it's only two months,' she says. 'Tony's the father. He answered the phone.'

'Tony! Your old flame?'

'The very same.'

'Well, congratulations Cassie. It's what you wanted.'

'It is,' she says quietly. And then there's an awkward silence, until I tell her it's cold on my terrace, that I have to go. Her last words are, 'I miss you.'

My last words, 'I miss you too.'

Before I leave the terrace, I look again upon the mountains, but the light has shifted, the face I discovered gone.

5

'WHAT THE FUCK!' BILL'S POSH VOICE DISAPPEARS IN THE THUNDEROUS ROAR of several hundred rockets set off simultaneously in the plaza. It's the night of Saint Jerome, the patron of my Catholic village; the night the sleepy pueblo of Purusha turns into a madhouse. When the rockets are spent there's a wild cheer, followed by a concatenating chain of deafening firecrackers that circle the main square; a firework display in an enclosed space so violent that tiles fall from rooftops, framed photos from walls. Briefly I lose my friend in the ensuing fog of cordite smoke, the press of villagers jumping up and down to welcome their saint out of the church. When I espy his Harrovian boater in a sea of behatted faces it takes me more than a minute to reach him.

'Did you enjoy the fireworks?' I ask.

'Yes and no,' he replies. 'Yes, now that it's over. No, while it was going on. Why didn't you warn me?'

'And spoil the fun!'

'Fun! I was petrified. When I felt the ground shudder I thought the church tower would tumble.'

'I've been told two chimneys fell one year.'

'Now, you tell me,' Bill responds with a nervous smile. 'That would never be allowed in England – Health and Safety would be on to this village like a ton of bricks.'

I laugh loudly, in agreement, for I had the same thought on my first St Jerome night. 'But it's different here,' I point to the camera crew from Canal Sur packing their equipment away on a balcony overlooking the plaza. 'Let's go,' I pull Bill by the arm into a doorway to allow the holy procession passage. 'It's going to be a long night.'

Our first port of call is to a house at the top of a steep street with a cusped archway on the other side of the village. The house is the home of Steffi, a twenty-one-year-old girl of considerable beauty, but the *escritura* or deeds are in the name of Blanca, her fifty-year-old mother, a local woman with a touch of Italian blood. The house is large, two houses knocked into one, spread over three floors. On the third floor there is a self-contained flat wherein, a seventy-year-old Catalan, Steffi's father, Blanca's ex-husband, spends his days. The Catalan's name is Manolo, but he's called Adolf behind his back. It's a nickname he has earned by eulogising everything German, oftentimes at the expense of the village, telling the locals that Germany has better women, better beer, that everything is better in Deutschland, from their football to their cars. Most of the villagers avoid him, think he's mad. I relate all of this to Bill before we reach the house, to put him in the picture. But my friend is a curious man, intrigued by tales of my village, he wants to know more. So I tell him that in my opinion Manolo is not a happy man, unlike the man he was, when he first met Blanca in a German car factory in Barcelona. How he never talks about Barcelona, so that everything I relate comes from Blanca. How he fell for her, an attractive Andalusian woman on the assembly line, how he used to wear a suit and tie, strut around the factory floor as if he owned the place. How they married in a church after a brief courtship, became parents a year later. How, against Blanca's wishes, he named their daughter Steffi, an unusual name in Spain. How the marriage went well for the next two years, until Manolo, who had been studying German for several years, was offered a new position in a Bavarian factory. 'She told me he said that it would bring in more money, but she wasn't concerned about money. She was happy in Spain and didn't want to go abroad.'

'And,' Bill prompts me when I pause to light a cigarette.

'The pair argued for weeks, Blanca with words, Manolo resorting to fists. She never knew that he had already accepted his promotion, accepted on the day it was offered.'

'He never told her?'

'No. That revelation lay in wait. He told her to think things over, take Steffi, spend a weekend with her parents. When she got back she returned to an empty flat. Her husband had gone and with him most of the furniture including the television, the pots and pans, the cutlery, even her bed.'

'A coward,' Bill shakes his head.

'He left his wife and child practically nothing, not even a note.'

'What did she do?'

'Unable to face the factory floor, she packed what little she had and with her two-year-old daughter returned to the village where she was born and bred. Nothing was heard from Manolo for eighteen years, no letter, no maintenance, no birthday card for Steffi, not a word. And then, out of the blue, he appeared at Blanca's door one very cold wintry morn. An old man now, with sunken cheeks, red-rimmed eyes, barely able to stand. "What do you want?" Blanca asked him without inviting him in from the howling wind. When he told her he'd returned to be a father she flew into a rage, almost hit him.'

'But he's here now.'

'He put up in a hotel for two weeks, returned to Blanca's house every day with a new ruse to get his foot in the door. He told her that he had changed, that he was a generous man, that his days were numbered, that he was a dying man with a fat pension, that Steffi needed a father, he tried every argument he could think of, but Blanca wouldn't budge. And that's when he changed his strategy, turned his attention to Steffi, showering her with expensive French perfume, boxes of chocolate and flowers, a promise of a pearl necklace after he had told her that he had always loved her. The poor girl was shaken; I saw it myself. She was confused, didn't know what to do, cried herself to sleep. I knew, and Blanca knew Manolo's game, but it broke her heart to see her darling Steffi torn apart, and so out of love for her daughter she relented.'

'So the fox wheedled his way back into the family.'

'But Blanca set conditions. He would live in his daughter's house not hers, pay rent for the flat, hire a maid to clean up his mess, a private nurse when needed, and if he ever upset Steffi would be shown the door.'

'A lucky man.'

'I couldn't agree more. In the twelve months he's been in the village his health has considerably improved - at least outwardly. He can shuffle to the local shops without a walking stick, he's got a new hearing aid and has put on weight courtesy of Blanca's cooking. However, inwardly, I'm not so sure. Every time I meet him he tells me he misses Germany, it's order and cleanliness. His biggest gripe against the village is dog poop. It's everywhere he complains, adding that the only time he's seen a dog owner pick up a turd was an old man who used his bare hand to put it in his pocket.'

'I can't wait to meet him.'

On a night that will last beyond dawn, it's early when we arrive at the house, barely nine, and yet the place is packed with villagers, most of whom are already drunk. Blanca and Steffi are delighted to see us, usher us like royalty to the table of tapas. It's a magnificent spread, from goat's cheese dipped in honey to Iberian ham; there's even popcorn for the kids. When I ask, out of politeness, about Manolo, Blanca tells me he's probably dreaming about dog shit because he's gone to bed. I marvel that anyone would consider going to bed early on St Jerome night, can sleep through the racket of the fiesta, the unending screams of exploding rockets, the sirens of car alarms being set off, but then Blanca winks at me as she refills our glasses with *ponche*, a liquor-laced punch. It's a conspiratorial wink that reminds me that Blanca controls her ex-husband by controlling his medication, that she spikes his food when he makes conjugal requests, asks for his passport or bank card. When I describe the set up to Bill he's shocked, says it's like the movie *'Whatever happened to Baby Jane?'*

'It's not as bad as that,' I laugh. 'Blanca has to control his finances. When he was in charge he never paid his bills. He gets his laundry done and meals thrown in with the rent. And besides he's a real handful. I don't know how she copes. A few weeks ago, on the road to Granada, he defecated in her car, soiled his pants on purpose.'

'He did?'

''I'm afraid so, and not for the first time. According to Blanca he gets pleasure from ruining her day. But it didn't work this time, his plan backfired. She kicked him out of the car and drove off. The Guardia Civil found him wandering up and down the hard shoulder of the motorway three hours later. And then there's another trick he plays, gets his penis out in front of her, pisses on the floor and then tells her to mop up.'

'How do you know all this?' Bill asks, but before I can tell him that village life is like living in a soap opera, the Devil himself appears on stage, making his entrance from a side door at the back of the room. Clearly befuddled the old fellow struggles to find a familiar face in the smoky atmosphere. Like his dentures, he's forgotten his glasses, without which he's as blind as the proverbial bat. His hair on end suggests a bird of paradise, his black and white pyjama top a prison, but it's not what he's wearing, but what he isn't that starts the sniggering. Naked from the waist down, he begins his awkward journey across the room, bumping into bodies, knocking drinks over, stepping on people's feet. A woman he shoves in the ribs says 'Heil Hitler!' When he starts to bawl like a baby for Blanca I know it's time to leave, wondering if this is the night she will show him the door.

Outside in the street it's bitterly cold. We stand by one of the huge bonfires that are blazing throughout the village. While warming our hands, Bill, still giggling, asks me why Blanca wouldn't go to Germany. 'I asked her that,' I reply. 'She told me that she couldn't live in the land of the Nazis.'

'That's not PC.'

'PC isn't high on Blanca's agenda,' I laugh. 'But then she lives in a country where Matamoros is a fairly common surname. There's even a village called Matajudios.'

'Good heavens! *Kill Moors! Kill Jews!*'

'In fairness, there's a campaign to change the name of the village.'

'And a campaign to get rid of the surname?'

'If there is, I haven't heard of it.'

21

'And I thought Brown Willy was bad,' Bill laughs. 'And Pratt's Bottom.'

When a rocket whistles above our heads, ricocheting off a wall into a tree we decide a bar is safer than the street.

'What's wrong with these people?' Bill asks, nodding in the direction of an elderly chap in a Stetson, setting off rockets from his hand.

'The villagers think a hand-held rocket sent to heaven bestows a blessing.' I answer.

'How odd!' Bill looks mystified. 'And dangerous!'

'Very,' I readily agree. 'Last year someone got greedy, set three rockets off at the same time and lost a hand. Another year, a neighbour of mine lost half his nose.'

The thought of someone setting off a rocket from a nostril stops Bill in his tracks. He can't help but ask for more details.

'It was in the plaza. The man wasn't wearing a hat. Unfortunately, he forgot that what goes up comes down. Tomorrow we'll find plenty of charred sticks on my terrace. I want to grow peppers in the summer, I'll use them as supports.'

The Olive bar is usually the quietest bar in the village - on an ordinary night somewhere old folk play cards, catch a game on the box. But on St Jerome's night everything's different, ordinary doesn't count. Tonight the TV's off, the bar's full of music, there are children with the pensioners and every age between. It takes a fair time to secure a beer, even longer a seat. But our repose is not long lived, for when a popular flamenco song comes on we are dragged to our feet. Bill is a good sport, up for the game, much keener than I am to join the gipsy ring. When it's his turn to dance in the centre, he lets out a yelp of *ole*, does a quick spin and then hops from foot to foot. I might be more familiar with flamenco steps, know how to snap my fingers and shuffle my feet, but I'm relieved when it's over. But it isn't over for long. I'm barely in my seat, when Ivana, the sole Ukrainian in the village, loops her scarf around my neck, and then as if I'm a fish at the end of her hook, tells me I must dance. Chivalrously I accept her hand, but I'm wary of the girl, especially when she starts to wiggle her hips like a seductive stripper. That her sixty-year-old beau, Ricardo, the richest man in the village, is dancing on a nearby table surrounded by middle-aged housewives egging him on, might explain her sensuous moves, it does little to relieve my discomfort. Then, just as I begin to panic that Ivana's getting too worked up, ready to bump and grind, our dance, mercifully, comes to a sudden end. A timely end, occasioned by the arrival of the St Jerome band whose music is so loud and discordant that it can't be challenged. 'Thank you Ivana,' I say, and quickly return to my seat. Bill, who has been studying my face, is in fits.

'I won't ask,' he says, with a roguish smile.

It's in the front room of a local butcher, our fourth open house, that I catch sight of Maria. She's with her sister, her brother-in-law, and their two children. I would like a moment with her, a few words, but there are at least thirty people between us, maybe forty, so instead I wave to which she responds by blowing me a kiss. Martha, the butcher's wife, watches the exchange with interest. 'Careful with that one,' she says for no apparent reason, and then pulls me aside, presses against me, tells me that her husband smokes far too much marijuana. 'In this very room, just a few nights ago, I caught him talking to the wall. "Reveal yourself," he said, over and over again. At first, I thought he was talking to me, had heard me get out of bed, knew that that I was hiding behind the door. But no! He thinks the house is haunted.' Why Martha is telling me this, where it's leading to, remains a mystery as the subject is swiftly dropped when her husband, the ghost-hunter, muscles his way through the merry gathering to join us.

Rafa is ginger-haired, a rarity in Andalusia, a short man with a fondness for tall stories. He once told me he went out for a drink and didn't come home for a year. Never shy of the superlative, his house is the oldest in the village, he knows the richest family in Madrid, the sexiest drag-queen in Seville, the most dangerous crooks on the Costa del Sol. I imagine him as a kid, addicted to comics, dressed as the caped crusader when he was put to bed. He tells me to tilt my head back to sample the best vino in the village. The jet of wine stains the white-washed wall behind me, splashes my cap, my chin, before it hits the back of my throat. My palate might be dead after so many hours spent drinking, but I play the butcher's game, tell him it's the best wine I've ever tasted. A friend of the hyperbole, he roars with approval, isn't put out when I decline a second shot from his goatskin *bota*. When *the host with the most* leaves my side, momentarily alone in the party, I turn to the far end of the room, scan the faces to find the one I fancy. But I turn too late, only in time to see Maria slip through a side door that leads to the street. She leaves without her family, her sole companion a swarthy, handsome man with black curls and golden earrings.

We pass the Red Cross ambulance on our way back to my house, where, drafted in for the fiesta, emergency workers are trying to resuscitate an old woman who has been hit on the back of the head by a rocket. 'I think I know that woman; she's deaf and dumb,' I say, somewhat dismayed by the blood running down her back.

'Probably didn't hear the rocket,' Bill responds in a gloomy voice.

'Are you ok, old fellow?'

'Well, I was – until I met that woman in the butcher's house.'

'Isabel!'

'You know her?'

'Not well, but I know her brother.'

'I offered to paint her, and do you know what she said?' I shake my head to indicate the negative. *'No podras encontrar un lienzo tan grande como mi chocho* - which means, if I'm not mistaken, I won't be able to find a canvas big enough for her fanny.'

'I'm afraid that's Isabel all over,' I say, trying not to laugh, for I can see that my sensitive friend is upset. 'She's a fire-fighter, works in an all-male team of ten. Her crudity is part of the shell she hides in to protect her from the constant smut she endures at work. She probably thought your offer to paint her was a come on.'

'It *was*,' Bill confesses. 'I always make the same mistake.'

'What mistake?'

'I wouldn't dream of getting juiced up to buy a house, a car or a second-hand TV, but I always chase skirt when I'm drunk.'

'Like a lot of men,' I respond.

'But it's a recipe for disaster. Remember Anelka, the girl from Berlin? I met her when I was pissed, and look how that turned out.'

I think of Anelka - how it took her a week to clean Bill's studio flat in Soho, a block away from the gallery I ran for seventeen years. How the poor girl slept on his sofa because he didn't have space for a double-bed, how she lived in a tiny space under the ferocious gaze of his towering sculptures, ate like a timid mouse on the floor. 'I thought she was nice.'

'You didn't live with her. And what about Patricia? I was so drunk I didn't even know she was a prostitute until she asked me to pay.'

'Patricia wasn't a prostitute; she was a high class hooker,' I stifle a smile, remind him that she went to Roedean. 'She admired your work, bought one of your paintings from my gallery. She was a connoisseur of fine art.'

'Art for fuck's sake. It was my bloody money.'

'That's your line.'

'My line! What do you mean? My line of work?' Bill gives me a quizzical look, and then bursts out laughing. 'Come on, let's get back to your house.' He wraps his arm around my shoulders. 'It's freezing here in sunny Spain. I need a stiff drink to sober up.'

It's five thirty in the morning when my first guests arrive, a batch of fifteen, stepping over the body of Carlos who is lying on my doorstep singing songs that were hits before the death of Franco. Carlos is where he wants to be. 'I'm not cold, I want to be outside so I can join the procession when I hear it pass at the bottom of our street,' was the rejection my invitation to drink in my house received.

It's my first open house so I've gone to a lot of trouble, prepared a stack of cheese and pickle sandwiches, a platter of spicy samosas, bowls of nuts and crisps, olives and dried fruit, a cauldron of creamy vegetable soup for those who want something warm. For drink, I've chosen Cava, Spanish champagne, for music, the Beatles and Bowie, the Stones, the Who, selecting racy tracks to suit the mood of the night. Within an hour it's standing room only on my ground floor – the event's an unmitigated success, even the samosas are eaten. When Carlos enters my front room to announce the arrival of the village saint everyone puts on a coat to join the tail of the procession on its last weary lap back to the plaza.

Outside the church Maria espies my baseball cap, breaks from her family group to link arms with me, to say sorry we didn't get a chance to chat in the butcher's house. Standing side by side, I put a protective arm around her when the last terrifying round of rockets goes off. Nestled into the crook of my arm, so close, for a few precious moments, I can feel her tremble when the fireworks explode. After the statue of St Jerome is carried into the church, the hallowed saint ensconced in his niche beside the altar, we walk hand in hand to the bottom of the village to watch the day break beneath the candyfloss striped canopy of one of the myriad food stalls that spring up like short-lived flowers at every Spanish fiesta.

Over paper cups of milky chocolate, a plastic plate of *churros*, sugary twirls of fried dough that Spaniards love to dunk in hot drinks, we sit at a foldable metal table, knees touching, to share snippets of our lives. I surprise myself by telling her of my mother's death, how she died in my arms, how hopeless I felt, like Mary at the foot of her son's cross. I learn of her time in Madrid as a teenager where she studied at the Conservatory to become a classical ballerina, how she fell in love with her teacher. She tells me about the night school where she studied English, something she had wanted to do since childhood but couldn't in her village, how the world is not for children, that if she ever had a child it would be adopted. When she holds me in a lingering gaze I lose myself in her almond-shaped deep brown eyes; it's as if I've known her for years, in another life, a feeling I've never had before. When I walk her to the street where her sister lives, stand outside the house where she always sleeps when she stays in the village, she enfolds me in her arms, kisses me on both cheeks ere briefly on the lips.

Standing in front of a shaving mirror, brushing my teeth, I notice Bill's wristwatch beside his washbag. It's ten forty-five in the morning. Five minutes later I go to bed.

The following afternoon I awake to find myself in a silent empty house. I recall Bill entering my bedroom several hours earlier, asking me if I wanted to go to the plaza, but the recollection is so misty that I can't be certain it actually happened or was part of a dream. On the terrace, in a gigantic I Ching pattern of rocket sticks, I eat the out of date porridge I bought last summer in a tiny British store in Roquetas called Arkright's. Frustrated in my search for divinatory meaning, I turn my attention to a rooftop in a neighbouring street, watch a pair of hoopoes dance along a stretch of guttering. I'm happy to see the hoopoes, remember Cassie telling me they were auspicious birds.

Around dusk I hear merriment in my street, followed by the familiar voices of Bill and Carlos. They find me by the kitchen stove preparing Dhal Bhat – a lentil, vegetable and rice dish from Nepal. The twain are like a pair of abominable snowmen, covered in flour from head to toe. '*Los fantasmas*,' I exclaim, in feigned fright. Carlos laughs, but Bill, not in the know, just smiles. Excitedly my English friend explains how everyone in the plaza was showered with flour, how Carlos set him up to participate in the piñata.

'The villagers blindfolded me, put me on a donkey, gave me a wooden pole to lash out blindly at clay pots strung across the square. And all for a shower of boiled sweets that the kids scooped up in seconds.'

'No,' Carlos, listening to Bill's Spanish, corrects him. 'That was your first prize. You won a juicy pigeon after the sweets.'

'That's right; I forgot about the bird. How did they get it into the pot?'

'Who cares how the Paloma got in the pot,' Carlos responds. 'You let it *go,*' he adds, giving Bill a censorial glance for he can't figure out such folly, how such a fine, fat bird escaped the oven.

'Bill's a Buddhist,' I explain, but it draws a blank expression from Carlos who doesn't understand what I'm talking about.

When the Nepalese food is ready, I present it on stainless steel thali plates, tell my guests to tuck in, warning them that the pickle is made of hot chillies. Bill says he's famished, tucks in heartedly, uses his fingers to make rice balls which sends Carlos into a bout of laughter, his eyes seeking mine for reassurance. Galled by the scent and sight of curry the *Andaluz* asks for a fork to fish out a few grains of turmeric-stained basmati rice, mumbles '*potingue extranjero*,' and then gets up from the kitchen table to tell us he's going to his brother's house where they serve proper food.

'What's *potingue extranjero*?'

'Foreign muck.'

'Not very adventurous,' Bill says as he dips a rice ball into the spicy pickle. 'You should have played Vilayat Khan to get him in the mood.'

After the meal, Bill says he's tired, has had enough of fiestas, suggests we stay in for the first time in two weeks. We sit in the front room, warmed by the *brasero*, watch an American sit-con on TV. I uncork a bottle of red wine called *las tetas de la sacristana*, the sacristan's tits. Amused by the name of the wine, Bill tells me he once ate a watermelon in Tuscany that was known as the nun's boobs. As we drink, we talk, the tireless flickering images of television fading into the background. Bill asks if I will be at Cassie's wedding in the summer. I tell him I won't be, that I'll send a present, that I can't make her future husband shake hands with his bride's erstwhile lover.

'I thought you two a good match.'

'We were,' I reply in the past tense, 'but she wanted to start a family and I didn't,' I add a little sadly, aware that days of love, near death, will be the ones that count.

'And the strawberry-blonde you slipped away into the night with?'

'Maria,' I furnish my friend with a name.

'A fine figure.'

'She's a dancer,' I respond, relating how I first saw her dance in the summer fiesta, how she comes to the village twice a week to give classes.'

'Do you speak Spanish or English when you are with her?'

'A bit of both.'

'And you can understand her Spanish?'

'Yes.'

'I ask, because today I had a twenty-minute conversation with a villager in the plaza and I couldn't understand a word he was saying.'

'Perhaps he was drunk.'

'Perhaps. But others seemed to understand him.'

'Then he was probably using the local dialect. I have problems with that too. There's one chap I know who speaks nothing else. Fortunately, he habitually ends whatever he's saying with the question *si o no?* I always say *si* and it usually works, but if it doesn't I quickly change it to *no*.'

Bill smiles, is about to say something, but his attention is diverted to the television screen, to a film set in London. 'Do you miss England?' he asks, '*Si o no?*'

'No.'

'*Nothing!* Nothing at all?' Bill persists so pleadingly that I'm moved to backtrack a bit, admit to occasional moments of nostalgia. I tell him that I miss a handful of people, the public libraries, the Tate, the National gallery, the smell of asphalt in central London after a heavy downpour, the green grass of White Hart Lane.

'When I first arrived I used to sit on my roof terrace trying to tune into BBC live sport. But I don't do that anymore. Not after I spent a whole hour one Saturday trying to find a good connection, and when I did, holding the radio above my head, the crackly commentary only lasted a minute before I was called to prayer by a mullah in a minaret in Marrakesh.'

'So you miss the Premiership,' Bill, who isn't a fan, responds dourly. 'But there must be other things you miss. You were born in London. You lived there for forty years. I've enjoyed every minute I've spent in this village. Everything is so different – it's like being on another planet. But I could never live here, not after London.'

'We're different Bill. I belong wherever I am. For me, living here is an adventure. You appreciate your home comforts; art is your adventure.'

Before we turn in for the night I put my hand on my friend's arm in the hallway. 'There's one other thing I miss more than most about England.'

'What's that?'

'You.'

For the next few days, before Bill's flight back to London, I join my friend on his holiday. We spent a couple of nights in Tabernas, the largest desert in Europe, not far from where '*Lawrence of Arabia*' was filmed. Against my better judgement we visit the boulder strewn Mini Hollywood, a mock up studio set of the wild west. Our last days together are in Almeria, in the fisherman's quarter, the gipsy *barrio*. During daylight, we explore the city, walk along the crenelated walls of the Alcazabar, look out to sea, one time, peer through a turret where a Moorish princess plunged to her death, forbidden by her father her Christian lover. At night, we're found in local bars, listening to Paco de Lucia. And then it's the Magical Mystery Tour; the house where Lennon wrote *Strawberry Fields Forever*, where he slept when he wasn't acting in Lester's anti-war film; downtown, the customary snapshot of the statue of the murdered songwriter.

At the airport, there's no time for emotions, barely time for a coffee and a shot of brandy, a few scribbled words on a last-minute postcard that Bill asks me to post when I get back to my village.

Driving back to my village, I'm in a reflective mood, somewhat divided, my eyes focused on the road ahead, inwardly watching a friend wave goodbye, a good friend not an acquaintance, a man of principle, someone who honours his word. I smile when I think of Bill's past, how he ignored his father's threat to cut him out of his will when he went to Art college instead of following his footsteps to Oxford, how he once told me that the greatest achievement of his adolescence was being kicked out of Harrow, after he set fire to an outbuilding on the estate of the elite school. He said it was a protest against privilege. I know I'm going to miss him – a rare bird indeed.

6

THE SECOND MEETING WITH MARIA'S MOTHER IS MARGINALLY EASIER THAN the first when all she did was glower at me for the best part of an uncomfortable hour. Since then, I've learnt that behind my back, Monse calls me a 'Hindu' because I've been to India, that she has warned her daughter in Spain I might pretend to accept her mini-skirts, her leotards on stage, but if ever I lure her over to London, she'll be forced to live in purdah and wear a yasmak. That she mixes up world religions, that I'm a free-thinking agnostic ruled by evidence not fancy doesn't enter the equation. Reality, it seems, isn't Monse's speciality. According to Maria, if something doesn't tally with her mother's version of events, it can go to hell. It's the reason Maria left home at seventeen to study in Madrid, why she moved to the other side of her village two years later when she returned from the Spanish capital, took up residence in a derelict farmhouse that she had inherited from her paternal grandfather. The old house is still her home when she is in her village, somewhere to sleep once a week - her other nights in the Alpujarras spent in villages scattered across the Sierra Nevada, wherever she teaches children to spin and stand on *puntas*, the slippers of a ballerina. It's a peripatetic life, Socratic, she often jokes, a compensation for the fact that she hasn't travelled.

Maria at thirty-one, on a good day, looks ten years younger, her pretty face unlined. Roberto, her eldest brother, is completely different, looks much older than his forty-five years, his visage weatherworn, deeply furrowed like the land he farms. It is Roberto's birthday, the reason why over thirty have assembled under his mother's wattle ceiling. All are blood-related; the screaming children, a widow, Monse's mater, all in black, with an ear-horn; everyone is family, but me. With an army of mouths to feed, Maria's mother hasn't time to spare a stranger. I'm barely acknowledged as she rushes hither and thither, her hostile glare replaced by lines of worry that a helping hand might burn the rabbits. I slice a few tomatoes, peel cloves of garlic, until Roberto takes the knife from my hand, tells me to go outside with the other men, not to meddle in the kitchen, upset the matriarch, his mother.

I sit with Alberto, Maria's father, and his cousin Alfredo, an innocent simpleton that Alberto's wife calls the village idiot. I remember Maria telling me that her father's cousin had a way with birds, that he could coax jays and magpies out of the trees to eat from his gentle hand. It's a gift I would like to see, but today there are no birds. Instead Alfredo's busy with flowers, which he picks and then carefully examines before he puts them in his mouth. When the simple soul spots, and then runs after a cat and her kittens, I ask Alberto if his cousin always eats flowers.

'Only when he's hungry,' he answers with a deadpan face.

'I see,' I reply, when I don't.

'Maria showed me your interview with Canal Sur on her machine thing.'

'Her laptop.'

'Whatever!' Alberto is dismissive, suspicious of new words. 'Your Spanish isn't bad for a foreigner,' he compliments me, and then tells me that he liked the bit when I said my village was so far behind the times that I tell friends who visit that they'll leave younger than when they arrived. 'It's even slower up here in the Alpujarras,' he laughs softly. 'I know because I'm a shepherd. You can come out with me one day into the hills, see the remote valleys and the villages. You'll see things that have been going on for centuries.'

'I'd love to.'

'Good,' Alberto smiles. 'Have a drop,' he offers me a swig from his hip flask. I'm not partial to whisky, but I accept, put the flask straight to my lips after his. 'Do you read the bible?' he asks.

'My mother was Irish. I was brought up as a Catholic.'

'Maria has never mentioned that. She should tell my wife.' Alberto falls silent for a few moments, searching for the right words to ask me what my intentions are with his daughter. When I tell him they're serious, that I've never met anyone like her, he nods his head, puts his calloused honest hand on my knee, tells me he'll have a word with his wife.

Throughout the meal, a riotous affair, laden with jokes and jugs of wine, I say little in the seat next to Maria. We eat our bread with an olive oil and vinegar-soaked salad, for in the short time we've been together Maria has become a vegetarian. It's something she'd thought about for many years, ever since her mother forced her to eat a piglet she'd named and befriended. No one in the family seems particularly put out by Maria's change of diet, only Monse, who thinks her child too thin, that a life without meat is unnatural and leads to rickets. She has completely forgotten the incident that marred Maria's early years, knows nothing about the childhood nightmares her daughter suffered, the disturbing dreams in which she saw her piglet on a baking tray, half eaten, but still alive, little pink piggy eyes looking for a friend.

The *postre* is all fruit, pomegranates and succulent pears, chunks of rosy red melon from local gardens, oranges from Seville. At length, the repast is done, the oak table swept clean to make room for a huge birthday cake. After the traditional song of *Feliz Cumpleanos*, Roberto blows out a single candle, slices and serves the cake, while Maria pours the café, neat for some, for myself and those more adventurous, diluted with *La Gloria*, a village-brewed hard liquor. After the café and cake, there's a lull in the hullabaloo, a palpable cloud of contentment in the room. Adults settle back into chairs with satisfied stomachs, children with sated bellies snuggle up to their great grandmother on the sofa. It's the perfect set up for a lazy Sunday afternoon siesta. It's the moment I've been waiting for, the moment to build a bridge, to congratulate Monse, for it's no mean feat to feed over thirty. Perhaps it's a mistake to stand up as if I'm proposing a toast – it draws too much attention, has the widow reach for her ear trumpet. But what follows is worse, as I confuse *cochinera* with *cocinera,* tell Maria's mother that she is dirty rather than a good cook. Mercifully, the family are quick to catch my malapropism, burst into a song of raucous laughter, but Maria's grandmother isn't impressed with the *guiri*, the foreigner, nor her daughter, especially when the children dance around the room, their squeaky, excited voices impishly woven into a chorus of '*cochinera, cochinera.*'

My faux pas lingers like a bad taste, follows me to Maria's farmhouse, where, beneath crooked beams, on an embroidered bedspread across her double bed, I apologise profusely. There's no need to apologise, Maria tells me, her mother will get over it.

'Are you sure?'

'She knows you didn't mean to insult her,' Maria giggles, and then tells me *cochinera* is related to pigs.

'Oh, no,' I groan.

'Don't worry Kim.' Maria smiles. 'It's just one of her nasty little games. She played them throughout my childhood; games of blame and guilt to manipulate the family.' I'm soothed by words meant to reassure, willing to move on, but Maria isn't finished. 'In our family she's the *gran dama* who pulls all the strings. When she can't get her own way, she plays the martyr on the cross to be seen from a greater distance.'

"Perhaps something happened to her in her childhood?' I say quietly, conjuring up the stern face of Maria's grandmother.

'Maybe,' Maria looks at me in surprise, 'but why drag the luggage of the past into the present?'

'Most people do.'

'I know, but I'm trying not to,' Maria laughs nervously, getting off the bed to stand by her bedroom window. 'Look,' she says, after a quiet moment, beckoning me to join her. 'Look at the passing clouds. When I was a little girl I used to stand by this window while my grandfather told me stories about the clouds. He said that clouds were like people in the sky; they changed all the time, came and went without leaving a trace. One day we were here when a storm broke out across the valley. There was lightning and thunder, but I wasn't frightened because my grandfather was with me. And then I saw a huge, dark raincloud shaped like a whale swimming through the storm. I was about seven at the time, and very excited because I had never seen a fish in the sky before. And then it changed, its tail broke off which seemed so cruel, and then so sad, when my grandfather said the tail was gone forever, that it was like the people we love and lose who go to heaven. That put me off heaven for about a year. Though my parents and the nuns at my school said it was a very nice place, I thought it sounded like a prison if the angels didn't let you come back, especially fiesta time to play with your friends. I was clever enough to keep that to myself, but I protested about the whale, said it would find its tail on its long journey around the world, that we only had to wait and see. But grandpa held me in his arms and shook his head. He never told me lies.'

'Your grandfather was a philosopher.'

'Yes, I think he was,' Maria smiles winsomely, 'even if he was *analfabeto*, couldn't read or write.'

We return to Maria's bed, where she tells me to undress, not only to make love, but because she believes people are more honest without clothes. When the sun dips beyond the mountain ridge to close the day, flooding the room with a kind, roseate light, we're still naked on her bed, sharing a pot of herbal tea, dipping wafer-thin biscuits in a jar of golden honey from a local hive. It has been an incredible afternoon on her creaking bed. A journey of discovery, of confessions, trusting each other with tales of tears. I've spoken of tempestuous times with my father, how his olive skin embarrassed me as a young child with racist friends, how he beat me and my mother with a buckle belt; but Maria has dug deeper, unearthed nightmares of her past to go beyond them, said things she has never said before. I've been told that she wasn't wanted, how her mother put knitting needles up her vagina, swallowed vinegar and raw mushroom concoctions to terminate her birth. How Monse, in temper, called her little girl a curse.

When the phantoms of twilight come out to play, as purple shadows creep about the crimson room, Maria turns her watery eyes to me to share another secret. I'm told she was born at night, in the heart of winter, entered the world on a rough *camino*, on the back of an old tractor that couldn't get out of the snow-bound village. 'My father cut my umbilical cord with his hunting knife,' she whispers softly, so sadly I'm moved to the edge of a tear.

'When were you born?' I ask in a croaky voice.

'On your birthday,' Maria says, burying her face into my neck as if the confession's so severe that she can't face me.

'But.... Why?'

'Because I don't celebrate my birthday,' Maria answers my unformed question, takes my face in her hands as she begins to weep. 'Would you if your mother told you that your birth ruined her Christmas, her life.'

'I would,' I respond. 'And you *will.*' I add emphatically, trying to mask the surge of rage I have for Monse, for all the monstrous parents who blindly scar their children. Parents, who, in moments of bellicose unforgiving, I would, if blessed with foresight, have sterilised, in the name of humanity, at birth.

As night settles upon us, as we ready ourselves for slumber, Maria enwraps me in her arms to tell me she has waited all her life to meet me. And then, in a coyness that is her own, relates a Spanish proverb – *El amor es siempre eterno mientras dura – Love is always eternal while it lasts*. A strange thing to share betwixt lovers, but I see through the fragility of one who has been hurt, tell her I love her, that I always will, even if we part.

7

AT EIGHT IN THE MORNING, PETE IS AT MY DOOR, FAR TOO CLOSE, FOR MY liking, to the hour of dawn. But it's typical of a man who proudly tells all and sundry, whether they're interested or not, that he has a timetable, lives by the clock, goes to bed at ten, gets up early, eats three meals a day, all at a set time. It's the way he structures his retirement. He advises me to follow suit, or I'll turn Turk, become like the locals. That he's a day late seems to have escaped his regimental mind. Fortunately, I don't have to get up to open the door, Kit, Jamie's boyfriend from New York is already up, plucking his eyebrows in the bathroom.

'Why, hellooo! I hear Kit's loud, theatrical voice in the hallway.

'Where's Kim?' Peter replies, ignoring the American's greeting.

'In bed, like Jamie. So it's just *me* and *you*.'

'Still in bed!'

'Oh, I love the uniform,' Kit projects his voice as he's learned to do on Broadway. 'So YMCA.'

'It's a boiler suit. I'm here to repair a tap.'

'And look at your matching tool-box. So twee! I bet you're good with your hands.'

'Steady on man, steady on.' I catch a note of alarm in Pete's fading voice as the pair make their way into the front room.

I'm called a lazy so and so, when, twenty minutes later, I make my appearance. It's Pete's version of *good morning*, a reminder that it's his way or no way. I smile, wonder how he would get on with Maria's mum. 'Where's Kit?' I ask.

'In the bloody bathroom, shaving his legs. Had the bloody cheek to ask if I'd help him shave the bits he couldn't reach.'

'He'll be out soon. Then we can turn the water off and tackle the tap.' I respond, disappearing into the kitchen to make coffee, to hide a wide grin that's guaranteed to provoke my irascible neighbour.

The tap works with a new washer; for once, a job without complications. I offer payment, but Pete declines, prefers to make a note in what he calls his book of favours. As he is about to leave, Jamie comes downstairs in a pair of Indian pajamas, says he has an announcement to make – Kit's going to prepare a special dish tonight and would like Pete and his wife, Pat, to be there.

'Will it be halal?' Pete asks, for though he carries a British passport, he's really Polish, from a Jewish background.

'A Mughal dish – vegetarian,' the Californian replies.

Without a moment of hesitation, Pete accepts the invitation, says Elishera loves a good curry. It's a surprise, for Pete's not a social fellow, rarely goes out, and when he does, usually picks a fight. In his first week in the village, a year before my arrival, he so enraged one neighbour that he had his son aerosol a wall outside the main supermarket with the words – *Espana para los Espanoles – Ingleses fuera, Spain for the Spanish – English out.* A month later, someone set his mailbox on fire.

'Who's Elishera?' Jamie asks, when my handyman's beyond earshot.

'Pat, his wife. Elishera is the pretty Hebraic name he's given her. He calls their dog Shulamit. I think it means peaceful.'

'*In the beginning was the word, and the word was with God.* Name it, claim it.' Jaime's good with words.

I keep out of harm's reach, spent most of the sunny afternoon on the roof terrace, reading, as best as I can, Irvine's *Tales of the Alhambra*, in Spanish. It isn't long before Jamie joins me, banished from the kitchen by his flustered, apron-clad lover, who seems to need every pot and pan in the house to concoct the perfect curry. 'He has to turn everything into a performance,' Jaime complains between gritted teeth. 'If you couldn't smell the onions, you'd think he was an alchemist in search of the philosophers' stone.' I chuckle inoffensively, not wishing to enter a lover's tiff. 'So what's the score with Pete?' Jaime asks when he's more composed. 'Kit says he's a prickly type; fun to tease.'

'Prickly is an understatement,' I tell my friend of twenty years. 'When I first moved here I spend a fair amount of time with him and his wife. I got to know them well. My Spanish was rusty; it was a relief to speak English. That was a few years ago. Nowadays, I hardly ever see them, and when I do, I keep it brief, especially in public.'

'Why?'

'He's got enemies all over the village. He's been beaten up twice.'

'Beaten up! The Spanish seems such a placid bunch.'

'Under most circumstances they're fun-loving and peaceable. But it's wise to remember their recent history's seasoned with a civil war. It's best not to provoke them; and Pete's a master of provocation. Once we were in a bar in the village and he started mouthing off – said the Spanish were all thieves, liars and cheats – in *SPANISH*. Another time, I was having a coffee with him and his wife in the main plaza in Guadix, when a coachload of German pensioners turned up. He can speak German, and went from table to table, asking them what they did in the war. And then, he goose-stepped across the square, signing off with a Nazi salute. It was ugly, and nasty.'

'He's Jewish, isn't he?'

'Every bone in his body. A Zionist through and through, more pro-Israel than Netanyahu, says the only good Palestinian is a dead one.'

'Shame I didn't bring my *Keffiyeh,* my Palestinian scarf,' Jamie says, and then shakes his head, wondering if dinner is such a good idea.

Maria's the first to turn up for what Kit calls a soiree, says she needs a shower, that she's all sweaty after her class. While she's shampooing her hair, Pete and his English wife arrive, bearing a bottle of local white wine. Kit's at the door to greet them, his hair in a bun with a Geisha clip, a flimsy, thigh-length kimono over his boney body, on his dainty feet a pair of black, velvet slippers. I'm glad we are eating in, and not out, as he looks like Ziggy Stardust on speed. 'You look nice,' Pat says, not knowing what else to say. Pete's less forthcoming, gasps, but can't find any words as he hands over the wine.

While Jamie and I entertain our guests in the front room, offering small talk and salty titbits to go with the wine, Maria disappears to the first floor to help Kit put the final touches to the Kabuki face he wishes to wear. When everything is just so, the white powder and eyeshadow settled, the table artistically laid, she returns downstairs in a low-cut silk evening dress to call us to dinner, to invite us into a warm ambience bathed in soft-scented candlelight. Kit has been through my collection of CDs; found a *raag* by Ali Akbar Khan, so there's the sound of a sarod in the background to go with the meal.

We begin with parathas stuffed with thin slices of eggplant, paneer koftas in mint sauce, a lime pickle found at the back of my kitchen cupboard. The pickle is extra hot, so hot it almost chokes Pete, has his wife gulp down a whole glass of wine to put out the flames. The main course is a biryani, a lightly spiced vegetable and basmati rice, streaked with crimson strands of saffron, a spice more valuable than gold. Everyone is full of food and compliments for the chef, but there's still room for dessert, a falooda, rose syrup and milk, mixed with vermicelli and sweet basil, served in a chilled glass. Maria says it's the best dessert she's ever tasted, asks Kit for the ingredients and how to make it. I suggest we leave the plates for the morrow, go downstairs for café and liquors, open the box of thin chocolate mints that Maria found in *Mercadona*, a Spanish supermarket.

As we shuttle downstairs in convivial spirit, Kit retires to his bedroom, only to reappear a few moments later, laden with a gift for each and every one. I'm given a coffee-table, hardback book of black and white photographs of the Sierra Nevada, thanked for my hospitality, for putting up with him and Jamie for a week; for the *girls*, there's a box of Belgium chocolates, a Cuban cigar for Pete, and a peck on the lips for his long-suffering lover. Pat is overwhelmed by Kit's generous gesture, says, almost tearfully, that she's having the best night she's had in ages, that it reminds her of Christmas, the festive time she loves best, but hasn't been allowed to celebrate in the eight years she's known her husband. Whether wine has liberated her tongue is difficult to say, but her comments, on an evening that has been a great success, mark a change in the atmosphere. Apart from cussing the lime pickle, throughout the dinner, Pete's been on his best behavior. Only on one occasion has he lost the plot, irrelevantly reminding us that his people are the chosen ones, gave Spain what little culture she has before being kicked out in the fifteenth century, that Dylan's real name is Zimmerman, that Einstein, Marx and Freud were all Jews, but the mention of Christmas is too much for him. 'What did you say?' he bellows at his wife.

'Sorry Pete, I forgot, Pat replies timidly, a tear threatening to roll down her crumpled up face.

'What's wrong?' Kit asks in alarm.

'We don't mention Christmas, or Christ in my house,' Pete snaps at the American.

'But this is not your house,' Jamie snaps back.

'I meant figuratively in the house of marriage.'

'Why ever not? Of all the Jews who have ever walked upon this earth, he's the most famous.'

'He's right Pete,' Pat tries to placate her husband, 'Jesus was a Jew before he became a Christian.'

It isn't the moment to point out that Jesus was no more a Christian than Siddhartha, a Hindu prince, was a Buddhist, for all eyes are on Pete who has turned a puce colour as if he's about to implode. Somehow, he manages to contain himself, erase the deep furrow from his brow.

'You mustn't misunderstand me,' he says in a quavering voice, 'I respect all religions.' And then, proceeds, somewhat predictably, to contradict himself by telling us that he calls Corpus Christi Corpus Crispy, that he hates Jesus because he betrayed his people, that there was no virgin birth, that Mary was a Jewish whore, who cuckolded Joseph by screwing Roman soldiers.

Of Chilean descent, brought up in the Catholic faith, abused in childhood by a Jesuit priest, Jamie hates the church of Rome. It's a morbid hatred that's grown tentacles to smother all religions. A passion that has prompted a rigorous study of all forms of faith, not unlike a General at war who marks his enemy's every move to know where best to strike. When he opens his mouth, I don't know what he's going to say, but I know Judaism is in for a rough ride. 'So who's your man? Abraham, Micah, Moses?'

'Moses gave us the ten commandments,' Pete says proudly, with a touch of hubris, unaware that he's stepping into a minefield.

'Moses was a psychopath,' Jaime doesn't beat around the burning bush, goes straight for the jugular. 'Thou shall not kill, *unless I say so*. Your prophet was a mass murderer, up there with Hitler, Pol Pot and Saddam Hussein.'

As something akin to the white noise on a wireless, a silence that isn't silent, descends upon the room, Maria scoops up a bottle of Frangelico in one hand, grabs Pat by the other, leads the poor English woman into the kitchen, where she says she has something to show her. 'Explain yourself man,' Pete, watching his wife disappear, finds the right frequency to reply.

'It's all there in your forefathers' book,' Jamie responds, and then quotes the Biblical passage where Moses sanctions the slaughter of tens of thousands, and then another part of the Old Testament that Catholic priests don't talk about, how the great prophet celebrated another victorious bloodbath by sparing thirty-three thousand virgins for the pleasure of his troops. 'No one else was spared, not even pregnant women. Their swollen stomachs were slashed open by swords, their babies ripped from their wombs.' Kit, who believes in God, but isn't very religious, has never heard such things before, wonders what other commandments Moses might have transgressed. Innocently he asks if that's the reason Michelangelo's statue of Moses has horns.

Although Pete regards the American with undisguised malice, he doesn't bother to respond to his enquiry. Instead he turns to my Californian friend, mutters, barely audibly, something about primitive times and tribal warfare, before launching a personal attack, figuring like some chess masters, that it's the best form of defence. 'Look at the state of *you*,' he opens with his customary diplomacy, 'And *him*; or is it a *her*?' he nods in the direction of Kit. 'You're rudderless, out at sea without an oar. Your ways are unnatural, go against God's will. That's why you're being punished by the plague of Aids.' Jamie, familiar with the Old Testament argument, smirks, before telling Pete that he reminds him of the homophobic Catholic church. 'You mean the church of queers,' Pete scornfully snickers. 'Look! I'm not judging,' he continues judgmentally, 'but look what happened to the children of Sodom and Gomorrah. It's all there in the greatest book ever written, the book that guides me in everything I do.'

'Pete's telling porky pies,' Pat, swallowing her third shot of Frangelico, calls out from the kitchen. 'He eats chorizo on the Sabbath,' she adds, before succumbing to a fit of giggles. It's the wittiest thing she's said all night, but I wouldn't want to be in her shoes when her husband gets her home. When Jamie informs my Jewish guest that his old scriptures are fossilized, that the gruesome ritual of circumcision arrived before the invention of soap, that his holy book was written by ancients who knew nothing of the telephone and television, nothing at all about the internet and Facebook, or men on the moon, that to follow it by the letter was like heeding the counsel of a child on matters of adulthood and death, the day of Pat's judgement draws nigh, for Pete's on his feet, accusing the 'yank' of being anti-Semitic.

'Anti-religion, not Semitic,' Jamie tries to hide the laughter in his eyes. 'If you had stuffed the Koran down my throat, I'd have spoken of the hypocrisy of your sensual heaven, if a Hindu, how Krishna made out with married women, if a Buddhist, how the man who became the Buddha abandoned his wife…'

'I've heard enough,' Pete cuts the American short. 'Elishera,' he bellows, 'we're going.' At the door, I'm told my house is for heathens, chastised for entertaining faggots.

'Goodness! That went well,' I say to Maria, after our guests have gone, the North Americans tucked up in bed, after a tongue-in-cheek dispute in which Kit accused Jamie of stripping poor Pete bare, of ruining the soiree he toiled so tirelessly to prepare.

'Like Christmas at my mum's house,' Maria says, with so serious a face, we both burst into the relief of laughter.

'So what did you talk about in the kitchen?' I ask.

'I didn't talk, I listened.' Maria replies; and then tells me how Pat has to hide the Christmas cards her ninety-year-old parents send each year. How she'd like a few paintings on her walls, paintings of flowers, seascapes, anything but the tattered, torn map of Israel that adorns her front room. How her husband's idea of a good night in, is watching a film about the holocaust. How, after watching one of his horrible films, she had a nightmare, found herself in a concentration camp, surrounded by giant snails with swastikas on their shells.

'Poor woman,' I sigh.

'I didn't ask, but I thought it. Why doesn't she leave him?'

'She almost did two years ago,' I reply. 'Pete came round after the threat; said he told her, he'd kill himself if she did.'

The following morning, while Jamie and Kit are upstairs packing suitcases for Almeria airport, there's a light rap on my front door. When I open the door, I find Pat and her dog on the doorstep. 'I won't come in,' she says, handing me a bunch of roses from the local florist. 'I just came round to thank you and everyone for a wonderful evening, and to apologise for Pete's behavior.'

'There's no need.' I smile. And then, looking into her sad, grey eyes that match her husband's hair, add, 'Pete got what he gave.'

8

WHEN SOMEONE DIES IN SPAIN BILLS FALL LIKE TICKER TAPE FROM HEAVEN. There are fees for the undertaker, the funeral parlour, the requiem mass, the memorial service, the cost of a cortege, a coffin, wreaths of flowers, the price of a tomb. When Rosa's mother died, Carlos was so shocked by the expense of everything, he told me he couldn't afford to die. The only good thing about dying, he added, was when the fateful day arrived, he wouldn't be there to foot the bill. But that was false bravado on his part. In reality, he worried about his death, how much his passing would cost his family. He told everyone that he wanted a simple service, no great fuss, no great fee, his body laid under an olive tree. I don't know if he meant it, or knew, but only the rich and powerful can bury their loved ones where they wish.

His death comes as no surprise; everyone knew, including Carlos, that it was coming. There had been the usual pattern of decline, one thing going wrong after the other, in and out of hospital for almost two years, the sudden loss of weight, the sunken eyes. But when the dark day arrives, it's still one of shock and sorrow; for me, the saddest day I've known in Spain. It's the loss of my first friend in the village. Although we didn't always see eye to eye, especially when he would call out *vete a la mierda*, invite me to go fuck myself, for no discernable reason, I always remained polite, and fond of him, his mischievous eyes and peculiar ways.

Before I visit the *tanatorio,* the parlour for the dead, I cook a tortilla for the family, knowing, unlike the *tanatorios* in the big cities, the one in our village has no restaurant or bar. After shaking hands with neighbours and distant family members, hugs and kisses for those I know best, I take a last look at my old friend behind the plate-glass window. That there's no sign of suffering etched into his features is a comfort, but small, as I make the sign of the cross out of respect for those around me. 'At least, he's out of pain,' his brother says, laying his hand on my arm.

When the black hearse arrives in the plaza the following morning, I'm outside the church with Maria. We wait for the arrival of a small procession of family and clan members bearing religious banners before we raise the coffin. I'm the only pallbearer who isn't related by birth. Before I came to Spain I had been to four funerals. Today is my fifth in as many years. And like the previous four, the name of the deceased is the sole concession to originality throughout the service. The church is, however, full to the rafters. The *alcalde*, the village mayor, stands at the back in attendance, like Diego, and the early morn tipplers who have left their half-empty glasses in nearby bars to pay their final respects. For at least a day, all grievances are forgiven, in remembrance of *un hijo del pueblo*, a son of the village. I can't imagine such a turn out in a large city like London. When the requiem is through, and the more devout have had their *papa tapa*, as Carlos used to call the host, two thick queues of mourners line up, men to the left, women to the right, to offer a handshake, a hug, their condolences to the family.

Outside the church, there's time to have a cigarette before the final journey to the cemetery. After the penumbral gloom of the church, it seems strange to stand in the sunny plaza, to know it's where Carlos spent a considerable part of his life, but will stand no more. 'He could've had a few more years.' I hear one villager say to another.

'Aye, if he had stopped drinking before he pissed blood.'

The cemetery is hidden from the living, perched on a lonely, windswept promontory about a mile outside the village. The tombs are two-tiered, stone cubby holes for coffins, laid out in rows like tiny streets. At night, I imagine a hobbit-like village for hobgoblins. I'm informed, that once a year, on All Saints day, the cemetery is tidied up, but when we arrive there's an air of neglect; a few flowers, mostly plastic, scattered on paths of weeds and cigarette butts. It's not the sort of place where I want to end up; a thought that has me whisper to Maria my wish to be cremated, with no service or cut flowers, my body burnt in a cardboard box, my ashes cast to the wind over the mountains. 'Me too,' she responds, staring at an eerie photograph of a young girl above a tomb that bears her family name.

The tomb is empty for Carlos, a solitary sepulchre for a bachelor's casket. It's a blessing for some of the mourners - those who remember the last funeral in the family, when the coffin of a grandmother was opened to put the remains of her husband, wrapped in a pall, beside her. The husband had died twenty years earlier, too many years for the skeletal frame to support the skull that rolled out of the tomb across the cemetery floor.

We decline the offer of a lift to the village, prefer to make our own way back. Our walk is one of few words. We leave the dusty path, cut through a thicket of aloes, watch a snake slither up the bough of a fig tree, a cloud of butterflies above the flowering shrubs of myrtle. Maria seems sad, her spirit subdued. When I ask for her thoughts, she tells me she is thinking of Carlos, how he will lie in his darkened tomb, alone, and forever. I assent to her bleak perception in silence. But then, removing my black tie, I tell her, with a brave face, I prefer her grandpa's way, to think of passing clouds.

BEFORE I ARRIVED IN PURUSHA THE CLOSEST I EVER GOT TO A BULLFIGHT was in Madrid, walking past the imposing towers of Las Ventas, the biggest bullring in Spain. I was nineteen at the time, a backpacker, touring Europe, when a barker approached me outside the famous bullring. He told me, somewhat cryptically, that for a handful of pesetas I could procure a seat in the sun, peer into the heart of his country, that if I wanted to understand Spain, I had to see a bullfight. Alas, for the tout, I was too young to appreciate his poetry, too young to find anything in his spiel but strangeness. I was familiar with Hemingway, but knew nothing of the American's ideas on Spain. How the celebrated writer thought the Spanish, unlike the English and French, had an obsession with death, that bullfighting was an art, a spiritual spectacle in which the common man could taste the God-like enjoyment of killing. And it was the same with Picasso. I had admired the boldness of his *corrida* collection in *El Prado* only two days earlier, but no one had told me that he thought the life of a Spaniard was mass in the morning, a bullfight in the afternoon, and the whorehouse at night, that all three were linked by a chain of sadness, that bullfighting was an expression of what it meant to be Spanish. Had I been more worldly I might have parted with my pesetas, but I was a student with a poor pocket, more interested in a *tortilla* than a ticket. Perchance, seeing disinterest in my face, the tout changed his approach, told me a little of the history of Las Ventas, how the Beatles had played there in sixty-five. He didn't tell me that Ringo hadn't enjoyed the concert, drumming in front of an audience with more plain-clothed police than genuine fans, nor how the arena had been turned into a concentration camp during the civil war. At length, growing impatient with the man, I told him I'd think things over, and if I wanted a ticket, to see into the heart of his land, I'd turn up the following day, at three, outside the box office.

I never did return to Las Ventas, but two nights later, in a tiny backstreet bar off Plaza del Sol, I saw my first, and last, bullfight, from start to gruesome finish. It was an experience that dispelled any illusions I had about the so-called sport. Naively, I had conceived the *corrida* as a battle betwixt a single man and a beast. I knew nothing of chain mailed horses, *picadors* with lances, *banderilleros* with barbed darts, the torture that weakens the bull before it falls to its knees. I couldn't deny the drama of the ring, but to find pleasure in the spectacle, let alone spiritual enjoyment, was completely beyond the range of my comprehension. As I watched the bull's carcass chained, and then dragged out of the arena by horses, all I felt was an overwhelming sense of hopelessness, revulsion and utter disgust. When I considered how the magnificent beast, bursting with life, had charged into the ring, and after, imagined its last sight of life, a crowd celebrating its slaughter, I found myself so profoundly upset that I told a French student at the hostel where I was staying that I felt ashamed of being a member of the human race.

Admittedly things have improved a bit since my youthful flush of misanthropy. Catalonia has banned bullfighting; a few groups dedicated to animal welfare have sprung up here and there. But sadly, my aversion for blood-sports isn't pervasive in Spain. Most Spaniards live the old way, see no harm in the bullring, no barbarity in fiestas where bulls' horns are set on fire, or worse, in televised fiestas where the terrified animal is tortured till it drops, and then, unable to defend itself, stabbed to death with a thousand knives by revellers, including children, in a frenzy of violent madness.

And then there's hunting, killing for fun, not food; another stain on the soul of my beloved country. I can't count the times I've heard the crack of distant gunshot in the forested hills around my village, seen blood-dripping deer draped over jeeps in the countryside, eaten under the stuffed heads of stags, looked into the glassy eyes of wild boars and mountain goats in bars with display cabinets piled high with hunting knives. I might wish to turn a blind eye, but I can't; killing animals is a popular pastime in Andalusia. Even Maria's mild-mannered brother-in-law, Paco, a meek man, has his collection of guns. Though his wife likes to believe her *Paquito* keeps six dogs in the *corrales* next to their house because he's an animal lover, Maria and I both know he has them holed up in a primitive, flea-infested animal pen for hunting. Just like the pair of female *perdices* he keeps in whicker and wire cages so cramped that they can't turn round. Partridges that never see the light of day, unless they are taken to a stretch of greensward in the heart of the woodland, their love ditties used as bait to lure the males out the bosky environs so Paco can shoot them. It's something his father, grandfather, great grandfather did. An unquestioned tradition, even though the lifeless partridges are no longer grilled, but thrown to a pack of panting dogs. And it's not only birds that are tossed to the dogs. I've come across a rotting donkey in the *ramblas,* parts of boar, a deer's thigh bone, a half-chewed pig's head, left out on the backstreets of my barrio for rodent and canine teeth. It's not that I am squeamish; I know the sad ways of the world. I've seen Thais eat barbequed eaglets at cockfights, cobras in bottles of Cambodian whiskey, walked next to dogs and cats crammed into cages outside restaurants in China, and in the Congo was offered the hand of a mountain gorilla as an ashtray. Knowing the gorilla as the nearest living creature to human beings, that only three hundred remain in the wild made my day in a remote Congolese market one of the saddest in my entire life. But I can't help feeling disheartened in modern day Spain, when I hear that boys in my own village have been caught tying fireworks to the backs of stray dogs, or come across an emaciated donkey tethered to a post by barbed wire, a defenceless beast of burden wilting in the midday sun.

Maria thinks man's contempt for animals is because we don't befriend them. Instead of making them our friends, we use them, chop them up and eat them. We are in a bar when I tell her about the donkey covered in maggots in the dry river bed. The intelligence upsets her so much she asks the barman if he knows the owner. Of course, the barman knows nothing, just like when someone scratches your car. I admire her for trying. Mostly I keep my opinions on such matters to myself, wouldn't dream of broadcasting them in a bar, but on bullfighting I make an exception. My stance is constant, and unequivocally clear. I might not advertise my view, nor proselytize, but if I'm asked, my response is always honest. Thus it comes as a great surprise, when Pepe, a mutual friend, drives Maria and me to a bullring in a neighbouring village, gifts us a pair of expensive tickets that he can barely afford to buy. '*No te preocupes,*' he tells me not to worry, reading panic in my eyes. '*Es un gran prix, no una corrida.*' And so we ascend the steps into the open air, makeshift arena, assembled overnight like a circus tent for a local fiesta.

'What's a gran prix?' I ask Maria as we take our seats on an upper tier.

'A competition with prizes for the winners,' she explains, 'apparently this one is with bulls.'

Listening to our confab, conducted in Spanish on his behalf, 'Baby bulls,' Pepe interjects. 'Mani and Pep are in our team,' he adds proudly, speaking of his sons. 'Us against Champa and Chakora.'

After a song, sung out of key, by a fat Chakoran housewife, the games commence; the boys, from the competing villages, running around the arena trying to put ribbons on the bulls' horns, pull a tail or two. The young bulls seem to enjoy the sport. About the only danger in the sawdust ring is when the spirited bulls go for the boys, try to toss or spear a teenage backside. Whenever that happens the crowd erupts into wild applause, far louder than any occasioned by this or that village kid scoring a point.

When the games come to an end, the *alcalde* of Chakora steps into the ring to hand out the prizes. Purusha are the clear winners, at least in the eyes of the numerate. The team from Champa, awarded the third prize, aren't particularly put out as they know it reflects their score. But the boys from my village, able to count, are less than pleased with second place, notwithstanding their prize of red and white rosettes and a bottle of whisky. Pepe tells me the mayor is as bent as the rigged elections in Spain were over a century ago. 'The results were published in Madrid before the people had even voted,' he shouts in my face as if I might have had a hand in the political corruption. But his protest is mild, drowned out by the chorus of insults and chants concerning the mayor's sexuality and the wanton ways of his mother. Someone from the crowd hurls a cabbage at the mayor, but it misses, hits the fat singer on the bum; a fist is thrown. It looks like things might get out of hand, until the mayor, fearing for his safety, summons the Guardia Civil into the fray to reestablish order.

'*Agua fiestas,*' a woman screams out, meaning killjoy. It appears to be a fair reflection of the mood around me. What better way to cement old rivalries than a punch-up, icing on the cake, a fitting finale to round off a great day out. The sight of cops manhandling his sons has Pepe on his feet, riles him beyond belief; a farmer has to restrain him. Wisely, he sees reason, decides it's time to leave. He knows he's drunk, driving without the licence he lost for drunk driving. At his behest, we stop at a bar on the way back to our village. I smile, Maria doesn't, when he informs us he needs a *copa de coñac* to steady his nerves.

We have barely settled into our seats, when we're joined by Cebolla. Born in Malaga, Cebolla is a supervisor in an olive oil factory just outside the village. He isn't a popular man; in the twenty-nine years he's lived in Purusha he's failed to make a single friend. At the factory where he works he's hated by his co-workers. Too macho to prepare his own pack lunch he scrounges from those beneath him. On one occasion, chomping on someone else's sandwich, he moaned that there wasn't enough meat between the bread. It was a complaint so offensive to the factory hand that he drew a knife, offered to make a different sort of sandwich, stuffed with plenty of meat after he had cut the Malagueño's balls off. A smoker who cadges cigarettes, but never buys a packet, a drinker who never stands a round, his meanness is legendary. Someone told me the blind shell out more for girlie magazines than Cebolla spends in a year. According to rumours, in his apartment there's a lightbulb he moves from room to room, in emergencies, a candle in his bathroom when he can't wait for the bulb to cool down. But it's not only his stinginess that sets him apart. His body odour doesn't encourage propinquity. He's called Cebolla, which means onion, because of the oleaginous stench that emanates from his neck, chest and armpits. Every morning, smearing his body with the juice of freshly crushed onions, he thinks he's discovered a cheap perfume that drives women crazy. Judging from Maria's reaction to his peculiar scent, he might have a point, but not in the way he thinks. He is, however, undeniably popular with dogs. They follow him everywhere in the village; oftentimes try to shag him.

A malodorous, tightfisted man can be forgiven, like any fool, his faults. But a charitable disposition is more elusive when Onion airs his views on women. Even in a village such as Purusha, where the wind of feminism has yet to fan the thoughts of many, his Neanderthal views are conspicuous, or, in fairness, his nerve to express them. Openly, he espouses the view that women are inferior to men; vassals put on the earth to serve them. If he had the money, he'd live in Afghanistan, convert to Islam, take four wives, settle down in a country where women know their place. Known in the village as a *pulpo*, an octopus, he paws at married women, practices frottage in the fiestas, stands behind lone, teenage girls to perform a little war dance of pelvic thrusts. A fount of lewd comments, he boasts of his conquests in local bars, how he bedded someone's grandmother, shaved the hairy thighs and armpits of a plump, middle-aged fruit-picker from Romania before he could mount her. In a country with the most punters in Europe, where knocking-shops aren't hidden, but advertise their trade under garish, brightly coloured neon lights, smutty vignettes aren't uncommon, late at night, in village bars. But they are usually reserved for the ears of men, many beyond their rutting prime. What marks Onion out from others of his sort, is that he doesn't give a fig if a member of the fairer sex overhears his sordid stories. Thus we're not surprised when he tells us that he's had '*a bit of black*' in a brothel over the weekend. 'I pity any women who bears your weight,' Maria looks at him with disdain, weary of his eyes caressing her bust. Unaccustomed to women who stand up to him, Onion doesn't offer a riposte. Instead, with tongue and fist tied, he turns to Pepe and me for moral support, tells us that all women are *putas*, whores who can't be trusted, that he's a generous man, pays good money for his vices. I tell him to piss off, that he needs to be sectioned; Pepe that he needs to buy us a drink. My hostile response doesn't seem to bother him in the least; he's used to insults, has a thick hide. But the idea of buying a round so alarms him, that he's on his feet in a flash, says he's late, would love to stay, but has to go. When we're rid of his reek, Pepe tells us that Onion hasn't the *cohones* to go to Cadiz, let alone Kabul, that he's a kerb crawler rumoured to like underage girls, who, some whisper, he beats up in the back of his car.

'Why isn't he arrested?' I ask.

'You can't cart people off to prison because of rumours,' Maria tells me, 'the Inquisition has come and gone.'

'Yeah, she's right.' Pepe says, with a thoughtful expression. 'If you could, there'd be no one left in the village.' It's an observation without humour, but because it's true, has me convulse with laughter.

We don't stay long in Pepe's house, merely tarry for a baked potato in the fire he lights to prepare a barbeque. While we are sitting by the pool in his garden, his boys turn up with their team-mates, and an empty bottle of whisky. Still smarting from their recent brush with injustice, Pepe throws fuel on the barbeque, and then their fury, by telling them they were cheated. Out of disgust they ceremoniously tear off their sportswear, toss their shirts into the fire, along with their prize rosettes, all the while discussing the mystery that Chakora's *alcalde* has managed to father children when he's a *maracon*, a queer. A cathartic pantomime, recorded on mobile phones, downloaded to Facebook accounts and YouTube, something to share with their friends. But it's a grave error, as the youngsters discover, when they each receive a magistrate's letter the following month with a one thousand euro fine – their videos, alongside the testimony of 'independent witnesses' used against them.

On our way home, walking through the village, we pass the bar on the ground floor of the *tercera edad*, the centre for senior citizens. It's late; the patio tables and chairs are already stacked; the manager is mopping the floor. But for a dejected figure, sitting with hunched shoulders on a bar stool, there are no customers. Staring at his feet, rather than the walls of an empty flat, I'm the first to recognize Onion, the man who can't make friends. 'It's sad,' Maria says, somewhat clairvoyantly, following my regard. But her sympathy is thin for she's known such men throughout her life. At home, over a pot of tea, she tells me that in the tiny *aldea* next to her village, a settlement of barely thirty houses, there's a plaque in memory of a fourteen-year-old girl. In her time, the girl was said to be the prettiest flower under the sun. Her name was Angelica, a beautiful name to match her face. And yet her beauty destroyed her. Denounced as a witch, she was burnt at the stake, after she spurned the advances of an old, ugly money-lender. According to the stories that sprung from the flames that consumed her, she was stretched on a rack, tortured in every conceivable manner, before the *auto-de-fe*. The money-lender paid the Inquisition a coin to enjoy her, as did others; the last, a wizened hunchback who used the fallen limb of a tree as a grotesque phallus to ram into her broken body. The poor child was already half-dead when the priests dragged her by the hair into the public square to burn her. A day later, unable to expunge the memory of Angelica's screams, the flames erasing her face, her father hung himself outside the Catholic church in Maria's village.

I heave a huge sigh of sorrow, but can't find words to respond to such a tale of horror. It's only when we are lying in bed, an hour later, that I tell Maria her legend is famous, that I once read something similar in a novel. 'My village, this village, it happened all over Spain,' she says sadly, and then tells me that women have always been downtrodden in her country. How, in the dark years of the civil war, innocent women were thrown into prisons, fed on rotting vegetable peels, worked as slaves, tortured and raped, used as bait to flush out their men. And then, after the war, half the women in Madrid, often with their daughters, were forced to stand on street corners to feed their families. Branded *rojos* by the Francoists, men who could satisfy their lust and at the time confirm the fascist prejudice that all Republican women were whores.

10

SPAIN HAS A TRADITION OF NAMING HER CHILDREN AFTER CATHOLIC SAINTS, often the first son taking his father's name, the eldest daughter her mother's. Thus in a village as small as mine, there might be fifty Joses to match fifty Marias, a score of men called Antonio to go with twenty Antonias. In my own barrio there are half a dozen men with the name Juan in a cul-de-sac of four terraced house. Hence the *raison-d'etre* of the *apodo* or *mote*, the nickname attached to each and every family in the village. While it's customary, a matter of common courtesy, to address a Jose by his Christian name when face-to-face, the same Jose, in the third person, to avoid confusion, is always denoted by his *apodo*.

Not all *apodos* are pleasant. In Purusha there's a family known as the *Caga Zanahorias*, the family of 'Carrot Shitters'; another family burdened with the nickname *pulga*, meaning flea, yet another called *Oreja de Burro*, 'Donkey Ear' – an *apodo* that traumatized one boy in the Donkey Ear family so much that he trimmed the top of his ears off with a pair of sheep shears. In Maria's mountain village, her family are known as *Los Gatos*, meaning 'The Cats', a nickname earned several generations earlier by Monse's great grandmother's habit of feeding stray cats. That Maria knows the origin of her family's *mote* isn't common; most are lost in the mists of time, passed down over the centuries. With newcomers it's completely different. Some, like Pete and his wife, don't even warrant a *mote*. As they hardly go out, their impact on the life of the village is minimal. But for the strangers who earn a nickname, having made an impression on village life, the connection between the name and the person is usually clear. Thus Cebolla is called onion because he smells like one. I'm known in reported speech as *El Londinense*, meaning 'The Londoner', because that's where I come from. If it's strange that I have a *mote* in the first place, given that there aren't any other men in the village called Kim, the mystery is magnified by the fact that Maria, behind her back, is now called *La Londinense,* even though she's Spanish, and has a sister in the village with a completely different family byname. The real complication will arise in the future if we have kids, Maria tells me jokingly one day. No matter how thick their Andalusian accents might turn out to be, they will always be known as the *Londinenses,* as will their children if they have any. Fortunately, it's a hypothetical consideration, parenthood isn't on our horizon. We both love children too much to have them. And then there's *El Oso*, 'The Bear', for Pablo from Jaen; so named as he stands over two metres tall, looks like a beast, has long, shaggy hair and a fiery temper.

On the rumour mill I've been told that Pablo is a retired civil-rights lawyer. A man who spent several years in South America where his family lived in exile until the death of Franco. It's also on the wind of gossip that I've learnt that he acquired his unusual appellation with unwonted swiftness. Out for his first beer in Purusha, he tore into a bunch of villagers foolish enough to admit that they had voted for PP in the last general election, a political party, in Pablo's eyes, with fascist roots. A staunch republican who lost two grandparents in the civil war, Pablo called them rednecks, accusing them of licking the hand that whipped them. When one of the villagers protested, Pablo rose to his feet, cast his huge shadow over the man, stared into his eyes until he fell silent. Challenged by his friends, once Pablo had departed; called a *cobarde*, a coward for not taking a stand against the newcomer, the villager defended himself by saying he couldn't argue with a bear.

Although I'm intrigued by Pablo's reputation, have seen his redoubtable figure in the village a few times, always in a sombrero, his eyes shaded by sunglasses, our paths have never crossed. But all that changes one night in a bar, where, between a dozen tapas, I chance upon him haranguing a group of five men at his table. Of the five, four I know by sight, the other, a father of three, by his byname *Tonto*, which means fool, a sobriquet he lived up to one night when he got into a fight after someone told him he was heterosexual.

Reading a newspaper, nursing a cup of coffee, alone at a table, even against the din of the TV, I can hear Pablo's every word. 'Get off your knees,' he yells at the frightened villagers. 'The so-called crisis is a conspiracy cooked up by the corrupt elite. Their plan is to rob you of your pensions, to scare the shit out of the poor buggers lucky enough to have a job, so they're happy to accept longer hours and lower pay, grateful to work until they drop dead.' I catch myself behaving like a local, looking up when he pauses to drink, looking down when he continues. 'Look at the kids in our village, all over Spain – they *are* the future, and yet over half of them are out of work, their jobs in the hands of sixty-seven-year olds. Who wants a sixty-seven-year-old fireman?' Someone at his table puts his hand up to speak, but Pablo ignores him. 'Is it our fault that we live longer?'

'No,' the man who wanted to speak replies, putting his hand down.

Again Pablo ignores him. 'They've divided the poor into those who have a job and those whose hands are idle. They'd love to make us all destitute, but they can't. Without us, who'd do their face-lifts, put implants into their rotting gums, build their mansions, police their property, sweep their streets, grow their food, cook and clean for them, wipe their rich arses.'

'Yeah, that's right.' The man who wanted to speak finally makes a contribution beyond the monosyllabic. 'But what can we do?'

'Rise up against the handful of multi-billionaires who pull the strings, whose wealth is greater than the wealth of half the world's population put together. Rise as one, and shout *"No Mas."* And this 'crisis', in which the rich have got richer, will be over in the blink of an eye.'

'But where will the jobs come from?' The man who has found his voice has the temerity to ask another question.

'They're already here. All we need do is share them. A two-day working week for all.'

'The bosses won't like that.' The man with the voice interjects.

'Idiota!' Pablo calls the man an idiot. 'We are the bosses,' he shouts, thumping the table to spill his and the others' drinks. 'How long has your brother worked in the paint shop?'

'Years,' the oldest man at the table replies.

'How many?'

'I don't know. Twenty, maybe more.'

'And he's married, with kids and a mortgage round his neck.'

'Aye.'

'And yet *el carbon*; the bastard, who owns the shop, doesn't even pay his full social security; his Saturday staff less than the minimum wage.'

A thought, in a small village, best left unsaid; Pablo's explosive accusation falls on deaf ears, warrants no response, other than a wall of silence erected by an uncomfortable awareness that *el carbon* is at the other end of the bar drinking a glass of beer.

Dismissive of the hush he's engendered, Pablo calls the men slaves of their own making, pays his bill, and then turns to my table. 'Hi,' he says to me in English. 'I'm Pablo,' he introduces himself, crushing my hand in his enormous paw. 'And you're *el Londinense*,' he laughs. 'I've heard of you. You're famous, must be someone of consequence to have earned a title in this God-forsaken pueblo.' He laughs again, heartily, like a Rabelaisian roar. He notices that I've finished my coffee, says I need a beer, orders one, and then tells me that he has to go, that he's late for his supper, but we must have a chat sometime, talk about what really matters.

'I'd like that,' I respond, after I've thanked him for the beer.

'Hasta luego,' he bids me farewell, adding before he steps into the street, 'You know we've met before.'

'We have?'

'I gave you a postcard.' He removes his sunglasses to allow me to contemplate his dark, piercing eyes. And then, all of a sudden, it's clear – the *bicho raro* in Almerimar.

'That was you?'

He nods with a smile.

'That postcard changed my life.'

'I know.'

When Pablo's out of sight, Joaquim leaves his seat to ask me what we talked about. Like everyone else in the bar he doesn't speak English. 'Nothing! He just introduced himself.'

'Good,' Joaquim says, and then warns me to keep away from him, or I'll be banned from his paint shop.

When I get home, Maria's there waiting for me. I tell her about Pablo and his nickname, how he fired me up, how he reminds me of the protagonist from a book that Bill asked me to read years ago.

'What book?'

'It was called 'The Ragged-Trousered Philanthropists.' A book about the plight of the poor in England at the beginning of the last century, about a worker who saw things how they were, but was mocked by his fellow workers when he tried to open their eyes. Orwell called it a classic of working-class literature.'

'Orwell! He's the English novelist who fought for the Republican army in our civil war. I've read his 'Homage to Catalonia.' But who wrote the other book?'

'Tressell. A pen name used by an impoverished Irishman for fear of the workhouse if his work had him blacklisted. I remember that no publisher would touch his hand-written book, that he died young, of a preventable disease, never saw his book in print, never knew it would sell over a million copies.'

'That's so sad,' Maria responds with a lachrymal look. 'But what's a workhouse?

'A place where those without work were housed. A place where families were segregated, with conditions so dire that some men were forced to sell their wives. Orwell called them prisons for the poor.'

'And that happen in your country during the British Empire?'

'Spain's not the only country with dark pages in its glorious history.'

'I guess not,' Maria says, looking downward with widened eyes.

We succumb to silence for a short period, both absorbed in pensive thought, but I'm far too excited to allow sadness to creep over our mood. 'But there's more to this night than I've mentioned. Pablo's the man who gave me the postcard in Almerimar.'

'The postcard that brought you to me?' Maria responds to my disclosure with open-mouthed astonishment.

11

AS MY FATHER FOUND OUT IN MY MID-TEENS, I'M NOT THE TYPE WHO CAN BE told who I can or can't see, but it's nigh two months later, in the heart of spring, when I again chance upon Pablo, near an olive grove, a short walk from the country house that he calls his *cortijo*. He's out with his dogs, a piebald bull terrier and a beautiful, black and white collie with a golden chest. Both dogs are on extendable leads that he holds in one hand, in the other, a tiny shovel to scoop up their mess, the first one I've ever seen in the village. 'That's the man who gave me the postcard,' I inform Maria, as I shift into reverse to park in a street that sees a car once a year, but has a Zebra crossing.

At first, Pablo doesn't recognize me, my face obscured by the visor of a baseball cap. But then his face lights up, as we draw nearer, to give sense to my shadowed features. 'Hi,' he smiles broadly, releasing his dogs to shake my hand, to bend down to kiss Maria after I've introduced her. He invites us to his house for coffee, brings his dogs to heel by bellowing into the olive grove; calls the bull terrier Mahatma, the collie Maya. When he opens his front door, he shouts a warning to his wife that he's not alone. We are removing our shoes in the hallway when a slim-figured, *Mia Farrow* lookalike, probably in her late thirties, appears at the top of the stairs. Dressed in a pair of frayed jeans and an oversized woolen jumper, her descent is greeted by a flurry of wagging tails. '*Hola*,' she says in a chirpy, friendly voice, trying to control her dogs and kiss us at the same time. '*Me llamo Maite.*'

'*Me llamo Kim, y esta es Maria.*'

'*De donde eres?*' Maite asks where I'm from; my accent evidently not *Andaluz*.
'*Londres.*'

'Oh, I love that city!' she immediately switches to English, tells me that she spent a year in Camden Town as an au pair when she was twenty. How she got to know all the famous landmarks, Buckingham Palace, Big Ben, the British Museum. How she made extra pocket money busking with her guitar in Covent Garden on her free weekends. When Maite talks of Berlin and Bratislava, a honeymoon suite in a gothic palace overlooking the Grand Canal in Venice, poor Maria, who's spent her whole life in Spain, looks a little subdued. But like me, she can't help warming to Pablo's wife, especially when she tells us that they settled in a village where first cousins fall in love with each other – to forget the world, to grow vegetables and walk their dogs.

'We're here to lose our egos,' Pablo calls out from the kitchen where he's grinding coffee beans from Colombia.

With slippers to warm our feet, Maite leads us to the back of the *cortijo*, into a large, brightly-lit room with a prospect of the garden. There's a paved patio with flower beds, garden furniture, an alabaster fountain next to a pair of hammocks – somewhere to stretch out to enjoy the mountainous vista. 'We have a *pozo*, our own source of water,' Maite smiles, pointing to a well. Beyond the patio, shaded by orange and citron trees, is a vegetable patch with the first green shoots of spring. In the distance, I make out a shrubbery of Japanese loquats, a pair of holm oak trees and a Spanish chestnut that looks as if it has been there for centuries.

'It's like a picture canvas,' Maria remarks.

'Our slice of paradise.'

I take the risk of sounding erudite, tell Maite that the Arabic word for garden shares the same root for heaven.

Maite receives my comment with a smile, says she has another garden she'd like to show us. Following her into an adjoining room, we are led to a bonsai collection on a long, pine table, under a jalousie window. I recognize Japanese maples, a baobab and a banyan, but have to be furnished with a name for the Chinese elm, juniper and jade trees. Maria, unfamiliar with the oriental art, can't believe the beauty before her; nor the banyan a single tree, its aerial roots spread across a porcelain tray like a little forest. When Maite informs us that the banyan is eleven years older than she is, neither of us are surprised. The room is no less a surprise, scattered with art and artifacts from South and Central America. A collection of Aztec masks covers the wall opposite the bonsai garden. Inca tapestries embellish other walls; above an open fire, a jaguar mask from Mayan Guatemala. In a glass-panelled display cabinet I find clay shards of pre-Colombian Gods, pottery from Peru, jade models of Mexico's pyramids of the sun and moon, next to a calabash mate mug from Chile, a set of spoon-shaped, pure silver straws. 'It's like a museum,' Maria says, looking at black and white, framed photographs of Angel and Igazu Falls.

'Oso loves the Americas,' Maite says, using her husband's *mote* rather than the name his parents gave him. 'We might go and live there.'

'Or India,' Pablo joins the conversation, entering the room with a coffee percolator in one hand, four mugs in the other.

'Have you been there?' I ask of a land I know fairly well.

'I spent two years there in my mid-thirties,' he answers as he pours the coffee. 'Mostly in the southern state of Tamil Nadu. In an ancient temple town called Tiruchirappalli.' Impressed, somewhat stunned, as I know the town, I ask why. 'To study yoga and meditation with the wisest man I've ever known. I'm who I am because of what my Guru taught me.'

'Whoever you are, you're a man of surprises,' I respond. 'A Sufi of secrets.'

'Sufi!' Maria looks at me with questioning eyes.

'People of the path.' My answer doesn't alter the look in Maria's eyes. I add to her confusion when I elaborate, 'One who has mastered the art of invisibility.'

'Are they ghosts?'

'Teachers seldom seen,' I try a plain answer; before adding that Sufi masters aren't prophets, out to save the world; oftentimes, live as simple shoemakers, bakers or beggars, seen by only those with eyes to see.

'Beauty is in the judgement of the eye,' Maite misquotes the Bard to gauge if she's grasped my point.

'In a way,' I respond. And then, speak of a Sufi who could express different emotions on different sides of his face. At the same time show himself as a Sheikh to one, a fake to another; aware that one might be ready, the other not, to look at the sun.'

'How two-faced!' Maite shows wit by crossing her eyes.

Clearly confused by our chatter, Maria turns to Pablo to say, 'Your wife's very funny.'

'She has her moments,' Pablo responds, looking at Maite with affection in his eyes. 'And she makes great cheese omelets.'

'Madre mia! He's always thinking about food. That's why I call him the bear,' Maite laughs, standing up to slap her husband's ponderous belly. 'Would you like

to eat with us?' I'm inclined to divulge my reserve, say we don't want to impose, but Maria's Spanish, more forthcoming, says we'd love to as long as she can help.

Alone with Pablo I ask him about his Guru. He tells me that he was called Balaji, that he wasn't famous, had but a handful of followers. How he died twenty years ago at the age of ninety-five, in an act of *mahasamadhi*, fully conscious, willing his spirit to depart the body.

'Did he write anything?'

'No,' Pablo replies with a wistful smile. 'He taught breathing techniques and meditation, gave *satsangs*, but mostly just sang songs to God.' Not wishing to appear intrusive, I hear myself humbly ask of his Guru's teachings. 'Better Balaji speaks for himself,' Pablo responds, laughing at the effect his words have on me. 'Come,' he says, leading me to the first floor, where we tread gingerly between Mahatma and Maya enjoying an afternoon siesta. We enter a small room without bed, table or chair; bare, but for a stack of battered up suitcases and a bronze statue of Nataraj with his six cosmic arms frozen in the dance of death. While I admire the exquisite detail of the Indian sculpture, Pablo rummages through a suitcase full of old papers, photos and documents until he finds what he seeks. 'Here,' he says, handing me a cassette tape in a broken case. 'When I was in India my English wasn't as good as it is today,' he laughs. 'Sometimes I found it difficult to understand Balaji because of his accent, so I asked him if I could record his *satsangs;* pause, rewind and play a hundred times until I understood every word. This is the only recording that has survived, the others eaten up in cheap Indian cassette players, or lost over the years.'

'This must mean a lot to you,' I say, looking at a cassette case that has travelled the world.

'Don't worry! If it breaks, it breaks!' Pablo says with an engaging smile. 'I know every word by heart. I want you to have it.'

The moon is up when we leave the *cortijo*. We thank Pablo and Maite for their hospitality, invite them to dinner the following week, before we hug and say goodbye. It's still warm, a pleasant night, so we take the long way home, drive to the *pantaneta,* the pretty reservoir a few miles beyond the village. 'Maite didn't know anything about the postcard,' Maria says in a quiet voice as I turn off the engine.

'Maybe Pablo forgot to tell her.'

'I don't know. She just shrugged her shoulders, and said that she wasn't surprised.' Maria sighs before she continues, 'In the kitchen she told me that she spent three months exploring the three Guianas of South America. She travelled by herself. She was only twenty-three. Don't you think she's amazing?'

'She's great,' I reply. 'And Pablo too. I meant it when I said he was like a Sufi. Who would have thought I'd meet a man like that in a tiny village?'

'It must be fate!' Maria exclaims in a strange voice, almost as if she's brooding. Her voice is no less peculiar when she suggests we take a *paseo*, a moonlit walk. We take an ancient pathway, pass through silent olive groves, following a stream where once a river flowed, until we come to an abandoned mill. 'Let's look inside,' Maria suggests, 'see if we can hear the faint echoes of the family that once lived here.' Apart from shafts of moonlight spilling out of the crumpling roof, the mill is full of shadows. A gloomy abode, fetid and musty, with no sign of life, but an empty beer bottle and a bat hanging from a rotting rafter. When I light a cigarette, Maria snatches it from my lips, throws the cigarette to the floor, stubs it out with her foot. 'Later,' she says, as she unbuttons her blouse, unclips her bra, hitches up her denim skirt to remove her panties. Arching her back against a stone wall she pulls me into her breasts. When her passion is spent, the panting all but over, puzzled, but pleased, I ask her what has got into her. *'You,'* she says, biting my ear. 'You, you, you,' she repeats in a husky whisper like a bitch in the distance baying at the moon. In the car, on the way back to the village, she tells me she has a plan.

'A plan!'

'Yes, a plan. I'm going to master the world language so that we can always speak English when we're alone.'

'Bueno, tu eres la Londinense,' I reply, to make us both laugh.

At home, Maria says she has another plan. She tells me that she'd like to see something of the world before she dies; asks me if I'll take her to Africa.

'Africa!'

'Yes, why not? Except for Morocco, I don't know anyone, apart from you, who's been there. Not even Maite and her husband.'

'Say where and when, and I'll take you.'

'Promise.'

'I promise,' I reply, and then seal the pact with a kiss.

An hour later, in bed, with my eyes closed, on the verge of slumber, I hear Maria whispering into my ear that she loves me, that I'm *her* Sufi who writes love poems in the sand. With my heavy eyelids sealed I can't know if she thinks I'm lost to sleep.

12

THROUGHOUT THE SEASON OF SUN, I FOLLOW MY LOVE, UP INTO THE SIERRAS, down to the coast, wherever she dances on stage in village fetes and fiestas. In the blue sea, on lazy, cloudless, long days, I teach her to swim and snorkel; the name of the stars and constellations on short, sultry nights. Not weeks, but months pass before I sit down, on a cool evening in autumn, to listen to Pablo's tape.

The tape is so old that it takes several minutes before anything emerges from the dialogue recorded. The first voice heard is that of an Indian, presumably in response to a question. 'Unlike the poet, the dancer can't be found outside her art. When the dance begins, the dancer comes forth. When it ends, the dancer disappears. The world is the dance of the Lord – that's how you can see him.'

'But from the day I was born to this one, men have been killing men. So much suffering, one war after another. Is this God's choreography, part of his plan?'

'There's no plan, my child,' the Guru chuckles. 'Only *lila*, the cosmic dance.'

'But Balaji...' I hear the same sanyasi's voice rise plaintively before the tape falls silent, returning a few seconds later with a truncated answer.

'You might see it waxing or waning, but the moon is always full.'

I switch off the cassette player to consider the Guru's response. For some reason I find his words unsettling, but can't put my finger on the reason why. Not until I remember a school day, when a boy I had never spoken to, asked a priest why God had allowed his sister to die of leukemia when she was only eight years old. At the time, I had already suffered three or more years of Bible studies. But this was different, the first time I was fully alert in catechism, had heard a question worthy of a decent answer. When the priest told the boy that God saw the whole picture, whereas those of his creation only parts, I was so disappointed that I asked the priest if he saw what God saw, for if he didn't, how could he know what he said was true. The response from the Catholic father was immediate, and fraught with fury. With the full force of the Old and New testaments he thumped me on the head with an unabridged Bible. Unable to imagine an Indian Guru using the holy book of Hinduism in such a forceful manner, I return to the tape, catch a mumbling chant, before someone with an American accent asks a question about God and meditation.

'When mind is, meditation isn't. When meditation is, mind is not. When you are, God isn't. When you aren't, God is. With light, darkness disappears. This is the journey from the sixth chakra to the seventh. When water boils it turns to steam. This is the moment of transformation.'

The message seems clear enough, apart from the bit about chakras, of which I know little. But it is evident that the American struggles, for the Guru appends his address with a short, but charming tale. 'This is the story of the mosquito and the wind,' Balaji begins. 'How the little fellow went to the court of the King to complain that the wind never allowed him to go about his business.' The Guru stops to clear his throat, before he relates how the King was fair and just, summoned the wind to give his account. How, when the wind swirled into the court, the mosquito was nowhere to be seen. 'You can't find darkness with a torchlight,' Balaji laughs out loudly. And then his voice fades into a whisper, metamorphosing into a monotonous, crackling hiss that persists for nigh three minutes, until broken, by a young seeker's quest to help humanity.

'Turn to the one beside you. Humanity is an abstraction. People exist, not abstractions. To save the forest, love the trees. Above all, be a light unto yourself, and you'll be a light unto others.'

'But...'

'No buts. The light from a single matchstick can burn a great city to the ground.'

After that passage, there is little else on the recording. Merely a word, here or there; without context, fragments devoid of meaning, like random pieces from a jigsaw puzzle. Just before the play button clicks into a horizontal realignment with the other keys, I hear Balaji admonishing a female student, telling her that she asks too many questions, that if she could drop all questions, she'd become the answer.

I press rewind, listen to the ancient tape screech as it spins back to where it began.

13

I CAN'T BLAME MARIA FOR HER FRIENDS' BEHAVIOUR, OR HER INNOCENT WISH that they might join us on our African adventure. On the surface they seemed a personable couple; suitably paired. Indecisive and vague, with a need to be smothered and mothered, not a confident man, Antonio wanted a woman to order him about, someone capable of making his decisions. Dolores had all the traits he lacked and admired. A bossy headmistress by profession, in her private life, someone who had to be obeyed. On the evening we got together, to discuss where we might go, everyone was in high spirits, the wine flowing freely until we had emptied three bottles. Aware that people love to talk about travelling, especially when they're drunk, but rarely do anything about it, I expected nothing to result from the evening other than a sore head. For me, it was all hot air, alcohol-fueled 'pub talk'. A term I had coined, somewhat bitterly, at the age of seventeen, when, after a night of ale with two friends debating how to hitchhike around Europe, I found myself alone, a month later, waiting in the port of Dover for a ferry. One of my friends, I later discovered, didn't even have a passport. But on this occasion I was wrong. To her credit, Dolores meant business, she wanted to go to Africa and her husband was going with her. Thus I was faced with the prospect of flying to Durban, a city with an unenviable murder rate, with not one, but three fledglings of the road. I was up for the challenge, but if I envisaged difficulties ahead, especially when Dolores started phoning me to read out hotel reviews three weeks before the date of our departure, I wasn't mistaken.

'Yes, dear,' Antonio meekly responds, when Dolores screams at him for getting lost after he's followed her directions. It has been a constant theme between the newly-weds; an amusement for the onlooker if it's wasn't dangerous. But spinning round in black townships, where Afrikaans daren't stop at red traffic lights for fear of being carjacked, is anything but a joke in crime-ridden South Africa.

'Yes, dear,' Antonio provides his stock response, when Dolores instructs him to pull up in a one-dirt-road settlement in the middle of nowhere. When I ask why we are stopping, Dolores informs me that she's hungry.

'But you had steak for breakfast not two hours ago,' I protest. 'And three fried eggs.'

'That was *then*. I'm hungry *now*.' Dolores puts me in my place.

Fortunately, there's a tiny market in the settlement to which Maria and I repair to share a tepid coke and a packet of crisps. Declining the offer of a pet macaque, we wait under the blood-red flowers of a sausage tree, while Dolores and her chinless husband, ignoring a cloud of flies, tuck into an African stew. It's a mistake, as we all discover the following day in Kruger National Park. 'Stop the car,' Dolores yells in the middle of the bush. 'I need to have a shit!'

'There might be lions nearby,' I warn her. 'Can't you wait?'

'No, I *can't*. It's out *there*, or in the *car*,' she shouts with a twisted grimace, ordering Antonio out of the car to keep watch.

'Can't I watch from here?'

'Get out of the car *now*. This is an emergency.'

As it turns out, there's no pride of lions in the vicinity, no leopards or hyenas, but while Dolores is busy with her bowel business, another hired car arrives, full of

German tourists. As we pull out of the shadows, the Germans moves into our parking space as is the custom on safari. But if the tourists anticipate a glimpse of wildlife, they're sorely disappointed, for the only extraordinary sight on offer is an enormous, steaming quagmire of human waste. Things might not be so bad if our pit, or shit stop, were the only ramification of the unfortunate African stew. But over the course of the next few days, there's another consequence - a variety of odoriferous perfumes to entertain us in the enclosed space of the car. Needless to say, Dolores doesn't acknowledge her wind, leaving the three of us to wonder which of us has mastered the vaudeville act of anal ventriloquism. It's during one of her less vociferous, but lethal farts, that I finally lose my cool. Having careered off the road to avoid an oncoming juggernaut, swerved into a pot hole that almost flips the car onto its roof, I shake my head solemnly as I put my hand out for the ignition key. '*What!*' Dolores bellows, 'it wasn't *my* fault. The truck driver was a maniac.'

'He was on the correct side of the road; *you* weren't,' I raise my voice to match hers.

'How dare you speak to me like that,' she shouts in my face.

'I speak to you as you speak to others,' I shout back, citing several occasions when she has addressed the Africans we've encountered as if they were slaves.

'Did you hear that,' she turns round to her husband sitting in the back of the car next to Maria. 'This man is insulting your wife.' When Antonio doesn't respond, she orders him to speak up. But for once her demands aren't met. Suffering from a near-death experience, he's too shaken up to utter a word. When I ask for the key a second time, the neurotic reverts to a childhood tactic by turning on the tap of tears. For the rest of the afternoon, mysteriously transcending the constant plaint of car sickness that has bagged her a front seat throughout the journey, she sits with her husband at the back, her head on his lap, intermittently shedding tears whenever his hand tires of stroking her matted hair.

After another wonderful afternoon on safari, followed by a short, but spectacular sunset, we find ourselves on a benighted road, heading back to our lodge. Everyone is elated, chatting ten to the dozen about what we have seen, nothing more dramatic than a battle between two bull elephants in musth. But then, everything changes when Dolores spots a neon light, tells her husband to pull into a parking lot outside a shopping mall. 'I'm famished,' she tells us. 'I fancy a pizza.'

'It's late! There aren't any whites about,' I make audible my observation, but Dolores, already out of the car, isn't listening. Despite the alarm bells going off in my head, I join the others to follow her to the entrance of the near-deserted mall. When I espy a gaggle of red-eyed black youths eyeing our every move, I suggest we return to the car, eat at our lodge, which is only a thirty-minute drive away.

'Why?' Dolores demands.

'Because it's dangerous,' I reply forcefully, reminding her that we're not in Spain, but in a country that doesn't bat an eyelid at fifty homicides a day.

'I don't think it's dangerous,' she argues without rhyme or reason.

'Then why's that parked behind you?' I point to a bullet-proof van that advertises twenty-four-hour armed security.

'Kim has more experience than you,' Antonio addresses his wife quietly. 'He's been here before; to Africa fifteen times. I think we should go,' he adds softly, aware that he's broken the rules.

In the car, driving on an unlit road, a tense silence prevails until Dolores puts the radio on, finds a news station in Swazi, and then starts to talk to herself in Spanish. When we arrive at the lodge, hapless Antonio, who only wanted to save his skin, is frog marched into their bedroom, where behind a closed door, he's given the lecture of his life.

Sharing a bottle of Stellenbosch wine, in the privacy of our bedroom, Maria opens up, beginning with her concern for her friend's state of mind. 'What happened tonight? I thought Dolores was having a nervous breakdown in the car.'

'She's a control freak who freaked out because she lost control.'

'In Spain I thought I knew my friends, but now we're here, I realize that I don't know them at all They're like strangers, especially Dolores.'

'Many a couple have broken up on a package holiday, I laugh. 'And travel, with all its demands, swiftly lowers the mask on the face of so-called friendships, revealing the warts and pimples you only glimpse at home. I've lost a friend or two on the road.'

'I guess you're right; but it's still a shock.' Maria sighs. 'Dolores convinced me that her weight problem was due to a medical condition, but I've never seen anyone eat so much. She's obsessed with food. She's like a walking stomach.'

'Behind all that blubber lurks a very insecure human being. She's not sure of herself, or her husband. Not unlike a sea lion, her blubber is her line of defence against a hostile world.'

'You mean the bigger her belly, the smaller the world?'

'That's one way of putting it,' I laugh, amused by the idea and image. 'There's metaphysics in her obesity. An attempt to control a hostile world by eating it. Of course, she doomed to fail like Sisyphus, for the universe isn't constant, but expanding.'

'But Kim, what are we going to do? Is there any way we can part? They're ruining our first journey together, or at least trying to.' I laugh out loud, say I can think of several options, that it's a temptation, but if we abandon them anywhere in black Africa other than the departure lounge in Durban, they won't survive.

'Morally, we're stuck with them.'

For the sake of what remains of the journey, I try to keep a low profile, ignore Dolores' incessant gibes and provocations, walk away when I catch her and her redneck husband laughing in the face of a simple chambermaid who doesn't understand their demands for Wi-Fi. I only step in when things look like they might turn nasty. One such incident occurs the following week in a market in Lesotho, near the South African border. Instead of following Maria's lead in modest attire, Dolores shows her ponderous bust off in a skimpy, skin-tight halter neck top, her enormous, short sausage legs cellophane wrapped in a pair of see-through leggings. When she bends over to prod a jackfruit, to reveal knickers so stretched as to appear as a G-string, the local men howl out in delight. 'That mama likes Africans,' screams an old man with thick, grey dreadlocks, openly pointing at her gigantic rump with a rusty machete.

'Na'man! Her *ma* knows black,' says another, with a salacious grin. When he puts out a hand to sample what he calls an elephant's bum, I move swiftly, grab the man's wrist with an indulgent smile, tell him to calm down in a strong South African accent. Aware that we are vulnerable, the only pale faces in town, I turn to Antonio, switch to Spanish, tell him to get his wife back to the car, not to hurry, not to show fear. For once, Dolores doesn't play the *sabionda*, the know-all game, but does what she's told. I take the wheel, snake through the busy market in first gear, order the others to lock their doors, roll up their windows when a stone hits the side of the car.

A few miles out of town, on a narrow, twisting mountain road pitted with pot holes, with more men on donkeys than other cars, Antonio, regaining a hint of colour, does the unthinkable. 'Why do you have to dress like a black man's whore?' he yells in anger. None of us can quite believe what we've heard, least of all Dolores, who looks at the trembling wreck of a man next to her with thick eyebrows arched in utter contempt.

'I can't help it if other men find me sexy,' she says, her small, beady, brown eyes catching mine in the rear-view mirror. A wave of nausea passes through me as I return my eyes to the meandering road.

'I feel like I'm dreaming,' Antonio says, as we enter the village where he was born and has spent most of his life. He doesn't seem to realize that in a week or two, when his life has returned to normal, Africa will turn into a dream. When we bid the couple farewell, I contain myself, say goodbye instead of good riddance.

But for sand from the Sahara on the terrace, a dead cockroach on the kitchen floor, my house is homely, just as we left it. We unpack, throw our dirty clothes in the washing machine, prepare a light lunch. 'I can't wait,' Maria says, searching for a USB socket at the back of my TV. And so we sit on the sofa to relive our trip through video clips; see again two tuskers at war, a pride of lions snarling in their sleep, a buffalo carcass ripped to pieces by a pack of hyenas, a cheetah on a rock surveying the savannah for potential prey, a baboon taking a green mango from my outstretched hand. When the more intimate moments of our journey, mostly remotely recorded, appear on the TV, Maria finds it difficult to control her emotions. Watching us kiss on the banks of the Zambesi; wrapped in each other's arms, under a celestial rainbow rising out of the mist of the mighty Victoria Falls, she struggles to hold back her tears. 'What memories!' she says, when the television screen turns blue and silent. Climbing on to my lap, holding my face in her tender hands, she thanks me with a lingering kiss, for making her dreams come true.

14

A FEW WEEKS AFTER OUR AFRICAN ODYSSEY, WE FIND OURSELVES IN A DANK, candle-lit bodega, sitting with Pablo and Maite, in the *barrio de cuevas*, one of the oldest quarters in the ancient town of Guadix. On the heavily scarred table of oak before us, there's a platter of *bravas*, roast potatoes covered in spicy tomato sauce, and two carafes of wine – one, a red from La Ragua, a mountain pass into the Alpujarras, the other, a sweet white from the Moscatel grape. 'Africa!' between mouthfuls of *bravas*, Pablo mutters a word that's the same in English and Spanish. I take a back seat, allow Maria to narrate our tales, how we saw herds of elephants, giraffes, buffaloes and hippos, four of the big five; how her first passport lost six pages to visas and stamps.

'It sounds wonderful,' Maite says with delight, when Maria ends her story with the hornbill we tamed with titbits, how the exotic bird waited for us every morning outside the rondavel we hired at the end of the trip. 'But you haven't once mentioned Dolores and her husband.'

'A team made in hell. Not my cup of tea,' I give my opinion succinctly, leave Maria to explain her friend's penchant for getting lost in dangerous places, how she gassed us with farts throughout the journey, stole items, ashtrays and towels from every hotel and lodge we slept in, purloined a packet of peanuts in a store in Swaziland with a security guard on top of a stepladder with a submachine gun; how, at the end of the trip we were barely on speaking terms, and haven't spoken since. Pablo nods his head knowingly, strokes his shaggy beard, before he tells us he doesn't know the woman personally, has only seen her from a distance, but if the mind and body are intertwined, it was obvious we would have a hard time.

It's a surprise when Maite suggests we try another wine, but an even greater surprise when Pablo vetoes the idea. 'If we don't leave now we'll be late for the midnight procession.'

'You know I'm not keen on religious processions,' Maite smiles at her husband. 'Not after the coffin!'

'Coffin! What coffin?' Maria asks.

'Shall I tell them?' Pablo turns to his wife as he begins to laugh.

'If you *must*.' Maite doesn't look impressed.

'While you were away we went on a driving tour; hopping from village to village along the northern coast.' Pablo begins his narration with a wicked grin. 'Quite by chance we stopped for lunch in a village in Asturias on a local saint's day.' He pauses to chuckle.

'And!' Maria prompts our friend.

'And so, after our lunch, we joined this strange procession where the pilgrims carried artificial limbs that corresponded to their body parts they believed had been healed by the saint.'

'And the coffin?'

'That was the idea of an old man who had been told he had a month to live after being diagnosed with terminal cancer. Apparently, he had prayed to the saint for another year, and had had his prayers answered. To thank the saint, he got his family to carry him at the back of the procession in a coffin. When the procession ended the coffin was placed outside the church, and to the shock and horror of everyone who didn't know the story, the old man popped out of his box like a reanimated corpse. Maite, who was quite drunk at the time, and like me knew nothing about the old fellow, nearly had a heart attack.'

'That's a great story,' I manage to say, before joining Pablo in an eye-watering bout of belly laughter.

'Pobrecita.' Maria gets up from her chair to give Maite a cuddle.

We reach the sixteenth-century baroque church of Santiago the apostle just after twelve, but being in Andalusia, in good time for the midnight procession. We aren't long outside the church, in a plaza of cypress trees, before we're approached by familiar faces from our village.

'Hola, mis amigos,' Rafa, the village butcher, greets us merrily. *'Toma,'* he hands me his goatskin full of wine. 'I'm not religious,' he says with a serious face, 'but I had to get out the house.'

'A change of scene,' Maria suggests.

'A change of family more like,' he responds, before explaining that his wife's family are down from Barcelona for *semana santa*. 'I had to sleep in my van last night.'

'Why?' Pablo asks.

'Because it's the only place I can get some peace, smoke my home-grown, escape the bloodhound who gave birth to my wife.'

'As bad as that!' I exclaim, thinking of Maria's mother.

'Worse!' Rafa takes a huge draught of wine. 'Even the phantom in my front room has buggered off.'

'Your house is haunted?' Maite enters the confab with a question.

'For centuries, till *she* moved in the other day with her crucifix and bloody rosaries.'

'Don't talk about my mum like that,' Martha prods her husband in the chest. 'You know she was brought up by nuns, and is very religious.'

'I've seen more religion in an ant,' Rafa scoffs at his wife; and then tells us about a painting of Jesus his mother-in-law owns. How it hangs in her saloon, next to the bathroom. How, after a shower, naked under a towel, she apologises to the painting when she passes it on her way to her bedroom. 'As if *He* would be interested in a scrawny, old plucked chicken.' Martha's mouth opens, but no words are forthcoming. 'In my house, I don't even close the door when I'm on the throne.'

'No one wants to hear about your dirty habits,' Martha prods her husband's chest with a disapproving frown rather than a finger.

'I've nothing to hide. My bum is God-given.' Rafa lifts the *bota* to his lips. 'It's your mother who has the weird ways; *she's* the Catholic stripper.'

'Sinvergüenza!' Martha calls her husband shameless.

'Well, if the painting bothers her so much, why doesn't she move it – put it in the pantry, out of harm's way.' Martha tries to keep a straight face, to continue the domestic battle, but before she can wipe the ghost of a smile from her lips, the lights go out, bringing a sudden hush to the plaza. It's an orchestrated outage, for as the street lamps go out, firebrands are ignited on the crenelated ramparts of the Moorish castle above the plaza. A light show to transport the devout congregation to another century, to set the scene for a solemn procession of penitents in black, pointed hoods, black cassocks with red crosses splashed across their chests.

'This is the spookiest sight,' Rafa says, reverting to the superlative, but for once isn't wide of the mark.

When the ghoulish figures filing out from a narrow passage in the seigneurial palace above the church, taking two steps forward, one step back, finally reach the plaza, the ominous beat of a dozen drums grows louder. Children who should be in bed, cry out in fright, hide behind their parents, while grandparents lower their heads before making the sign of the cross. Maria, who looks as frightened as the children, sidles up to me, hooks her hand on to my arm, asks me what I think Julia would've made of the men in black with their burning torches. The question pleases me, reveals a traveller's perspective. But when I think of the jolly maid who swept our room in Zambia, how she sang Christian hymns all day long, my answer makes me shudder.

15

I'M IN THE MONTHLY MARKET, BUYING APPLES FOR A PIE I WANT TO BAKE, when Nabo, a rabbit farmer, runs up to me with a red face. *'Ven conmigo,'* he tells me to follow him, after I fail to make sense of his gibberish. Holding my elbow, he leads me to the end of the market of thirty-two stalls until we stand face to face with two scruffily clad strangers. Stubble-faced, dirty and dishevelled, the men look like vagabonds out of an American novel set in the nineteen-thirties.

'Buenos. Puedo ayudaros?' I greet the strangers, ask them if I can assist them.

'Si, Señor! ¿Hay... un restaurant... aquí?' The tallest of the two strangers asks me if there's a restaurant in the village.

'Would you prefer to speak English?' I respond, having detected a cockney accent behind the faltering Spanish.

'Cor blimey! Yeah!' The cockney grins in surprise. 'Can't understand the lingo round here.'

'There's somewhere to eat at the top of the village.' I begin to give directions, but lose the strangers after the third turning through the alleyways of the village. Instead, I offer to take them, as it's easier, and on my way home. There's little conversation climbing the steep hill to the plaza, but the cockney, noting that we're being trailed by Nabo, tells me we're being followed. 'That's Nabo. He's harmless.'

'Strange name!'

'It's a nickname. It means turnip.'

When we reached the restaurant in the *tercera edad*, Frank, from East Ham, offers to buy me lunch. 'The least we can do.' I decline politely, but accept a beer. John, from Silkstone, somewhere in South Yorkshire, opens his mouth for the first time, says he's starving when he picks up the menu card. 'I'm starving too,' Frank responds, says he fancies two menus of the day not one.

'Me too,' John says, putting down the menu card. 'And a couple bottles of the best wine.' When Antonio, the bartender, takes the order for two bottles of Duero and four menus of the day, he's confused as there's only three of us at the table.

'My friends are hungry,' I explain, but Antonio, looking at the bedraggled Englishmen, doesn't seem convinced. He tells me that Duero's expensive, that before he uncorks a bottle, they'll have to pay up front.

'What's up with the waiter?' Frank asks.

'He wants payment in advance.'

'No problema!' Frank produces two crispy fifty euro notes when one will do. Feeling slightly embarrassed by Antonio's unwonted request, I explain that the village is off the beaten track, not on the tourist map.

'He was confused by the order. I had to tell him you were very hungry.'

'That's no lie! We ain't 'ad a proper meal in a week,' Franks responds. My look of surprise brings forth their story. I learn that they both live in the ex-pat enclave in Albox, that John has an Irish wife, and Frank, a long-standing girlfriend from Leyton. Despite spending several years in Spain, their Spanish is poor because in Albox they don't need it. To make ends meet, John's a mechanic, but being ex-SAS, runs survival courses in his spare time. 'And I'm a plumber who likes hiking. If there's a mountain, I'll climb it. So a survival course is right up my street.'

'So you've been in the mountains?'

'Up and down mountains all week long. But *gawd* knows where we've been. He'll 'ave to tellya.' And so it's left to the taciturn Yorkshireman to relate their route. As he tucks into the bread that comes before the meal, I learn that their course began in the Badlands of Tabernas, in a landscape of karsts and caves so weird that Frank thought they were on the moon. 'Tell him about the cactus,' Frank interrupts.

'Someone left a cowboy hat on a cactus. Frank thought it was an alien.'

'Too bleeding right I did.'

'Anyway, after the desert, we climbed into the Sierra Filabres. Six days and nights wandering through pine forests, hiking in and out of gullies.'

'What did you eat?'

'Not much,' Frank, his mouth stuffed with bread, interrupts a second time. 'John trapped a rabbit on the first night, but after that our diet went downhill.'

'It's true,' the Yorkshireman nods solemnly. 'For six days we had to make do with prickly pears and berries, washed down with infusions of wild herbs boiled in billy cans from dewdrops.'

'Did you see much wildlife?' I ask, caught up in their adventure.

'Foxes, hares, rabbits, a viper and a couple of scorpions in the Badlands,' John answers.

'And plenty of birds,' Frank interjects.

'Yes, lots of birds,' the Yorkshireman responds. 'Golden and booted eagles, griffons, Egyptian vultures, falcons, one or two peregrines, and a spoonbill.'

'And an eagle owl.'

'You saw the beast, not me.'

'I sure did! It was on our third night in the Filabres. In the half-light I thought it was a rock until it took off when I approached it. I've never seen a bird so big! I nearly shit myself! It had talons big enough to grip a man's head, rip his face off.'

'Yeah,' John smiles. 'But in the pine forests we saw more fauna than in the desert. Deer, mountain goats, wild boar and their spotted piglets.'

'But they were always in the distance – glimpses in the pines.'

'Except one night, when we made a fire, and found ourselves surrounded by a pack of wild dogs.'

'Wild dogs!' I exclaim. 'I know there are a few wolves roaming the Pyrenees, but wild dogs in Spain. Do they exist?'

'They do now,' John assures me. 'Ever since the *Junta* decided to clean up the pueblos, round up the strays and put them down.'

'Those that escape the noose head for the forest to form feral packs,' Frank adds knowingly.

'Were they aggressive?' I ask, remembering a case in Sri Lanka where a tourist was torn to threads by a pack of pariahs.

'Not really,' John says, 'just inquisitive; skeletal, flea-bitten, mangy mutts.'

'Que dijo sobre pulgas?' Pulga enters the conversation he's been following with his friend Turnip, from a neighbouring table. Having recognised the one word in English he knows, namely 'flea', he's keen to show the rabbit farmer he has a handle on a foreign language he doesn't speak. I translate what has been said; and Flea confirms my intelligence. He tells me that his cousin is hired to hunt the dogs. I continue my role as translator, relate that Flea thinks it reduces road deaths.

'Wot's the geezer going on about? Frank gives Flea the eye. 'Dog or man?'

'I don't know; he didn't specify; or, if he did, I didn't understand.'

'No, you're doing alright mate. All I hear is grunts and groans.'

When Flea tells me that some of the dogs his cousin kills aren't strays, but domestic dogs let out for the day, family pets without chips or collars, like most of the dogs in our village, I nod my head sadly, but refuse to translate his words, as Antonio arrives at our table with plates of food. Turnip is astonished by the amount of food on our table, especially when he realises that all the dishes are for the two tramps he found in the market.

'Wot's Igor staring at?' Frank asks, with his mouth full of salad. 'And why's he leaning to one side? He could be a *bleedin'* gargoyle on the tower of Pisa.'

'I'm afraid the villagers tend to stare at new faces,' I attempt to answer the cockney's first question before I address his second. 'A chronic neck ache forces him to lean to one side. It's somewhat ironic as he makes a living by snapping rabbits' necks.'

'Karma, you mean!'

'Perhaps!' I respond to an idea I've previously considered. 'But according to Turnip it's nothing to do with his profession. He believes it's the work of his dead wife. He claims she tries to strangle him every time he sleeps in the bed they once shared. For this reason, he has given up sleeping in his bedroom, prefers to spend the hours of darkness by a fire in his front room, propped up in a hard-backed chair. The local doctor has told him this is why he has a problem with his neck. But Turnip has no time for quacks. His hope lies with the Catholic church. He wants an exorcism. So far he hasn't been able to persuade an ordained priest to perform the ritual.'

'Gordon Bennett!' Frank exclaims. 'It's like the dark ages round 'ere.'

'Bell-bottoms have just arrived,' I respond with a titter.

'You seem to know a lot about the locals.' Having devoured two dishes, John comes up for air with a comment. 'Are you staying with friends?'

'I live here.'

Frank puts his fork down, looks at me in surprise. Essaying to digest my reply instead of fried chicken, 'Do they accept you?' he asks.

'Sort of! I've got a *mote,* a local nickname.'

'I don't know how you do it,' John scratches his grizzled chin. 'When my wife and I first arrived in Spain, we rented an apartment in Calpe, and bought a second-hand car to go touring. We wanted to look around, to see where we might set up shop. We went south, along the coast, and then up into the mountains. One day, somewhere above Berja, we took a twisting road into the sierras, and found a white-washed village in an isolated valley. It looked so picturesque that my wife told me to drive down to the village. She thought we might have a coffee, ask if there were any houses for sale. It was a small village, perhaps a hundred inhabitants, all of whom, from baby to grandma, were gathered in the main plaza when we arrived. No one spoke, or moved, except to turn their heads in unison to stare at us.'

'I read about a village near Salamanca that was so remote that the villagers only heard about God at the beginning of the last century.' Frank chortles, before shovelling down the first of his two rice puddings.

'There was a church in this village, so I guess they knew about God. But the weirdest thing was that they all looked alike, as if they all came from the same family. We thought we had found the village of the damned.'

'What did you do? I ask with a mischievous grin.

'We didn't do anything. I just drove around the plaza, and took the only road in and out of the village. It was the most surreal experience I've had in Spain.'

'I reckon there's a fair bit of inbreeding goin' on round 'ere,' Frank says, looking at Turnip.

'A bit, I dare say,' I concur, before my mobile starts to sing. 'Excuse me,' I stand up to take Maria's call outside. When I return to the table, the boys are on the brandy. 'Where did you sleep?' I ask, for their mud-caked knapsacks look too small to accommodate a tent.

'Under the Milky Way,' John replies, 'in thermal sheets.'

'And tonight?'

'In our own beds. I called my wife from the phone box in the market. She'll drive here when she's finished work. We've arranged to meet outside the town hall at five.'

'I'm having a hot bath when I get home,' Frank smirks, scratching his leg. 'I'm covered in flea bites.'

'Are they racist?' John asks.

'Who?'

'The villagers here?'

'They don't seem to like the Moors, but they put up with them. Someone's got to harvest the grapes.'

'But you! Have you had any comments?'

As John's question is particular, I don't mention Pete's myriad clashes with the locals. 'I've been called a *guiri* a few times, suffered the odd snide remark about El Peñón, or Gibraltar, as we prefer to call it. But apart from that, the only time my place of birth has been an issue, was when a miserable fellow told me the British were worse than the Arabs.'

'Why'd he say that?'

'Because his grandfather told him about the Rio Tinto massacre in the nineteenth century. How the British owners had their Spanish workers slaughtered when they asked for better conditions.'

'What did you say?'

'The bar owner stepped in on my behalf, so I didn't get the chance to respond. He told the fellow I was born in the twentieth century, which resulted in a handshake and a game of darts.'

'So you're happy here?' Frank takes a turn to ask me a question.

'It's hard not to be,' I reply, thinking of the disgruntled Jesuit monk who complained in the seventeenth century that it was difficult to be miserable in Andalusia.

'But you're a Londoner! Why here?'

'I'm about to cobble together my usual colourful answer when Maria enters the restaurant. She's finished her *Sevillana* class for bored, middle-aged housewives, showered at her sister's, shampooed her hair, put on a floral frock, and looks beautiful, fresh as a spring flower. 'That's why,' I reply, taking the easy way out, for the two Englishmen smile knowingly, which I doubt would've been their response if I'd mentioned a Sufi and a postcard.

15

THE EASE WITH WHICH PROMISES ARE BROKEN IN MY VILLAGE IS AN ASPECT of my life in the sun that I've never fully come to terms with. I might have grown accustomed to the Andalusians', at times, healthy disrespect for arriving on time, their endorsement of Wilde's observation that punctuality is the thief of time, come to accept that television programmes might not appear on the box as scheduled; or, not at all, as when a live chat-show I was hoping to see was cancelled at the last moment because the host hadn't recovered from a *Resaca*, in other words, was too drunk to appear before the camera. But when a friend invites you to dinner, and then forgets all about it, isn't even at home when you turn up with a bottle of wine, is a little difficult to understand. To compound the enigma, if I wait for an apology, I'll wait forever. Not that this seems to bother anyone in the village but me. In a neighbour's kitchen, I remember how it was almost impossible to reach her sink. There were boxes of self-assembly kits everywhere, no room to swing a cat. Proudly, my neighbour told me she was having a new kitchen installed; it was just a question of when her cousin could find the time to do the job. When I asked her how long she'd been waiting for her cousin to show up, she told me, without a hint of embarrassment, a year. I couldn't help laughing, but quickly redeemed myself, by telling her at least her cousin would turn up one day, being blood-related, in a village where family counts.

But waiting for a new worktop and a set of kitchen cupboards is quite a different kettle of fish from waiting for an electrician to repair a faulty fuse box, especially when half your house is without power. I've waited three days for Juan, three days down the drain, trying to contact a man who refuses to answer his phone. Admittedly, it's not an insuperable problem; I can live without electricity on the first floor, do without air-con or a fan, get around with a torch, read in bed with a candle, but it's annoying. And yet, no matter how I try, I can't quite work the flames of anger up, for Juan, notwithstanding his unreliability, is an agreeable fellow, loveable in many ways. Two years earlier, I recall, how, after I had declined his offer of paella, he went ahead and cooked the dish, brought it to my house, carried the huge pan in sweltering heat to my front door. No, I'm not angry, just irritated that instead of waiting for Godot, I could've been with Maria, in Cadiz, where she is staging a dance programme she's been working on for months. I'm annoyed because I know she wanted me at her side, for love, if not moral support.

When the working day is over, hope evanescing with the sun, I'm seized by a sudden burst of bottled-up energy. Three days cooped up in my house inspires me to shave my chin, put on a clean shirt, and march to the nearest bar, which just happens to be my electrician's local.

Of course, there's no sign of Juan, only an unruly crowd for a game on the box. As far as I can gather the match is a friendly, a kickabout in the park between the Spanish youth team and their French counterparts; hardly *'El Classico'*. I arrive just in time for a penalty shootout. For some reason, the meaningless game seems to be of the upmost importance to a farmer known as Rana, which means frog, so much so that he removes the picture of St Jerome from behind the bar to put it next to the TV.

'But he's French!' Flea barks.

'St Jerome was born in the village,' a member of the Donkey Ear clan counters.

'Yeah, that's right!' Alberto, the barman adds his pennyworth. 'That's why he's our saint.'

Out of harm's way, I sit at the back of the bar, hidden behind yesterday's local tabloid. When the Spanish miss their first penalty, I'm glad they're up against the French and not the three lions of England. Having once made the mistake of watching England beat Argentina in a bar in Buenos Aires, in a game the locals called *'La batalla de las Malvinas'*, I've learnt to stay at home in my village whenever England play Spain. Sadly, after a beer was thrown in my face by an angry Argentinian, I've reached the conclusion that football doesn't always bring out the best in people. Fortunately, the missed penalty isn't costly as the French youngsters don't seem up for the job, but when the Spanish miss another penalty, Frog leers at the patron saint of the village. 'Jerome doesn't sound very Spanish,' he mutters angrily, his faith in the saint shaken.

'He might be Italian! A neutral!' Flea suggests when the French centre forward sends his spot kick into the stands, a miss that leads to a sudden death shootout. I put down my newspaper to watch as a gangly, acne-faced youth from Valencia puts the ball on the penalty spot, note the deadly silence that permeates the bar.

'He can't miss,' Frog makes the sign of the cross. With the ball going in off the post, Frog's faith is restored; the bar's timbers rattled by an enormous roar, so mighty, it has Eva, the cook, pop her head out of the kitchen to see what all the fuss is about. Just as a golfer might sway to one side to influence the direction of the ball he has already struck, a jeer goes up to unnerve the French teenager who must score to keep his team in the game. Of course, the booing doesn't work – the Spanish keeper goes the wrong way as the ball hits the back of the net. Or, perhaps it *does,* for despite the ensuing groans of deflation, there's a twist in the shootout when the referee, for no apparent reason, orders the kick to be retaken. Again, the jeering of telekinesis is called into play, and this time, at least according to Frog, it's efficacious, as the Spanish keeper palms the ball over the bar. The victory has the farmer off his stool, running around the bar, arms in the air, screaming with delight as if Spain have just won the World Cup. I, of course, do my part, cheering on the team of my adopted country; a celebration that brings me a large beer on the house, and companions to my table. When someone shouts *'Viva San Jerome,'* I join in the chorus of *'Viva, Viva,'* – a sort of Spanish version of 'hip-hip-hoorah.'

Although it's mildly disturbing to witness, I'm pleased to see Frog wear a happy face, for he hasn't by all accounts been having the best of times recently. After discovering the internet, following in the footsteps of three other middle-aged men in the village, it's common knowledge that he ordered a bride from South America. But his bit of skirt, as he likes to call her, didn't quite match the photo he saw online. Instead of the gorgeous blonde he dreamt about, he got a frumpy, bad-tempered, cross-eyed woman in her mid-forties from Manaus. Having forked out a fortune on agency fees, legal documents, visas and air tickets, he drove to Madrid airport in high spirits. Admittedly the flight from Brazil, delayed by five hours, had ruined her make-up and hair-do, added a year or more to her already weathered face, but had he not written her name on a piece of cardboard to be held aloft at the arrivals gate at Barajas, he might never have found his future wife. It was at that special moment, when the online lovers met, that he discovered the photo in his wallet had been taken twenty years earlier. Struggling with the four trunks that contained her past, he led the Brazilian woman and her five-year-old daughter to the airport car park. It was there, on the fourth floor of the dimly-lit car park, feeding coins into a machine, that he recovered from the initial shock. Aware that he was no oil painting himself, that he hadn't ordered a virgin, he reasoned that after being alone throughout his adult life, something was better than nothing. Driving out of the airport, he was in a good mood, convinced everything would run smoothly with his new woman and her daughter. What he didn't know at the time was that there were seven more kids to follow.

The transformation from being a carefree bachelor, who, during the weeks of winter, went to bed without removing his shoes, to a married man with responsibilities was, within a few months, enough to thin out his hair. That was at the beginning of the marriage. But now, a year on, crowned the head of one of the largest households in the village, without actually fathering any children, has rendered his comb completely redundant. It has also turned him into the butt of a host of horrible jokes. It is this change in his local standing, rather than finding the confines of the bar too constricting to contain his joy, that compels him to run around the village square like a madman. As he stops by the fountain to issue lung-bursting cries of celebration, and at the same time deliver uppercuts to an invisible enemy, I realize it's his way of putting a finger up to the world. When, red-faced, puffing like a steam engine, he returns to the bar, I watch with compassion, as he rushes up to the picture of St Jerome to kiss the image of the saint.

'It had nothing to do with San Jerome, Turnip mutters. 'We were the better team, and deserved to win,' he adds, to pour scorn on Frog's idea of a miracle.

'No miracle!' Frog explodes as if he's been stabbed in the back by a protestant.

'Yeah! No more a miracle than the Chinese shutting up shop on the night of San Jerome.'

'Now, that *was* a miracle,' an Antonio I don't know butts in, and then invites me into the conversation by asking if there are any Chinese stores in England.

'Plenty,' I reply. 'There's an area in central London known all over the world as Chinatown.'

Alberto, the barman who claimed St Jerome was born in the village, considers my contribution before sharing his thoughts. 'It's an invasion. They're pouring in,' citing immigration figures he saw on the news.

'Their plan is simple,' Antonio interjects. 'First, they visit a village to study the shops. They note the price of everything; and then a month later they open a store with the same "Made in China" goods, only ten percent cheaper. Within a few months all the competition is dead. That's when their prices start to creep up.'

'They put Imma's shop out of business,' Alberto wags his finger.

'And Raul's hardware store,' a man with a pepper and salt goatee raises his voice.

'It's the same in Madrid,' Frog says with authority, having been in the capital, especially in the area around the airport, several times recently. 'Even traditional Spanish shops, butchers and boutiques have been bought out by Chinese businessmen. I had a beer and a tapa in a bar run by the Chinese. There wasn't a Spaniard in sight. I couldn't understand a word they were saying – I had to point to the menu to get a slice of chorizo.'

'It's not right!' Alberto shakes his head. 'What do you think?' I'm asked for my opinion.

As a foreigner I'm not sure how to answer. 'It would help if they took on Spanish staff,' I respond, hoping my comment isn't contentious.

'Yeah! My boy needs a job,' Antonio supports my suggestion, and then drags me back into the dubious debate by telling me the Chinese store in the village is selling Union Jack doormats.

'And on the coast, in resorts where the British are the main tourists.'

'Let them make a doormat out of the Spanish flag and we'll kill them. Aren't you offended?' Antonio is determined to get my opinion.

'Not really; although I think it's in bad taste, and not good business.' My response doesn't appear to impress my audience, so I explain how Britain and China have a long history. How, during the time of their empire, the British exported opium to China in exchange for silk and silver. How the Chinese lost Hong Kong, and more importantly, face. How, centuries later, they still have a problem with opium addicts.

'But they got Hong Kong back,' Antonio responds angrily, leaving me to wonder if Gibraltar is next on the agenda.

'They are taking over; trying to dislodge the yanks.' The man with the goatee moves the conversation in another direction. 'We should torch their shops.'

'Yeah, and then we're get our shops back,' Turnip, with his hand on his neck, wakes up. 'And Raul'll be back at work. What do you think? He looks at his fellow farmer. But Frog has other things on his mind, matters far more important, namely the lottery results. And so the incendiary debate peters out as all eyes turn to the box, reminding me of Pete's uncharitable observation that the locals have the attention span of grasshoppers.

From wind-swept Tarifa on the southern tip of Spain to La Coruna in northern Galicia it's nigh impossible to find a bar without a slot-machine. There are casinos in the big cities, betting syndicates in every village. In that sense Spain is like China; two nations that love to gamble. In my village, the locals will bet on anything; even, as I have witnessed, how to correctly spell Australia in English. It's the thrill of the flutter that counts. And there's no greater rush of adrenaline throughout the whole of Spain than when the lottery results are announced, especially at Christmas, when a ticket can cost a hefty twenty-five euros. Apart from me, the only other person in the bar without a lottery ticket is a man called Pedro. A pensive man who thinks the game is fixed, that the balls are weighted, that the only winner is the government who slap a twenty percent tax on the prize money. But Pedro has another reason, a darker reason to loathe the lottery, for he is the first cousin of Senor Fernando Garcia-Lopez, the only person in Purusha who ever hit the jackpot.

A jack-of-all-trades, described by his friends as an ordinary *campesino*, Fernando wasn't cut out to deal with the advent of sudden wealth. The first thing he did with his winnings, to the dismay of his family, was demolish the house where he had lived for forty years, replacing it with an extravagant folly that looked like a birthday cake with towers and turrets. Having owned a van and a tractor throughout his adult life, the next eccentric decision was the purchase of three expensive foreign sports cars. In front of his burgeoning claque of friends, showing off, by racing up and down a dried up river-bed, he wrote the first car off within a month. And then, somewhat inevitably, the women arrived; none more local than a manicurist from Malaga, with breasts so pronounced that the locals cruelly nicknamed her *los melones*, the melons. Monica was the name behind the melons, and when our paths crossed, I found her pleasant and unassuming, hardly the gold-digger I was led to believe. But *la Malagueña* apparently had another side to her, one I never saw, only heard about, namely a craving for cocaine. When she introduced her beau to the magic of the white powder, it was, according to Pedro, the beginning of the end for his cousin. Within two years, Fernando's fascination with Colombian powder was so strong that it altered the shape of his nose. The first thing to go were the cars, followed by watches and jewellery; eventually everything his lucky lottery ticket had given him was sold to feed his habit.

I never knew Fernando when he was high on the powder. When I met him he was clean, for the money had gone. All that he had left was the peculiar mansion in which he lived. It was there that I met Monica, still at his side, living with him in his large kitchen, the only room he could afford to heat. I was invited to his home after a mutual acquaintance, introduced me as *el Londinense*, the foreigner who could support himself without working. To butter me up, Fernando played the only English music he had, a CD by the Nolan Sisters; and then, as I opened the bottle of wine I had brought, he offered to sell me his house. When I explained that I already had a house in the village, he told me his garage, with room for five cars, was also on the market. After I had declined the offer of the garage, he said it was time to get down to business. By business, he meant a loan of a thousand euros, which he would pay back in a week with ten percent interest.

It was a few months after that brief exchange, when I heard that Monica had left him. Some said she walked out on him because the good times were over, others that she couldn't support his violent outbursts. Whatever the reason, her departure marked a dramatic acceleration in his decline. He was frequently kicked out of the village bars, oftentimes sleeping on the street in pools of congealed vomit. It was at this low point in his life that he turned to crime; enlisting as an accomplish, a good-for-nothing Bulgarian living in Champa; an alcoholic, who, to keep himself befuddled on cheap cartons of wine, put his wife on the game, selling her for as little as five euros for hand relief to punters on pensions. Together the pair targeted the most vulnerable, the very old, who were easily taken in by false ID cards, and the report of a gas leak. They even broke into three tombs in the local cemetery in the hope of finding a valuable heirloom. In all, their crime spree lasted six months, coming to an abrupt end, when someone recognised the wedding ring they were trying to sell in a bar not far from the house from which it had been purloined.

The Bulgarian was deported, but Senor Fernando Garcia-Lopez was given a three-year jail sentence that he cut short by swallowing a two-litre bottle of bleach. Pedro's cousin was barely fifty when he took his last drink. According to Flea, who went to school with Fernando, he was *'un hombre sinvergüenza que murio de vergüenza,'* – a shameless man who died of shame. Pedro, on the other hand, is more understanding, tells me that those with an interest in money beyond ordinary need, rich or poor, never have enough.

'Cono!' Turnip swears in disgust when the first number comes up, for even with the little sense he has at his disposal, he knows tonight is not the night when he will become a millionaire. It's a ghastly word that grates on English ears, for it refers to a woman's vagina. And yet, throughout Spain, it's a word casually employed in all sorts of situations, by both sexes, old and young alike, whenever the need to curse arises. There are more groans of scatological interest in the ensuing moments as tickets are torn and crumpled up. No one wins a penny. But the disappointment won't last, won't deter anyone from buying another ticket of

hope for tomorrow's game. No one gives a damn that Pedro is smirking in the corner.

'*Cono!*' It's my favourite word again, this time hurled from the mouth of the barman. 'Look at the time,' he yells, pointing to the clock above the slot-machine. It's almost ten thirty, the time when the cops turn up for their coffee. Turnip is assigned the role of 'look-out', something he cherishes as it makes him feel important. The whole palaver reminds me of my school days, when a nerd was posted outside the boys' bog, to keep watch while the 'in crowd' smoked their cheap cigarettes.

It's the government's second attempt to ban smoking in enclosed public spaces. The first time was voluntary. Left to the discretion of bar owners whether or not to ban smoking on their premises, it was completely ignored. One pub owner in Almeria was so annoyed by the EU directive that he put up a poster of Franco with a caption that read '*Cuando yo era el jefe podiais fumar tanto como queriais.*' – 'When I was the boss you could smoke as much as you liked.' But now the law has returned, '*en vigor*' this time, which means it's compulsory. '*No nos dieron ningun voto!*' - 'We weren't given a vote!' is something I must have heard a thousand times. For the Spanish are proud of their traditions, and smoking in a bar is one of them. Any intervention by a foreign power is guaranteed to cause resentment. I remember the actual day the ban became official. I was sitting in a bar in a very small village in the province of Granada. I fell into conversation with a retired English teacher who was openly flaunting the new law. When I asked him if I too might smoke, he told me it was up to me. 'Ban cars, not fags,' he said. And then had to repeat his opinion in Spanish, after an ancient, sitting at the other end of the bar, clutching a *sol y sombre,* demanded to know what he was talking about.

'Why cars?' the old timer asked, before taking a sip of his lethal concoction.

'Smoking might damage *my* lungs, but cars damage the lungs of the world. That's why.' The retired pedagogue equably replied. And then, as far as I could understand the local patois, he invited the greybeard to try an experiment that involved chain-smoking a packet of cigarettes in a car with its windows rolled up. 'It will take you an hour or so. Sure you'll feel lousy at the end. But get out of the car, walk around for a bit, and in no time at all you'll be as bright as rain. Now, try the same thing with a hose-pipe attached to your exhaust. You'll be dead in ten minutes.'

'But I need my car,' the old fellow protested. 'How else will I get to Granada?'

'Like you did when we were kids – on the back of a donkey.'

'The cops!' Turnip shouts into the bar, whereupon Alberto stubs his cigarette out. 'Sorry! False alarm.' Turnip sticks his head into the bar with an awkward smile.

'*Joder!*' Alberto swears before he lights another cigarette. Pedro, still smirking, offers Turnip his glasses.

Accepting a cigarette from the man with the goatee, I return to my reverie, wonder how the old schoolmaster has fared in the two years that have passed since our interesting *tete-de-tete*. I imagine that he still sparks up openly in a bar reached by a spider web of barely traceable mountain tracks. As Maria's father once told me, the mountain folk of the Alpujarras have their own ways. Proud and independent, Brussels could be on the moon for all they care. Until the beginning of the civil war, women regularly left their homes in veils, I recall reading in a book on the region. How, in remote villages pagan beliefs still mingle with papist dogma;

how the *curandera,* or healer is consulted to ward off the evil eye, asked to prepare love potions, or grind the cantharides beetle into an aphrodisiac mixture – a powder so potent that it once killed a Spanish king.

Of course, it's different in larger settlements like my own. Autonomy has been lost to a network of secondary roads connected to a motorway. There are daily buses to Jaen and Almeria. A train station, albeit unmanned, three miles from the village, that serves the coast and Granada. I'm told it was very different in the old days. Fifty years ago there were only two cars in the village. Now, it's difficult to find somewhere to park. And so, we play a game of cat and mouse with the local cops. In fairness, the cops are rather sporting, happy to turn a blind eye to a cloud of smoke in a bar as long as no one has a fag in his mouth while they drink their coffees.

As it turns out, the game is off for the night, forcing Turnip, who looks quite put out, to give the 'all-clear.' 'Someone must've lost a peseta,' Alberto says as he lights a cigar, insouciantly blowing smoke over a customer's tapa. On the TV, the news comes on. It begins with the usual soporific prattle of politicians, followed by sport, a murder or two, some wife-beating in Burgos. I lose interest when a reporter talks about a scandal involving a bald man whose fame doesn't spread beyond the shores of Spain.

'Wow!' Look at that!' Flea bellows, watching a report from a courtroom in Girona, where two teenagers are faced with a crippling fine or imprisonment for burning a photo of the king. Known throughout the village as a staunch royalist, a man who jumps to his feet whenever he hears a distant strain of the national anthem, he turns a shade paler, as he confesses to using his wife's old copies of 'Hola' magazine to kindle a fire in his kitchen.

'So what,' Pedro looks at his friend doubtfully.

'So, I'm a criminal. 'Hola' is full of photos of the royals.'

'Don't be daft,' the man with the goatee laughs. 'It only counts if you do it in public. Like having sex.' At the mention of sex, Turnip's ears prick up, as Flea considers the loophole.

'Are you sure?' the monarchist asks, but no one bothers to address his concern. Instead they tell me what they would like to drink after I offer to stand a round before I leave.

On the way home, I wonder where Juan has spent his night. Somehow, with my belly full of beer, not having a bedside light doesn't seem so important. *Manana*, I mutter to myself.

16

GLIDING INTO A SPACE BETWEEN A PINK CADILLAC AND A RED MUSTANG, Maria drives as gracefully as she dances. Not far from mini Hollywood, we make a pit stop in a roadhouse called 'Route 66'. A barn before it fell into foreign hands, the diner's popular with bikers. The cavernous dining hall is crammed with American memorabilia, mostly from the fifties. There are pinball machines, Wurlitzer duke boxes, Texan and Californian car plates, black and white photos of James Dean, Buddy Holly and a young Elvis Presley. We take a table next to a statue of Marilyn Monroe with the flowing hem of her dress frozen to her thighs. Studying a menu card that stirs the memory, for it's full of T-bone steaks, hamburgers, and other forms of meat, Maria and I opt for a bowl of tacos with an avocado dip, a side salad with a thousand island dressing. Maite orders barbequed spare ribs, but Pablo goes the whole hog with two giant hamburgers and a huge platter of French fries. Everyone drinks Budweiser from the bottle, except our driver, who is happy with a coke.

After the meal, we smoke over expressos, as Pablo tells us of Jorge, whose home we will housesit for a week. How he met the Andalusian in Tamil Nadu, in the ashram of all places. How they soon became great friends, were drawn to each other as the only Spaniards under the Guru's tutelage. He informs us that his friend is eccentric and unpredictable, likes to live on the edge, but that he's a soulful man with a heart of gold. And then he tells us that Jorge spent his late teens living in the Rif mountains of Morocco. How, every time he crossed the Straits to visit his family in Algeciras, he smuggled a lump of resin; just for the fun of it, as everyone knows the southern coast of Andalusia is never short of hash, no matter how many boats the Guardia Civil impound.

'A risky hobby,' Maria interjects, nervously twisting the straw in her coke cola can.

'That's why he did it,' Pablo laughs. 'But that was over thirty years ago. He stopped when his mother found him sorting through his waste with a kitchen fork in the family bathroom.'

'Why was he doing that?' Maria asks.

'Because on the ferry to Spain the ball of resin was in his stomach,' Pablo laughs again. 'His father was furious, called his son a wastrel who mocked the noble tradition of smuggling.'

'The *contrabandista* was the poetic hero of the common folk,' I mention the words of Irvine Washington. 'A swashbuckling Errol Flynn, a man among men.'

'But isn't smuggling illegal?' Maria evinces the innocence I love in her question.

'It *is* if you get caught,' Pablo clutches his belly while he hee-haws mirthfully.

Before we leave the diner, I pay a visit to the *servicios*. The toilet seats are decorated with the famous highway that cuts across America. Somewhat more uplifting than the urinal with a naked woman I once found in a bar in Purchena.

Passing a disquieting array of cliff-top houses, Maria suggest that if Jorge likes to live on the edge he should buy a house in Sorbas. 'I'll tell him that,' Pablo's laughter fills the car as we head for the coast.

When we reach the twisting road that curls around the Sierra Alhamilla, we catch our first glimpse of the Mediterranean Sea. The tang of salt in the light breeze, the sheen of the sun-speckled sea in the distance, a cloudless blue sky, sends a wave of excitement through the car as we drive up to the foot of the jagged mountain peaks into the charming white-washed pueblo of Mojacar.

The site of several ancient settlements, the pueblo, like my own, has a colourful history. But nothing lasts forever. By the middle of the previous century Mojacar had fallen on hard times. With barely a few hundred inhabitants, mostly old folk, retired weavers and fishermen, the pueblo seemed doomed, oblivion written on its crumbling ruins. But then a certain Senor Jacinto Alcaron, the local mayor, came up with a brilliant idea to save his community. He offered free land to those who would work it, abandoned houses to those who would refurbish and take up residence. It was a stroke of genius that attracted artists, musicians and writers, and a host of adventurous entrepreneurs. Jorge's grandfather was one of the first to move in. It was a perfect opportunity for a *contrabandista* fed up with his trade, a man fat with five thousand peseta notes in a goatskin money belt wrapped around his waist. That was over fifty years ago, since when the little town has been transformed into one of the prettiest and most prosperous white-washed pueblos in the whole of Andalusia. 'Park over there,' Pablo points to a rare parking space outside a seafood restaurant with a patio decorated with colourful flowers.

We follow Pablo's lead up meandering alleyways lined with fashionable boutiques, bars and cafes, pass under bowers of bougainvillea and arbours of rambling wisteria and wild rose, until we reach the *Castillo* and its pleasantly shaded courtyard. 'Not far now,' Pablo says, as we climb a promontory perched above the main cluster of white-washed houses.

'We're here,' our guide announces puffily, as he knocks on a heavy wooden door patterned with polished, metal studs. Half-hidden by a profusion of pink geraniums, Maria discovers a ceramic plaque mounted by the arched doorway. The plaque is decorated by interlocking flowers that encircle two proverbs in English. The first, allegedly German, reads:
 'If one man can do it, so can I. If no one can do it, I can be the first.'
 The second, the Andalusian version, is slightly different:
 'If one man can do it, let him do it. If no one can do it, why should I bother.'

We are still laughing when the door creaks open to reveal a sleepy-eyed Jorge. He's dressed in a loose-fitting, striped *jillaba* and a pair of bright yellow *babouches*, leather slippers from Morocco. A short man with shoulder-length grey hair, lean, but wiry, sporting a pencil-thin moustache, reminiscent of Dali, under a prominent hooter, Jorge's not the picture I had conjured up of a venturesome buccaneer. But appearances can, and often are, misleading. '*Mi alma*,' Pablo greets his friend by calling him his soul. Jorge returns the salutation as Pablo drowns him in a bear hug. Recovering his breath, Jorge showers me and the women with wet, wine-flavoured kisses, before inviting us into his house.

If Jorge's appearance is deceptive, his home follows the same theme. On the outside, white-washed and typically Andalusian, the interior resembles a traditional Moroccan inn. When we are led into the marble-tiled courtyard, the focal point of the house, I marvel at the two-tiered fountain, the orange and apricot trees in huge ceramic pots, the columns linked by arabesque arches that lead to pastel-coloured rooms and a sumptuous saloon that opens on to a terrace with a prospect of the sea. Contemplating the vista beyond the castle and the terracotta rooftops of the village I tell our host that his home reminds me of a *riad*.

'You've been to Morocco?' Jorge responds to my observation.

'Yes; and I've stayed in a *riad.*'

'Where?'

'In the labyrinthine medina in Marrakesh. I can't say exactly where as I always needed a guide to find it.'

'Ah! Marrakesh!' Jorge exclaims with evident pleasure. 'The pink city of my dreams.' Momentarily, peering out to sea, our host is seemingly lost in fond memories. *'El Maghreb,'* he sighs, before collecting his thoughts. 'Please, sit and smoke,' he directs us to a circular copper and brass table, before excusing himself to prepare refreshment. On the table there's a bowl of dried fruit, a silver, embossed ashtray from the kasbah of Mednes, two identical boxes inlaid with bone, one full of *kif* from Ketama, the other stuffed with vanilla-flavoured tobacco. While Pablo fills the bowl of a beautifully designed water pipe, his wife and I stick to *Fortuna* fags. Sending out clouds of scented smoke, long after our cigarettes are squashed dog-ends in an antique ashtray, Maite looks at her husband lovingly, tells us he is never in a hurry.

'Do you know the joke about the yank in an Indian taxi?'

'No,' Maria answers on our behalf.

'He asked the driver if he could go faster, only to be told he could but wasn't allowed to leave his taxi.' Familiar with Indian roads, I laugh more heartily than Maria. 'Pablo would never ask such a question, he's too busy in the present. Aren't you dear?'

'What!' Pablo looks at his wife, somewhat mystified, vaguely aware that he has been asked a question.

'See, he's lost in the moment.'

'There's nowhere else to be,' Jorge enters the room and the conversation. Bearing a platter of what he calls *cornes de gazelle*, crescent shaped pastries full of ground nuts and cinnamon, he's followed by a middle-aged woman with a tattooed face half obscured by the hood of a dark-coloured, baggy *jillaba*. 'This is Safiyya,' he introduces the wizened-faced Berber as she pours mint tea into gold-rimmed goblets. 'Our families are entwined. Her grandmother cooked for my grandfather, her mother for my father, Safiyya cooks for me. But she won't be here when I'm in Barcelona. She's no good with strangers.' On cue, the woman gives a faint nod of the head before disappearing.

'So you're English,' Jorge addresses me with a smile as he sprinkles *kif* on Pablo's tobacco. 'I love the English. And long may the Union Jack fly over *El Peñón*.' It's not often you hear a Spaniard utter such words; for me, it's a first, so I politely press for an explanation. 'Democracy the name of the game. When asked, over ninety-nine percent of the Gibraltarians voted to stay under British rule. If they'd voted for independence, now that they've got a football team, that would've been ok by me. Anything but the Rock in Spanish hands. That would be a disaster; ruin the whole coastal economy.'

'How's that?' I ask.

'There be no more smuggling, or wheeling and dealing on the money market.'

Maria wisely keeps her views to herself, but the cat hasn't got my tongue. 'What about the money the tourists bring in?'

'Tourists come and go. Where were they before and during the civil war? If it hadn't been for smuggling, we'd have gone under. I know families who had to rob rabbits from the eyries of eagles to survive. But not my family with its noble tradition of smuggling. My forefathers were dealing in contraband three hundred years ago; centuries before the first bikini graced our beaches.'

'As long as that?' I raise my eyebrows.

'Possibly longer,' Jorge pauses to suck on the water pipe before giving another thumbs up to Gibraltarian 'free trade' as he calls it. 'They gave us birth control.'

'Really!'

'Yeah! Condoms were prohibited in Spain. My family made a fortune selling *preservativos* to the peasants. And when the pill was invented, the only way to get hold of it was through the Straits. There would've been a population explosion if it weren't for *El Peñón.*'

'And today?'

Jorge's lips are briefly sealed with sadness. 'It's not as profitable as before; at least not for the honest smuggler,' he sighs. 'A few cartons of cigarettes, bootlegged whisky, electronic gadgets, that sort of thing. The real money's in the flesh and bone business, but Gibraltar's clean. The boats come directly from the *Maghreb*, the *pateras*, sometimes as far away as Libya. I wouldn't touch it.'

Relieved, Maria loops a strand of golden hair behind her ear. It's a habit she has when she's nervous. Maite perceives Maria's discomfort, spares me the effort of shifting the confab in another direction, when she informs Jorge that I've wandered the ways of India.

'Where?' our colourful host asks me, swallowing the bait.

'From north to south, west to east, up and down the central spine of old Hindustan.'

'Tiruchirappalli?'

'I spent a week there,' I reply.

'In the ashram?'

'No; but I've heard of Balaji.'

Clearly stunned by the mention of his erstwhile Guru, Jorge asks me with protruding eyes of my acquaintance.

'Pablo lent me a tape.'

'A magpie and his treasure,' he smiles at his old friend. 'To know that you don't know is to know,' he says, looking at me with the same warm smile.

A thought twister, I surmise Socratic, but Jorge assures me the words are those of his Guru.

'*Ole!*' Pablo pipes up. 'Where is the child you once were?'

The question catapults Jorge to his feet, whereupon he sways back and forth, clapping his hands as he rises to the challenge. 'With the teenager I once was.'

'And where might I find that adolescent?'

'With the man I was a moment ago,' Jorge shoots back, using his hands like a pair of cymbals.

'*Ole!*' Pablo roars with delight. 'And who is the man who thus speaks?'

'The witness speaks,' Jorge prances before his friend with a forceful clap.

'*Ole!* And who is the witness?'

'The observer is the observed; the watcher the watched.'

'*Ole!* And of the mind?'

'More the mirror, less the mind.'

'*Ole!*' Pablo bows his head, apparently in humble defeat. Rising to his feet he embraces his friend.

Maria looks nonplussed, until Pablo explains the pantomime as a parody of novice monks from the high Tibetan plateau who always clap and sway when scoring a philosophical point.

'And the '*Ole*'?'

'A Hispanic twist to the maroon-robed tradition,' Jorge butts in, and is about to elaborate, when his attention is diverted to a huge, fierce-looking cat that suddenly appears in the Moorish patio. But for its snowy white paws, the cat is as black as soot, the size of an adult badger. 'This is Fiji, my familiar,' Jorge introduces the cat that looks like a miniature puma. With ominous yellow, saucer-sized eyes the cat surveys the scene, before arching its fiendish back to rub itself against Maria's leg. 'He likes you,' Jorge smiles pleasantly, as he watches the tom make its majestic way to Pablo. Foolhardily, Pablo puts out a hand to stroke the beast, whereupon he receives a nasty left hook that leaves three razor-thin rubescent stripes on his forearm. Not much of a mauling, but enough to inspire Maite to freeze when it's her turn to be scrutinized by the cat's horrible yellow eyes.

'Now, you know why Mahatma and Maya are boarding with my sister,' Maite whispers from the side of her mouth. I nod my assent, glad that the cat ignores me, for Jorge snaps his fingers to summon his familiar to his lap, where it purrs as if powered by a battery.

'Oh, *Fiji*, be good to my guests while I'm away,' Jorge pets the feline on his lap. '*Tu eres el jefe*,' he addresses the cat, before turning to his human friends. 'He's the boss who knows no master. He hasn't a mortgage or a care in the world.'

'Like the monkeys at the Hanuman temple,' Pablo remarks.

'Just so,' Jorge responds with a look of nostalgia mantled on his gaunt features.

'The monkey temple was near our ashram,' Pablo explains. 'We'd watch them for hours – play, sex, sleep, raiding the local market and the mango trees when they got tired of the pilgrims' offerings. No possessions, no pockets, no fees to pay, no need of money. And never late, always on time.'

'Yeah! Imagine a tree asking a monkey what time it was,' Jorge begins to laugh.

'I can't,' Pablo responds.

'And dolphins don't need dollars,' Jorge adds to the theme.

'Nor birds, a visa or passport, to go where they please.'

'And yet, we're the bright ones,' Jorge stops laughing. 'The good book tells us so.'

'Yeah,' Pablo smiles sadly. 'The only animal on the planet that has to pay rent to be here.'

Our bedroom is one of three on the first floor, in a passage that leads to a spacious terrace at the back of the house, shaded by palm trees, with a blue-tiled pool that reflects the sombre mountains above the village. Like the rest of the mysterious house, the bedroom has a Moorish flavour. There are horseshoe arches to the bathroom and balcony, on the marble floor, cool to the touch, hand-woven kelim rugs and pouffes of camel skin. The window frames are carved in Arabic symbols, the mirrors set in Moroccan mosaics; above the bed there's a soft, delicate watercolour of the kasbah in Fez.

While I take a siesta, Maria slips into a skimpy bikini, repairs to the balcony with the dog-eared copy of *The Tibetan Book of the Dead* that she found on a sun-lounger by the pool. I sleep briefly, perchance an hour, but such are my dreams, it seems like I've been asleep for a lifetime. According to the book in Maria's hands, my idea is probably nearer the truth that any tale a clock might tell. I'm still sleepy, imbued with the dreams I've lived, when Maria tells me of the *Bardo*, the journey one makes at the end of one's life. 'There are demons and angels on the path beyond,' she tells me. 'But you must always remember that everything you see is in your mind.'

'Are you in my mind?' I ask playfully.

'And then, at the final moment, you come face to face with the lord of the dead. The Tibetans call the God of death Yama.'

'So too, the Hindus,' I interject, but Maria, animated by what she has read in the ancient tome, ignores my comment.

'Before his gaze you cannot lie,' she stares hard into my face, 'for his eyes are *your* eyes, the mirror of *your* soul, the sum of *your* past deeds.'

'No more self-lies,' I remark as I finally wake up.

'There's no more lies of any sort. It's everyone's moment of truth,' she says with a vulnerable look. 'Liberation or incarnation, another spin on the wheel.'

'And as death can call at any time, it's best to be ready.'

'You understand,' she says so sweetly, so soulfully with a sad smile in her eyes that I almost want to cry.

The light has begun to fade when we gather around the cedar table in the *comedor*, or dining room. Shortly after the sun slips into the sea, Jorge ignites stained-glass lanterns to provide a magical illumination under which we listen to the tinkling song of flowing water from the fountain in the courtyard. We drink our coffee in near silence until our host decides it's time for music. 'This is black music, the soul of Moroccan slaves,' Jorge explains. 'The Arab traders stripped their captives as locust strip the land. They took everything from the blacks; their land, their animals, their Gods, even their woman and children, but they couldn't silence their music. The music of Sub-Saharan Africa was too powerful for the slavers. When they slept the rhythm of their slaves seeped into their dreams. Today, Gnaoua *is* the music of Morocco. Listening to the pre-Islamic lute and drums, the cymbals and handclaps, the hypnotic chants, the music appears to seep into Jorge's dreams. Donning a red fez, he rotates his head to swirl a tassel like the blade of a helicopter.

'It makes me giddy,' Maria says, tapping out the dark rhythm on the cedar table.

'It's supposed to,' Jorge laughs wildly. 'Join me,' he says offering Maria a golden fez.

With itchy feet Maria doesn't need a second invitation. With music in her bones my love knows the choreography of the ancient rite. Effortlessly, she leads the dance, Jorge aping her tottering motion, their heads swaying like a pair of intoxicated snakes. When Saffiya's daughter alights on the unlikely scene, pushing a trolley into the *comedor*, laden with the cuisine of the Maghreb, her face lights up. Beneath an embroidered kaftan headdress, fringed with silver coins and coral beads, the Berber girl gives Jorge a coruscating smile; and then, unable to resist the terpsichorean game, squeezes in between the Spaniards, slapping her hands for want of cymbals. With his eyes greedily glued to the teenager, I remark Jorge's obsession with the square pendant between the girl's breasts. It looks as if he's hypnotised by the girl and her niello jewellery, on the edge of a trance, for the dance is alluring, one that could lead anywhere. But whither it might go remains a mystery, as the dance is brought to a sudden halt by the ominous silhouette of Saffiya under an arched doorway.

'Sakuna,' the mother hisses through stained teeth, lest her daughter betrays her honour. Having spent most of her life in Spain, the girl isn't pleased, but the pendant is brought to rest on her bust out of deference to her mother's wish. Casting a mysterious glance from her hooded, dark eyes at Jorge, she leaves the room, in what looks like a teenage huff.

Saffiya, sure of her step, places two tajines, earthenware vessels with conical lids, on the table. And then, to show she's not a bad sport, retires to the shadows of the room, where she rests on a leather chair, beating her feet to the music of her mountains, while she smokes a cigarette.

Jorge calls the meal his last supper. Though he might love Barcelona as much as he loves Morocco, his heart forever remains in Andalusia. 'Where else can you find champagne flowing in the fountains of a fiesta,' he declaims with outstretched arms. 'Where else can a young lad learn the facts of life pretending to be asleep under an olive tree.' Maite giggles, but I'm left in the dark, whereupon Maria explains that in bygone days olive picking was women's work.

'No men were allowed near the trees, especially when the women were in the branches beating the olives.'

None the wiser I ask, 'Why?'

'Because we didn't wear knickers during the harvest,' Maite laughs.

'But things change,' Pablo sighs with apparent regret.

'But ever so slowly in my beloved Andalusia,' Jorge grins at his friend. 'We were the last Spanish province to accept the wheel.'

'Indeed, we were,' Pablo chuckles. 'We preferred to do it our way; on foot or on the back of a donkey. We only accepted the wheel when somewhat convinced us that an *Andaluz* had invented it.'

'Come! Let us feast,' Jorge waves his hand theatrically above the table, before opening a pair of Moroccan wines; the first a Medallion red, followed by a dusty bottle of Gris de Boulaouane, a light, fruity rose.

Notwithstanding Pablo's appetite, there's more food than we can handle. The plates are piled high with dates and figs, thinly-sliced tomatoes, onions and cucumbers covered in parsley and yogurt. Another plate is covered by briouats, small fried pastries stuffed with almonds. There are bowls of carrots and turnips marinated in honey, aubergine and garlic puree, a deep tureen full with unleavened bread the size of frisbees, and finally the tajines. When Jorge lifts the conical lids, I can almost see the fragrance of Morocco rise up into the balmy air. The first tajine contains a pyramid of steaming couscous, studded with dates, sweet onions, olives and slices of marinated lemon, covered in a stew of garlic and tomatoes. The second tajine is the same as the first, but with chunks of succulent lamb for the meat-eaters. I turn to the back of the room to compliment the cook, but the leather chair is empty.

'That's her way,' Jorge notes my concern. 'She comes and goes as my cat.'

'I hope we didn't offend her.'

'How?'

'Her daughter dancing ...'

'No! No!' Jorge shakes his head. 'She's been round the block a few times. She knew me in the Rif mountains, has been with me in Spain more than ten years. She's seen everything there is to be seen under my roof,' he laughs like a March hare.

'Were you homesick in Morocco?' Maria asks, perchance, fearing that Jorge might reveal what Saffiya has seen.

'Never in the mountains where the people live the life of *Al-Andaluz*. The only difference was that prayers were said in mosques instead of churches,' Jorge replies, his eyes clouded with nostalgia. 'And strangely enough, I felt completely at home in India, especially in the mud villages of Rajasthan.'

'Where our dark-eyed gypsies began their journey,' Pablo responds with words I've heard before.

'Without doubt,' Jorge agrees eagerly. 'That's why the first thing I'll do in Barcelona tomorrow is climb up to the sanctuary of Montserrat. I'll lay flowers at the feet of the black Madonna, the Durga of the gypsies, our own Kali-ma.'

After the repast, we retire to the terrace at the front of the house, where the warm air is scented by jasmine and the briny perfume of the distant sea. Jorge serves us a dark, sweet liquor, pours strong, black coffee from a silver pot. It isn't long before the conversation turns to travel and adventure. Animated by the coffee, Maria tells the others about a pair of cheetahs we saw in Zambia. How they lost their kill to a pack of hyenas. It's pleasing to see her at ease in company of wide experience. I contribute a little tale about a blind man next to me on a crowded mini-bus in Gambia. How the locals, annoyed by his incessant need to know where he was, put him off in the wrong village. 'I got off the mini-bus to stretch my legs. We were only there for a few minutes. The last I saw of him, he was wandering around a market, lashing out with his white stick, screaming at the top of his voice, "Auntie! Auntie! Is that you?' It's not much of a story, but Pablo finds it so funny that there are tears in his eyes before he stops laughing.

'By now, he's probably somewhere near the Cape of Good Hope,' Pablo succumbs to another wave of hilarity. Jorge, moved by his friend's laughter, links into the conversation by telling us that the blind have an advantage over the sighted in that they are less distracted by the world.

'They are obliged to look within. Not like me when I first arrived in India. I was full of questions; who, why, where, when, knocking on the door of the world to find my answers. But the door never opened. Not until meditation taught me that the door wasn't locked, opened inwardly not out, that I had been knocking from the inside, that I was already there with all the answers at hand.'

'Ole! Ole! Ole!' Pablo sings in jubilant voice. 'When you are at the Kaaba, you don't need a compass to tell you which way to pray.' We're all well-fed and spent, ready for slumber. It's a fine thought to wrap up the evening.

17

SITTING LIKE A BLACK SPHINX, GIVING ME THE EVIL EYE, I WAKE UP TO FIND Jorge's cat in our bedroom. When I try to get out of bed, the old tom puffs up, snarls and spits. 'Maria,' I call for assistance.
 'What!' Maria pops her head out of the bathroom.
 'Li Shou won't let me get out of bed.'
 'Who's Li Shou?'
 'A Chinese cat God.'
 'Fiji's just a pussy cat,' Maria laughs, as the feline tilts its sable head, seals its sinister eyes, to be tickled under the chin.

We join our friends by the pool to breakfast on coffee and hot croissants, splattered with butter and home-made apricot jam. After breakfast, the girls dive into the water, leaving Pablo and me to plan out the day. We decide to head south to Aguamarga, a crescent-shaped cove, so upmarket that Spanish royals have been seen on its beach of pebbles. With towels and beach chairs in the boot of the car, we are about to leave, when Maite calls us back into the house. 'I've found something *very* interesting,' she says, leading us back to the pool, to show us a beautiful headstone adorned in hieroglyphics, hidden behind a pair of palm trees. 'Who died?' she asks as Pablo changes the cryptic epitaph into English:
       Linger not before this stone of moss,
       For I'm not here, and never was.
       On wind, your wings, fly far,
       For you are not, and never are.
 'No one died,' Pablo is the first to find his tongue.
 'But what does it mean?'
 'I don't know what it means. It's just Jorge's way of preparing for the final day.'
 'It's a bit morbid,' Maria says, with a puzzled look.
 'We all have to blow a farewell kiss to the sun before it sets.'
 I smile sadly, impressed by the sagacity of my friend's lovely line.
 'It's still a bit strange.' Maite is as unconvinced as Maria.
 'Strange in Spain perhaps,' Pablo respond with a grin. 'But not everywhere. On remote islands in the South Pacific it's a custom to build your own burial chamber before you die; spend the nights of your last year sleeping in a coffin.'
 'That's horrible!' Maria exclaims.
 'Oh, I don't know,' Pablo tries to keep a straight face. 'When death calls where better to find you than asleep in your own bed.'

On a display table by the front door, just as we're leaving for the second time, we find a note and a small plastic bag. The note informs us that the house is our home, and is signed with the sacred symbol of OM, rather than Jorge's signature. 'Even with the long drive up to Barcelona, he thought of us,' Maite smiles, as Pablo takes an old Indian cassette tape out of the plastic bag.
 'Just like Jorge,' he laughs joyfully.
 Sitting up front with Pablo at the wheel, I notice scratch marks on his left hand to match those on his right forearm. 'Been playing with the cat, have you?'

'Hardly! It was in our room last night. Don't know how it got there. I shooed it off our bed, and got clawed in the process. Maite had a nightmare about Fiji last night. But when we woke up the cat was nowhere to be seen.'

'That's because it was in our room.'

'Was your door open?'

'It was locked.'

'Strange animal,' Pablo frowns with a grimace.

The road across the coastal mountains is extremely picturesque, with sweeping vistas of a cerulean sea hazily melting into a pale blue sky on the horizon. We pull into a *mirador*, a viewing point, to take photographs, and stop a second time to look at a monstrous, half-finished, concrete hotel, covered in 'Greenpeace' slogans. Despite having all the 'legal' papers, work has stopped on the hotel as it's situated in a National Park. Now, everyone, from the central government in Madrid to the hierarchy of the Andalusian *junta*, is arguing about who is going to foot the bill to have it demolished. 'Didn't anyone notice that it was being built?' Maria asks.

'Of course,' Pablo smirks. 'But underhand business comes with a blind eye.'

We plant our parasols on the beach, take a dip in the warm water, drink a couple of beers, and then, all four of us fall asleep. When I open my eyes, I find the sun has shifted, giving me a tan up to my knees. We lunch in a *chringuito*, a beach bar. Pablo orders grilled sardines, fresh from the sea, while Maria and I enjoy a *tortilla* with salad. After coffee and cognac, we lie in the sun, swim when it's too hot, and then take a leisurely *paseo* through the pretty village. Around mid-afternoon, it's time for another collective siesta, which in my case is so profound and peaceful that it lasts almost to sunset. When I finally rediscover the world, I find myself alone. With a cigarette in my mouth, I scan the shoreline for my companions. I soon descry Pablo, sitting cross-legged, on the fringe of the beach, in meditation, facing the dying sun. At the other end of the beach, I make out Maria and Maite, in bikinis, talking to a fisherman repairing his nets. When a low, elongated cloud, resembling the outstretched wings of a might condor, turns from flamingo pink to crimson, its silver-lined under feathers to a warm golden hue, I take a photograph with my mobile phone. Of course, I'm not surprised that the photograph is a disappointment, for I know that a photograph can never truly capture a magnificent sunset, a frozen image the beauty of shifting light.

The next day, we all get up late, take coffee by the pool, and then set off for Cuevas del Almanzora, a little town, full of history, and in the months of summer, unbearable humidity. We don't linger long in the uninspiring town, can't be bothered to visit the castle or any of the famous caves. It's far too hot in streets of dust for sightseeing. Instead, we head to Vera, in search of a light lunch.

We buy baguettes, cheese and tomatoes in a local store, mangoes and a papaya from a market stall. Sitting on a patch of frizzled grass, next to a dried up fountain full of beer cans, we eat our lunch, share fruit with a colony of ants, bread with pigeons and sparrows. After the meal, Pablo suggests we escape the sun, spend a peaceful hour in the silence of the city's cathedral.

On the *autopista* to Mojacar, I espy a British supermarket I often used in London because of its wide range of vegetarian products. Although Spain is a land of meat-eaters, to my delight, the supermarket has a vegetarian section, well stocked with products I haven't tasted in years. There's not much change from a hundred euros for a spending spree on Linda McCartney sausages and burgers, Quorn pies, pieces and mince, kilos of mature Cheddar cheese, and three jars of my favourite brand of 'extra hot' lime pickle. As it is on offer, by the till, I also add to my fifth carrier bag, a jar of Branston pickle, even though I don't really like it.

Back in Mojacar, after a quick, refreshing dip in the swimming pool, I commandeer the kitchen to prepare a *'chicken less'* chicken korma. Pablo says it's the best curry he's had since leaving India. Quite a compliment as he hasn't been in India for decades. After dinner, we gather in the courtyard, to drink chilled white wine, and listen to Jorge's tape. Fiji, starved of human company the previous night, after we closed our balcony doors, having discovered his knack of scaling the bougainvillea vines that laced the walls up to the first floor, sits purring contentedly on Maria's lap.

The thirty-year-old tape is in the same pitiful condition as Pablo's, but ten minutes near the end of side A, the dialogue is perfectly clear, at least to a native English speaker. The first intelligible words are those of Balaji, presumably in response to a disciple who has spoken of loneliness, something many westerners feel in India.

'You are lonely because you cannot face yourself, your aloneness.'

'But I'm not alone,' the *sunyasi* protests mildly in a French accent.

'We are all alone,' the Guru counters. 'Aloneness is inescapable. It is a condition of Being. You feel lonely when you cannot cope with this condition. Loneliness is social, it is related to the outside. Aloneness is spiritual, related to the inside,' the Guru pauses to have a good laugh. 'We create families, clubs and countries to escape our aloneness, to hide from ourselves. We crave for these groups, and when we can't find them, we feel lonely. We run in herds, hide in crowds, wave our flags; we desperately want to belong to this or that church or congregation, any club will do as long as we can escape our aloneness. Isn't this a club you have formed around me?' Balaji appears to be enjoying himself, for he stops to have another good laugh. 'But it is a false dream, for you cannot escape aloneness. Your aloneness is who you are. Like your own death, you have no choice but to face it.'

Maite reaches over to the cassette player to press the pause button. 'This is depressing,' she says' looking at her husband for reassurance.

'It probably gets worse before it gets better,' Pablo smiles at his wife, but doesn't press the play button. Instead he takes the stage himself, by telling a story I recognise as plucked from the *Tales of Arabian Nights*. 'The younger of two brothers went to a market to buy bread. In the market he saw a stranger of shadows, standing by an old woman who had collapsed with her final breath. When the stranger turned from the old woman he looked at the brother. The cold glare of the stranger froze the brother to the spot, made him forget all about the bread. At home, he told his older brother about the stranger whose look had send a shiver through his whole body. He said he was scared by the stranger, that he would take his horse and ride to Samarkand, stay with their uncle for a few nights, somewhere safe and secure, to recover from his fright. Later that afternoon, the older brother went to the market to buy the bread his brother had forgotten. He too saw the stranger of shadows, lurking in a dark doorway. He approached the stranger to ask him why he had frightened his brother. "I didn't mean to scare your brother," the stranger replied, "my expression was one of surprise, seeing your brother here in this market, when I have an appointment with him tonight in Samarkand." '

'That's a horrible story,' Maite scrunches up her face in dismay.

'Ancient, but not horrible,' Pablo looks kindly at his wife. 'We can no more escape our aloneness than the stranger of shadows, for the stranger is within. The point of the story is to know the stranger, to look into his face, to behold his eyes, to turn the stranger into a friend, for the stranger of shadows is yourself.'

'You mean death?'

'Yes, I mean death. But not death as you know it, or perhaps don't. I mean the death that is always here, always with us. She has always been with us. I say *she* because, unlike Scheherazade, I see death as feminine – life is yang, death, yin. Like a mother, she is here with us to give us life, a full life. She is our true friend, always loyal, though most shun her, pretend that she is not. I say, know her, love her. Friends might come and go, but she is with us from the beginning to the end. She is with us to make us whole, to complete our lives. Don't deny her. Embrace her. She is the only one who will be with us throughout our entire lives. Without her, our hearts cannot be one.'

After the paean to Kali, as I construe it, the girls are speechless, wrapped in a solemn silence that prompts Pablo to restart the tape.

'Even in a crowd you are alone. You can't escape yourself. And why the wish to belong? To belong is so restricting, so limiting. Belong nowhere. Let the universe belong in you.'

Pablo pauses the tape, looks relieved, 'I told you it would get better.'

'After what you said, it couldn't get worse,' Maite responds with a wry expression.

'Celebrate your aloneness. Your aloneness is virgin territory. Your aloneness is unique. A vast continent that belongs to you. To explore this land is the greatest of all adventures, and such a privilege…' - the Guru's voice begins to waver unintelligibly, finally giving way to the sound of screeching spinning wheels.

'Well! What did you think of that? Pablo asks when the tape ends.

'I loved it, especially the last part' I respond. 'I often think I don't belong to any country, or particular place, even if I'm forced to carry a passport. I'm at home wherever I am. My home *is* who I am.'

'Ole!' Pablo lets out a mighty roar. 'And what did you make of Balaji's words?' he asks Maria.

'I'm overwhelmed,' Maria responds in a quiet voice. 'More by what you said than the words of your Guru.'

'And you?' Pablo turns to his wife.

'I don't feel alone, not when I'm with you.'

Maite's response paints sadness in Pablo's eyes, before he tries to explain. 'Do you remember the beautiful sunset we all saw in Aguamarga yesterday?'

'I couldn't forget it.'

'You were at one end of the beach, I was at the other, Kim was in the middle, under the parasol.'

'That's right.'

And as the sun dipped into the sea, its light tipped the undulating waves, and made a beeline to *your* eyes.'

'I remember.'

'Well, that light made a beeline to *my* eyes too, and to *Kim's*, and *Maria's*, and everyone else's who was on the beach watching the sun die its daily death.'

'So we all had our own sunset.'

'Ole!' Pablo bursts into laughter, 'Each of us our own show. The creator looking at creation through our eyes. Or, for the less religious, the universe using our eyes to look at itself.'

'The privilege your Guru talked about,' Maria smiles at Pablo.

'Ole!' Pablo smiles back. 'But it only works for those whose eyes are open. The sleepwalkers amble through life and never get a glimpse.'

'But it's still a little sad,' Maite says, 'to think we're all alone, not connected.'

'Not connected!' Pablo looks at his wife. 'Pinch your nose, and hold your breath for as long as you can.'

'Now!'

'Yes, now. Hold your breath till you're bursting.'

Despite her social smoking, Maite manages a full minute, before gasping to fill her lungs with air.

'Now, tell me you're not connected,' Pablo laughs, and then goes into song: 'Outside is in, inside is out; in, out, out, in, the twain are never apart.' Returning to his normal voice, he adds, 'It's not so difficult to understand.'

Around midnight, lying side by side, with Fiji curled into a ball at the foot of the bed, Maria asks me something that has been troubling her for most of the evening,

'Are we really alone?'

'We are, and we aren't,' I give an answer that doesn't really help. 'If the universe is infinite, everywhere is the centre. That includes you, me, your mum, your dad, the whole lot of us. In ancient India, the holy men talked of Indra's net, a sort of spider's web that stretched across the skies of infinity, on each vertex a pearl that reflected every other pearl in the net *ad infinitum*. In Pablo's words, each of us a point through which the universe can slip through to see itself. But at a higher level, where the self is dissolved, the raindrop surrendered to the sea, it doesn't make much sense to talk about aloneness, a point or a centre, for the only thing left is *you*.'

'Me!'

'You, but not as *'me'*. Better to think of a pearl that contains all other pearls. Being, consciousness and bliss, all wrapped into one. Years ago, in my mid-twenties, I had a flash of indescribable light during a session of meditation. The experience confirmed what I believed in; a taste of truth infinitely more profound than reading about transcendental states in a thousand sacred books. In Sanskrit it's called *satchitananda*.'

'Will you teach me to meditate?'

'Of course. Ever since we met, I've been waiting for you to ask.'

Cooing with delight, Maria turns on her side to bite me on the neck. For both of us it's a crossroad, a magical moment. Even Fiji, certain that he's the centre of the universe, alert to any movement, opens his yellow ochre eyes, but for once, doesn't appear to mind our intimacy.

For the rest of the week, time speeds by, as it tends to in congenial company. We spend our daylight hours on beaches, each with a different charm. At San Juan de los Terreros, we wade out from the shore fifty metres to find waves at our waists, a few feet from the sandy beach of los Muertos, the dark depths of the sea. Along the wild coastline of Cabo de Gata, we watch great flamingos sail across the sky, a solitary dolphin looping out of the waves from a nudist beach in Villaricos. As a rule, our nights are spent at Jorge's house, dining on food from every corner of the world, talking about things that matter. But, as Pablo constantly reminds us, with an impish grin, rules are there to be broken, so not every night is spent under the stars by the pool or in Jorge's charming courtyard. One night we visit Aguilas for a fiesta, the first town in the neighbouring province of Murcia. It's not a particularly inspiring fiesta, somewhat run-of-the-mill, but we're there to give the women a chance to dance. I ask Pablo if there's a music academy hidden away, somewhere in the heart of Spain, like a secret CIA training ground. 'Not that I know,' he replies, before asking me why I ask.

'Because I've been to literally hundreds of fiestas, up and down the breath of this country, and the music's always the same. An hour of *pasodobles*, old fashioned music for the old folk, a few hits from the Gipsy Kings, one or two songs from *Saturday Night Fever*, and, if the group is really good, *Another brick in the Wall* by Pink Floyd.'

'You're right,' Pablo grins. 'I've never thought of that before.'

'And the set-up is always the same too. A lead singer, usually a man in a glittery jacket, supported by a back-up band and two pretty girls in mini-skirts who dance about the stage, sing in the chorus, but whose real purpose is to entertain the party revellers with their legs.'

'You're right,' Pablo reiterates his first response, pointing to an old fellow, clearly drunk, clinging to the stage, tilting his head to look up the girls' skirts. 'I bet he wishes they were olive pickers,' he adds with a wild laugh.

Our last night is spent in a British pub on Mojacar playa. Our timing isn't great as the place is packed with English fans watching a rugby match between England and Italy. Maria, who has never seen a rugby match, asks me to explain the rules. I try my best, but am completely flummoxed when she asks me why the game is played with a lemon-shaped ball. Watching the ball bounce unpredictably, she concludes that the game is completely ridiculous. 'All sport is absurd,' Pablo adds to her comment, 'unless it's your own. Like Kim, I like football, but I have to suspend my sense of reason for ninety minutes to enjoy it. It's a game of make belief. You have to pretend it's important, because if you don't, it isn't.'

When the Italians convert a try, the atmosphere turns nasty. Embarrassed by racist remarks from my fellow countrymen, when a group of drunks start to sing the controversial song *Swing Low, Sweet Chariot*, I suggest we take a table outside the bar, on the pavement. We aren't long at our table, before a drunk in a Union Jack T-shirt, staggers out of the pub, to vomit in a pot of geraniums. 'Perhaps, he's homesick,' Pablo remarks wryly. A nonsensical comment, until he explains his play on words, informing us that the first settlers in that part of Europe known as Britain today, were from Spain. 'They came from the caves of the Almanzora region. The same caves that none of us had an appetite to visit the other day.'

In the car, on the way back to the house, I relate a story about a professional golf instructor I knew in England. How, on his first trip abroad, he went to Majorca for a weekend with three school chums. How they got so drunk on their first night in Palma Nova, they couldn't remember where their hotel was, so decided to take a taxi. 'But the taxi-driver wouldn't take their fare.'

'Why? Because they were so drunk?' Maria asks.

'No. It was because he was parked outside their hotel,' I reply with the mirth that always accompanies my story.

'At least there's one honest taxi-driver in the world!' Maite exclaims, from the back seat.

'Perhaps he was one of those Sufis you are always talking about,' Maria remarks.

'Sufi!' I exclaim in puzzlement.

'Someone who knows you don't need to travel to find your way home.'

'Ole!' Pablo celebrates the light-hearted comment by thumping the horn.

18

IT'S A LOVELY SUMMER EVENING IN THE VILLAGE. CHILDREN ARE PLAYING football in the street, Sergio, a neighbour, his bald head dappled with birdshit, is hurling abuse at the swallows in the sky, Rosa and Rubin, sitting on their doorstep, like a pair of lovebirds, are stringing red peppers. In the distance, I hear a donkey braying for a bale of hay, a peacock singing for its lost love. Closer at hand, the church bells announcing the death of a villager, either that, or thirty-seven o' clock. Everything considered, a typical summer evening in Purusha, not a cloud in the sky. But that will all change in a few hours, when the shadow of dark clouds from the north sweep over the rooftops to confect a storm just for me, Pete and Pat, a couple I haven't seen or spoken to in years, not after Onion told them I'd been badmouthing them in the village, and they chose to believe him.

It wouldn't be so bad if I wasn't alone, but Maria's in her village, preparing a group of schoolgirls for a dance competition in Granada. Admittedly, like so many British ex-pats, scattered across the continent of Europe, I haven't cast a vote, in my case because I thought I didn't have to, but when I switch the television on, I wonder if I've made a mistake, my faith in the good sense of the British people severely misplaced. The early results, in what has become known as the 'Brexit' referendum, aren't too worrying, with the 'leavers' just ahead of those who want to remain with Europe. But at three in the morning, when I finally fall asleep on my sofa, nothing has changed. Several hours later, when I open my eyes, it's all over. A trading nation, Britain has voted itself out of the biggest free trade agreement on the planet. I can hardly believe what I'm seeing on the BBC world News. I switch channels, watch news bulletins from Spain, Germany, France, Italy, Qatar, Japan, South Korea, Australia and America. It seems, like me and millions of other British expatriates in Europe, the world is in shock. As the value of sterling tumbles on the money market, one commentator in America says the history books will look back and call it the day Britain shot itself in the face. I don't know what to think. But I'm upset, almost angry, with myself, for looking at my country through rose-tinted glasses. I had relied on the Britain that gave the world Shakespeare and Darwin, Blake and the Beatles, not to mention football. I had turned an indulgent blind eye to the other side of the UK, the Britain that loved the 'Globe', a foreign owned newspaper, that once published a list of what made Britain great based on a survey of its readers, a list that included a diurnal page of tits, the royal family and pork scratchings. To confirm my worst fears, just before I turn the TV off, I watch an interview with a Brexiteer, who, when asked why he voted to leave Europe, tells the reporter that he's sick and tired of seeing women in *'burpers'*.

Maria calls to tell me that she's heard the news. She tells me that she misses me, that whatever happens in the future, she'll stay with me, even if we have to live in a cardboard box in the heart of Africa to be together. It's a fillip I need, loving words to lift me out of my gloom, but barely an hour later I'm back in the dumps, the throb of foreboding returning like a toothache when the anaesthetic wears off.

Taking a coffee in the plaza, everything seems the same in the village. The high pitch whistle of a knife sharpener challenges the church bells. A Moroccan with a gigantic holdall, tries to sell me a pair of sunglasses. Villagers, walking through the plaza, smile at me, say hello, no one mentions Brexit. The only difference is the way I look at things, wondering if I'll still be here in a year or two.

Barefoot, in a pair of denim shorts and an old T-shirt, Maite opens her front door. She smiles, invites me in, tells me Pablo is out with the dogs, asks me if I'd like tea or coffee. 'Tea would be nice.,' I reply, 'I've already had three coffees this morning.'

'Late night?'

'I was up half the night.'

'Whatever for?' Maite turns from the kitchen counter to face me with a look of surprise.

'Watching telly. I stayed up to watch the Brits vote themselves out of Europe.'

'Is that what they did?'

'You didn't know? It's all over the news.'

'We don't have a TV.'

'*Really!*'

'Well, strictly speaking we do. It's in the garage, but it doesn't work. When they switched the signal from analogue to digital, we didn't bother to buy a box. We get our news from the radio. Fewer murders on shortwave.' I must look puzzled. 'Haven't you noticed? There's always blood on the box. Wherever you are in the world, switch on a TV, flick through the channels, and within minutes, you'll find scenes of violence, usually someone killing someone else. I don't know if the television producers are pandering to the blood lust of their viewers, or if they're all suppressed serial killers, sublimating their wicked ways when there's no war on. It's definitely one or the other, probably a mixture of both,' Maite creases her brow. 'But it doesn't seem very healthy.'

'Like the kids' video games.'

'*Exactly,*' Maite responds, as she serves me a cup of tea. 'To me, it doesn't seem natural, but Pablo has other ideas on an animal that killed over one hundred million other members of its own species in the last century. He thinks there's something wrong with humanity, that we're deluded and arrogant to think of ourselves as homo sapiens, wise monkeys, when our real name is homo sacaria, the killing ape.'

'Perhaps, he's right,' I respond quietly. 'Perhaps murder on the box softens us up, weakens our moral resolve, so we're ready when Lord Kitchener comes calling. And he will call, sooner or later, he always does.'

'Who's Lord Kitchener?'

'Britain's answer to Uncle Sam,' Pablo explains, as he steps into the kitchen, followed by Mahatma and Maya, and Alberto, a neighbour and local baker. 'Coffee, or the usual?' he asks his neighbour. The usual, a glass of brandy, is the preferred option. 'Fancy a tipple?' Pablo puts the bottle of *Soberano* on the table in front of me.

''I'm happy with tea,' I offer a weak smile.

'You don't *look* happy,' Pablo observes my gloomy mien. 'What's up?' he asks kindly.

'Brexit.'

'I heard about it this morning on the radio. That's democracy for you, my friend. Didn't one of your former leaders call it the best worst system we've got?'

'Probably Churchill.'

'It's an old thought; something that has bothered thinkers for centuries. Why should Einstein's vote be worth no more than a moron's? Plato thought a benign philosopher king might be the answer. Perhaps he was thinking of himself, as he didn't offer any names.'

'Bhutan has a king who measures his country's wealth in terms of Gross Nation Happiness instead of Product,' Maite says chirpily, with her back to us, as she's peeling potatoes at the sink.

'Bhutan! I've never heard of it. Where is it?' Alberto looks up from his brandy.

'In the Himalayas,' I provide the geography.

'Oh, yes!' the baker exclaims, but doesn't ask me where the Himalayas are. Instead, he turns to Pablo, 'So what's wrong with democracy?'

'The people.'

Alberto knots his brow to chew over the answer, but it's clear he's all at sea.

'Put it this way,' Pablo smiles at his neighbour. 'Imagine a family of five, three kids, two parents. The kids want to light a bonfire in the front room so they can toast marshmallows and watch cartoons at the same time.'

'The parents wouldn't allow it,' Alberto, considering the unlikely scenario, shakes his head.

'But democracy does, by giving everyone a vote.' Pablo transforms his expression into a broad grin. 'And so the democratic house goes up in smoke.'

'It wouldn't happen in *my* house,' the baker responds grimly. 'I'd put my foot down straightaway.'

To me, Maite whispers, 'We've tried that already in Spain. It's called fascism.'

'Anyway, I'm off,' Alberto drains his *copa*. 'I need my siesta.'

'A bit early for a siesta,' I remark, when Pablo's neighbour departs. 'It's barely one.'

'He's a baker,' Pablo reminds me of the man's profession. 'Up all night working, sleeping all day.'

'There's dough in bread,' I say light-heartedly. Pablo smirks at my colloquial wordplay. 'He can't be short of money.'

'He isn't. Have you seen his house? It's one of the biggest in the village.'

'So why does he carry on? He must be in his mid-seventies. Why doesn't he retire?'

'He's been baking bread for over sixty years. He thinks if he stops, he'll die.'

'He's also saving up,' Maite interjects.

'What for? His funeral.'

'That's a question he can't answer,' Pablo responds.

'He's like Maya when she was a puppy. She spent all day chasing her tail. Of course, she never caught it, but that didn't stop her from trying. Nothing stopped her till she dropped down exhausted. She's a bit wiser now. Aren't you, my love?' Maite bends down to stroke her dog, who seems more interested in potato peels than in her tail, or affection.

'And so are we. About seven years ago we dropped out of the game, stopped chasing our tails.' Pablo puts his arm around his wife's waist. 'Let the wheel take us whence it will.'

'Followers of the Way,' I mutter, grappling with a point I should know well.

'Greet each dawn like a blessing, each sunset as a gift, and life's a holiday. Each day, a *holy* day,' Pablo claps his hands. I'm still waiting for the 'Ole!' when he invites me to lunch, tells me we need to celebrate.

I accept the invitation, lay the table, sit down with my friends, to enjoy a bowl of pureed carrot soup, a plate of *papa a la pobre*, sopping in olive oil, and a stick of sweetened bread, still warm from Alberto's ancient oven. I go through the motions, clink glasses to celebrate the day, but in truth, my heart's elsewhere, a lugubrious cloud over me.

'You're brooding because you don't know where you will be tomorrow,' Pablo looks me in the eye. 'It's the same for all of us. No one knows when they go to bed if they will get up the next day, or for that matter, next week's lottery numbers.'

'That's the adventure,' Maite pats me on the hand. 'There's no interest in a game if you know the outcome before you play.'

'I didn't sleep well last night,' I make a pathetic excuse for my downcast face. 'I'm not at my best.'

'It's this Brexit business, isn't it?' Pablo sits back in his chair to light a cigarette. It's so obvious, that I don't bother to reply. 'You can learn a lot from someone's face, the pattern of their deportment. Small clues from which you can make an educated guess. And my guess is you'll stay on, whatever Britain decides to do.'

'I'd like to, but how?'

'When Coward abandoned the island of *'mad dogs'* to settle in the Caribbean, Churchill told the playwright, it was the inalienable right of every Englishman to live wherever he wanted. It's your right too.'

'There are no borders for the rich and famous.'

'Ah! Borders! The lines drawn up by kings and queens, politicians and priests, scribbled in the mad pursuit of their own interests. They're everywhere, and nowhere. Where's Prussia gone? Or Yugoslavia? Now you see it, now you don't. Like football, it's a game of make-belief,' Pablo begins to laugh. 'Borders are all in the mind. There are a thousand ways around them.' I'm about to ask for one, but Pablo's one step ahead of me. 'Apply for Spanish citizenship. You've been here long enough, you own property here, you pay your taxes, it shouldn't be a problem. I've still got a few contacts in my old trade. I'll make a few calls to see who can sort out your papers.' It's an option I hadn't considered; an option that hundreds of thousands of British ex-pats will weigh up in the months ahead. But even with a speckle of light on the benighted horizon, I'm not quite ready to give up my gloom without a feeble fight.

'But my Spanish is awful.'

'Then you're in the right place,' Maite splutters, choking on a lump of bread in an attempt to contain her laughter. 'Sometimes, *I* can't even understand the locals.'

'Or *me*,' with nothing in his mouth, but words, Pablo's volcanic laughter is unimpeded, and so explosive, that I have no choice, but to join in.

At the front door, I hug my friends, kiss them the Spanish way, thank them for lifting my flagging spirit, helping me to get things into perspective. 'Your company was therapeutic, your council like medicine,' I say as I climb into my car.

'A word with an interesting origin,' Pablo responds mysteriously, as I start the engine.

At home, over a *manchada*, a weak, milky coffee, I find a website on etymology, to discover that medicine shares an ancient root with the word meditation. I'm more pleased than surprised. In bed, just before I fall asleep, I think about what Pablo said about borders. I think of the border between Tanzania and Kenya; a fairly straight line but for a curve to accommodate the tallest mountain in Africa. How Queen Victoria gave her grandson, the Kaiser in Tanzania, Mount Kilimanjaro as a birthday gift. The thought of giving or receiving a mountain is so absurd, I find a smile on my sleepy face, but there's sadness too, to think the world I live in is so full of fools.

19

OVER THE FOLLOWING WEEKS, IT'S HARD TO FORGET ABOUT THE BRITISH referendum. It hogs the headlines, is mentioned on every news channel I watch. Even when I make a conscious effort to avoid newspapers, switch the TV off, I get phone calls from England to remind me that it's a British obsession. Cassie, who I haven't heard from since her wedding, phones me from a call-box. Expecting a second child, her happiness swelling like her belly, she tells me that I shouldn't worry, that I'm resourceful, will find a way through the mess. She talks about a romantic weekend in Paris that she's just got back from. How, when asked where she came from, she told her husband's friends that she was a Londoner, for the first time in her life, too ashamed to call herself English. And then, there are the frequent calls from Bill, whose fury with his fellow countrymen, and a host of right-wing politicians, is giving him sleepless nights. His first call wakes me up in the middle of the night, with a string of national types - Huguenots, Picts, Flanders, Normans, Saxons, Romans, Iberians, Celts, pre-Celts, Jews and Jutes – the list seems to go on forever, and doesn't make any sense, until the cloud of slumber lifts to reveal the landscape of his point, when he concludes that the English are a bunch of mongrels, a potpourri of mixed blood, a people, not a race.

I'm about to tell him what I know of the Beaker people, but I can't get a word in edgeways, as he jumps on to the back of 'Dick', the British Prime Minister, telling me he's one of the main culprits behind the fiasco, having put the fate of the nation in the hands of the mob. 'Thatcher was against a referendum on EU membership, said it was too complicated for the masses. And for once, the 'Iron Maiden' was right. A survey published yesterday showed that eight out of ten adults in the UK couldn't define the single market, with a fair proportion having the honesty to admit that they hadn't heard of it. One idiot said it was a market where you could only buy one product, citing Billingsgate as an example. Everyone knows the British electorate are gullible, a sheepish folk with short memories, easily seduced by snappy slogans, the PM, and his Etonian cabinet, more than most. But that didn't stop him from putting his own interests above the country's, offering a plebiscite to placate the Euro-sceptics in his divided party. It was a cynical decision that won him re-election, but divided the whole nation, turning us into the disunited kingdom. Already the SNP are clamouring for another referendum on Scottish independence, and across the Irish Sea, the whispers of a united Ireland grow louder by the day. The whole thing is a disaster. He didn't offer a popular vote on capital punishment, did he? The politicians never do; and you know why, don't you?' I think I do, but I'm not given the chance to address the question. 'Because they know within a week there'll be gallows up in Parliament Square, the mob foaming at the mouth, begging the hooded executioner to dampen the faggots around the stake, so they can enjoy a bit of toasting before the body goes up in flames.'

'You woke me up to tell me that?' I protest, my stomach churning, as I revisit the public flogging I once chanced upon in Pakistan as a young man.

'Sorry,' Bill swiftly brushes aside my protest, before launching a vitriolic attack on one of the leading light in the 'leave' campaign, calling him a smug, two-faced, puffed up nobody of European descent. 'He's the one behind the vile, racist posters that sprang up across the UK before the referendum,' he yells down the phone, but I'm hardly paying any attention, my mind far away in the port of Karachi, watching parents with children munching spicy samosas under a blood-caked platform strewn with bits of flesh from a man's back. 'Are you still there?' Bill, aware of my prolonged silence, asks.

'I'm tired. It's very late.'

'God! You're right! Sorry!' Bill exclaims, and then hangs up without saying goodbye.

A few weeks later, I get another call, no less caustic, or confusing, even though it's made during daylight hours. 'Have you heard?'

'Heard what?'

'Dick's buggered off to write his unmemorable memoirs.'

'Buggered off! Where?'

'Probably pissed off to Panama to check his off-shore accounts. Who cares where? Have you seen what we've got instead?'

'Edith March.'

'That's the one. Voted 'remain'; now, to hang on to her footnote in British history, she's talking about a 'hard Brexit', gabbling on about how the people have spoken.'

'Fingers up to the establishment and its bankers.'

Maybe! Maybe!' Bill briefly considers my point. 'But what about the other half – we spoke too. Every major city in the UK voted to remain. Take London, our city, for example; the most dynamic, diverse city in Europe, the most open-minded, cosmopolitan place on the planet. We voted overwhelmingly for Europe, and what do we get? *Brexit,* fronted by a frump with a grey tan, a cadaver from the Tory boneyard. Her highlight from the swinging sixties was dancing in her socks to a hit by Herman's Hermits.'

'She must've been a kid in the sixties.' I defend the lady with a smile on my face. 'And she can't help the way she looks.'

'Man! It's not *how* she looks that I'm worried about. It's *how* she thinks that keeps me awake at night. Have you seen who she's chosen to be the foreign secretary?'

'Bill Butler.'

'Yeah, Butler, the bungling buffoon. Now, this once great nation, has a comedy act strutting across the world stage. He'll turn Britain into a laughing stock. And then deny it, because he's a pathological liar. Did you see him on top of the double-decker bus lying his head off? Promised the nation a new hospital every five minutes from the money we're going to save from leaving Europe. He didn't mention the rebate we get back from Brussels, or the fact that he's descended from Turks who sold shish kebabs in the grand bazaar in Istanbul.'

'I thought he had Russian and French blood.'

'Who cares,' Bill bellows down the phone. 'He's not from Shepherd's Bush, is he?'

'I thought you liked some of his liberal ideas.'

'Not me, old bean. You must be confusing me with someone else. The clown has no social conscience, no principles; he's a sociopath. I know someone who went to Eton with him. He told me the other boys called him Billy Bunter behind his back. No one trusted him. He was too selfish, always thinking of himself. He doesn't even believe in Brexit. He just jumped on the populist bandwagon to further his political career. I wouldn't vote for him if he promised free joints on the NHS to alleviate insomnia.' I guess that Bill hears me chuckling, for he quickly adds, 'In any case, given his track record, they'd probably be laced with dried parsley.'

'I take it; you don't like him.'

'*Kim!* He's an accident waiting to happen. I don't know why we don't go the full hog, and make the Queen's consort the Prime Minister; we'd be at war in a week.' I'm tickled by the thought of the Prince leading parliament, but my levity remains unaired, as like Bill's previous call, his second is a monologue. 'And what about his wife? Mrs Bratwurst.'

'Who's Mrs Bratwurst?'

'The Queen, who else? Don't you know your history? The royals changed their German surname to Windsor during the First World War. They got a bit hot under their ruff collars when the teenage Tommies were falling like ten-pin skittles in the trenches.'

'I didn't know they changed their name.'

'Well, it's true. The British monarch is as German as that piss water wine called Liebfraumilch. The way things are going, we'll have to cart her off to Berlin before the Brandenburg Gate closes. And then, we can give her husband a paddle to show off his naval skills on a banana boat to Corfu, or wherever he comes from. He can sell souvlaki wraps to the tourists on the beach, strike up a free trade deal with Billy Bunter in Istanbul.' My friend's politics were never entirely orthodox, but I've never heard him use such dubious points to support an argument. It's so strange that I mention the fact.

'Listen, old bean, PC is out of the window over here, gone out of fashion. Without the support of racists, the leavers wouldn't have won. For many, it was all about race, for or against immigration. Sadly, as you know, this country has always had its racists, but the result of the referendum has emboldened them, brought them out of the woodwork. Since the referendum, attacks on foreigners have soared, on the football terraces, the monkey chants are back. Only the other day, a group of French schoolgirls were manhandled by a bunch of louts for speaking French on a British Rail train. The incident happened near Batley, where a pro-EU MP was murdered on the street by a maniac yelling "Britain first." The Keep Britain British brigade are having a field day. As for the royals, you know I'm not a monarchist, but I've nothing against them personally. They're people, like me and you, and like us they have their own problems. Even the Queen's grandson has been targeted by racists for falling in love with a beautiful girl who's not Snow White. I only mentioned them as they're so beloved by the bigots who want the Europeans out, and Billy Bunter's exotic background, for the leavers to chew on the fact that their foreign secretary's veins are awash with foreign blood. Personally I couldn't give a fig where someone comes from. My interest in people is in their hearts.'

'Point taken,' I respond conciliatorily, regretful of forcing Bill to make it, fearing I've needled a friend who I know hasn't a racist bone in his body.

Bill's voice is quavering, as if tears might be welling up, as he closes the call, by telling me he doesn't know what's happening to his country, that London should go to the polls to seek independence, become a city-state like Singapore, but more liberal.

It can't be more than an hour later, after I've made a pot of lemon tea, watered the ferns and flowers on my terrace, when my mobile phone starts vibrating across the table where I left it. It's Bill again, penitent, apologetic, calling to say he's was only joking about the kebab shop in Istanbul, that he's sorry for being so negative, that he understands that like attracts like, that pigeons never play with crows, that I must have enough on my plate without him adding his woes. I hear him sucking in his breath, before he tells me he loves and misses me, that he finds solace knowing I'm still on the planet. "I'm always here,' I respond breezily.

'Thank God,' he replies with a shallow laugh, 'My head is spinning. The other day I caught myself swearing at the box when a UKIP bigwig popped up gloating. I need to get out of my flat, take a stroll, clear my head, fill my lungs with the smog of Soho. Or perhaps, I'll buy an air-ticket, jump ship, and have a beer with you.'

'That's my boy,' I tell him, before he hangs up.

20

ONE LATE SUMMER MORNING, BLESSED WITH A BRIGHT BLUE SKY, I WAKE UP agog with puzzling wonder over the fragments of a peculiar dream. Maria's side of the bed is empty. She's stretching her lissom limbs on the terrace. I listen to her footsteps on the tiles above the bedroom, as I examine the dream I've barely emerged from. The first thing I remember about my dream is that the little boy is called Joe Cole. A delicate child of six, with pale, almost translucent skin, and straight hair in a fringe so fair that it's practically white. If I discount the strange quietness about the little boy, a sad seriousness in his face that doesn't match his years, there's nothing peculiar about the star of my dream. Nothing peculiar, until he tells me that I'm dreaming, that his short life will end soon as he dying from a terminal cancer, that when I wake up I must remember him, for if I forget his face, it will be as if he never lived at all.

I've always had a fascination for dreams, not only their content and significance, but the unlikely fact that we have them in the first place. How, each night we effortlessly conjure up different worlds in which to live. I recall a Vedic text that revered the ability to dream, spoke of it as a mirror of the key that could unlock the mysteries of Maya. How the ancients in India believed that even with our eyes wide open, we were still living in some sort of dream. It is with such thoughts swirling in my head, that I slip on a pair of shorts, and head for the spiral staircase.

When I join Maria on the roof terrace I tell her about my dream. She listens attentively, marvels at my vivid account, tells me she rarely remembers her dreams. She says her dreams are like lives lived but forgotten, just like the days of her early childhood before she had learned to speak. 'But what does my dream mean?' I ask pointedly, determined not to be side-tracked by her interesting remark.

'It's obvious,' she replies gaily, staring into my eyes.

'Not to me, it isn't,' I respond with an involuntary frown.

'The little prince in your dream is the child within you telling you not to forget him.'

I'm dumbfounded by her insight, stunned by the precision of her perception. It's akin to remembering the name of something on the tip of my tongue. And like the forgotten name, once it's remembered, everything is settled. I'm still pondering her exegesis, when she tells me that those who sacrifice the child on the altar of adulthood, end up forgetting who they are. 'Do you remember Angel, the farmhand who lives just outside my village? He always wears a straw hat,' she adds, furnishing a detail to jog my memory.

'He has a firm handshake,' I smile, in recalling the man who crushed my pampered palm in his calloused hand.

'His heart's as hard as his hand,' Maria sighs sadly. 'I used to play with him when I was a little girl. He was a delightful child, in awe with everything around him. He kept a grasshopper as a pet, and when it died he cried like a baby. I had to go to the funeral. He made a wooden cross for its shallow grave. He recited the Lord's prayer and three hail Marys, with a strip of white paper glued to his neck with honey, so he could look like the parish priest. And now, look at him,' Maria sighs again, 'a brute who drinks brandy for breakfast, bitter with the fists that drove his wife and daughter away. People avoid him in my village; today, his only company is the pack of half-starved dogs he keeps chained up in an outbuilding. When he's blind drunk, he beats them with a horse whip for the fun of it.'

'Why doesn't someone report him?'

'They have, but no one turns up,' Maria responds forlornly. 'The poor dogs sleep in their own waste. He only unchains them so they can mate with each other. And then, when the bitches give birth, he treads the little mites underfoot, feeds the litter to their parents. He's a monster who believes *los hombres no lloran*, men don't cry. That's the price of killing the child within you.'

21

I DECIDE THAT I CAN'T SIT AROUND BROODING ON SOMETHING THAT MIGHT not even happen. Maria tells me to focus on the moment, to deal with tangibles, things in front of my nose, to be here now. One evening, when I tell her about a book I read in England that described Spain as a country of *'little Spains'*, that I would like to discover some of the cultural pockets of her country that I've never experienced, she encourages me to buy an air ticket to Catalonia, to see what lies between Barcelona and the Pyrenees, to visit places I've never seen.

I buy a return air ticket to the capital of Catalonia that's cheaper than travelling by train. But there's another price to pay. I arrive in the busy city centre after nightfall. The hotel I find on foot is expensive, although conveniently located in a quiet backstreet in the Gothic quarter, the oldest *barrio* in Barcelona. From the hotel, it only takes me a few minutes to walk to *La Rambla*, where I order a glass of wine in a pavement café. I linger awhile over my wine to watch the tourists walk up and down a street that Lorca once described as the only one in the world that he wished would never end. I'm not sure that I agree with the poet, but being downtown in the second largest city in Spain, after spending so much time in a small pueblo that no one has ever heard of, is certainly, for a city boy like myself, exciting. I phone Maria to tell her I miss her, that I've changed my plans, that instead of one night, I'll spend two in Barcelona. She thinks my idea is great, tells me that she wishes she were with me.

The following morning, after breakfast in the hotel, I make my way to the National Art Museum of Catalonia, somewhere I've never been before. Most of my time in the museum is spent admiring Romanesque murals, but I still find time to contemplate Fra Angelico's masterpiece, the 'Madonna of Humility', and climb to the rooftop viewpoint for a panoramic picture of the sprawling city. One art gallery a day is enough for me, so after arranging a hired car for the following day, my afternoon is leisurely spent near my hotel, exploring the Gothic quarter, taking photographs of the cathedral and other medieval churches. Just before dusk, standing in the road, I almost lose my life to a passing bus, not far from where Gaudi lost his to a tram. When, around midnight, I phone Maria to tell her about my day, how I nearly got knocked down by a bus admiring the *Sagrada Familia*, she tells me to be careful for her sake, warns me to keep my head before beauty.

Mistakenly pressing dismiss instead of snooze on my mobile phone alarm I oversleep by two hours. I miss the set breakfast in the hotel by ten minutes, but still manage to enjoy an instant coffee in my room as I always travel with a small element and a stainless steel mug – items I bought in an Indian market over a decade earlier for such emergencies. The only real inconvenience of oversleeping is that I get caught up in Barcelona's mid-morning traffic. But once I'm out of the city it's plain sailing on the road to Ripoll, and from there into the foothills of the Pyrenees. I'm in no hurry, and stop several times to take photographs of the picturesque countryside. I arrive in Setcases, a small village near the French border, early afternoon, having spent three hours on the road, when most drivers from the Catalan capital would have taken two. Located near the source of the river Ter, the ancient village is very pretty, as I discover wandering through its cobbled narrow streets. I take a table in a street café and order a plate of *setas*, huge greyish brown mushrooms, a seasonal dish. The café is near a narrow canal so while I eat I can hear the babble of running water. I'm tempted to stay a night, look for a hotel, but change my mind, after a conversation with a couple from Madrid who tell me that in every hotel they've tried, even those with vacancy signs, they've been turned away. One hotel manager even when so far as to tell them that his hotel didn't accept Madrileños, as their city was full of thieves. The intelligence doesn't surprise me. I'm aware of the history between the Catalan state and the central government in Madrid, but I'm disheartened to learn of such nastiness between ordinary folk. When I'm overcharged for my mushrooms, I return to my car, leaving a leaflet on hiking trails from the village next to a saucer of small change to settle my bill.

The drive to Compradon is less than half an hour, and it is there, not far from a magnificent Roman bridge, that I find a bed for the next two nights. The hotel receptionist, a local, middle-aged woman, seems to like me, tells me I can have the attic room, her favourite room in the hotel, at a discounted price as I'm alone. After Setcases, I can't help wondering how I would have been received if I had been born in the Spanish capital.

The room at the top of the hotel is full of character, just as the receptionist described it. There's a huge double bed for me to flop on, creaking polished floorboards, on the walls, black and white photographs of local scenes, and best of all, a small balcony overlooking the plaza below.

After a refreshing shower, I'm ready to explore the little town. The receptionist is at the front of the hotel, smoking a cigarette, when I leave. She asks me where I'm going. When I tell her that I have no plans, that I'm just going out to look around, she tells me that I must visit Beget, where she was born. According to her, it's the prettiest village in the whole of Catalonia. 'But you will need a car,' she warns me, 'unless you like hiking, as it's at the bottom of a valley.'

With little over twenty inhabitants, the receptionist's village is an unspoilt gem. Walking across a hump-backed bridge, down cobbled lanes lined with stone houses with Arabic roof tiles, I find myself in an apple orchard. An old woman, dressed in black, is sitting under an apple tree, knitting a scarf. When I look at her, she puts her knitting needles down, bends her ancient limbs to rummage in the sack of apples at her feet. I accept a rosy-red apple from her frail hand. '*Muchas gracias*,' I thank her, and in return receive a sad smile and the sign of the cross made with a hand that wears a wedding ring.

Back in Compradon, I take a coffee in a square that used to be, until recent times, known as the Plaza de Espana. At the risk of appearing odd, or at best eccentric, I chortle over my coffee, when I think of Kolkata, where the local authorities renamed the street where the British and American consulates were located to Ho Chi Minh street.

There are plenty of reasonably priced, decent restaurants in Compradon, but I can think of no better way to have my dinner than to sit under the Romanesque bridge. There, beside the river, I eat a stick of bread stuffed with goats' cheese, followed by a roseate apple. Against the soothing burble of the flowing river, I hear a boy's voice in the distance, singing a romantic song that takes me back to my village.

At the hotel, the receptionist is still on duty. She smiles, when I tell her that I loved her village, that it was like a medieval village frozen in time. When I mention the old woman in the apple orchard, she looks at me quizzically. 'That was Maria, my great grandmother,' she tells me. 'She died years ago of a broken heart.' As I don't respond, or for that matter, look surprised, the receptionist feels the need to elaborate. I'm told that her village has more ghosts than anywhere else in Spain, but that they usually come out at night, when the tourists have gone home. 'To show her face in daylight, Maria must have liked the look of you,' the receptionist closes her account of the strange affair with a suggestive wink.

After an instant coffee and a sugary bun on my balcony, the following day I set off early to drive through the mountains with the vague ambition of reaching Cadaques on the coast. Despite the blind corners, the twists and turns, I prefer the secondary roads, as I pass through villages I've never heard of, settlements so small that they aren't even on the road map that came with the hired car. At one unknown village I pass a young man, standing by the side of the road, with his thumb held aloft. He tells me that he wants to get to Besalu, a small town, according to my map, on my route to the coast. Patrick, the young Frenchman, speaks English, but like my French, not very well, so we converse in Spanish. He tells me that he's from Paris, but once a year spends a week hiking in the Pyrenees in search of meteorite rocks from his planet. 'So you are an alien?' I ask light-heartedly.

'We all are!' he exclaims with a serious mien. 'We might even be from the same planet.' When I ask him to explain his ideas, he enthusiastically responds that all life on Earth began in outer space, the building blocks of life arriving here on meteorites full of organic compounds. 'I'm not alone in my extra-terrestrial theories,' he adds defensively, 'the scientist who discovered the structure of DNA believes in panspermia, and he's a Nobel laureate.' Perhaps, because I have no immediate response, Patrick drops the subject. 'Do you mind?' he asks, leaning from the passenger seat to turn the radio on. 'I hate Spanish pop music, and French,' he volunteers as he scans through the stations. 'That's better,' he says when he finds a station dedicated to American and British rock and roll. As I listen to a song by Led Zeppelin, he tells me that I come from an uptight country that makes good music. It's a paradox I'm not unfamiliar with, but Patrick's take on British musicality is new to me. He tells me that at the dawn of time there were no continents, only one land mass in the form of a human body. 'Britain was an ear.'

'And the other ear?' I ask innocently.

'I don't know. It's not my speciality.'

When I drop Patrick off, near the Roman bridge of Besalu, he gifts me a small grey fossil of what looks like the skeleton of a fish. 'I'm sure we've met before,' he says as he gets out of the car.

'On another planet?'

'Of course!'

There are no other hitch-hikers on the road to Cadaques, but near Figueres, I see a signpost to France, and just for the hell of it, take a detour and drive across the unmanned border to drink a *café au lait* in the first French village I chance upon. An hour later, I'm back in Spain, laughing at the wheel. I'm sure my unplanned excursion on to French soil has something to do with Brexit and the passport in my pocket, but the exact connexion escapes me as I nearly have an accident, when a bull, without care of cars, bolts across the road in front of me. After that close encounter, my second of the day, I drive carefully and cautiously on the small country road to Cadaques.

With difficulty I find somewhere to park my car, and then stroll through the white-washed little town in search of a restaurant. It might be immoderately priced, but the pizza I enjoy for lunch is delicious, as is the small carafe of chilled white wine. Alone, the sweeping vista of the bay, justifies the exorbitant bill I pay for my table. I could and would spend the whole afternoon, looking at the fishermen in the harbour, the moored yachts with sails glittering on a deep blue sea, but there's a queue for the restaurant, so when my wine glass is drained, I reluctantly go in search of somewhere else to enjoy myself under the cloudless cobalt sky.

Having read a little about Cadaques the night before, I know that John Cale, the avant-garde musician, played chess in the little town, that Picasso loved the place, like Miro, extolled the quality of light, that the bay is mentioned in a novel by Marques, Columbia's greatest writer. But of all the illustrious names associated with the small coastal town, one name stands out above all the rest. Born in nearby Figueres, Salvador Domingo Felipe Jacinto Dali I Domennech, or just Dali, as he is known to the world, played in the narrow streets of Cadaques when he was a boy. As an adult, he lived in a house on the edge of the town, where he created some of his greatest works of art. The house still stands, but it's always crowded with tourists, so I settle for a cigarette next to a statue of the Spanish artist. With riverlets of perspiration running down my back, I return to my car, turn on the air-conditioning, and drive to a nearby cove, fringed by pine trees. I might be on the Costa Brava, but the beach is without tourists. I strip down to my boxer shorts and plunge into the sea. Without a towel, I roll my jeans up to make a pillow, and lie in the sun to dry out. I have no recollection of falling asleep, but when I turn on to my back, I find a plump woman in a bikini, lying on a towel, with a book folded over her face, who certainly wasn't there when I came out of the sea. Parched, I need something to drink, preferably a coffee, poured over ice. After the problem of parking in Cadaques, I take the country road back to Dali's birthplace, and from there the main road to Compradon, stopping in an *aldea* to quench my thirst.

After a cold shower, I take an early dinner by the river, and then return to my hotel, where I spend the rest of the evening on my balcony with a bottle of wine. When Maria calls, I tell her about my perfect day; how I went to France, swam in the sea, sat next to Dali, and had a memorable meeting with a young Frenchman called Patrick. I don't mention the close shave with the bull. When I outline the conversation I had with Patrick, how he thought we might have met before on another planet, Maria bursts into laughter, before reminding me that our bodies are made of stardust. Before we finish our phone call with declarations of love, she tells me that she's bought tickets to a music festival, that when I get back, I'll have a day to rest before we drive to Cartagena.

'Who's playing?'
'That's a surprise. But it's someone you love.'

My last afternoon in the province of Catalonia is spent in Girona. I find a cheap room in a pleasant *pension* in the oldest part of the city. I'm very fortunate, as the *pension* isn't easy to find, hidden in a labyrinth of lanes. The manager tells me his *pension* is in the *barrio* where Jewish families lived for nearly five hundred years. When I ask if there are any Jews left in the neighbourhood, the manager responds by shaking his head, tells me the Jews of Catalonia were kicked out at the beginning of the sixteenth century, hounded from their homes, after unfounded, despicable rumours accused them of kidnapping Spanish children to eat them in diabolical rituals.

My room is on the second floor, a corner room with two balconies, overlooking a restaurant on the ground floor. I won't have to look far to find my dinner. Without plan or map, I stroll down to the river Onyar that runs through the city, walk across a bridge that looks as if it might have once spanned the more famous river Kwai in Thailand. On a plaque in English, I read that the bridge was designed by Eiffel, before he constructed the tower in Paris. For want of direction, I follow signs for the *Passeig de la Muralla*, which turns out to be an undemanding walk along the city's medieval walls, with watchtowers affording expansive views. Sighting the cathedral, I climb the steps to the old church, ignore the tourists, to meditate as if I'm at prayer, beneath the magnificent, rose-shaped, stained glass windows. Happy with what I've seen, I return to my *pension,* prepare my bag for the morrow, and then descend two flights of stairs to sit in the restaurant. There isn't much on the menu for a vegetarian, apart from vegetable soup, which I order with a glass of cold beer. Two girls. who look like students, catching my English accent, start up a conversation. At first, I'm asked standard questions; where do I come from? Do I like Girona? Do I like Catalonia? What do I think of Barcelona? But it isn't long before the conversation turns political. I'm told that 'Dick', Bill's favourite politician, is popular in Girona, because he allowed Scotland a referendum on independence. 'That's what we want,' one of the girls explains, 'the chance to run our own country.' Thinking of recent events in Britain, I warn them that they might not get the result they want.

'Oh! We'll win a clear majority,' a young man, who introduces himself as Jordi, joins the conversation. 'And Madrid knows it. That's why they won't give us a referendum,' he adds somewhat aggressively. 'We are the economic powerhouse of Spain, the only ones who work in this country.' Not knowing enough about what is obviously a sensitive issue to my young companions, aware that the last thing I need is to get into a fight, I essay to make intelligent, but neutral comments, preferring to listen, rather than talk. I keep my fears of nationalism to myself, how in the nineteen thirties, Germany thought it was better than her neighbours, how that sense of superiority led to war. How, I fear, that the appalling nationalism sweeping across Britain, somewhere down the line, might have a similar result. While I'm being informed how a Catalan politician with an unpronounceable name was arrested for refusing to speak Spanish when questioned by the police, my strategy of nodding sympathetically seems to work. Or at least, it works with the girls; Jordi is less impressed; he wants a positive response. In quest of that response, he has a word with the barman, whereupon the opening bars of *'Give Ireland back to the Irish'* blare out of the speaker above our table. 'Do you know this song?'

'It's famous. It was written by a British icon.'

'But it was banned in Britain. Even your so-called independent BBC refused to play it,' Jordi says with a bitter snarl. 'Do you think 'Give England back to the English', written by the same man, would be banned?

Thinking how some Englishmen would have loved such a song, made it their anthem, I finally make a verbal commitment. 'No, I don't.'

The flight back to Granada lasts barely ninety minutes. Sitting by the window, I look down, through the thin clouds, at the mountains of Spain. From the air it's easy to accept, that apart from Switzerland, the land I love so much is the most mountainous in Europe. Breezing through the airport with hand luggage, there's another reason why Spain and her beautiful peaks will always be in my heart; Maria, waiting for me, holding back her tears, with arms outstretched as if we have been apart for years.

22

FOR MOST OF THE JOURNEY TO THE ANCIENT CITY OF CARTAGENA I'M FAST asleep, rolled up like a foetal ball on the backseat of Maria's car. Mid-afternoon, just past the midway point of the trip, Maria breaks the journey for a bite to eat. When she leans over the driver's seat to shake me gently from my slumber, I'm in a hypnopompic haze, removed from everyday reality. 'Have we arrived?' I ask in confusion, still half asleep.

'No,' Maria giggles. 'I need to have a sandwich and use the loo. We're in Lorca.'

'Lorca!' I think of the poet Franco killed, before the town. 'Isn't this where people died in an earthquake?' I ask in sleepy alarm, my memory not fully restored.

'Yes,' Maria giggles again. 'Sit up, and look out of the window.'

'Is it safe?' I ask, looking at a street with derelict buildings, a church without a roof.

'*Quien sabe*? Who knows?' Maria looks at me with a radiant smile. 'The earthquake was *only* five years ago.'

Founded two hundred and twenty years before Christ appeared on the planet, Cartagena is a paradise for historians, but staggering around Roman ruins under a sweltering sun is not my cup of Earl Grey. Fortunately, it isn't Maria's cup of EG either, as she readily agrees with my suggestion to return to our three-star hotel room, turn on the air-conditioning and take a siesta.

There's time for a cocktail before the concert of world music begins. When we take our seats, there's a group of musicians from Senegal on stage playing West African folk songs with unusual instruments that Maria's never seen before. The African act is followed by two Japanese women, petite figures in crimson kimonos, one on a zither, the other with a bamboo flute. And then the lights go down, the thick red velvet curtains sweep across the stage to hide the hands that prepare the props for the final set. Above the murmur of subdued voices, I catch the strain of sixteen strings being tuned, and as the curtains part, my first glimpse of a sitarist I've heard so many times, but never seen live, unlike her father, Ravi Shankar, whose musical magic I once had the privilege of listening to in a concert in Calcutta.

Alone on stage, barefoot on a cushioned dais, dressed in Punjabi garb, a deep red tikka on her forehead framed by black, lush hair held by a sparkling band of gold, Ravi's daughter looks like an Indian Goddess, perchance Lakshmi caressing her sitar. 'She plays like an angel,' Maria whispers in the middle of the short *raag*, weakening a personal fancy, fashioned in my pueblo, that the Spanish have no ear for Indian music. When a host of elite Spanish musicians, including Duquende, a famous flamenco singer, walk on to the stage, the half-baked notion crumbles into dust, disappearing into thin air like the twirling smoke of joss sticks surrounding the musicians.

The following day, on route to the eponymous capital of Murcia, listening to a fusion of ancient Indian music and modern flamenco, Maria tells me that music is the language of God, that the musicians, the *real* musicians, are angels in a world full of demons. In Murcia, after a coffee near the gothic cathedral, Maria hands me her car keys, asks me to drive for the rest of the day as she's tired. 'You won't get lost,' she says as she types in 'Fortuna' on the GPS, changing the language to English.

Like Barcelona, once I've escaped the city traffic, the drive to the small spa town is easy, the last stretch a countrified road lined by prostitutes, mainly African, sitting in deckchairs. Two girls, young, obviously desperate, stand stark naked rather than sit by the side of the road, using their knickers to flag down passing cars. It's a sad sight, and I'm glad that Maria is dozing in the passenger's seat when we arrive in the tiny town surrounded by a dusty forest of pines.

There's no shortage of accommodation in Fortuna, especially in the scorching months of summer, but we shun the expensive hotels, settle for a bungalow on a so-called campsite instead. The bungalow, resembling an oversized garden shed more than the photo in the glossy brochure in reception, is clean, and most importantly, has a powerful air-conditioning unit. Ignoring the poolside warning, we spend hours in the thermal pool, our weariness pounded by heavy jets of water. Lying side by side, tickled by *burbujas,* on a bed of bubbles, Maria tells me we've had enough, when she discovers her hands are covered in pink cherry-blossom wrinkles.

Opting for the set menu in the campsite restaurant, rather than one of the upmarket *balnearios* in town that cater for the well-heeled, Maria tells me that she has only two more classes before her summer holidays start. 'I was thinking we might tour Galicia,' she says in a tentative, quiet voice, 'perhaps Asturias as well, somewhere I've never been.'

'I'd love to!'

'So we can go?' Maria's face lights up.

'Yes.'

'Just like that! You don't want to think about it?'

'I don't need to think. I'll go with you wherever you want.'

After another plunge in the thermal pool, followed by a cold shower and a light breakfast, we drive into the hinterland of Murcia to visit a town sacred to Catholics. The name of the town is Caravaca de la Cruz, which, to the amusement of secular tourists, means 'Cowface of the Cross.' There are innumerable religious sites and monuments in the pretty town, but after an enervating climb up to the fortress-like Basilica and a drive-by peep inside the church where a pope once performed mass, we head to the pedestrianised centre to settle our thirst for an iced coffee. Inspired by caffeine, Maria finds the energy to visit a few shops to buy a two-barred cross as a gift for her 'religious' mother; a cross that Pablo once described as more suited to the four arms of Kali than the more familiar anatomy of Christ.

In the province of Granada, at Caniles, near the former Moorish stronghold of Baza, we follow a country road through the sierras to the semi-deserted village of Escha. Just beyond the eerie village, we stop so I might pee in a cluster of pine trees. When I emerge from the shadow of the trees, there's a man with a hooked staff, presumably a *pastor*, or shepherd, standing by the car, talking to Maria. As I approach the car, the man looks at me suspiciously, and then suddenly walks off, casting a grunt in my direction. I'm not in the least put out, as I know that *pastores* in the mountains of Andalusia are oftentimes more comfortable in the company of their animals than with a man who says *hola* in a foreign accent. 'What did he want?' I ask Maria, as I climb back into the car.

'He wanted to know if I had seen any sheep in the pine forest,' she responds. 'He said he'd lost one of his flock, that he'd been looking for it since sunrise. He described the sheep in detail, said it had an orange brand on its neck, and a black stripe on its left rear leg. The poor man was desperate. He told me that if he didn't find it, he would make a loss this month.'

As I slowly drive down the mountainside, zigzagging past huge wind turbines, to find the old road back to my pueblo, I think of Jordi, the young man I met in Girona, of the ireful confidence in his voice when he told me that in Spain only Catalans know the meaning of work.

23

FROM THE PARCHED OLIVE GROVES OF ANDALUSIA TO THE SWEET-SMELLING apple orchards of Asturias is a gruelling drive. Most travellers would take two days, but we're determined, by sharing the driving, to complete the journey in one, starting pre-dawn to finish beyond dusk. With this in mind, we turn the engine off only three times on the journey north, once to fill our tank with petrol, twice to rest. Our first break is taken on the outskirts of Valdepenas, alas not for its celebrated wine, but two large coffees and a plate of *pestiños*, fried fritters that look like donuts, covered in honey. Then, somewhere in Castile and Leon, a few hundred kilometres further north, we take our final break, by leaving the highway in search of a village for a very late lunch. We find a *venta,* a sort of old-fashioned inn, that was once a watering-hole for muleteers. It's musty, and surprisingly dark inside the *venta*. With a heavy curtain over the doorway, the only natural source of light is filtered by jalousies on two small windows. When I remove my sunglasses, I notice a calendar with a topless woman on the wall behind the bar, on another wall, a sad-looking stag's head, moth-eaten, one-eyed, with a string of garlic hanging from a broken antler. The only clients in the *venta*, a knot of *campesinos*, working men from the surrounding fields, are gathered around a wooden bench, eating *morcilla*, black sausage, with lumps of bread, washed down by local wine from a barrel beneath the stag's head. Our sudden appearance, altering the dramatis personae in the enclosed space, dries up the conversation at the wooden bench. Aware that we are surrounded by patent hostility, being scrutinised with undisguised suspicion, for the briefest moment, I'm tempted to return to the car, and head for another village. But things improve considerable, when Maria opens her mouth to ask the barmaid for a *bocadillo* and a glass of beer. '*Andaluz*!' the barmaid picks up Maria's accent.

'From the Alpujarras.'

'And him?' the barmaid looks at me warily.

'*Ingles.*'

Turning to the bunch of men, who, following the exchange with so much interest, have actually stopped eating, the barmaid says something in a local dialect. Exactly what's said escapes us, for even Maria can't fathom the dialect. But we aren't out of the loop for long. '*Me llamo Maruja*,' the barmaid gives us her name, returning to *Castellano*. 'Angel,' she nods in the direction of a bearded man in a French beret, 'and his men, thought you might be snooping around to see if anyone is selling tobacco without a licence.' Maruja notes my glance at the row of cigarette packets beneath the bombshell with enormous tits above her head. 'Not that sort of tobacco,' she laughs. 'I'm talking about *real* tobacco. The stuff we grow and sell round here without a *duro* going into the treasury's pot. Fifty euros a kilo of the best *rubio* money can buy. Do you smoke?' I produce my packet of Fortuna as an answer. 'That stuff kills,' Maruja looks at my cigarette packet with disgust. 'Smell this,' she hands me a bag of tobacco, watches me inhale deeply, before asking me what I think.

'Fifty euros,' I reply, as I fish out a flesh-coloured note from my back pocket. It's a happy transaction, one that completely alters the atmosphere in the old inn. When our *bocadillos* turn up, they're so large as to make an American sub look like a paltry titbit. Overflowing with cheese, fresh tomatoes, slices of oily, sweet red pepper, topped with so much *alioli*, a sort of garlic mayonnaise, the sandwiches are impossible to eat without making a mess. Not that anyone, now that I've bought some tobacco, is standing on ceremony. We are asked where we're heading.

'Asturias,' Maria replies, whereupon Domingo, the oldest of the men, writes out an address in Gijon where his brother lives. Forgetting to add his brother's name to the address, he gives Maria the scrap of paper, and then tells us if we turn up at his brother's place, he'll look after us, especially if we want any more tobacco. Angel is even more friendly, handing me a cigarette rolling machine that he insists I accept as a gift. For *postre*, we're served a stodgy pudding soaked in thick black syrup, and a second beer, hauled up from a *pozo* in the kitchen, where bottles are stored to keep them cool. After a very strong black coffee, served in a bowl, it's time to hit the road. When I ask for our bill, Maruja, with a mischievous grin that wipes years off her kindly face, repairs to the bar to tot things up. It seems arithmetic reckoning isn't her forte, for several minutes later, she hands me a torn serviette, on the back of which, in pencil, is written the excessively modest sum of five euros.

'This can't be right,' I protest mildly, not wishing to offend.

'That's the price, the *local* price,' Maruja smiles at me. 'Not more, not less.'

Somewhat awkwardly, I settle our account, before I'm struck by a bright idea. Leaving Maria to entertain the troupes, I return to the car, to rifle through our luggage. When I return to the *venta*, I plant two fine bottles of red wine on the wooden bench; disown them, say I don't know how they got there. 'That's the way to do it!' Maruja exclaims brightly, before throwing her arms around me. 'That's the way we do it around here, the *old* way.'

After a round of hugs and kisses, everyone in the *venta* follows us to our car. Despite Maria's protests, a bag of luscious pears is put on the backseat as a farewell gift. While Maruja and the men stand in the sun to wave to us as we head out of their lives, Maria thumps the horn twice to say goodbye.

It's dark when we arrive in Cangas de Onis, one of the prettiest towns in Asturias, if not the whole of Spain. For once, I'm glad that we have pre-booked our accommodation, instead of pursuing the adventurous game of playing everything by ear. Our room, at the back of the hotel, away from the road, has pine floorboards to match the furniture, an attractively tiled bathroom, and a generous balcony overlooking the river Sella. Maria, the first to stand under the shower, suggests we spruce up, go in search of a *sideria*, drink a cup of local cider to celebrate our arrival in the land of apples. When it's my turn in the bathroom, I shower, shampoo my hair, and shave, wondering where Maria, who has been behind the wheel since we left the *venta*, gets her energy from. With a towel wrapped around my waist, I'm resolved to ask her, only to discover, when I return to the room, that she curled up in bed fast asleep. It's beyond me to disturb her slumber. Rather, I drink in her angelic features in defenceless repose, before tiptoeing to the balcony to try my new tobacco as I listen to the babble of the river. Dog-tired, I think I'm already asleep when my head touches the pillow.

The following morn, I wake up to the song of blackbirds, open my eyes to a room suffused with soft zebra stripes emanating from the wooden shutters on the window. Maria's already up, sitting at the table on the balcony with a cup of instant coffee. 'Hi sleepy,' she jumps to her feet to hug me in my underpants. 'It's so lovely here,' she warbles, 'the air's so crisp and fresh.' I concur with a smile, think of the hairdryer winds that sweep over the villages in the south at this time of year. 'So, what shall we do today?' Maria asks, pouring me a coffee from the flask she's prepared.

'Whatever you want,' I reply. 'But hopefully nothing too strenuous.'

'No! After yesterday, nothing too strenuous,' she laughs like a little bird. 'Let's leave the car in the forecourt, have a day without hurry or worry.'

Inspired with Maria's vision, we amble along the riverine path at the back of our hotel, stopping whenever we feel the need, to admire wild flowers, to make friends with a collarless dog, to watch an iridescent blue kingfisher dive-bomb into the river, to steal playful kisses under the dappled light of tall birch and beech trees. When we reach the edge of the town, it has taken us over an hour to cover a distance that an octogenarian on crutches might have walked in twenty minutes.

Although it can claim to be the first capital of Christian Spain, Cangas de Onis remains a small, provincial township. Even without a guidebook, it isn't long before we find ourselves facing the town's oldest church. Much as we might wish to explore the ancient house of worship, our desire is thwarted by a heavy padlock. 'It's the times we live in,' Maria sighs, before relating an incident that happened in her village ten years ago on her saint's day. How thieves removed roof tiles from the village church, lowered themselves down with ropes from the rafters to make off with a pair of seventeenth-century silver candlesticks. Recalling my disdain in a funeral service in my own village, when a bronze dish was passed from hand to hand to squeeze donations from mourners, I'm less sympathetic to a super-rich religion that can't spare a few coppers to keep its doors open.

We cross the river, stroll down a few pleasant streets lined with shops well-stocked with postcards and tourist knick-knacks, until we reach the famous hump-backed Roman bridge. Maria asks a passer-by to take a snap of us on the bridge with the rolling hills in the background. Thanking the stranger, we scramble over rocks to sit by the river's edge, where, like a pair of kids, we splash each other with cold water. A couple of cigarettes later, our shirts bone-dry, we return to the hump-backed bridge, to wander into the town centre. In the main square, we find a *sideria*, opposite a stone church with a tiered bell-tower. The waitress, a local lass in her early twenties, pretends she's not bored performing the region's party trick. We watch as she pours cider from a bottle above her head into a glass held just below her waist. 'The idea is to drink the cider while it's full of bubbles,' she explains with a well-rehearsed smile. When it's my turn to try the trick, the point becomes somewhat moot, as most of the cider lands on my shoes. There's a bucket and mop at hand to clean the floor tiles, as it seems I'm not the only tourist in town to make a fool of himself. Pouring my second bottle of cider into a tilted glass, like an old hand pulling pints, I settle down at a table with Maria, to enjoy a tortilla in tomato sauce, followed by an assortment of local cheeses.

On the way back to the hotel, Maria suggests we take a taxi as she's keen to catch a TV documentary on Isabel Duncan, an American dancer I've never heard of. Although happily acceding to her wish, I can't help jesting in the back of the cab, reminding her that Pablo doesn't have a television. Maria, being who she is, tells me as much as she admires our friend, she's her own woman, that TV is neither good or bad in itself, but only made so by how it's used. 'Like the internet, mobile phones, or an aeroplane that can take us to Hawaii for our honeymoon or drop chemical bombs on innocent civilians in Syria,' she adds to hammer her point home.

'*Ole!*' I clap my hands softly to avoid startling the taxi driver.

Back in our hotel. I sprawl across the bed, while Maria is glued to the set. As the documentary is in Spanish, I follow the plot half-heartedly. My main interest is Maria, watching her shed tears, first of joy, in appreciation of Duncan's unusual talent, and then those of sorrow over the ballerina's untimely death when her neck was snapped after her scarf got entangled in the wheels of a car in France. It's a poignant reminder how fragile our grip on life is, how, at any moment, it can all end. Before I succumb to a siesta, I apology to Maria for teasing her in the taxi, tell her I'd love her no less if she had an addiction for Mexican soaps.

With plans drawn up to visit Gijon and Oviedo the following day, we forget the car, and dine in the hotel's restaurant, opting for a buffet that includes unlimited local wine. There's not much on the menu for a vegetarian palate, but we make do with a combination of side dishes, including a bowl of *fabada*, a thick stew of white beans, flavoured with garlic cloves, paprika and slices of sausage. When a waiter sees Maria fishing out the sausage pieces, he approaches our table to ask if there's a problem with the food. 'No,' Maria responds with an engaging smile. 'It's just that we don't eat meat, but we know a dog who does.'

'In that case, would you like a doggie bag?' the waiter grins to show his sense of humour.

We both enjoy exploring the old quarter of Gijon, but after a stroll along the promenade that ends with a photograph of the façade of the San Lorenzo church, neither of us are sad to say goodbye to the Bay of Biscay and its screeching seagulls.

Miraculously, it stops raining as soon as we arrive in the capital of Asturias. With no interest in modern buildings, we head for the historic centre of the city, for a spacious plaza named after a Spanish king. Outside the gothic cathedral of San Salvador, we are informed by a tout that for only seven euros each, he's willing to show us an ancient cross encrusted with precious gems, apparently the most valuable of all the priceless treasures contained within the church. 'Another day,' I decline the generous offer, 'when it's raining.'

'I promise,' the tout shouts aggressively as we leave the plaza, 'it will rain soon.' When it begins to drizzle ten minutes later, just as we enter the Museum of Fine Arts, Maria remarks, somewhat wryly, that the barker outside the cathedral would make a good weatherman. After spending time studying the work of Titian and Goya, I discover a painting by Sorolla, one of my favourite Spanish painters. Hiding my mobile behind Maria, I take a forbidden photograph, for although I'm not much of an artist, great paintings always inspire me, at least for a week or two, to pick up a brush. Back on the street, an hour later, it's still spitting, so we head for a restaurant, choosing a table under a parasol in a pedestrianized street. Our main dish is a pasta of some sort, followed by a fruit salad that doesn't come out of a tin. Maria selects the wine; a fine dry white that costs as much as the meal. As the wine is so expensive I imbibe a third glass to empty the bottle; peradventure one glass too many, for twenty minutes later I drift off on a bench in a city park named after San Francisco. Wisely, Maria sits behind the steering wheel for the drive back to our hotel on the banks of the river Sella.

Early, the following day, our last in Asturias, we set off to visit the sanctuary of Covadonga. Arriving before the daily convoy of coaches, we are first in line to buy a ticket to explore a cave grotto surrounded by waterfalls dedicated to the Lady of Covadonga, otherwise known in the Catholic world as the Virgin Mary. The shrine has a beautiful setting to match its historical significance, for it marks the site of a David and Goliath battle that changed the whole course of Spanish history. As Maria reads from the leaflet we were given with our tickets, I learn how, against all odds, an army of Moors was defeated by a small band of *Asturianos*; how the unlikely victory marked the beginning of the *Reconquista*, a campaign that lasted seven hundred and seventy years. 'A thousand-mile walk is shortened by the first step,' I quote a Chinese proverb as Maria puts the leaflet down. But the leaflet doesn't give the whole story, fails to mention the flipside, how, eight hundred years after the famous battle, a Galician despot, mindful of Spanish history, sent an army of mercenaries from North Africa into Asturias to slaughter those who opposed his rule. An historical irony not lost in Asturias, where, if not with the strident tones of the Basque country and Catalonia, there is still talk of an independent state.

   Happily, it isn't a long drive from Covadonga to the western fringes of the Picos de Europa. It's one of the wildest regions of Spain, where packs of wolves and solitary brown bears still roam. Our itinerary isn't overambitious, just Ercina and Enol, two very picturesque glacial lakes set against mountainous backdrops. Both lakes would be ideal sites for a picnic if they weren't surrounded by soggy grassland. At Enol lake, in the safety of our car, as it begins to pour, we eat cheese sandwiches, washed down with fresh orange juice. I know I ought not to laugh, but I can't help myself, when I see a rather large woman in a pair of purple hot pants lose her balance trying to extract one of her high heel shoes from the superglue grip of the boggy marsh.

   As on our first night, we dine in our hotel's restaurant, eat the same food, drink the same wine, ask for a doggie bag. Not far from the place where we first met our collarless friend, Maria empties the contents of the doggie bag under a tall poplar tree.

24

GALICIA, THE NORTH WESTERN CORNER OF THE IBERIAN PENINSULA, IS ONE of my favourite Spanish provinces. It is a region coloured by everything Spain has to offer. And a bit more, if Celtic inspiration is considered. There are mountains and verdant vales, beaches, cliffs and coves that face the sea of Cantabria and the Atlantic Ocean, historic cities and picture-postcard villages, lakes and lagoons, rivers that run like ribbons across the land; and then, there's the music, quite different from anywhere else in Spain. I'd fain live in a Galician village, but for one significant drawback – the weather. But then not everyone is bothered by the constant need of an umbrella. On my first visit to the province, a camping trip in my early twenties, a red-eyed Galician in the caravan next to my tent, told me he loved the rain. It painted the rainbows over the mountains, fed the waterfalls, the rivers and streams, fatten the cows, and clothed the forests and rolling hills in every shade of green. 'The rain defines us; without it we are nothing,' I remember his exact words.

St James is the patron saint of Spain; and it's to his city, Santiago de Compostela, we drive, oftentimes in third gear, through splendid countryside, following the old trunk road into town. Barely touching the accelerator, we pass hordes of trekkers and tourists on the ancient path, pilgrims from every corner of the world, some on horseback, one eccentric leading a mule decorated with a Manchester United flag. When we trundle passed a pensioner using a walking frame, Maria says she feels guilty sitting in a car. 'That's what happens when you go to a primary school run by nuns,' I laugh throatily.

A rarity in Spain, if not in the whole of Europe, we find a free parking space not far from the centre of the city. I can hardly believe our luck, scan the street for hidden parking meters. It is only when a local tells us that we can park where we are all day and night, that I can escape the conviction that the rain has washed away the yellow lines that all motorists detest. *'Un Milagro!'* I give the Galician my warmest smile. Sadly, there are no more miracles in Santiago, at least for us, not unless I count the price of the ticket to the cathedral which has gone up a thousand fold since my last visit. To me, it seems the height of hypocrisy, to pay to enter a church. It's a belief I've harboured for most of my life, a conviction converted to a rule I rarely break, even when the cost is high, like my one time in Rome, when I refused to pay to see Michelangelo's masterpiece in the Cistern Chapel. But rules are there to be broken, not solely in the words of Pablo, but also in those of many others. Thus I break my rule, for the sake of Maria, who confesses coyly she would like to see a religious relic. Of course, she doesn't get to see any relics. Even on the tips of her professional toes, she's hard pressed to see anything at all, except the back of Germanic heads, as the place is teeming with tourists from the north. Abandoning all hope of reaching the celebrated altar, we slip into the chapel of Salvador for a respite from the bustling crowd, before launching an all-out attack on the Romanesque masterpiece known as the *Portico da Gloria*. The *Gloria* is an exquisite work of elaborate carving, but without the arms of a gibbon, there's a fat chance of embellishing a future conversation by touching the feet of a saint set in stone, as we are literally swept off our own by the noisy arrival of at least fifty tourists from China. Following a woman in a black uniform carrying the flag of their nation, the tour group are so unruly that the grandfather of the group feels free to spit on the hallowed floor of the cathedral, before blowing his nose like a trumpet.

I don't suppose we are under the cathedral dome more than thirty minutes, but our sojourn coincides with the visit of an overweight Australian woman, who, crashing into a gaggle of Japanese tourists, bellows at the top of her voice, 'Swing the burner, swing it high and low; scatter the heathen bastards.'

Outside in the sun-baked fresh air, I'm still chuckling, when Maria asks me what the Australian was yelling about. 'She wanted the thurible, the biggest incense burner in the world, swung to flatten the tourists.'

'Not such a bad idea,' Maria smirks gleefully.

'It was built centuries ago to mask the stench of unwashed pilgrims.'

'*Que pena!*'

'*A shame!* Why?'

'We didn't see it.'

'It can be dangerous.'

'*Really!*'

'There have been plenty of accidents over the years. None more famous than when it flew out of a stained glass window on the occasion of a royal visit.'

Unable to find a decently priced *menu del dia* in the medieval city centre, we drive out to the modern suburbs to secure a table in a restaurant that offers a three-course lunch with a glass of wine for only six euros a head. Although we're the only tourists in the restaurant, we're still in Santiago, so there's little surprise to see a painting of St James on a wall above a display of tempting pastries. Usually portrayed as a gentle apostle, the painting above the cream cakes, captures the saint's other guise, as a slayer of Moors with three decapitated heads beneath his blood-stained sword. The painting is so gory, Maria struggles with her tomato soup. 'I thought the message of Christ was love,' she says with knitted brow. 'Aren't we told to turn the other cheek?'

'We are,' I smile glumly, before relating my confusion in an English primary school, when I was forced to sing a hymn that began with the words '*Onward Christian soldiers*'.

'I'm not surprised you were confused.'

'My first school, unlike my second, wasn't Catholic. They might have had a first edition of the Tyndale bible.'

'*Tyndale!*'

'The scholar behind the first translation of the bible into the English language. The Catholic church had him burnt at the stake for his labour.'

'Why?'

'Apparently, the first edition suffered from several printing errors, including the omission of 'not' from the two commandments concerning adultery and murder.'

'They *killed* him for printing errors?'

'Probably not,' I laugh. 'The Catholic church didn't approve of a vernacular bible. They wanted to keep the sacred book in Latin to mystify the masses. Remarkably, in America, the first Catholic service held in English was in the mid-sixties.'

Over coffee, poured into glasses full of chunks of ice, Maria informs me that she's had enough of the Catholic church for one day, and her schizophrenic saints.

After Santiago, Noia, a working town, built around the mouth of a river, is perfect. After finding a small, but pleasant boarding house with rooms overlooking the river, we shower, and wash our dirty clothes, wringing, as if making rope, the larger items of our laundry, before hanging them out to dry on a makeshift line on our balcony, Maria suggests we spend the rest of the afternoon in bed, do what lovers do, and then sip instant coffee, while we translate the poetry of St John of the Cross into English. The game of passion is easily accomplished, but even with the stimulus of coffee, we struggle to stay awake tackling the first stanza.

The sun is setting, when, in a fresh set of clothes, we take a *paseo* along the riverfront, before taking a table outside a local bar. I order a bottle of Estrella de Galicia, for me, the best beer in Spain, while Maria opts for a glass of *orujo*, the local firewater. Unlike in Britain, where every drop of whisky will snatch a pound from the purse, there are no mean optics in Spain. Unburdened by strict measures, our waiter is generous, fills Maria's glass to the brim. It's the first time Maria's sampled *orujo*. I surmise it's the reason why she guzzles the drink. Unaccustomed to hard liquor, it isn't long before she succumbs to a bout of giggles. It isn't something that bothers me in the least, but as I've never seen her in such a ridibund state, I ask her if everything is all right. 'I'm drunk,' she replies with a silly smile. Wisely, she only takes a few sips from her refilled glass, patiently waiting for me to polish off my second beer, before asking me to take her back to our room. Fortunately, we aren't far from home, for the last few hundred metres are a bit of a struggle, as she leans heavily on my supporting arm, unable to walk in a straight line. In the room, although it's a balmy night, she suddenly complains that she feels very cold. In bed, shivering, she asks me to cuddle her, to wrap my arms and legs around her body to keep her temperature up until she falls asleep.

In the morning I awake with renewed vigour, but Maria, nursing a huge hangover, tells me her head feels like fragile glass. 'What happened?' she asks. 'Did I make a fool of myself?'

'No. You were dignified throughout,' I give her a peck on the cheek. 'You just had a bit too much to drink, that's all. We've all been there.'

'I've never seen you like that.'

That's because you didn't know me as a teenager,' I grit my teeth in remembrance of a bad night in Athens. 'Do you remember the gap-year I told you about when we first met?'

'The one before you went to University, or the gap-year after University that turned into three?'

'The first one; when I was eighteen.'

'I remember.'

'Did I mention Greece?'

'I can't remember,' Maria responds with a pensive expression. 'You mentioned a lot of countries that night.'

'Well, one of the countries I went to on my first gap-year was Greece. After a month travelling around the islands by ferry, I ended up in Athens. It was to be the highlight of my Grecian adventure. I'd just finished Plato's 'Apology' on a beach in Kefalonia, and my head was spinning with admiration for Socrates. I couldn't wait to climb up to the Acropolis and stand where the great man had once stood. But first, I had to find a room for the night. I must have spent hours tramping around the dusty city before I found a dorm bed in a doss house for causal workers. It was high season and it was the only bed I could afford. I didn't know at the time, but I needn't have bothered.'

'Why?'

'Because once I got to the Acropolis, I stay there until the sun had set, and then went back into the town centre to buy a sandwich and a bottle of booze before making the long trek back to the doss house. The booze was called *ouzo* and easy to drink. I finished the bottle off before I had finished my sandwich. Decidedly still in the grip of sobriety, I bought another bottle of the local brew, selecting as before the cheapest brand.'

'What's *ouzo*?'

'It's what you call *anis* over here.'

'Isn't that quite a strong spirit?'

'That's what I discovered half way through my second bottle, when I tried to stand up, but couldn't.'

'You couldn't stand up!'

'Well, I *could*, just about, but like you last night, I couldn't walk in a straight line. Worse still, I couldn't remember where I'd left my bag, or ask for directions as I hadn't memorised the Greek letters that made up the name of the doss house.' I pause for a wistful sigh as I look back on my youthful folly.

'So, what did you do?'

'My recollection is full of holes, but I remember falling in love with a girl's face in a painting I saw in a shop window, and then, sometime later, being slung out of a nightclub for climbing on stage to ask the singer if he knew any English songs. After that, it's a blank. But I guess, I passed out, for the next thing I remember is being woken up by a shower of cold water.'

'Someone poured a bucket of water over your head?'

'No. The water came from the municipal workers hosing down the street in which I had chosen to spend the night.'

'I'm *glad* you were with me last night!'

'Me too,' I respond to the look of concern on Maria's face. Essaying to move on from the past to a new day, 'Would you like to go out for something to eat?' I ask, to change the subject.

'I'm not hungry,' Maria replies, 'but you go out. I'll be fine if I can sleep a bit longer.'

'That's a good idea,' I nod knowingly as I draw the curtains to swathe the room in semi-darkness. Just as I'm about to leave, Maria lifts her head up from the pillow, switches on the bedside light. 'What was she like?' she asks with eyes feigning indifference.

'Who?'

'The girl in the painting.'

'A real sultry stunner,' I grin teasingly. 'But not nearly as beautiful as you.'

Sitting in a pleasant square in the centre of the old town, I order an orange juice and two toasted sandwiches, one to eat, the other, wrapped in foil, to take back to the boarding house for Maria. Waiting for my breakfast to arrive, I watch a team of workmen erect a stage in front of the Romanesque church that gives the plaza the name of St Martin. 'Is there a show tonight?' I ask the young waitress when she returns to my table.

'A concert,' she flashes me a metallic smile, the early sunlight catching the brace across her upper teeth. 'You English?' Her intonation tells me I've been asked a question.

'*Si*,' I reply. 'How did you know?'

'Book,' she points at my novel on the table. 'My boss English. He like to talking,' she adds before leaving to serve another customer. A few minutes later, Bert, her boss, emerges from the café, to bestow meaning on uncertain grammar.

'Anabel tells me you're English.'

'I am,' I confirm Anabel's intelligence.

'We get plenty of Spanish tourists this time of the year, but hardly any English,' he looks at me suspiciously as if I might be up to something underhand. 'A bit off the beaten track,' he makes a statement that sounds like a question. 'Shame really, it's lovely round here.'

'It is,' I nod in agreement. 'Have you been here long?'

'Twenty-six years. I've owned this café for twenty years, and I run an English academy on the side. All the kids round here speak English because of me, even if they're too shy to use it. Anabel's one of my students,' he nods proudly in the direction of the girl with the disfigured smile, serving two old ladies at another table. 'Are you on holiday?' Bert makes it clear he wants an answer.

'I'm having a holiday within a holiday, but I'm not really a tourist,' I reply, before giving a summary of my Spanish story.

'So you're an ex-pat like me,' I'm afforded a brief smile, before another question is fired in my direction, 'Do you go back often?'

'I haven't been back in years.'

'Since you've been here?'

'Not once.'

'And you *live* in Andalusia!' Bert exclaims, looking at me as if face to face with a fugitive living incognito on the costa del crime. Wondering if he was in the detective business before he came to Spain, I ask him the same question. 'I go back once a year; family, that sort of thing,' he replies.

'And do you miss England?'

'No, not a thing. Everyone's so miserable over there,' he unites his bushy eyebrows into a thoughtful frown. 'If you ask me, it's a *bloody* mess.'

'What is?'

'This *Brexit* nonsense,' he frowns more deeply, before telling me the referendum was about Britain's future, and yet those nearest to the grave, in other words without a future, cast the deciding votes. 'Many of them won't *even* be there when it happens, *if* it happens.'

'*If* it happens!'

'It was an advisory vote, not legally binding; if it had been, it would've been declared null and void, as the 'leave' campaign broke a whole bunch of electoral laws.'

'If that's true, it should be headline news.'

'No chance! Britain might call itself the land of the free press, but in reality, most of the newspapers are in the hands of a few press barons who want us out of Europe. It's a sham show with a sour cherry on the cake as some of them aren't even British. In short, the media back home, is *bent*; even the BBC, craving butter for its bread, leans to whoever is in power.'

'So the key is to change who's in power.'

'No chance!' Forcefully, Bert repeats his earlier exclamation. 'There was a poster I remember in one general election that said "Whoever you vote for, the government always gets in". The farcical *first past the post* system maintains the status quo, keeps the Brits under the thumb of a political duopoly. Do you know it takes just over thirty thousand votes to secure a seat in the House of Commons if you stand as a Conservative candidate, just over fifty thousand if you represent Labour, three times that if you're with the Liberals, and if you're mad enough to support the Greens or any other alternative party, just under a million votes might, and I emphasise the word *might*, get you a voice in Parliament. And they call *that* democracy. It's a *bloody* joke! It should be called a mockery of democracy, taking the piss out of the masses.'

Despite his bitterness, I'm beginning to warm to my fellow countryman. In some ways he reminds me of Bill, but before we can develop our political rapport, he's on to another subject, a personal bugbear, according to him, a vice the Spanish have perfected, namely their inclination to gossip. 'If it were an Olympic sport, they'd win the gold medal hands down,' he tells me with a grimace on his face. 'To close me down, my next-door neighbour spread a rumour that I used rats in my home-made hamburgers.' Bert swivels his head to stare at the house next to his restaurant with undisguised malice. 'And I'm not the only one to suffer the lashes of her twisted tongue,' he continues excitedly, his eyebrows twitching like rabbit's whiskers. 'One old fellow, a close friend of mine, took an overdose after she accused him of fondling himself while he spied on her with a pair of binoculars whenever she put her bloomers out on a washing line. She whipped up an old-fashioned charivari, had the neighbours banging pots and pans outside his house.'

'He died?' I ask, somewhat startled.

'Dead as a dodo when his daughter found him a week later.'

Momentarily, I'm tongue-tied, unaccustomed to an Englishman disclosing intimacies so freely to a stranger. In an attempt to offer support, I tell him that tongues in my village wag wickedly at the drop of a pin.

'Rumours are like so many feathers in a high wind, scattered hither and thither so no man knows where they will land, or what damage they will do when they've landed.'

'Well put,' I say of a simile I've heard before.

'Thanks,' Bert smiles, licks up the compliment as might a cat, milk. Drawing the tips of his eyebrows to the bridge of his nose to form a facial victory sign, he tells me it has been a pleasure, but he must return to his kitchen to chop up the rats.

It's around the witching hour when I return to the plaza San Martin. Bert's restaurant is doing a roaring trade, as are all the bars in the crowded square, but there's no sign of the Englishman, only Anabel, still on her weary feet, darting from one table to another to take and serve orders. Maria's not up for an alcoholic beverage, so I queue up outside a kiosk selling ice-creams.

Fortune smiles on us in the form of two empty plastic chairs a few rows back from the stage. The first group to appear are a local band with plenty of family support in the crowd. A folk band of some sort, their first song is the best in their limited repertoire, so when their gig is spent, and mum and dad call for an encore, it's repeated, brothers, sisters, cousins, uncles and aunties joining in with the irritating chorus. The next group are an altogether different pair of shoes, well worth the price of a ticket if one was needed. Much older than the first act, with more musical experience, the band has nine members, each with a different instrument. Their first number is decidedly Gaelic, a lively jig that wouldn't be out of place in a country fair in Kerry. When the drummer provides an unlikely backbeat to the bagpipes, the music becomes so infectiously rousing that I'm sorely tempted to join Maria and the handful of other dancers at the foot of the stage. 'I'm glad we came,' Maria says when she returns to her seat. 'They are very good, aren't they?' And they get better as the night wears on; one song reminiscent of the 'Dubliners', another, an emotive dirge, and then my favourite, a simple composition for tin flute and fiddle that transports me to the green fields of farmland where my mother grew up as a child. When the last chord is struck, we, like everyone else, jump to our feet, to cheer and clap until our palms sting. On our way home, to round off a perfect evening, we linger by the river, to kiss beneath the silver smile of a crescent moon.

Our last day in Galicia is spent in Caldas de Reis, another charming little town built on the banks of a river. Famed for its thermal spring, we take the hot water, and then, following directions from the townsfolk, head out across the rolling hills and woodland to the site of a magnificent waterfall that should be famous, but isn't. Amazingly, there's no one about when we arrive, leaving us free to choose the best of the huge boulders at the foot of the falls, to eat our lunch, sit and stare at the water cascading out of the forest into a lagoon of translucent beauty. 'It's enchanting,' Maria says, 'like something out of a fairy story.'

'It is,' I reply, shortly before the spell is shattered by the arrival of a bunch of schoolkids, well-behaved, but boisterous, followed by a family of four with two Labradors, one, black as a crow, the other clad in a golden coat. Almost as one, the schoolchildren plunge into the water like synchronised swimmers, the dogs not far behind, diving to the depths to retrieve the very same rocks thrown into the middle of the lagoon by their master. 'How can they do that?' Maria asks.

'I don't know,' I make an honest reply, as I think fondly of my first dog, who never ceased to amaze me by waiting at the front door twenty minutes before my mother came home, no matter what time of day, who knew before I did that I was going to take him for a walk. 'Their senses are different to ours,' I conclude weakly, without insight into the canine mystery.

25

ALL IT TAKES IS A ROAD SIGN TO ALTER THE COURSE OF OUR JOURNEY. ON MY part, a spur of the moment decision, for Maria, a few minutes of reflection, before she can surrender to the flow of traffic that sucks us into the centre of Madrid. Maria seems a little surprised by my enthusiasm for the big city, especially as she knows I kissed my life in London goodbye because I was weary of city life. 'But we're only here to visit. We're not putting down roots,' I try to explain my position.

'But you seem so excited to be here.'

'I am, but only because I know I'm not staying. After a lifetime in London, no city in Spain tempts me, no city in Europe, not even Paris.'

'No city in the world?' Maria, who doesn't appear convinced, asks.

'Well, I might be tempted by a clapboard house facing the sea in the suburbs of San Francisco, or a townhouse overlooking the harbour in Sydney.' I sometimes forget Maria grew up in a small village in the Alpujarras, that despite her youthful chapter in Madrid, for her, Almeria is a big city. To reassure her, I take one hand off the steering wheel to stroke her shoulder, tell her that I love living in the mountains, that it's only in the playful world of 'what if?' - if I had to live in a Spanish city, it would have to be Madrid. I remind her that before I moved to Andalusia, I knew the city inside out, had explored its parks and galleries, walked along its tree-shaded boulevards, tasted the city's racy nightlife several times. 'Being in Madrid, is like visiting an old friend.'

'I think I understand,' Maria responds, looking less worried. 'It's just that my memories of Madrid are mixed, not all of them fond like yours.'

We book a room for two nights in an overpriced, but comfortable hotel in the trendy barrio of Chueca. It's a colourful area, popular with gays and trans, artists and film makers, would-be poets and drug addicts, and a whole host of wonderful weirdos, including a drunken cop who cross-dresses when he's not on the beat. If sunshine replaces rain, in some ways, it's a bit like Soho.

Already in the city centre, we eschew the metro, walk to Puerta del Sol, to touch the bronze bear that stands on a plinth not far from a stone slab that marks the centre of Spain, even though there's a hillside in Getafe that claims the same status. From Sol, we follow Calle Mayor, to the plaza that bears the same name. Although unquestionably the most celebrated square in the whole of Spain, a site that has seen the coronation of kings, famous bullfights, heretics swinging from the gallows, their corpses displayed in gibbets, when we arrive there's no sign of entertainment except the antics of street performers, buskers and beggars. With our eyes already smarting from the polluted air, our feet sweating on soles scorched by burning flagstones, Maria happily falls in with my suggestion to seek shelter in a bar to refresh our parched throats. As the dice rolls, the first bar we encounter, according to a gilt-edged plaque, happens to be the watering hole where Hemingway often drank in the nineteen twenties. Though she still shudders from Hemingway's account of the civil war, in particular a scene in Ronda when he described how the townsfolk forced the landowners to walk a gauntlet of pitchforks before hurling them from the bridge that spans the gorge that makes the town so picturesque, Maria is more than happy to sit in a bar where the famous American writer once sat.

After a cold beer and a triangular piece of cheese as tough on the teeth as a slice of leather, we are ready to face the heatwave once again, only this time, sagaciously, not on foot. With a *bono*, a ticket that gives ten rides on the city's public transport system, we take the metro to the station of Gregorio Maranon, a commercial hub in the heart of the city. Emerging from the bowels of the metro, we are greeted by the sight of a well-dressed man, on his knees, begging for alms outside a bank; a poignant reminder that where there's wealth, there's always poverty.

Hemmed in by high-rise buildings, mostly offices, we arrive at the house of Joaquin Sorolla, only to discover that it's closed to the public due to renovation work. After I spin a cock and bull story about travelling from England just to see the master's work, the foreman, a pot-bellied fellow from Segovia, takes pity on us. 'Ok! Just five minutes, while we're having a break,' he says, as he opens a can of beer.

'You're such a liar,' Maria remonstrates playfully, as we stand before '*La bata rosa*' a brilliant study of dappled light, a painting I love, but haven't seen in fifteen years. There's just time for a glance at a seascape before the foreman reminds us that our time is up. Shaded by exotic ferns, sitting on a stone bench in the brick walled garden outside the artist's house, the foreman joins us for a cigarette. He's a friendly man, offers us a beer from his icebox, tells us that he was once in a pub in Ireland where the owner let him and his friends drink until the wee hours behind a closed door. 'Rules are for bending,' he smiles, before finishing his beer to join his workmen.

On the way back to our hotel, we make a detour, so Maria can drop into a dance studio she once frequented. Of course, there's no one there from her past, but when she learns that Francisca Morena, a world famous flamenco dancer, is giving classes, she immediately signs up for a class the following evening, shelling out fifty euros for the rare privilege.

Spoilt for choice in terms of international cuisine, we dine in an upmarket Chinese restaurant that has the Spanish equivalent of two Michelin stars. After informing the waitress that we're vegetarians, it's a shade disappointing to find shreds of chicken in our noodle soup starter. When I complain about the meat, the waitress, instead of changing the dish, insists that chicken is a vegetable. 'Vegetables don't have eyes,' I protest, 'and they can't walk.' But the Chinese waitress is having none of my nonsense.

'This *bery good* Chinese restaurant, *two star*,' she tells me crossly. 'In China, chicken vegetable.' I give up, fearing she might spit on our main course if I persist in my stupidity.

The following day we are up early for a light breakfast on Gran Via, one of the most famous thoroughfares in Madrid. Fortified by two strong cups of coffee, we head to El Prado, stopping but once to buy ice-creams at Cibeles, where the fans of Real Madrid gather at least once a year to celebrate yet another title.

Under a single roof, housing one of the finest collections of works by Spanish masters on the planet, it's no surprise to find the museum packed with foreign tourists. What is surprising, however, is that so many of them, rush from the work of Zubaran to that of Goya, from paintings by Murillo to those of Luis de Morales, running up and down marble stairways in a mad quest to see every famous painting in the gallery. 'They're like the *all-inclusive* holiday makers on the *costas*,'

Maria chuckles, 'stuffing themselves silly.' Our ambition is somewhat more modest, a mission to see less than a dozen paintings, mostly from the gifted hand of Velaquez, Maria's favourite artist, and in the eyes of many, the greatest of all Spanish painters. Unfortunately, when we enter the room wherein hangs his celebrated depiction of the crucifixion, we're forced to share the space with a coachload of Argentinian schoolkids.

'Hush,' the smallest of the three nuns in charge of the group, glares at an adolescent in a football shirt with the sacred name of Maradona printed on the back. And when that fails to summon silence, '*Callate*,' she yells, telling the teenager to shut up in a peremptory voice of authority.

''*Pero madre, no es una iglesia*,' a spotty kid with an attitude to accompany his heavily-gelled, spiky hair, informs the nun that they are not in a church.

'*Mira*,' the bird-sized nun commands, her tiny, arthritic forefinger pointing to the painting of Christ on the cross. '*Nuestro Senor dio su vida para salvar la nuestra.*' Reminded that Jesus gave his life to save our souls, the kid backs off, puts his nervous hands on his head, before hiding behind his friends. Unseen by the diminutive sister, his spiky hairdo flattened like the quills of a porcupine out of danger, he redeems his status with his schoolmates by poking his tongue out at Maria.

Outside the museum we are dazzled by the fury of the midday sun. It's too hot to walk, too hot to take the metro, so we hail a cab, enjoy an air-conditioned ride to El Retiro, Madrid's answer to Manhattan's Central Park. At a table overlooking the boating lake, we order soft drinks and a bowl of peanuts, a snack particularly popular with the park's permanent residents. With a flurry of scruffy feathers pigeons gather around our feet, while a pair of red squirrels entertain us with their acrobatics, before settling on our table top to tackle the nuts with their tiny hands. Before we leave for our hotel, Maria purchases another bowl of peanuts to scatter on the grass for our new-found friends.

It's not the first time I've sat in on one of Maria's classes, but it's certainly the strangest. Senora Morena, refreshingly untouched by international fame, is overjoyed to have an Englishman in her class, Caressing the back of a chair next to her desk, she indicates where I should sit, dashing my hope for a seat in the wings, or better still, in the gallery above the studio. The dancers, perhaps a dozen, are all young females, dressed in leotards and revealing tops; the majority, like Maria, teachers in their own right.

The class begins with the usual warm-up routine, followed by an exercise on the use of castanets, before the teacher introduces the unconventional steps that have made her technique so famous. It's a treat to witness an authentic display of flamenco, for even with an untrained eye, it's obvious that the room is full of wonderful talent, the same talent conspicuously lacking in the tawdry shows that tourists put up with. But then, all of a sudden, near the end of the hour-long class, things seem to go lopsided, *literally.* As if at sea, on a tilted deck, with the exception of Maria, all the dancers gravitate to the desk next to my chair. Had I been a single man, with fewer years behind me, I might've welcomed such a move, felt flattered by so much female attention. But I soon grow uncomfortable playing the honeypot around which the bees swarm, especially when one saucy girl shoves another dancer out of the way, to strike her feet, swivel her brown, sensuous hips right in front of me, the tip of my nose almost touching her diamond-studded navel. With heat rising to my face to reveal my discomfort, I'm actually glad when Senora Morena brings the class to an end. Bestowing my gratitude on the talented teacher, I swiftly escape to the street to smoke a cigarette, to cool down in the humid heat.

An hour later, in Lavapiés, over an Indian dinner, Maria finally shares the secret behind the scene of my acute embarrassment. 'The girls though you were a foreign musician, scouting for talent for a forthcoming tour.'
  'Why would they think that?'
  'Because one of them said she had seen you on TV.'
  'But *surely,* you put them right, told them I was your boyfriend?'
  'No,' Maria pouts coquettishly. 'Why would I do that?'
  'Because I thought I was in a film directed by Almodóvar.'
  'I thought you liked his movies.'
  'I do. But I prefer to *watch*, not be in them.'
  '*Really!*' Maria feigns surprise. Tucking into a pistachio-flavoured kufti with the pleasure and face of an innocent child, she eggs me on to order a second 'Kingfisher' beer. 'They're imported from India,' she tells me, smiling mischievously, something I already know.

26

THERE ARE MYRIAD WAYS TO MARK THE BEGINNING OF AUTUMN IN OUR village. For some, it's when the bee-eaters disappear to decorate African skies, for others, when the swallows leave their nests under the eaves of the town hall. For me, it's finding chestnuts under crispy leaves, fewer nights with mosquitos, strewn across the surrounding countryside, pomegranates split open like exotic red stars. And yet, the sun still shines, and the sea remains warm. With the kids back at school, and so few tourists about, in some ways, it's the best time to visit the coast. Thus, when one of Maria's midweek classes is suddenly cancelled in a neighbouring village due to a plague of fleas, it's a simple decision to jump in the car and drive to Cabo de Gata. Designated as a *Parque Nacional*, a protected area of natural beauty, Cabo de Gata has my sort of beach; backed by a chain of mountains, instead of high-rise blocks, just how I imagine the Spanish coastline before the tourists arrived in the mid-fifties.

Before we turn on to the coastal road, we stop at salt flats to watch a colony of greater flamingos wading through the murky water for the crustacean life that sustains them. Maria puts a coin in a high-powered telescope, tells me she's spotted an albino flamingo with white plumage instead of pink. 'Probably a white stork,' I laugh, pointing to a board with illustrations of the local birdlife. After a coffee in a local bar, we set up camp on the beach. Maria builds a sandcastle, using shells as windows, before I coax her into the waves to look at the baby octopus I've found in the rocks. It's early afternoon when we settle under our parasol for lunch. Sated with simple fare, a chunk of bread, a lump of Manchego cheese, a handful of tiny apricots, and a plastic beaker of *tinto de verano*, I'm about to drop off, when Maria draws my attention to an expanding knot of people gathered at the edge of the water. 'What are they looking at?' she asks, as if my eyesight is keener than hers. 'It might be a stranded dolphin?'

'It looks like a black bin-liner,' I reply with sadness. 'The sea is full of plastic. In Scotland marine scientists recently found kilos of the stuff, including supermarket shopping bags, in the belly of a dead whale. In the middle of oceans, cruise liners pass floating islands of plastic several kilometres wide.'

'It must be more than a bin-liner,' Maria responds, brushing the coat of sand from her tanned thighs as she steps beyond the shadow of our parasol.

'*Que paso?*' I ask with rising alarm, descrying distress in her features when she returns ten minutes later.

'It was the body of a young black man,' she responds, tears trickling down her face. 'The body was bloated, part of the nose missing as if it had been chewed off. A fisherman told me it's the second time in three days they've found a dead body washed ashore.' I enwrap Maria in my arms, try to comfort her, feel her tears wet my neck. When the emergency services turn up to bag the body, she tells me that she'd like to go home.

On the motorway back to our village, tears return to Maria's eyes. 'How will the poor man's family find out what happened to him? How will they mourn him? Imagine him at night, alone in the sea, lost in the waves. What were his last thoughts.? He had nothing on the beach except a pair of underpants; there were no papers. No one knows his name. No one knows his story.' Her words are incontrovertibly true, there's little I can say to ease her distress, other than suggest we meditate and burn incense and a candle in memory of the unknown man. For the rest of the journey very few words are exchanged. My thoughts are with the only Senegalese man in our village, how he made it to Spain after spending eight days at sea. Whenever I see him in the village, I make it a point to sojourn in his company as he's always alone. I remember the photograph he once showed me of his village in Africa. The photograph showed his young wife, his childhood sweetheart, standing outside an ochre-coloured mud hut, in her arms their two-year-old baby boy. He told me that it was to provide for his family that he had left his country, his culture, his language, everything he knew, to pay every penny he had to risk his soul on an unseaworthy battered boat. 'One day I will go back,' he said quietly as we looked at the photograph. Until then, he will toil in the fields as a hired hand, will wear like a donkey a straw hat as the sun beats his back, queue up in the local post office once a week to send home half of what he finds in his paltry pay packet.

27

WINTER RETURNS, MARKED BY A SPRINKLING OF SNOW ON THE mountain peaks, a thin frost each morn sparkling on the rooftops in the village. It's the season of the *matanza,* when clans gather to slit the throats of the pigs they've fatten throughout the year. Maria invents a class to coincide with the slaughter in her village. When her mother phones to protest, she tells her she doesn't want to watch her family gnaw meat off the bone.

When Christmas arrives, we follow the Spanish custom, celebrate the traditional meal with Pablo and Maite on the twenty fourth. Somehow, the following day, I manage to cook a nut roast with all the typical English trimmings. Maria says she loves the Christmas pudding, but can't understand why anyone would make a fuss over stuffing. In the evening we sit under our Christmas tree to exchange gifts. Maria presents me with a beautiful hard-backed book full of wonderful photographs of the Himalayas. Shocked, she says she can't accept the gold bracelet shaped like a snake that my mother once wore.

Somewhere in the heart of January, the temperature drops dramatically. The mountains are covered in snow, a neighbour suffers a burst pipe, the water in the village fountain freezes over, the town hall clock stays at ten to seven until the icicles on the timepiece thaw out. A shepherd says it's a shame we need a clock in the plaza in the first place, when the sun tells us the time in a village where nothing ever changes. But things *do* change, even in Purusha. Babies are born, old folk pass away. One of the characters to leave the village stage this winter is Ricardo. A day after his funeral, I'm outside the *fruteria*, when I see his long-standing girlfriend struggling with a huge suitcase. When I leave the queue, to offer a hand, I ask Ivana where she's going. 'To Valencia to stay with my Ukrainian friends,' she replies, wiping her tearful eyes with a handkerchief.

'With so much luggage?'

'So much luggage! She exclaims with a sad, ironic smile. 'That's all I have.'

'What do you mean?' I ask, puzzled by her answer.

'That's all I've got in the world.' As I put her suitcase into the boot of her car, she tells me her sad story. How Ricardo's family threw her things into the street straight after his funeral, how his ex-wife suddenly appeared out of nowhere to orchestrate her eviction.

'But you were with Ricardo for twelve years.'

'I know, but the family never accepted me.'

'That may be,' I respond, unable to conceal my disgust. 'But out of common decency, they should've given you a bit of time to find your feet.'

'That might happen in your country, but that's not the way around here.' Her words remind me how a Guatemalan was thrown out of his cockroach-infested flat when he fell behind with the rent. There was no warning, nothing in the post headed with red letters from the bailiffs. Why bother with such formalities, when the owner had a key to the flat, and three strapping young sons to drag the Central American out of his bed.

'I'm so sorry,' I give Ivana a little hug before she gets into her car. I tell her to keep in touch, even though we both know she never will.

And then, a few days after Ivana's departure, the unthinkable happens, something that shakes the whole village, has local tongues working overtime for nearly two weeks. For the first time since the civil war, when three priests were shot outside the Church of Maria the Merciful, murder has the village in the headlines.

There are innumerable versions of what led up to the heinous crime, but most agree that Perrito was coerced at gunpoint to hand over his three-year-old daughter to his estranged wife. Some say, before she produced the handgun, she had pleaded with her husband for a second chance, swore that she had relinquished her adulterous path, others that she was cruel and direct, called him a wimp, told him he wasn't the child's real father. Warned that she would kill the child if he called the police, Perrito went back to bed, where, with his tail between his legs, he spent the whole afternoon pondering the dilemma. Unable to reach a decision, he eventually transferred the responsibility to his older sister. The same sister he had followed like her shadow throughout his entire childhood; a timid trait for a timid child that had earned a nickname that meant little dog. Putting down the phone in the office where she worked, Ana, the sister, picked it up again and called the police.

Two hours later, the police turned up at her brother's house. After scribbling down his statement, they asked for a photograph of his estranged wife. The only photograph he hadn't destroyed was taken on his wedding day. Everyone agreed it was a happy photograph, when they saw it on the 'Have you seen' posters that sprung up in the village. Twenty-four hours later, the photograph was on television, my tiny village mentioned on the national news.

For the next few days the village isn't the place I know. There are police everywhere, going from door to door in search of evidence or clues as to the whereabouts of the child and her deranged mother. A team of high-ranking detectives are drafted in from Madrid to lead the ongoing investigation. A Romanian, the only guest in the village *pension*, is asked to pack his bags, told to shove off, when a TV crew move in for a week. Outside the local supermarket, villagers are interviewed on live TV. A teenage housewife says it's like living in a circus. Another villager taps the side of his nose, tells the reporter that the woman has fled with the kid to her village in Extremadura. When the reporter asks him how he knows, he taps his nose three times before revealing the fact that he's psychic. Nine days into the investigation, Flea appears on the eight o'clock national news, says there are too many police officers running around his village like headless chickens, mentions the 'Keystone cops' to divulge an aspect of his personality no one knew he possessed. The truth is that no one knows where the woman is; it's as if she's disappeared off the face of the planet. But that doesn't stop the rumours. Someone says she's been seen in Granada, shopping in a supermarket. Another swears blind he saw her in a car in a neighbouring village. Everyone has a view on her whereabouts. A tapestry of rumours engulfs the village. Day after day, the police follow the threads, but the strands of supposition fray in dead ends, all but one that no one bothers with until it's too late.

When the police arrive at the abandoned farmhouse on the edge of the village, they are surprised to find the heavy wooden front door locked from the inside. No one answers when they hammer at the door. A policeman smashes a window, picks up shards of glass, before he climbs into the kitchen. Seconds of silence, less than a minute pass, before the screech of a rusty bolt grabs everyone's attention.

'Que?' the sergeant addresses his young colleague as he emerges from the gloom of the abandoned house. The young man doesn't respond to his senior officer, staggers into the sunlight, says he wants to be sick. Inside the farmhouse, the sergeant and two other policemen, find a twenty-eight-year-old woman, leaning to one side in a broken chair. Near her shoeless feet, there's a shotgun on the floor, on the wall behind the chair, the remains of her head; balls of blood, unclassified parts of her young face splattered across the cobwebbed ceiling. Thirty minutes later, at the bottom of a dried-up well at the back of the farmhouse, a policeman says he thinks he's found the daughter. It takes a team of firemen three hours to get the little body out of the well. When the forensic team turn up, the tiny mite in Micky Mouse pyjamas is laid out on a sheet for the gruesome shots. The results from the post-mortem examinations reveal that the mother had been dead for two days, the daughter three.

The news stuns the village. Masses are sponsored for the departed, a handful of women dress in black, someone puts flowers by the fountain in the plaza, the town hall announces over its antiquated loudspeakers that there's to be a day of mourning. And then, nothing; absolutely *nothing*. No one talks about the tragedy. The dead are buried, and seemingly forgotten. Life moves on – a stage for the living. It's almost as if nothing has happened, the village once again, the place where nothing ever changes. Even Pablo, after cussing humanity, is taciturn on the matter. The silence upsets me, reminds me of a book I read a few years earlier about the Spanish reluctance to talk about their civil war. Troubled by the whole affair, Maria suggests that we plant an apple tree in her sister's garden, at home, burn a candle, light incense, meditate, perform our own little ritualistic ceremony in memory of the mother and her child.

28

AFTER THE HARSHEST WINTER IN YEARS, SPRING COMES EARLY, THE ALMOND trees at the end of February awash with the pink blush of blossoms. Almost a month on, a few days before the first swallows of the year appear in the village, I'm woken up one morning by the song of a nightingale. It's a wonderful time to be in Andalusia. The landscape facing my house is clothed in a variegated mantle of greenery, there's snow across the sierras, the clear mountain air full of joyful birdsong. At night I no longer need pyjamas, or a jersey while the sun journeys across the pale blue sky. It's the season of strawberries, my favourite fruit. Every Friday morning, I wait at the bottom of my street for a van loaded with punnets to replenish my stock. What we cannot eat, I freeze, or make jam, so many jars that all my neighbours have one. Maria jokes that I'll turn into a red Indian if I don't stop eating strawberries from dawn to dusk. Thus it's a surprise one morning when she wakes me up with a cheese sandwich instead of strawberry jam on toast, a mug of instant, rather than real coffee. 'Sorry, but there's a power cut. I had to use gas to boil the water.' Although it's a toil to carry the huge gas bottles up to our house, I'm glad that we're not completely dependent on electricity, as our so-called 'green' energy company, has a habit of cutting the supply off without warning. I've given up calling the company to complain as the age it takes to speak to a human being runs up a hefty phone bill. That, and the fact I've yet to receive a satisfactory response after I've listened to classical music for half an hour. The last time I got through, a woman with an Indian accent, probably sitting in a call-centre in Calcutta, told me I was mistaken, that there was no power outage in my area, even though the whole village was plunged in darkness. Thinking of the pensioner who fell down a flight of stairs during a three-hour blackout last year, I calculate the cost of a row of solar panels between sips of coffee.

'Can you answer that?' I call out from my bedroom when I hear my ringtone downstairs, presumably on the coffee table in the front room, where I always leave my phone before I go to bed. 'Who called?' I ask, when Maria, fresh from her gas-heated shower, comes into the bedroom with a towel wrapped around her waist.

'Pablo. He said Dani, his friend who works in the pharmacy, has four spare tickets for a night of music from the sixties. The organisers are calling it 'A blast from the past.'

'*In English?*'

'Yes, In English,' Maria laughs.

'Where?'

'In a bar in Champa, Saturday night. He called to see if we wanted to go.'

'I suppose so,' I respond flatly. 'I'll phone in a minute; tell him we *can't* wait.'

Roughly half the size of my village, full of farmers and fruit-pickers, Champa doesn't look like the sort of place where anyone would know, let alone celebrate the music of the sixties. But I'm mistaken. It seems everyone is familiar with the music that was on the radio over half a century ago. The problem is that the music Spain loved when Franco was the alpha dog isn't the music an Englishman might have heard on 'Top of the Pops'. The highlight of the musical night is an album by the 'Duo Dynamico', according to The DJ, Spain's answer to Simon and Garfunkel. But in reality, the *duo* are a couple of crooners, who, had they lived in Brooklyn in the sixties, would've been lucky to earn a bagel at a bar mitzvah. If I'm surprised by the set-up, I'm not alone. Vicente, the biggest Beatles fan in my village, is livid. Sporting his *'Abbey Road'* T-shirt, he tells me how as a kid in Almeria he ran errands for John Lennon, how the celebrated songwriter always gave a handsome tip before removing the filters from the fags he had bought him. I've heard the story before, maybe five times, like everyone else in my village. I've also heard several times before that he is a co-founder of the Beatles fan club in Almeria, that he's met Cynthia, Lennon's first wife, on two occasions, and that he's a good friend of the Spanish teacher, who according to Andalusian legend, is the man who persuaded the Beatles to print their lyrics on their albums.

As it would be rude to interrupt Vicente, inform him that what he's telling me is yesterday's news, I listen to his tales politely. It's only at the end of his lengthy monologue I hear something I haven't heard before. How he took his wife on holiday to Liverpool three years earlier. With photos on his mobile phone to corroborate his story, I'm shown pictures of the houses where Lennon and McCartney grew up, the street sign of Penny Lane, and the interior of the Cavern, a photo presumably taken by his wife, as Vicente's on stage giving the peace sign. 'I should've known better than to turn up here,' he concludes his narrative, before inviting me to the bar to drown his sorrows. At the bar, we are joined by Pablo, another disappointed soul.

'I thought this would happen,' he tells us. 'So I came prepared,' he adds, showing us a CD by the Rolling Stones. But when he offers the DJ the CD he's told it's a family night, so the '*Rollins*' are definitely out. 'What kind of sixties is it without the Rolling Stones?', everyone at the bar hears Pablo yell. 'I've got an English friend with me, and you're embarrassing me, bringing shame on our country.'

Ingles! the DJ repeats, obviously in shock, perchance by his gamble to advertise his event in English actually paying off. Impressed that his show has managed to draw an international crowd, he relents. 'Ok! I play song for *El Ingles*, but no '*Rollins*', not tonight, there's kids here.' And so Abba comes on, followed by a Boney M hit from the seventies.

'What can you do?' Pablo shrugs his shoulders, as he downs his fourth straight scotch of the night. 'Anyone for another?' he asks as he orders a fifth Scottish drink.

'I'm fine,' I respond, waving a bottle full of beer. 'I'm going to sit with the girls for a bit.' At the table, I turn to Maite, who, as our driver for the night, is on her second orange juice. 'Pablo seems hell bent on getting drunk tonight.'

'He'll pay tomorrow,' she laughs at my observation. 'Booze is his bridge to the mob,' she laughs even louder. 'He thinks going out is going down; staying in, going up.'

'Are we the mob?' Maria asks, looking a little crestfallen.

'No, of course not,' Maite smiles to reassure her friend. 'He thinks the world of you guys. If you hadn't come, he wouldn't have come either.'

'But he seems a little grumpy,' Maria responds, not wholly convinced.

'That's because he's pissed off with Dani.'

'But Dani's not here.'

'That's why he's pissed off. An hour ago, he called him a descendent of Fernando and Isabel.'

'Dani's got royal blood?' Maria asks naively.

'In his dreams,' Maite laughs. 'Fernando and Isabel were first cousins. Medieval Spain got started on an incestuous bed. Upset the pope at the time.'

'But if he doesn't like Dani, why is he so upset that he's not here?'

'Because he set the night up. Pablo has called him several times for an explanation, but all he gets is an answering machine asking him to leave a message.' I'm reminded of Diego, my electrician, but keep my trap shut.

With her husband still at the bar, engaged in what looks like a heated exchange with a pair of fierce-looking fellows, Maite excuses herself to answer a call of nature. 'I still don't think Pablo should allow the shortcoming of others to alter his disposition,' Maria shouts over the blare of a song by Antonio Molina.

'I dare say you're right,' I respond, before reminding her that our friend is a man of flesh and blood, not a saint from another planet. 'I might forgive the villagers their want of punctuality, but I've never really understood how easily they betray their word. For me, it remains a mystery. Remember Diego; how he turned up a week late to fix my fuse-box.'

'It's a Spanish thing. You'll never understand because you're not Spanish.'

'Are you like that?' I ask, looking directly into Maria's eyes.

'Not with you,' she replies, reaching for my hand.

Not long after our romantic exchange, Maite returns to the table, followed shortly after by Pablo, who tells us it's time to leave. 'Already,' I protest, even though it's around two in the morning.

Outside in the car park there's an argument brewing. Isabel, the firefighter, wearing her prickly, provocative mask, tells Vicente she hates hippies, and is glad John Lennon was gunned down. She might be drunk, but some things shouldn't be said, even under the influence of liquor. I'm about to give her a piece of my mind, when Vicente gets in first with a piece of his own. *'Me cago en la leche que te dio a mamar'*, which loosely translated means, I shit on the milk you suckled. Hardly an *'All you need is love'* approach, but I can't stifle a smile of satisfaction as I take my seat at the back of the car.

On the short journey back to our village, Maite asks her husband why we had to leave so suddenly. 'Because there was a storm on the horizon,' he answers cryptically.

'Go on,' she prompts him for a fuller picture.

'Those men at the bar I was talking to were Moroccans, seasonal farm workers. One of them said that all Spanish women were whores. I told him I was married to one, that I liked women to wear bikinis on the beach, rather than hide under a medieval sack. I also told him I believed in same sex marriages. That's when the other one butted in, told me it was an abomination, against their holy book. Things started to get a bit nasty when I asked them if they'd have faith in a book on farming that had sold millions, but if followed by the letter, rarely resulted in a good crop.'

'I don't understand what you're saying,' Maite admits she's lost.

'It's almost unheard of for someone to attain Godhead by reading the Bible.'

'But why did we have to leave?' Maria asks. 'You're entitled to your opinion.'

'Because one of them showed me a knife, after I asked why, if they were so religious, they weren't on their knees in a mosque, instead of drinking whisky in a bar surrounded by Spanish whores.'

At home, in bed, Maria asks me if I had a good time. 'With you, I always have a good time.'

'Really?'

'Yes, *really*. Besides, it could've been a lot worse. At least the DJ didn't play the Nolan Sisters.'

29

I FIND IT HARD TO KEEP TRACK OF TIME IN MY VILLAGE. WEDNESDAY MIGHT be Saturday, Sunday seem like Tuesday, the sun rises and then sets, days just come and go, melt into weeks, weeks into months; without clock or calendar, if someone asks me for the date, I have to consult my mobile. When Bill calls me, I know it must be at the end of spring, not because he tells me, but because the bee-eaters are back and the snowline is retreating. It's the first time we've spoken for months, but the song's the same. I'm told that sovereignty is as empty as the seashells that litter the Suffolk coast, that we live in the age of globalization, that the nation state is a thing of the past. 'There must be another referendum,' he yells down the line, as if I'm against one. 'Measure, and measure again, before you cut the cloth,' he tells me that the UK needs to follow the tailors' code. 'The biggest search on Google the day after the referendum was "What does it mean to leave the EU?" The day *after* the vote, not the day before. People were misled; they didn't know what they were voting for.'

'The young voted for the future, the old for the past,' I play with the words of an ex-pat, having looked up the demography of the referendum online, when I eventually got home from Galicia the previous year.

'You're right,' my comment is succinctly endorsed, before my friend pushes on with his endless list of woes. 'Even the Bank of England, the CBI, the very pillars of capitalism, think whatever deal we get will sink our economy. There will be shortages, prices will go up, not down, as the 'Daily Post' predicts. And it's my guess it will end in tears, in other words, war.'

'Whatever makes you say that?'

'Because it's happened before.'

'You're being alarmist,' I respond. 'You're going a bit over the top?'

'*Hardly!*' Bill brushes aside my suggestion. 'Those who don't learn from their past mistakes, tend to repeat them,' he paraphrases Santayana, a Spanish philosopher. 'Already, there are Tory grandees rattling their sabres over Gibraltar, threatening to send warships south to keep the Spanish at bay.' I don't know if he hears me groan, as the connection is poor, his voice clear one moment, distant, indistinct, as if he might be having a shower, the next. I think I hear him mention an ex-Tory leader as the main culprit, a bitter politician I haven't heard of in years, in truth, someone I thought was dead.

'Can you speak up?'

'I was just saying that the seeds of the EU were planted in the ashes of the Second World War; that there hasn't been a war between member states since its inception. When Britain breaks the union, who knows what the future holds?' I shudder at his words, remember where and how the last world war got started. 'Aren't you worried?'

'I am *now*,' I try to make light of what he's saying.

'And your plans?'

'I haven't got any specific plans. But maybe I'll apply for an Irish passport.'

'*Yes,* that's the ticket. You've Irish blood in your veins. That's the solution; I don't know why I didn't think of it.'

'Don't worry.'

'*Don't worry*! You're my best friend; I can't help worrying,' he says with affection. And then, somewhat sternly, adds, 'Get the forms off *at once*,' reminding me that

Article 50 has been triggered, that the clock is ticking. 'I'm *serious* Kim. Do as I say because I love you.'

That night I find it hard to fall asleep, mulling over Bill's words. I realize that I haven't really thought about Brexit in recent months, my idea of a new passport just a passing thought. Living in a small village in the mountains of Southern Spain, it's easy to forget about what's happening in the rest of the world. Unlike Britain, where everyone seems obsessed by the result of their referendum, in Spain, Brexit's no big deal. The last time I saw it covered in the Spanish press was in the form of a political cartoon depicting two Englishmen rowing a boat across the English Channel. With the white cliffs of Dover on the horizon, the pair were in jubilant mood, singing *'Royal Britannia'*, drinking beer, grilling sausages on a barbeque, unaware that their wooden boat was on fire and sinking.

The worst, and best moments of my troubled night are just before dawn. In the dead hour before the first glimmer of a new day, I take the bull by the horns, contemplate the inconceivable, bring to the fore of my conscious mind, a nightmare tucked away in the darkest cellar of my consciousness. What would happen to me and Maria, if somewhere down the line, Britain and Spain crossed swords, perchance the duel triggered by the contentious issue of Gibraltar. Where would we go? France, maybe; Switzerland, if we could afford it. And then, a spark of light in my darkest moment, a thought that puts a smile on my face. The Indian sub-continent; India herself, Nepal, the beautiful island of Sri Lanka. I fall asleep for two full hours, lulled into slumber by dreams of a mud house facing the Himalayas, a cabana of bamboo overlooking the Arabian Sea.

Knowing Bill as a night bird, I wait until midday, before dialling his number. 'Have you got those forms off?' he immediately asks.

'Not yet, but I will.'

'*No mas mañanas!*' he responds gruffly. 'Put your skates on. Get your head out of the sand.'

I accept the admonishment with good grace, if a little hurt by the suggestion that I can't face reality. I recount my pre-dawn crisis, and how it ended in a smile on a beach in Sri Lanka.

When Bill reminds me that Spain and Britain haven't always been happy allies, I list the Anglo-Hispanic wars I've read about to show him I'm up to date.

'You might lose your house,' Bill ignores my history lesson.

'I might; but that's not the end of a life, only a chapter.'

'No problems, only solutions!'

'That's right.'

'I was being sarcastic.'

'I know.'

'*Look Kim!* I've just got out of bed, and I'm not at my best. But you've got to start taking things seriously. With an Irish passport, you've have more security, more options. If everything goes pear-shaped, you could live in a farmhouse in County Mayo. Drink a pint of Guinness a day, write a book, paint a picture, rear free-range chickens in your free time. And when it's all over you could go back to Spain. There are plenty of cheap flights from Eire to Madrid or Malaga. Your idea about India is pie in the sky. You *might* love it over there, but Maria *won't.*'

'She'll love it.'

'You forget. I'm talking *from* experience.'
'Your package holiday to Goa!'
'That's right. Two weeks in India, and a month on the throne when I got back.'
'We'll cook our own food.'
'*Oh, I give up*! You've got an answer for everything,' Bill responds, before matching my laughter, when I remind him he lost six kilos in Goa. Not by going on a diet, but by eating a dodgy prawn curry for breakfast.

It takes me several weeks to gather all the documents I need to support my application for a new passport. When I return from the Post Office without an A4-sized envelope addressed to the Irish Embassy in Madrid, I'm without a care in the world. Perked up, I phone Bill and Maria to share my good news. My friend in London is delighted; Maria says she's on cloud nine.

At home, I sit on the edge of my bed, staring at the framed photograph of my mother that I keep on my bedside cabinet. Looking into the blue eyes I've inherited, I mirror her wistful smile, kiss the photograph, press it to my forehead, to thank her, convinced her caring hand has guided me from beyond the grave.

When Maria arrives home in the evening, I tell her I want to make another journey, this time within the boundaries of Andalusia. I ask her if she can cancel her classes to come with me. At first, she says it's quite impossible, that she's never been so busy. But seeing the disappointment in my eyes, she gradually comes round to my idea, tells me she might know a dancer who can step into her slippers, hold the fort while she's away. 'I can't promise, but I'll phone her first thing in the morning. I'll do my best.'

Just after midnight, propped up in bed, Maria fast asleep on her side of the bed, I find myself wide awake. I'm tired, having hardly slept in the last twenty-four hours, but my head is buzzing with thoughts of travel. Quietly, I slip out of bed, tiptoe downstairs, open the fridge door to find a carton of milk. Sitting on the sofa in the front room, sipping cold milk, I discard thoughts of travel as my mind goes in another direction. 'Every disadvantage has an advantage,' I recall the words of the gardener of my youth. Like Pablo's vision of death, everything has a flipside, even the nightmare of British folly, in my case, the inspiration to explore the province of Andalusia, *today*, not tomorrow. I have no need to consider where we might go; the adventure is all that matters. Smiling, I sit cross-legged, put a cushion at the base of my back, to travel with my mantra.

30

WE BEGIN OUR JOURNEY IN THE REGION OF JAEN, FAMOUS FOR HIGH QUALITY, virgin olive oil. Our first two nights are spent in Ubeda, before we move on to the neighbouring town of Baeza. Both towns are on UNESCO's list of World Heritage Sites, blessed with Renaissance architecture, but of the two, we prefer Baeza. Home to the fabulous Jabalquinto Palace, Baeza is smaller, more easeful than its sister town, the scales tipped in its favour by a charming public garden where we spend a week of mornings reading Spanish poetry over pots of coffee. We would fain stay another week in the pretty town, had we not arranged to meet up with Pablo and Maite in Seville the following weekend.

After settling our bill at the hotel, we call on a couple on the ground floor, newly-weds, in their seventies, who fell in love after a date on a TV show. 'You're an inspiration to us all,' Maria says, as she presents a potted geranium as a parting gift.

Built on the banks of the Guadalquivir, one of the great rivers of Spain, Cordoba was once the capital of a powerful Moorish dynasty. There are traces of the quondam rulers scattered throughout the city. As we cross the river we pass under the shadow of the Islamic tower that was built to protect the Roman bridge. Nearby, the baths of Hamman Al Andalus are still in use. But the undisputed jewel in the crown of Moorish rule is the Mezquita. Constructed at the end of the ninth century, on the site of a Visigoth church, the mosque is a marvel of Moorish architecture. Wandering through a great hall of double-tiered horse-shoe arches, Maria says it's like being in a dream. When Spanish soldiers conquered the city in the thirteenth century their regal leaders were no less impressed. Rather than raze the mosque to the ground, priests were brought in to consecrate the fane, turn it into a place of Christian worship. Over the centuries, chapels were built, and finally a Renaissance Cathedral that squats to this very day in a sea of Islamic arches. Peradventure, as I've been to the ancient Inca capital of Cuzco, sat in the Catholic cathedral the conquistadors built from the stones of the great Inca temple they had destroyed, I can tolerate the peculiar juxtaposition of a church within a mosque. But Maria isn't convinced. Even when I mention how the Taliban blew into smithereens the wonderful sixth-century stone statues of the Buddha in Bamiyan, she remains adamant that her ancestors should have left the mosque as they found it, built their imposing cathedral somewhere else in the city.

With our rendezvous with our friends on the horizon, we only spent two days in Cordoba. Our first day is devoted to the magical Mezquita, and ends with a romantic candlelit dinner in a restaurant overlooking the Guadalquivir. The second day is more strenuous. In the morning we visit the ruins of Madinat al-Zahra on the outskirts of the city; in the afternoon the patios and gardens of the Viana palace, followed by a walking tour of La Juderia, the maze of narrow alleyways that make up the old Jewish quarter in the heart of the city. By nightfall, we're so foot weary that we happy to dine on our hotel room balcony. Brown bread softened with red peppers and cream cheese, and a bottle of wine, is all we need.

The journey to Seville shouldn't take long, but for some reason, perchance my preference for secondary roads, we get lost, and end up in a hilltop town called Osuna. At first, Maria is a little put out by my suggestion that we spend a day where the road has taken us without a map. But when I remind her that we aren't due to meet our friends until the following day, and that travellers, unlike tourists, never know where they're going to spend the night, she sees where I'm coming from.

'Let's stroll around, see what this town has to offer,' I suggest with a cheeky smile.

Although the little town has an eighteenth-century arch, and an interesting coat of arms featuring a topless young woman, in truth, there isn't much to see in Osuna. In a matter of minutes, no more than ten, we come upon a handsome church with a *hospederia*, or inn, next door. The inn has a restaurant with a stark dining hall of bare stone walls. Maria says she likes the look of the place as it reminds her of a cloister, somewhere centuries earlier monks might have broken bread. Lunch is a plain affair, but the wine is good, and like Maria I enjoy the monkish ambience. When we ask to see a room, we are pleased to discover it simply, but well-appointed with the same bare walls found in the restaurant. Drowsy from our bottle of wine, we both decide we need a siesta.

Around the crepuscular hour, we emerge from our protracted slumber. After a quick shower, we put on a set of clean clothes, and then repair to a patio area with a bar and a swimming pool. Although no one is in the pool, the bar is crowded. To me, it seems strange to see so many people gathered in a small space in such a small town. At first, I surmise it might be a wedding reception, but Maria dismisses my idea, pointing out that the ladies aren't wearing funny hats. 'It might be a birthday bash,' she suggests, looking at a cake on a foldable metal table.

It turns out we're both wide of the mark, as we discover when a short man with a grey goatee and receding hairline, approaches with a booklet of raffle tickets. '*Es una fiesta*,' he explains, a one-off affair, set up by the priests to raise funds to repair the roof of a local church. Although we have no interest in winning a leg of ham or the cake on the display table, Maria finds her purse to buy a ticket. When we're asked from whence we come, I mention London instead of Purusha, while Maria gives the name of her family's village.

'Tosca, near Bubion?'

'Yes,' Maria replies.

'*Why!* I was there many years ago,' the man illuminates his face with a smile. 'I spent a whole week there. I stayed with Javier de la Cruz and his family. We did the "*mili*" together in Tenerife. We didn't shoot anyone, but we drank a lot of wine.'

'*Javier de la Cruz*,' Maria echoes the name of a man from her village.

'Yes, Javi,' the man responds. 'How is he?' he asks, correctly assuming that Maria knows who he is talking about.

'Well,' Maria replies. 'He's married with three children, runs a small farm.'

'Is he fat?'

'Very.'

'*Always was!* Always eating the goodies his mama sent him,' the man laughs briefly. 'Tell him, Miguel Morreno sends his regards. Tell him I'm married, and have three *ninos* of my own. Come and meet them,' he invites us to a table where his family are gathered.

We are introduced to Beatrice, his wife, a fat woman with a warm smile, her parents and then Miguel's, and finally to three young women, his daughters rather than sons, the confusion arising through the masculine bias in Spanish grammar where *ninos* means boys as well as children in general. We are received warmly, regarded as if family, given wine and tapas, and then invited to Miguel's house. 'The fiesta won't get going for an hour or so,' Miguel informs us.

The family house is a little way down the hill, tucked away in a narrow alleyway, a town house not dissimilar to my own. 'Welcome,' Miguel beams with joy when we enter his tiny salon. *'Sentaros,'* he points to a sofa covered in a plastic sheet where he wishes us to sit. Sitting on the plastic sheet I remember Mrs. Barnes, a Jamaican Jehovah Witness I once had as a neighbour in London. How the good lady kept her three-piece leather suite under wraps, only removing the plastic covering once a year at Christmas. But it appears Miguel has his shabby sofa covered in plastic for an altogether different reason, as I discover shortly after a dollop of something very sticky drops out of the ceiling on to my head.

'Oh, no!' Beatrice exclaims in horror, rushing into her kitchen to fetch me a tea towel. 'You need to move,' she points to a pair of chairs on the other side of the room, and then tells her husband that his honey is dripping, castigating him for his idle ways.

'Honey!' I exclaim in surprise.

'Si, miel,' Beatrice confirms the nature of the sticky substance on my head. 'There's a beehive up there,' she points at the buckling ceiling. 'I don't know how many times I've asked Miguel to get the bees out, but he likes the honey.'

'Yes, it's the finest, the purest you'll find. Much better than the stuff you get in the supermarket,' Miguel doesn't contradict his wife, as he exits the room only to return a moment later with a sealed jar of his golden nectar. 'Take this as a gift,' he thrusts the jar at Maria as I'm busy trying to part my matted fringe. 'Something to remember us by,' he adds, as if a dollop of honey on my head wouldn't suffice. Presently, an expensive bottle of wine appears, followed by a tray of appetizing tapas. As I decline a chunk of black sausage, on the spurious, but reasonable ground of having already eaten, Miguel's daughters turn up, each with a *novio*, or boyfriend, followed by the rest of the family, members covered in fur and feathers. First to appear is a goat called *cabra*, which means goat in Spanish, followed by a baby lamb, then a pet weasel, a chicken and a pair of mangy, flea-infested dogs, and then finally the last member of the happy household, a dishevelled peacock, dragged into the room by its iridescent neck. When the bird lets out a piercing cry, Miguel tells us that 'Pedro' is pleased to see us. 'He only screams when he's happy.'

'You've got quite a family,' I say matter-of-factly to disguise my surprise. 'And so friendly,' I smile as I shove a dog off my lap.

'Yes,' Miguel beams un-self-consciously, as if the set-up is normal.

There are already angry lumps on my arms and legs, when, to my enormous relief, we're told the time has arrived to go down to the bottom of the town for the fiesta. 'I'm covered in fleabites,' I whisper to Maria as we trundle down the hill.

'Me too,' she laughs.

In my eyes, having your body covered in fleabites is no small matter. How Maria can laugh is beyond me. And yet, her attitude is in accord with those in my village, where most folk have a scrap of ancestral land to work on, keep a goat or two, fatten a pig for the annual *matanza*. I remember one farmer telling me that all farms with livestock have fleas, always have, and always will, but that his flock of sheep were free of fleas, as were his sheepdogs and the feral cats he fed on his farm to keep the rats at bay. It's a contradiction I've grown used to, living in a rural setting in Andalusia. No matter how compelling the evident, I wouldn't dream of informing Miguel that his dogs have fleas. My protestation would be pointless, at best draw a blank stare, or a shrug of the shoulders, for no Andaluz owns a dog with fleas. If there are any parasites about they always belong to his neighbour.

When we arrive in the town square, despite Miguel's theatrical remonstration, I'm first to the bar to order three carafes of sangria from a barman in a white dog collar. Beatrice's future son-in-laws help carry the fruity wine to the elongated table that her husband has managed to commandeer for their sizeable family. Pouring the rose-coloured wine into a phalanx of paper cups, I excuse myself, and head for the nearest public convenience. Miraculously, I manage to keep my balance inside the porta cabin, as I strip down to my underwear to give my shirt and jeans a thorough shake. In all, I count seventeen bites, mostly on my right leg. Half-naked, inhaling urinous vapour, I entertain the thought that without form fleas wouldn't bother me, nor mosquitoes, tooth or earache, not even cancer. It's a dark moment, hardly one to enjoy a fiesta, so I brush the lugubrious thought aside as I button up my shirt.

Back at the festive table, I discover that Miguel, not to be outdone by my generosity, has ordered a bottle of JB whisky and a pot of tea. 'You'll love this,' he tells me, 'because you're an Englishman.'

'Yes, an Englishman, but not a madman,' I remark quietly in my mother tongue, smiling as I sip the strange cocktail that Miguel calls a '*twhisky*.'

Our health is toasted, then the Queen of England's, followed by Freddy Mercury's, even though he's dead. Strangely enough, after my fourth cup of *twhisky*, I find the fire on my right leg somewhat dampened. When Beatrice stands up, grabs my hand, and says it's time to dance, I'm up for the challenge, ready to make a fool of myself, secure in the knowledge that I'll be in Seville tomorrow. Of course, the music is awful, the usual jolly crap the Spanish seem happy to put up with in their fiestas. When the band plays an old number, a favourite from heaven knows what dark century, couples spin in joyous abandon; at the bar, a man in a cassock rotates his hips in front of a pretty girl. To me, it seems a bit rich, the rich asking the poor to pay for a new roof, but no one else seems to mind, least of all the girl in the miniskirt dancing with the young priest. When the band takes a break, Maria and I return to our table, as the loudspeakers blast out the latest pop songs climbing up the Spanish charts. I watch a pair of very little girls, bop to the pop, under the loving gaze of their parents. The girls can't be more than six or seven years old, yet they sing along with the lyrics, know every word. Nothing unusual in that, I suppose, until I concentrate on the catchy refrain – *'Soy una perra calienta en la cama.'* – 'I'm a hot bitch in bed.'

In the bathroom in our hotel, I'm seized with a fit of laughter, almost choke myself on my toothbrush. 'What are you laughing at?' Maria calls out from the bedroom.

'I was just thinking about the DJs in Andalusia; the one in Champa who wouldn't play The Rolling Stones, and the one tonight.'

31

SEVILLE IS KNOWN AS THE FRYING PAN OF SPAIN FOR GOOD REASON. IN THE eccentric terms of temperature favoured by Americans and the bulk of older Brits, it's a hundred and eight degrees Fahrenheit when we arrive in the capital of Andalusia. There are people using umbrellas as shields against the sun, crowds outside wooden booths selling cold drinks, children with ice-lollies playing in street fountains. After our festive sojourn in Osuna, neither of us are up for sightseeing. There's no need of map or camera. We know the city well, have seen what there's to see several times. We leave the car in an underground parking lot, find a cheap hotel in a side street close to the biggest gothic church in the world.

I'm told, the cathedral, like so many Spanish churches, is built on the ruins of a mosque, the Giralda, converted from a minaret to a bell tower. Standing in front of the church, under the unwavering eyes of grotesque gargoyles, I'm impressed by the scale of the pile. If size alone, nor an imposing façade, aren't enough to draw the tourists in, there are other attractions. Aside from four score of ornately decorated chapels, an altarpiece considered to be one of the finest in the whole of Christendom, the church has history in its tombs, none more famous than the resting place of an Italian pirate. Known as Corombo in his homeland, Colon in Spanish, to the English-speaking world as Columbus, the remains of the celebrated slave-trader were carried into the church on the shoulders of kings.

As we walk alongside a row of horse-drawn carriages parked outside the cathedral, I ask Maria if she knows that the ships of Colon brought bubonic plague to the Americas, that more native Indians died as a result than lives were lost during the 'Black Death' that swept through medieval Europe over a hundred years earlier. 'No,' she replies; and again 'no,', when I ask if she's aware that his fleets introduced syphilis and smallpox to the *Indios*, brought gunpowder to their sandy shores, and the purveyors of the holy eucharist, the guilt merchants of Adam's apple. 'I went to the school in my village. Our history teacher told us Colon was the man who discovered the Americas.'

'That's what I was taught,' I offer a feeble smile to weaken my rant. 'But I was confused as the Indians were already there when he arrived.'

The sun is almost down when we walk across the Isabel bridge into the barrio of Triana. Once the home of famous bullfighters and flamenco singers, the district is sold as unique, that Seville, across the river, is another city. But the big names have gone, like most of the gypsies, replaced by memorial plaques, and hordes of tourists, with shops, bars and restaurants to empty their pockets. Before long, we discover Calle Betis, walk arm in arm beside the river, find our friends waiting for us at a table on a terrace with a view of the thirteenth-century Torre del Oro on the opposite bank. Maite, in a slinky, peach-coloured, sleeveless dress, greet us with the traditional double kiss. She looks stunning if a little weary. Dressed in a white shirt and a dark waistcoat, Pablo looks equally worn out, like a waiter after a long day. 'So how was it?' I ask of the first communion ceremony they've attended.

'Boring,' Pablo replies crisply. 'Like watching adverts on TV.' Maite nods her head to confirm her husband's summary. 'But there was a golden moment.'

'There *was*,' Maite chuckles with a furrowed forehead. 'The priest did the rounds in the reception, shaking hands, offering his congratulations. When he got to our table, our seven-year-old nephew, stood up to make the sign of the cross.

Encouraged by the child's show of faith, the priest asked him if he believed in baby Jesus, the Holy father, and the Holy ghost. "Yes, father," he replied three times, with his little palms pressed together as if he was praying. Beaming with pride, my sister looked like she'd gone to heaven.'

'But then everything changed, when the priest asked him if he believed in a life after death,' Pablo sniggers. 'The poor little mite didn't know what to say. His face took on a worried expression, his hands dropped to his sides. Marta, Maite's sister, froze in embarrassment. And then, Paco, God bless him, saved the day, or at least, made mine. Stretching his arms out in front of him, he did a little dance that he'd seen in a Michael Jackson video, and told the priest he believed in zombies'

'What did the priest say?' Maria asks with an open mouth.

'Nothing,' Pablo guffaws. 'He just left. We never saw him again.'

'That's a gem,' I roar with honest laughter.

'We thought so too,' Maite smiles sadly.

'But no one else saw the funny side,' Pablo says in a sullen tone. 'Least of all Marta and her stupid husband. She said that we were trying to spoil *her* day, that Maite was jealous of her fertility, that my wife was barren, like a desert.' In the corner of my eye, I catch Maite flinch, only for a split second, but Pablo sees it too, reaches out for his wife's hand.

'It hurt that she wanted to hurt me, not what she said,' Maite says in a girlish voice I've never heard before.

'*Families!*' I exclaim with a sigh. 'The furnace of anguish, the home of twisted games. We can't choose our family, but we can, *our* response.' I offer the advice I give Maria, when her mother upsets her by opening up old wounds. 'The scars of childhood can last a lifetime.'

'They can, but *needn't*,' Pablo fulminates with apparent fury. 'Few escape the crucible of conflict known as family life unscathed, but psychological scars can disappear, wounds heal with understanding. We're not dried up river beds, *ramblas* that flood every time there's a storm in the sierras. We have a choice. We *can* change the flow of the river, feed the flowers in our life.'

'I'm getting there, slowly,' Maria says, leaning over the table to stroke Maite's bare arm. 'I still struggle with the wild emotions my mum whips up in malefic moments. I'm of her womb; she knows exactly where to prod. I've never told anyone but Kim, but I left home as a teenager because of my mother.'

'You're very brave,' Maite caresses the hand on her arm. 'I had a good relationship with my mother. My problem at home was Marta. She's three years older than me. She always bullied me, put me down in front of my friends. I think she resented my birth. When I was five, I fell down the stairs. I never said anything to my parents, but I know she pushed me.'

'There's only the two of you?' I ask.

'Yes.'

'The fat chick that shoves the smaller fledgling out of the nest.'

'*Pangu!*' Pablo thunders. '*Pangu,*' he repeats the strange word, this time softly, as if savouring the sound. It's an unfamiliar word, not found in Spanish or English, so we must wait for him to explain its bitter meaning. 'In ancient China, Pangu was the name of a legendary creator who lived a million years ago. When he died the parasites in his body became the human race. We're the maggots of this planet, like the blind bacteria that feeds on our bodies but knows nothing of us.'

'*Maggots!*' Maria exclaims, her lips tight in a squeamish expression.

'Personally, I prefer to talk of sightless sleepwalkers, but maggots will do, or a cancer on the skin of the Earth,' Pablo laughs. 'It's one of the reasons why Maite and I remain childless.'

'And if everyone followed your lead?' an American woman, at the table behind us, listening to our conversation as there isn't one with her husband, asks rudely.

'It'd give our planet a rest,' Pablo replies smartly to see off the interloper. 'Of course, in reality, not everyone thinks like that,' he lowers his voice at our table.

'Our parents didn't,' I respond loudly, for the benefit of our nosy neighbour.

'Nor Marta,' Pablo burbles. 'She was pregnant a month after her wedding. "That's what people do," she told us, during her post-natal depression. For her, she was only following the prescribed course of a Spanish life. Find a partner, get married, have a kid, or in her case, three, the last, when she was in her forties. She actually said she was doing her duty, having children was the right thing to do. But the problem with Marta, is when she thinks she's right, anyone with an opposing view, is wrong.'

'Then, she can't be a fan of Nasruddin,' I mention the Sufi who found wisdom in folly. Maria looks at me questioningly, so I'm obliged to explain. 'When asked to judge in a dispute between two powerful men, he was ejected from the courtroom after agreeing with both sides.'

Maite knows the story, smiles faintly, tells Maria that he even agreed with the decision to throw him out of the courtroom. 'But my sister's not a mad mullah,' she concludes quietly, sadly, as if she might melt into tears. It's horrid to see a friend suffering. Maria, who has been reading my tattered copy of the Dhammapada on our road trip, suggests compassion, Pablo, after telling us those who hurt others, hurt themselves, that the murderer always takes two lives, his own as well as his victim's, the forgiveness Christ showed on the cross. 'You're both right,' Maite responds, her lips twitching with a hint of laughter while tears well up in her misty eyes.

A moment later, the American woman, having paid her bill, stops at our table before she leaves the restaurant. 'I'm a psychiatrist from New York. Like him,' she nods at Pablo, 'I tell it how it is. If the family screws you, I say screw the family. If you're ever in Manhattan, look me up,' she hands Maite her business card, 'You have good friends, Listen to them, not your idiotic sister.' The woman's husband, embarrassed by his extroverted wife, remains silent, staring at his feet. But before the ground opens up to save him, Pablo throws out a hand to build a bridge, 'Your wife's not too bad either.'

Alone again, just the four of us, Maite finds a handkerchief to dab her eyes. Studying the black stains of mascara on the white linen, she asks Maria to accompany her to the ladies' room. 'One of the mysteries of life,' Pablo remarks, as we watch our women disappear.

'What is?'

'Two women together in the bog. Imagine if we went to the toilet hand in hand,' he laughs, 'and didn't come back for half an hour.'

32

SURROUNDED BY MARSHLAND AND OPEN SHRUB, EL ROCIO IS A SMALL TOWN in the sub-province of Huelva. Ordinarily, the town entertains a few hundred souls, struggles, for want of children, to sustain a local school, but when we arrive the headcount surpasses one million. The biggest fiesta in Spain is called *'Romeria del Rocio*, and the pilgrims swarming into the little town, *Rocieros*. They come from every corner of Spain, arriving in flower-decked horse-drawn carriages, two-wheel pony traps, on the back of ox-carts, trailers pulled by tractors, in cars and coaches. The less fortunate, or more devout, arrive on foot in the thousands. Without a ticket to stay in one of the *hermandades* dotted throughout the town, we haven't a hope in hell of finding a bed for the night. If we had a tent we could camp in the surrounding countryside, or furnished with a blanket, curl up beneath a ceiling of stars. But all we have is our car, so it's to be a miserable night in a makeshift car park, hemmed in by coaches in a dusty field. To make matters worse, the fee we pay to park the car amounts to a small fortune.

Unable to locate a source of *agua portable*, with displeasure, Maria purchases water from a spring in the Pyrenees, bottled in plastic, for our overnight stay. 'I bought this from a strange, little man,' she hands me a wafer-thin booklet entitled 'The Secrets of the Virgin.' While Maria lines her eyes with a kohl pencil from Morocco, I leaf through the booklet, read that the *Paloma Blanca*, the White Dove, the colloquial name for the Virgin, possesses a cure for childless couples, a claim substantiated by the army of babies born nine months after her fiesta. A few paragraphs on, the author, seemingly unaware of what he's previously written, debunks the myth. The surge in fertility, according to the new paragraph, is the result of innumerable illicit assignations forged under the sultry skies of a pagan bacchanalia.

'This booklet reflects the man who sold it.'

'What do you mean?' Maria looks at me with one eye lined.

'It's strange.'

Dressed in denim, we're suitably attired for streets of sand. But there are plenty to challenge our sartorial sense, mostly women, in the colourful costumes of the countryside, a fair number with handheld fans, flowers in their hair, bodies wrapped in flouncy dresses, their beaus in the traditional *traje corto*, a tight-fitting monkey suit that doesn't flatter the flabby.

Outside one of the many brotherhoods, I count fourteen horses lashed to a hitching. When a stagecoach enters the street, Maria says it's like being in a Western movie. I laugh, couldn't agree more, even if there aren't any cowboys, apart from a naked opportunist selling baked spuds on a street stall. Famished, fatigued, we fork out for a stuffed potato, take a seat at an elongated table that DIY enthusiasts use for pasting wallpaper. We share the table with two young girls in matching polka dot dresses, their brown, bare shoulders covered in fringed shawls; between them and us, a farmer and his family. In their late teens, the girls tarnish the flush of youth with make-up, so heavily applied that they look like they're wearing masks. When the farmer's wife, a corpulent middle-aged woman in a mini-skirt, stands up to reveal her frilly knickers, I wonder how women would dress in a world without men. Sensing my distraction, Maria nudges me gently, tells me it's time to move on.

With the light falling, we plunge into the river of bodies pouring into the town centre. The brotherhoods, without exception, are full of music and laughter. While the women dance, the men, in conspiratorial knots, eye up the talent, cheer and clink glasses. The solemn face of religion doesn't seem to prey on the mood in any discernible fashion. We stop at a chapel ablaze with candles. Maria might wish to explore the incandescent light, but when a sudden breeze brushes the flames of faith to blow a fiery blast into her face, she accedes to my advice to stay without. 'Faith can heal or hurt,' I remark facetiously.

At length, we turn our backs on the dazzling chapel, to follow this or that procession, until we find ourselves in the main square, part of the huge crowd gathered outside the white church of Rocio. Reduced to rubble by an earthquake in the eighteenth century, I read in my booklet, that the church was rebuilt in the sixties to restore its former glory. A small fortune was lavished on the restoration, but I'm not impressed, not by the scalloped entrance that resembles the shell Botticelli chose for his goldilocks Venus, nor by the garish whiteness of the building. Floodlit, to me, the church looks as if it might have been assembled in a week, on a film set for a Bollywood blockbuster. Deafened by the drums outside the church, the songs and sway of the crowd, for a brief moment I'm not where I am, but back in time, in India, outside an ancient Hindu temple, waiting to catch a glimpse of a black stone idol possessed with psychometric properties. Here, I'm pressed into a fervid crowd, gathered to pay homage to a wooden doll. When Maria yells something into my ear, I suggest, in a voice above the sea of sound, we find somewhere we needn't shout to share our thoughts.

The bar, a few streets from the square, is packed, like all the bars in town. But lady luck is with us, for when we arrive, two elderly women finish their sherries to surrender a pair of seats at a table crowded with beer-drinking youngsters. Faced with the prospect of a long night ahead, we follow the lead of the youngsters, by ordering jugs of beer. Maria waits until I've wet my lips, before asking of the concern she read in my face outside the church. 'You looked distracted, a little worried.'

'Did I?' I smile, feign surprise, before I tell her about the Indian temple. How, in an ocean of Hindus, I felt like a ghostly spectator, a detached outsider looking upon the faith of others. How I imagine I'd be at the wailing wall of the Jews, the Kaaba of Mecca. How I couldn't see myself on my knees before the great tapestries of the Buddha that are unfurled, once a year, outside Tibetan monasteries.

'And yet you have statues, carvings and paintings of the Buddha, Krishna, Shiva and other Indian gods in nearly every room in your house.'

'And a Celtic cross in my bedroom, a framed copy of El Greco's Maria in the entrance hall,' I laugh. 'Knick-knacks to remind me of the teachings that help us. And, of course, on another level, art pleasing to the eye. But in terms of religion, they're only symbols, fingers pointing to the moon, not the moon itself.'

'I wish the priest who performed holy communion in my village had said something like that, told us that the host was a symbol, rather than the body of Christ,' Maria says thoughtfully. 'It's *not* what children want to hear. And yet, as an adult, I still find comfort in the silver cross I keep in my purse. Last night, when our friends walked us back to our hotel, Maite told me a story about a missionary in Africa. In an attempt to convert a heathen tribe, he called for a pot of water into which he threw their sacred stone. Waiting for the idol to sink to the bottom of the pot, he submerged a wooden cross in the same water knowing it would immediately rise to the surface to prove that *his* god was the one.'

'A cheap trick.'

'But it didn't work. A tribal elder lit a fire.'

'To cook the priest in the pot?'

'No,' Maria responds firmly to my dark humour. 'To put their stone god into the fire, along with the Christian's cross.'

'*Brilliant!*' I exclaim joyfully. 'Is that what you two were laughing about last night?'

'I suppose so. But I was thinking about my silver cross. Do you think I'm silly?'

'No, I don't think that. Maybe, your cross is the faith that heals? Who *really* knows about such things? I like to think of myself as a rational being, but alone, almost twenty years ago, in a tiny shrine in a place called Ayodhya, by the Saryu, one of India's myriad sacred rivers, I was stunned by the magnificence of a soapstone image of Ganesh. The statue seemed to exude a mysterious power. I don't know; maybe I had had too much sun that day, but the experience really unsettled me.'

'I'm not surprised,' Maria giggles at my grim face. 'If a statue spoke to me, I'd be terrified.' Lifted by Maria's laughter, I ask if Maite had any other stories. 'No, just the one. Mostly, we talked about her sister, how in her world, it's her reality or no reality. She told me that Pablo thinks you have to respect the reality of others, if you want others to respect yours. And that's when we really laughed, for Pablo, as you've probably noticed, really struggles with the reality of fools.'

'Pablo has a complex character,' I respond with a grin. 'He was awfully pleased when he heard your laughter. He said you were good for his wife, that she needed to laugh, not cry, after what she'd been through with her sister.'

'I'm glad to hear that.' The corners of Maria's lips lift into a smile. 'Maite really loves him. She said he was like a kiwi, tough on the outside, but soft within, the kindest human being she had ever met. To her, he's a tree without a forest, on a solitary hill, a tree that has shed its leaves, in, but not of this world, and she's the little bird that plays in his branches.'

'That sounds a little sad, but I'm sure she knows her husband.'

'She wasn't sad at all; as a matter of fact, she seemed rather pleased. I told her we weren't so different.'

'You did?'

'Yes, but with a difference. I told her you hadn't quite lost all your leaves, that in your foliage, there were plenty of juicy grubs for me to find and eat.' Struggling with the arboreal image in my mind's eye, I haven't time to reply, before Maria breaks my line of thought. 'Just girls' talk!' she slaps me on the back. 'Finish your jug, and order another.' I'm given a moist kiss on the cheek.

'And you?'

'This is enough for me,' Maria lifts her beer to take a tiny sip. 'This will last me another year.'

As it turns out, Maria is true to her word. The faces at our table might change, the drinkers swell or thin out at the bar, but in the hour it takes me to empty my second jug, Maria is still nursing half a pint of flat beer. But our time isn't wasted; in a reprieve from the tomfoolery all around us, I learn more of our friends' history. How, when her mother was dying, Maite and Pablo moved into her home to nurse her. How, in the six months they were there, her sister, who lived forty minutes away by car, only paid one visit to comfort her ailing mother. 'She called her sister on the last morning of their mother's life, begged her to come immediately, to say goodbye and tell her that she loved her. But she didn't come. An hour later, Maite called again. This time her brother-in-law picked up the phone, said he knew nothing about the previous call, informed her that his wife had gone shopping.'

'*Gone shopping!*' I wipe my forehead in sadness.

'Marta arrived at the house two hours after her mother had passed.'

'A weak spirit,' I sigh deeply. 'She will have to live with that for the rest of her life.'

'That's what Maite said.'

In the square outside the white church, the crowd has quadrupled in our absence. To me, it's a playground for pickpockets and the fingers of frottage. In the tight vice of perspiring bodies, I grip Maria's hand, warn her to hold on to her bag. Suddenly, the church bells ring out, the songs turn into screams, fireworks light up the sky. Someone lets off a firecracker that creates a wave that almost topples us. This is the fulcrum of the fiesta, the moment everyone has been waiting for, a glimpse of the Paloma Blanca. As the crowd surges up to the scalloped church entrance, Maria tells me in panic that her feet can't find the floor. 'Let's go back,' she releases my hand to grab me by the arm. Swimming against the current, a wild-eyed madman screams '*Paloma Blanca*' into Maria's face. I'm quick to act, put my hand out to steer the stranger back into the crowd. Somehow, still in one piece, we make it to the rim of the seething mass of humanity. Sheltering under a makeshift awning, with a wall behind us, in comparative safety, I survey the hysterical scene outside the church. When the revered idol finally appears, a child-sized doll with a white gothic face, the devotees lose all sense of reason in a savage scramble to touch a pair of pinewood feet.

'*Hombres*,' the barman greets us warmly, as he wipes the slosh off the table we vacated less than an hour ago. '*Me llamo Joaquin*,' he gives his name in Spanish, before switching to the foreign language he spent three consecutive summers studying in Folkestone when he was a teenager. We're told he heard us speaking English on our last visit, that he would've stopped to have a chat, but he was run off his '*bloody*' feet by the '*bloody*' pilgrims. 'They hunts the virgin like a pack of wolves,' he flops into the seat next to Maria. 'Haven't had a tink in two nights.'

'Wink.'

'That's what I says,' Joaquin dismisses my correction with a strained smile. 'And I won't have one tonight.'

'That's tough,' I respond, keeping my features in check to offer a straight face. 'How do you do it?'

'Easy,' Joaquin smiles spontaneously. 'With these,' he gleefully explains, rummaging through his pockets to produce a foil of tiny, sky-blue tablets.

'What are they?'

'My wife's slimming pills.'

'And they work?'

'Oh, yeah! They keeps me going, and the fat off her velly.'

'And where is the good lady?' I ask, resisting the suggestion he meant belly.

'Where she belongs,' he points his dirty rag at the alcove behind the bar. 'Cooking *cocido* for the ducklings.'

'What ducklings?'

'The *Rocieros*.' Joaquin offers the insincere smile he reserved for dullards.

'But why ducklings?'

'Because,' he looks at me with more disgust than pity, 'they follows the mother duck.'

'So, you're not religious?' Maria asks.

'Not since I married Charna.'

'Charna's not a Spanish name.'

'That's because she's not Spanish,' he snaps at the moron next to Maria.

'I just thought…'

'Well, you thoughts wrong. Charna's Israeli. I met her in a Kibbutz.'

'You've been to Israel?'

Joaquin doesn't lower himself by answering an idiotic question. Ignoring me, he addresses Maria, tells her that Israelis are clever people. 'They opens my eyes to Jesus.'

'How?' Maria asks politely.

'They taught me he was all man, not a god; only a prophet of flesh and blood who cries on the cross.'

'You mean dies,' I interject timidly.

'Yeah, that too. They taught me the Catholics got it mixed up and down.'

'Upside down.'

To silent the pedant, Joaquim narrows his eyes to deliver darts of resentment. 'The church sees God, but no man in Christ. So they makes up the angel and the funny birth.'

'The immaculate conception.'

'Yeah,' the barman responds without looking me in the face. 'Can't have God mixed up with the dirty business. That's why they invents the cult of the virgin.' Joaquin pauses to lick the gobbets of spittle that have settled in the corners of his dried lips. To me, the man looks like he's speeding. 'And now, the priests can't keeps their hands in their pockets. A man wants a woman, and a woman needs a man. That's the ways the world works,' he concludes his sermon with the lecherous look that Maria's so familiar with.

I'm denied the opportunity to mention Mary, the scarlet girl Jesus courted, or that the church was over a thousand years old before celibacy became the rule for Catholic priests, for no one at our table perceives the shadow of a fiery-eyed termagant, with a carving knife in her hand, until she's upon us.

'*Darling*,' Joaquin jumps out of his skin, much as a serf caught pilfering from the coffers of his cruel master.

'On *your* arse the minute my back is turned,' Darling bellows above the din of the bar. 'Move it, before I skin you,' she raises the knife like a cobra about to strike.

'But…'

'No buts, miserable worm. The ducklings are coming.' Never to be seen again, the would-be theologian is off like a whippet. 'And *you*,' the woman I assume to be Joaquin's wife, points her knife at a young waiter who has stopped to snigger at the domestic scene, 'fetch these people their drinks.'

'*Si, Senora*,' the youngster doesn't argue with a woman with arms as thick as her thighs.

Maria is barely halfway through her coke, when we notice that the flourboards are groaning, rumbling to the tramp of thousands, the thunder of booming drums. As Joaquin's wife foretold, when the procession passes the bar, scores of pilgrims pour into her parlour, popish celebrants who need to refuel before re-joining the

146

caravan of faith that will journey deep into the night. When a pair of rowdy drunks at the other end of our table, break into song, murdering the perplexing art of *cante jondo*, Maria says it's time for us to face the dismal prospect of spending the rest of the night in the back of our car. Although I'd like a close-up photograph of the thirteenth-century doll, Maria forbids it, insists we leave by the backdoor, steer clear from the path of the procession. In a sandy street, she tells me that the man who shouted in her face scared her, that he had the face of a fanatic. 'Perhaps he saw red because I had my back to the virgin?'

'*Perhaps*, but that's no excuse. I saw fury in his face, anger in his eyes, the faith that hurts. In another clime and time, twenty men like that can turn a crowd into an angry mob. How many have perished or killed in the name of God? Apart from Indonesia, India has more Muslims than any other country, and yet Islam spread through the ancient land of the Hindus on the blade of a sword. At one time, those who refused to accept the Koran were beheaded. Here, about five hundred years ago, the Moors got a similar deal. My religion is better than yours is a diabolical game; the concept of a holy war an abomination of contradiction, like talking about a married bachelor.'

'Kim.'

'I know,' I smile, somewhat sadly, 'I'm ranting.'

Although we avoid the procession, El Rocio just isn't big enough to escape the festive mood. When we find the field in which we are parked, our slender hope of repose is severely dashed, for the so-called carpark is now the site of a huge party. Maria calls it a *botellón*, a piss-up in a public place. There mightn't be jongleurs or dancing bears, but to me, it looks like a medieval carnival. Although forbidden by law, there are fires everywhere, some with roasting spits, the largest surrounded by convoys of carts and caravans; corrals assembled to ward off Apaches. And, of course, everyone wants to hear music, *their* music. Maria likens the babel of sound, different songs for different generations, to a dish saturated in conflicting spices, the worst ingredient, machine music known as techno, booming out of over-sized speakers from the back of a station wagon parked somewhere behind us. I open the glove compartment to fish out a flask of brandy from which I take a swig. 'Is that wise?' Maria asks, with a bottle of water in her hand.

'Everyone is hitting the bottle, why not me?' I laugh. 'If I'm to sleep, I might need a little help.'

'Don't overdo it; you'll end up with a headache in the morning.'

'I've got one *now*.'

Laughing with, not at me, Maria is about to compose a comment, when she's distracted by the shrill cries of a young girl, circling our car, pursued by a bearded youth with a *zambomba*. Playing the musical instrument by suggestively ramming a stick up and down through a rabbit skin stretched over a clay pot, the youth declares his love in a sozzled song. When the chase is over, the prey pinned to the side of a coach, the girl shrieks like a parrot, before offering her lips as a hand snakes up her skirt. Locked in a passionate embrace, the turtle doves, oblivious to the world, are interrupted by a pair of ogling, old hens, who, in truculent tone, remind them that the fiesta is in honour of a sacred virgin.

With a pair of earplugs and a blindfold, Maria curls up on the passenger seat. Within minutes, her soft breath tells me she's asleep. I try this and that position, end up on my back with my feet resting on the bar of the steering wheel. With years of experience travelling overnight on buses, trains and planes, I manage to escape the manic beat of techno for barely an hour.

Wending my way through the carpark in search of a public toilet, I pass a creaking van with steamed up windows, less coy lovers, hammering into the starlit night under cotton covers. Back in the car, I abandon any hope of sleep. Instead, I smoke a cigarette, close my eyes and rest, a technique I've perfected in airports waiting for early morn flights. When the first grey light of dawn heralds a new day, I go in search of a coffee. When I return to the car, Maria is still in deep slumber. When she finally removes her blindfold, the first thing she sees is a wild horse galloping across a marshland. 'Where are we?' she asks sleepily.

'I'm afraid I misread the map, mistook thin blue lines for ramshackle roads when they represented rivers. I could be mistaken, but I think we are in Donana National Park.'

'In other words, we're lost.'

'Lost! You could put it that way. But *Maria*, look around. Isn't it beautiful?'

THE SERENDIPITOUS SPELL FOLLOWS US INTO CHIPIONA, A SMALL COASTAL town, where, like so many good things in life, we find, without looking, just what we need. In my village we found each other; in Chipiona, a fine room with a comfortable bed and a view of the sea. Knowing if I sleep, I'll lose the whole day, I join Maria in the shower to find a second wind. Refreshed, we leave the car outside the pension, stroll along the beachfront, circumnavigate an impressive *faro,* or lighthouse, and then turn from the Atlantic coast to explore the town.

With almost twenty thousand inhabitants, Chipiona has the usual array of supermarkets that can be found anywhere in Spain, but we take our freshly baked sticks of bread from a local baker, and then step into a quaint delicatessen with a tinkling bell to announce our custom. The old-fashioned store is shelved with huge jars of herbs and spices, there are bowls of pickled onions and peppers and olives of every size and colour, a cabinet full of preserved meat in tins opened with little keys, a cornucopia of biscuits that Maria's mother would have known in good times, a selection of fine wines I've never seen before, and a fridge crammed with home-made pates and strange cheeses. I select a rose with a saint and a stag on its label, Maria, a slab of Swiss cheese, a tomato the size of an apple, and a plastic bag of olives, pickled and spicy.
 'Comida de reyes,' – 'Food of kings,' Maria happily declares, leading me through a warren of backstreets to the table on the terrace outside our room. With the azure sea spread before our feet, there's no better place to enjoy our fare. The glass tumblers from our bathroom might be mass-produced, cheap and chunky, but the wine is a delight with a shy magic that has us make love to the song of the sea. Exhausted, I sleep for hours, till a gentle hand stirs me to see the sunset.
 With elbows interlocked, we walk into the town centre, drawn like moths to light, by the sound of music to a marquee decorated with bunting, tinsel and flashing lights. *'Boda gitana,'* Maria tells me it's a gipsy wedding, as we approach the colourful carousal in the corner of a small square. I slow my step to take in the gathering, the children playing tag between grandparents' legs, wide-hipped mothers with missing teeth keeping a watchful eye on teenage girls with flowers in their jet-black tresses, young men, with a different sort of eye, in sharp attire, lined up with fathers dripping in the gold that has no faith in banks. On the edge of the party, upon a wooden chair with a wicker woven seat, an old patriarch with long, black-dyed hair, swivels his chin on gnarled hands clutching a handsomely carved walking stick, to size us up. I smile, and receive the faintest nod of recognition from the ancient warrior, before his dark eyes return to his flock of friends and family. A wild gipsy girl with hooped earrings steps into a circle to summon with castanets a middle-aged man to hammer the dust with his heels. 'Let's go in here,' Maria breaks the spell, by steering me by the arm into a bodega between two derelict houses.
 Stepping into the wine cellar, is like entering another age, turning back the pages, perchance, a whole chapter in the history of Spain. It's the sort of bar I adore, dark and fuggy, with the mighty smell of old wine and fried garlic. The broken tiled floor, covered in soiled napkins, plastic wrappings, toothpicks and peanut shells, doesn't look as if it has seen a broom in months. On white-washed walls that have turned yellow, there are posters of famous *corridas,* bullfights with tickets in the

sun for as little as fifty pesetas. An old woman with a plastic bottle comes in to buy a litre of sweet wine from a gigantic oak barrel covered in cobwebs. When the barman turns off the spigot, takes the woman's coin, he deigns to visit our table. Ploughing through the detritus of countless drunken nights, he tells us that *caracoles* are on the menu.

'We don't eat snails,' Maria responds, whereupon the man makes a confession that he doesn't like snails either, or gypsies.

'That lot outside have been at it for days,' he complains, before informing us that *Gitanos* breed like rabbits, don't do a stroke of work, yet can afford a '*Hindoo*' wedding. While the disgruntled barman is busy pouring Lerchundi moscatel, the most famous tipple in town, Maria tells me she admires the gypsies and their love of freedom.

'I hate the way they are downtrodden and disparaged in Spain. What would Andalusia *be* without their song and dance?'

'And what do you want for *tapa*?' the barman asks, placing a carafe of the local white wine on our table.

'*Bravas*,' I order on our behalf. Waiting until the barman is beyond the scope of her voice, Maria continues her paean to Romani people, how, when she lived in Madrid, she befriended a little gypsy girl who sold flowers outside the dance studio where she worked.

'Her name was Rosita, and she was like a little angel, the prettiest thing I'd ever seen. She couldn't read or write, had never been to school, but at twelve, she knew more of the world than I could imagine. I'd buy flowers from her, sit with her, and share a cigarette, while she told me about her life, how her family were evicted from wasteland near the airport, forced to live in a high-rise of social housing.'

'How did they get on in a block of flats?'

'They didn't.' Maria shakes her head. 'After a life under the stars, they couldn't adapt to living in such a confined space. And their neighbours hated them, especially when they used the lift to take their donkeys to the third floor.'

'Shame they didn't have a garage. They could've converted it into a stable.'

'They had a garage, but it was full of pigs. The donkeys had to live with them. Rosita told me they were part of the family, that they couldn't leave them out at night, tethered to a lamppost, lonely, and frightened by cars.'

'*Donkeys in a flat!*'

'Not only donkeys. Rosita told me she shared a bedroom with her two older sisters and four dogs, that their hallway was full of goats, their kitchen full of chickens that laid the most beautiful eggs. That was another problem with the neighbours.'

'Sounds like Miguel's house in Osuna.'

'But that was *his* house, not a council flat. Their cockerel woke the whole neighbourhood up at dawn.'

'What happened to them?'

'I don't know. But I think they were thrown out after the neighbours signed a petition. Rosita showed me the eviction notice, asked me to read it. That morning she said she hadn't any change for the flowers I bought, that I could pay her another day. But I never saw her again.'

'How sweet! She knew you would never again meet.'

'Probably. But it's not such a sad story. Rosita said her family would be happy back on the road, that living in a flat was like time spent in prison.'

I'm still ruminating on Maria's tale of Rosita, when the barman arrives at our table with a bowl of *bravas*. I'm asked if I've heard of the handkerchief of three roses, *la prueba del pañuelo*.

'I haven't,' I reply, noting Maria's unease.

'That's the bride-to-be's blood. Without proof of her virginity, there's no chant of *yeli*, and no wedding. It isn't decent in this modern age,' the barman screws up his miserable face in disgust. ''The sheet out of the bedroom window is bad enough, but at least the husband breaks the hymen, not the fat fingers of dried up witches who read tea leaves and sell sprigs of rosemary to gullible tourists.'

I'm left speechless by the outburst, Maria, flabbergasted, shifts in her seat to evince her discomfort. More by the hatred that drives the man, than moved by what has been said, the devil within me is tempted to ask the barman if his wife was a virgin on their wedding night. In the end, I let my face do the talking, stare at the man in stony silence. Bereft of a response, the barman reaches for familiar ground by asking us if we'd like to try another wine from the local grape.

'*Si*,' Maria replies to end the man's blushes.

The second wine is better than the first, but before the barman can win our approval, his attention is distracted by the loud arrival of a group of German middle-aged tourists. The Germans, four in number, three men and a woman, are in boisterous mood, obviously on the razzle. The fattest of the four, snaps his fingers at the barman. '*Vino*,' he yells at the top of his voice.

'*Rojo o blanco?*'

'*Rojo*,' the German replies, without lifting his eyes from the menu card. 'And *salchitas*,' he adds in Spanglish. Two carafes of wine arrive in due course, but despite innumerable entreaties, there's no sign of the sausages. Struggling to her feet, the German woman staggers up to the bar to remind the barman of their order. The possibility the barman doesn't speak German isn't entertained, especially as she recognises the word *salchitas* when he tells her in Spanish that sausages don't grow on trees. Satisfied her message has got through, she heads back to her table, stopping to stare at a poster. Unable to make out the small print, she leans forward, to steady herself puts her heavy hand on the poster. When her hand goes through the poster to reveal a gash in the wall behind the matador's face, she screams in horror to find a huge cockroach crawling up her bare arm. With a cascade of roaches pouring out of the wall like thick treacle, we calculate what we owe, put a blue note on our table, pick up our things, and leave. My only hope is that we haven't left a tip.

Twenty minutes later, outside our pension, I'm still in the wine cellar. When I ask Maria if she thinks the sausages have arrived, she punches me on the arm. My cackling doesn't properly cease until we're on our terrace. There, entwined, we marvel at moonlight spangling the sea with specks of silver, above us, a shower of sparks in a deep blue velvet sky. Maria makes a silent wish; thanks me for a day that began with a stallion to close with a shooting star.

The next morning, we are woken up by the call of an itinerant vendor of melons. On bare feet, surveying the sea, the beach beckons, breaking our resolve to spend the rest of the morning in bed. The scraps of yesterday's lunch are turned into breakfast, before we set off along the seafront for our first real coffee. I pick up a local newspaper to read an article about a ninety-year-old woman evicted from the house where she was born, how the police broke up a demonstration of angry neighbours trying to protect her. Maria, in another world, hands me the laminated menu, suggests we return for lunch to have a pizza.

Midweek, we find a deserted stretch of sand, unfurl our towels, spray each other with coconut-scented sun lotion, before burying our noses in our books; Maria lost in the metaphysical complexities of Buddha's message, while I, unhindered by missing syllables and impossible accents, tackle a Spanish novel set in the jungles of Tahiti. After our time in Rocio, the car, the crowds, it's wonderful to be alone. Stretched out on the sand, with the sun on our backs, Maria says it's like being on holiday. But it's hot; so hot, that when a bead of perspiration drops from Maria's nose to a page outlining the eight-fold noble path, she asks me to abandon the savage paradise of my novel to join her in the waves. And so the pattern is set for the next few hours; ten pages, perhaps a chapter, punctuated by a cigarette, a doze, perchance a dream, in my case, scenes of an artist searching for his soul on the islands of the South Pacific, and then the flight from solid ground into the cool caress of the sea. Watching the course of the sun, it must be around two in the afternoon when we leave the beach to take a table outside the restaurant where we had our morning coffee.

We order a jug of iced sangria while we wait for a side salad to accompany our baked bread topped with cheese and tomatoes. The other three tables on the pavement are occupied; two by workers in paint-splashed blue overalls, chomping through steaks from the menu of the day, the third, by a man of pensionable age, spectacularly overdressed for the season, wearing a black, double-breasted blazer with gold buttons, a British naval officer's cap on top of his silver hair. To me, he looks like George Cole, an actor who found fame in a British sit-com. Fluttering in the sea breeze, he holds an English tabloid, his eyes glued to a page devoted to horse racing. He folds his newspaper in half when he's joined by two elderly women in summer slacks and pink cotton blouses. The M&S ladies must favour the same beauty salon too, for their hairdos are identical, although one, the taller of the two, prefers a pink rinse to match her top, rather than blue.

'I'm sorry we're late Reggie, but Margo lost the key to her apartment,' explains pink rinse.

'Maureen, I didn't lose it. I just left it in the front door,' Margo corrects her friend.

'I suppose you left it there for your Latin lover.'

'*Oh*, Maureen, he's a one, isn't he?' Margo blushes.

'He certainly is. Have we kept you waiting long?'

'All my life, you lovely ladies,' Reggie replies as a man who likes to keep his options open. 'G and T girls? Our *paella* won't be here for another half an hour.'

'*Oh!*' Margo exclaims with delight, says she's likes Spanish food and is sick of fish and chips. 'How did your trip go? We missed you awfully. Quiz night wasn't the same without you.'

'Couldn't wait to get back. Everywhere I went, it was Brexit this, EU that. The whole country's gone mad.' The mention of politics seems to cast a shadow over the women, dampen the spirit of their luncheon.

'Did you manage to see Jim and Rose?' Maureen asks.

'No, I didn't have time. But I spoke to them.'

'How are they getting on?'

'They're living in a caravan in a muddy field, somewhere off the M6. It's so expensive back home, that's all they could afford.'

'I thought Jim's brother was going to help them out.'

'That's what Jim thought. But Rose told me there was some sort of family fall out, when Jim's brother said they deserved what they got, after living the high life in Spain for so many years.'

'That's not fair. Jim was on the buses for nearly forty years, and Rose at a market stall for almost as many. She told me it cost them everything they had to buy their apartment.'

'Like my Tony,' Margo interjects with a quaver in her voice. 'He was a milkman for thirty-seven years. He worked himself into an early grave. It was his dream to come out here. *And look what happened!* Not even a year before he had his stroke.'

'You lost him eight years ago, didn't you pet?' Maureen puts her mottled hand on the widow's.

'Next month, nine.'

Looking at his companions, Reggie's right upper eyelid begins to twitch. At his stage in life, talking about the deceased, isn't his idea of fun. He reminds the women that life is for living, tells them they're the *rock around the clock* generation, that whatever happens, they'll take it on the chin, and jive to midnight. It's a spirited little speech to enliven the ladies, help them to finish off their gin and tonics.

When our pizza arrives, I lose interest in our neighbours, as their conversation descends into gossip and rumours, how Sue and Mark who run the bingo nights might be swingers. It's only when we're on our coffees, and our neighbours are half way through their paella, that my curiosity is rekindled.

'Cross over to Portugal, and apart from the lingo, the different design of the churches, you wouldn't know you've left Spain. In Italy they eat pasta instead of *paella*. Take the ferry from Brindisi to Piraeus and the quality of wine goes down the drain, but the beer is colder. Travel north through Bulgaria, and then west into central Europe, hit the coast, take a train through France, Belgium and Holland, catch a boat to Scandinavia. And what do you find?'

Margo and Maureen stare at Reggie. Sensing the question rhetorical, they don't answer.

'Of course, all the countries have their own geography and weather, their own languages, their own food, traditional costumes and customs, but you won't have any problem recognising the way of life, as basically, it's the same as ours. From Sofia to Southampton, Budapest to Bromley, the ideas of what's right and wrong, what's acceptable and what isn't, is more or less the same.' Reggie pauses to remove a prawn shell from his gleaming dentures. 'That's because you haven't left Europe. And nor will Britain, even if it leaves the EU. We are part of Europe, always have been, and always will be. It's crazy to turn our backs on our own continent. The channel doesn't alter our shared values; Polish plumbers don't plant bombs in concert halls to blow up our kids, Germans say happy Christmas not happy holidays. And another thing,' Reggie reaches for a toothpick to deal with another shell, 'we won't get better deals than those we've already got with the economic might of the EU behind us. Alone, on the world stage, we'll be eaten alive.'

'But we're a rich country,' Maureen breaks the monologue. 'All the papers say we're got the sixth biggest economy in the world.'

'The German economy is bigger than ours, let alone the EU's. And as for being rich, the money is, and always has been, in the hands of the few. Britain has the poorest pensions in the developed world. The French work less hours, retire years before us, and yet their pensions are nearly twice the size of ours.'

Margo flinches, says her monthly pension has gone down thirty pounds a month since the EU referendum.

'But Bill's got a fat pension. He worked for BT.' Maureen looks at Reggie with hope in her eyes.

'BT isn't British. There might be British Gas, British Airways, British this and that, but none of them are British anymore. The family silver was flogged off years ago, mostly on the cheap to international investors. In a land famous for rain, the Brits don't even own the water in their taps. Even Rolls-Royce is in the hands of BMW.'

'BMW is German,' Margo remarks, to show that she's following the conversation.

'Our economy is interwoven with Europe's. Over half our trade is with our European neighbours. Imagine a shopkeeper telling his customers they have to fill in a form to buy a bottle of milk. To leave the EU is nuts.'

'Did you know that Lizzie voted to leave?' Maureen asks, her life and sun worn face a shade paler than when she arrived at the restaurant. 'She said she was being patriotic.'

'I heard,' Reggie bares his teeth in disgust. 'Like cutting the branch on which her sagging arse is perched. The poor old cow's senile.'

I might be imagining things, but I'm sure I catch Margo clenching her buttocks.

'Of course, there's problems in the EU,' Reggie adopts a more conciliatory tone. 'But our best bet is to stay where we are, *lead,* not leave. Sort out the unelected cronies in the commission, force the buggers in Brussels to put it to the people before they burden us with new members, make the ECB show its hand by publishing its minutes.'

'What's the ECB?' Margo asks, to show interest, hoping that Reggie doesn't think she losing her marbles like her neighbour Lizzie.

'Europe's answer to the Bank of England.'

'That's right. I remember now,' Margo, convinced she's not senile, smiles brightly.

'Do you think the pound will fall if we leave the EU without a deal?' Maureen asks.

'If I knew the answer to that, I wouldn't need the horses.'

'If the pound falls so will our pensions,' Margo responds with a worried look. 'It's already a struggle to make ends meet. I don't want to end up in a caravan like Jim and Rose. I'm too old for camping. What are we going to do?'

'Stay calm. That's what we are going to do,' Reggie says firmly. 'I'm sure the good old British public will come to their senses, and demand a second referendum.'

'And if they don't?'

'Then we'll revert to plan B,' Reggie winks at the old dears. 'We'll sell up, pool our money and buy a one-bedroom flat and live as a threesome.'

'Goodness! He's a one, isn't, Maureen? We're facing disaster, and all he can think about is sex.'

'Girls, another G and T?'

'Go on then. We might as well,' Maureen responds as if she 's considering Reggie's proposition.

'That's the spirit! Let's get drunk before they throw us out of the country.'

While I might admire the sporting frivolity of the old expats, gamely living in the moment, thanking their lucky stars for every day spent under the Spanish sun, when I get back to our hotel room, Reggie's words begin to haunt me. Try as I might, I can't find any peace in my siesta, not with the words of the silver fox spinning round and round in my head. Even at sunset, contemplating brushstrokes of magenta reflected in a sea as smooth as a mirror, my gloomy spirit holds sway. At dinner, I've no appetite; back in our room, when Maria switches off the light to burn a scented candle, I've no mood for amorous adventures, prefer to drink water rather than wine so as not to muddle my sullen thoughts. Unable to bear the strain of my suffering, Maria drops to her knees, puts her hands on my lap, stares into my eyes until tears brim up to blur her vision. 'Do you remember I once told you I wouldn't care if we lived in a cardboard box as long as we remained together?'

'Yes,' I reply, holding her watery eyes.

'I meant it,' she sniffles, twitching her nose like a mouse. 'We don't believe, but most do....'

'Believe!'

'In marriage.' Maria's eyes drop to her hands. '*Kim*, please make me your wife,' her eyes return to mine to reveal the vulnerability of an open heart.

'Are you proposing?' I ask dumbly, for her words are clear.

'I am; my soul is naked before you.'

Knowing the next moment will change the rest of my life, with tears welling up, I can't surpass her words. 'I accept,' I whisper, 'with my naked soul.'

'So why are we crying?' Maria squeals with delight, as she springs to her feet to throw herself into my arms.

'I don't know, maybe because we're so happy.'

'*Yes*, that's it,' Maria responds by burying her face into the nape of my neck, where, between quiet sobs, she declares her love, over and over again, until '*Te amo*' sounds like a magical mantra. 'Will we have rings?' she asks, at length, the wash of tears stemmed, her candlelit eyes before mine.

'If you wish.'

'Gold or tattoos on our fingers?'

'*Tattoos!* I've never had a tattoo,' I muse aloud; in truth, surprised by the unconventional option.

'You can't throw a tattoo into the sea after an argument.'

'You've convinced me. Your mum won't like it, but let's have tattoos.'

With glistening eyelashes, her face radiant in the lambent light, Maria has another idea. 'Let's go south tomorrow, forget Granada, drive to La Linea, cross over to Gibraltar, get our papers done in a day. We *could* do it if we get up early. The tattoos can come later.'

'Our honeymoon, a bed-in overlooking the canals of Amsterdam,' I mask my reluctance obscurely. 'No, not the rock. I don't want a Vegas wedding,' I smile as I shake my head. 'I wouldn't want a rent-a-crowd wedding, three hundred guests I've never seen before, but I'd prefer to do it the old Spanish way, Bill as my best man, your family in the front row in your village.'

'You would do that for *me*?' Maria looks at me with startled eyes.

'I would do anything for you.'

34

HOW MARIA STAYS COOL IN THE SUN IS A MYSTERY, BUT HER SHIRT IS DRY, unlike mine, clinging to my back in perspiration, when we finally reach the hilltop square with a gothic church and a vista that has been captured in a million postcards. It isn't the best view of the Alhambra; that's on another hill near a boys' prison, but it's spectacular, and goes way beyond the scope of picture postcards; the suddenness of the vast panorama of palace, mountains and open sky looming up to startle the newcomer to Granada. I remember the first time, almost thirty years ago, when I trudged up the steep hill to stand outside the church of St Nicolas. How I was startled by the famous prospect, the elation I had known but once before, when I stepped out of the train station in Venice into a painting by Giovanni Antonio Canal, commonly known as Canaletto.

The square is crowded with tourists and the hawkers who hound them, but we find a space on the knee-high wall that overlooks the rooftops and gardens that tumble down into the chasm through which the thawed snow of the sierras in summer flows. Maria gives me her bag for safe keeping, says she'll be a minute or two, that she wants to buy a pair of hand-made earrings. I watch as she approaches a band of hippies playing bongo drums, walks through a cloud of marijuana smoke, to a young girl with beaded hair, sitting on a Peruvian rug. I watch as she tries several earrings on, looks at herself in a hand-held mirror, laughs with the girl. For a moment I lose her, my view obstructed by a group of tourists, a moment to think of Europe without England and the marriage I've agreed to. Although I still feel as if I'm in a Kafkaesque quandary, I pour scorn on my erstwhile self-pity. I smile, when Maria's minute or two stretches to ten, turn my inward gaze out across the vale to what a Moroccan poet termed a pearl set in a sea of emeralds – the jewel of Moorish Spain surrounded by groves of myrtle, elm and cypress trees. I recall the day I spent in the palace, a shabby backpacker wandering from courtyards into patios lined with fountains and flowers, the sour orange I plucked from a tree, the photograph a stranger took of me cuddling a stone lion. And then, fancy usurps memory, for I go beyond my time. First, to the ghosts of a nineteenth-century American writer, then to Napoleon who wanted to destroy the building, finally, to the sultan who, to save the palace, surrendered the keys of Granada to the Spanish. Legend speaks of the last sultan as an effete man, a horseman on a mountain pass beyond the city, turning back to look one last time at what he had lost. How his hardened mother never forgave him, told him he wept as a woman over what he couldn't hold as a man. I'm still on the *El Puerto del Suspiro del Moro,* standing next to Boabdil, when Maria skips into my dream, smiling widely to show me the silver pendant she preferred to a pair of earrings. 'It's an Inca design, a symbol for happiness,' she informs me. 'And I'm so happy,' she says, removing her bag from the wall, to sit beside me. 'So *happy*, I feel guilty.'

'There are deserts that burst into flower once a year; the inhospitable terrain of the Great Karoo in South Africa, for a few weeks, covered by a carpet of wild flowers. In Namibia, at the same time, the rippling red dunes of the Kalahari lie beneath a riot of colour. Happiness is never a crime, not even in hell. If your heart swells with smiles, share them with the world Maria; only think twice before you glare.'

'And these fellows?' I follow Maria's eyes to a pair of gypsies working the wall, eliciting coins for a few chords on a guitar. Maria keeps her mouth shut when it's our turn to be fleeced, leaves it to me to explain in poor French that we don't speak Spanish or English. *'Aap kaise hain?'* I ask the gypsies how they are in Hindi. My little performance earns a withering look, but does the trick, although I still end up with an embossed card, an invitation to spend a night, and a fortune, watching flamenco over a candlelit dinner in a cave in Sacromonte.

On the heels of an oriental globetrotter, consulting a map on his smartphone, we find our way down to the foot of the hill. From there, Maria knows the lay of the land, leads me to the Renaissance cathedral. In the imposing shadow of the sixteenth-century church, she tells me she has some serious shopping in mind, points to the Capilla Real, the royal burial chapel, suggests I buy a ticket to look at the mausoleum of Fernando and Isabel. 'I'd prefer to wait for you over there,' I point to a *teteria*, or teahouse, to a tent for smokers, remind her that I've no interest in royalty, dead or alive, of whatever nationality.

I take a cushioned-cane seat under the awning, order a hookah pipe, a slice of carrot cake to go with a pot of jasmine tea. The waiter, a Moroccan in his sixties, with a worn out face, asks me if I want a newspaper, tells me he has a copy of yesterday's New York Times. *'El Pais,'* I respond, explaining I prefer a Spanish take on current affairs. I read a page-long report on the rise of the far-right in Italy, a revolt against the flood of refugees arriving from Libya; how, in Andalusia, there are early signs of a similar movement. And then, to sour my mood further, I find a short article on child poverty in England. How teachers in Lancaster have found children looking for scraps of food, rummaging through rubbish bins during playtime. Dismayed by the politics of the day, I discard the paper, take a sip of jasmine to quieten the ireful bile bubbling up in my belly. The waiter brings the water pipe, stuffs the bowl with blueberry-flavoured tobacco. He stands at my side while I light the pipe, opens his mouth to say something, but is distracted by the arrival of a car that splutters into the street. We both watch the car as it comes to a halt right in front of the teahouse with squeaking brakes.

The first to get out of the car is the driver, a woman with wizened features under a beehive of grey hair. As if I might be a traffic warden off duty, she looks at me with a challenge, aware that she's parked on a yellow line. Without removing her cigar butt from rouged lips, she looks up and down the street, before yelling something at her passenger. It must be the all-clear, for a woman immediately emerges from the car, a woman covered from head to toe in silver paint. With argent hair and fingernails, it could be psyche on the pavement, an angel of some sort, someone or something from another planet. 'That's Juanita,' the waiter with the furrowed face whispers. 'She used to be so beautiful,' he sighs. 'She disappears in the winter, but comes back every summer.'

'As a statue?'

'No, no!' the waiter shakes his head. 'Last year she played the violin like a sorceress.'

'Sorceress!'

'Yes, like the gipsy in Hugo's Notre Dame.'

Surprised by the literary reference, I might press the waiter to elaborate, but he's at another table before I can put my question. Instead, I stare at the strange figure, tall and elegant, watch as she takes up her statuesque position on the corner of the street. I wonder what passes through her head, as she stands as still as a blue heron. Her performance might not be on par with the fakir I once chanced upon outside the Golden Temple in Amritsar. According to his coin-collecting assistant, a living scarecrow who had stood on one foot for over a year, but I marvel at her volition to stand stock still for ten minutes, broken but once to twitch a sparkling eyelash, and with an invisible wire flutter diaphanous wings, when someone puts a coin at her frozen feet.

'Wouldn't you like to lick her?' the waiter, passing my table, noting my interest, says with a sinister smile.

Our hotel has more stars than we are accustomed to, but after our matrimonial pact, we're willing to pay a little bit extra for a decent room. A room with air-con, a mini-bar to cool our cheese and wine, a coffee maker, a telephone that works, free Wi-Fi, and best of all, a balcony overlooking a pretty plaza.

Maria serves me a cold beer on the balcony, spreads our takeaway dinner on a table surrounded by potted palms. We eat with cheap plywood chopsticks that have to be prized apart, and the plastic spoons that come with the coffee maker. Although there can't be more than one egg in the oversized aluminium tray of fried rice, accompanied by a watery chop suey, it's a satisfying meal, recognisable Sino-fast food, available anywhere in Western Europe, but never found in China. To finish our inexpensive repast, we smoke cigarettes, share a small bottle of rose, followed by a chocolate biscuit and a cup of processed coffee. When a mariachi band turns up in the plaza to entertain diners on the terrace below our first floor room, we close the door to our balcony, lie side by side on a king size bed to watch a black and white film that's so boring I fall asleep in the middle of a love scene.

In the morning, I'm awoken by Maria, fully dressed, with a coffee and a plate of biscuits. When I ask why she's dressed, I'm told she wants to visit a store that sells books on ballet, that she has an appointment with a hairdresser. 'Don't look in the shopping bags I brought home yesterday or you will ruin the surprise,' she wags her finger at me.

'Surprise!'

'Yes, surprise. Have you forgotten we're getting married?'

I haven't forgotten, but I'm sleepy, remember to ask her what time she'll be back, after she's gone. I sit up in bed to drink my coffee, smoke a cigarette to garner my senses. I think of Maria, her serene surrender to life upstaged by thoughts of today and tomorrow, how happy she seems, lively with purpose. Aware that her happiness guarantees mine, I wonder, in a surge of gentle affection, if a childhood spent in a remote mountain village makes it difficult to see wedlock merely as a pantomime to procure a piece of paper. Missing her already, I get up to visit the bathroom, shave and shower, before sitting on the balcony in a clean pair of underpants to watch the people in the plaza go about their business. Hidden by a profusion of palms, spying like a houri in a harem behind a lattice screen, I watch, with amusement, a young man in fashionable garb kick up a fuss when he discovers that pigeons have besmirched the bonnet of his car. An old woman, selling flowers, shares my humour, laughs silently behind his back. A group of schoolgirls stop to look at a middle-aged woman in slippers and a faded dressing gown feeding scraps to a stray, three-legged dog. Wondering why people find other people so interesting to look at, I return to the room to prepare for a forenoon stroll.

Not long abroad, I find myself in an open square shaded by palm fronds and tall cypress trees. I sit on a bench opposite another on which a tramp twitches in dream. I hope he dreams well, of better things than he will see when he opens his eyes. I finish my cigarette and walk on, reach *La Avenida Divina*, the Divine Avenue. I'm puzzled by the name until I stand outside a museum dedicated to a Capuchin monk who spent most of his life wandering the streets of Granada in service to the poor. There's a photograph of the man outside the museum, an old man in a coarse brown cassock, bald with a long white beard, and kind twinkling eyes. It's the eyes of Fray Leopoldo that draw me in, persuade me to offer a coin for a ticket, only to discover that the entrance to his crypt is free. I find another photograph of the monk in a hallway, a face that reminds me of the abbot who looked after me, when, as a young man, searching for heaven knows what, I spent a week in a Greek Orthodox monastery in Mount Athos. A few minutes more than twenty, I'm not long in the old friary, most of my time spent contemplating the small cell in which the monk slept. A simple room with a single bed, a chair and a desk, the cross of Christ on a bare wall. The room speaks of a path I'm aware of, takes me to the sheltered corner of my heart that made Cassie tremble, prompted Maria to suggest in the home we'll build together, there has to be a room without furniture, a room for meditation, somewhere I can be alone with the fairies, my mantra and little Joe Cole.

Back on the busy streets of Granada, I take a seat at a sidewalk table, order a small glass of beer to water down monkish thoughts. I watch a young African man with dreams of a better life, struggling with a heavy suitcase, a scamp rattling down the road with a supermarket trolley, a well-heeled woman stoop to scoop up her Chihuahua's poo. *'Senor, es tu dia de la suerte,'* a blind man, who knows my sex, breaks my daydream, tries to sell me a lottery ticket, tells me it's my lucky day.

'Si Señor, soy un hombre con suerte, tan afortunado que no necesito ningún billete.'

'I'm glad to meet a lucky man,' the merchant behind the sunglasses smiles at my response.

Distant chimes of church bells tell me it's beyond noon when I return to the hotel. Maria is already on the first floor, on the balcony, in a pale green dress I've never seen before. Her hair is braided, pulled from her face, a silk red rose embedded in the fair locks tucked behind her left ear. I take her in my arms to banish the thought of a cloistered life in a silent cell, tell her I love her, how I find her more beautiful each dawn of each new day.

'And when my bones creak and I'm old and grey?'

'We'll live and die together.'

'Don't,' she says, 'you'll make me cry.'

'Then, we'll cry together.'

'But this day isn't for tears,' she takes my face in her hands, stares into my eyes to see my reality. 'Today, we celebrate. We're going out, and you need to get changed.'

'Do we have to go out?'

'I've reserved a table for lunch.'

'And I need to get changed? Changed into what?'

'You'll find what you need in the bathroom.'

With a beautiful woman on my arm, sporting a new shirt and a touch of polish on my shoes, I walk with a measure of confidence that is only marginally diminished when we enter a sumptuous French restaurant manned by waiters in bowties. There aren't cruel lights in the wood–panelled dining-room, only dim wall lights and chandeliers, so I'm not sure my shabby jeans are remarked, but it's still a relief to sit at a table where my faded denim kneecaps are hidden from view.

'Can we afford this?' I look up in dismay from the wine list.

'If we skip the soup, I'm sure we can make it,' Maria laughs daintily. 'And if we can't, we can always sell the car.'

'Or end up in the kitchen washing plates for a month,' I try to smile. 'And the table! Why's it laid for four?'

'Because we aren't lunching alone. We've got guests.'

'Oh dear!'

'I had to tell someone about the happiest day in my life, so I thought about Pablo and Maite,' Maria grins. 'It's a one-off to celebrate the day I found someone to share the rest of my life with. I've asked Maite to be my maid of honour.'

Aware of a waiter, ignoring his approach, I reach across the table for Maria's hand, tell her that if she's happy, I'm happy too. 'I'll ask Pablo to be my best man.'

'What about Bill?'

'There's no rule against having two.'

'My mother won't understand.'

'Don't worry about your mother. She'll be in a state of shock after she's seen our tattoos.'

We're on our second glass of Chablis, dipping *camembert au four* in cranberry jelly, when Maite, in an elegant, dark blue, satin dress, arrives at our table. 'You look great,' I say, as I stand with Maria to greet her.

'You too,' she kisses me on the cheek, and then Maria.

'You haven't seen the faded patches around my knees,' I laugh when I'm safely back in my seat.

'You haven't seen Pablo.'

'Where is he?'

'He's with the manager in reception. He'll be along in a moment.'

'There he is,' Maria turns her head to the far end of the dining-room.

Accompanied by the maître d', apparently in deep debate, I watch my friend shamble across the plush, thick red carpet, in crumpled attire, gnarled toenails poking out of his scruffy sandals. At first, I wonder if there's an issue with his footwear, a dispute over the dress code. But my fears are unfounded, for when Pablo claims the high-backed chair between Maria and his wife, he's in fine spirit, full of good cheer. Pouring himself a glass of wine, he congratulates us, says he knew this day would come, raising his glass to toast our future, our well-being.

'You knew this day would come?'

'As much as I know my hand will burn if I put it in a fire.'

'Can you see the future?'

Pablo laughs as he considers Maria's guileless question. 'Not in the mists of a crystal ball. *No one can.* In India, an astrologer once told an emperor he had days to live. Troubled, the emperor asked how long the astrologer would live. When the astrologer said he would enjoy a long life, the emperor had his head cut off, there and then, to show the imposter he didn't know the future.' Pablo finishes his first glass of wine, wipes the breadcrumbs of the deep fried cheese from his lips with the back of his hand, ere he continues: 'But I can read faces, read the lines to see what way a man will take. That's how I knew this day would come. There's no magic in my perception.' Pablo cackles when a waiter arrives at our table with a bottle of vintage wine. Uncorking the bottle, the waiter asks if Pablo would like to sample the wine before filling our glasses. 'No need. I know the year and the label.'

'Very good, sir,' the waiter responds with a false smile.

'We all read faces, animals too; we do it all the time, search for clues in the eyes of others, look for a faint smirk or smile to guide us. But with me, it's a special skill, one that I've honed, shaped and sharpened to keep me safe in my skin. Without it, I wouldn't be here.'

'I saw that the waiter who served us just now didn't like us,' I remark. 'He smiled, but with resentment.'

'But what do you mean you wouldn't be here if you couldn't read faces?' Maria asks before Pablo can address my remark.

'I've been in war-torn countries, Maria.' Pablo's tone changes, coloured by memory. 'In Afghanistan, Iraq and Iran. I've witnessed countless revolutions in the Americas, looked down the barrel of a gun, had a machete held to my throat. I might be able to change like a chameleon, carry false papers, switch language and accent, fake an allegiance to this or that crown, play the sage one moment, the fool the next, but none of my thespian trickery would've been enough if I hadn't the gift of reading faces. It's the gift that has kept me alive, the same trained eye that saw you and Kim as a match made in heaven.'

Maria, her expression like one who has just seen a horror film, puts a tremulous hand on the broad shoulder of our friend to thank him for his kind words.

'Yes,' I echo Maria's position. 'And thank you both for coming.'

'The thanks are all *ours,*' Pablo refills our glasses with vintage wine.

When the soufflé arrives on gold-rimmed plates, followed by a creamy cauliflower gratin and a satsuma salad, in deference to French cuisine, there's a lull in the conversation. It's only as we approach our last mouthfuls, that Pablo, after summoning the miserable waiter for champagne, picks up the tread of his theme. He tells us that we are made for each other, that between us we have love and meditation, the two things in life that really matter, without which human beings are merely beasts. 'By love, I mean its highest form, what Christ meant when he spoke of laying one's life down for a friend.'

'And meditation?' Maria asks.

'By meditation, I mean the path to self-realization; to know who you are.'

'Om Mani Padme *bloody* Hum,' Maite, evidently tipsy, interjects with a sing-song voice to show her husband there's no room in her house for a prophet. Heedful of the wide grin on Pablo's face, she begins anew her chant, but is dissuaded from a third mantric round by the approach of the waiter who doesn't like us.

'Your champagne,' the waiter announces, as he puts four fluted crystal-cut glasses on our table.

'Thank you,' Pablo takes his adoring eyes from his wife, to address the waiter. 'Would you mind opening the bottle?'

'Of course,' the waiter replies. 'We wouldn't want to disturb our neighbours,' he adds, somewhat haughtily, casting a sycophantic glance at three suited businessmen at a nearby table. 'Will that be all?' he asks, having expertly opened our Dom Perignon without a cascading mishap.

'Yes, we'd like coffee with our desert,' I reply with a cultivated smile. 'And could you bring me the bill please?' I add, before he can slip away with his sullen face.

'*The bill!*' the waiter looks at me blankly. 'Your bill is already settled.'

'By *whom*?' I respond, my forehead creased in confusion.

'By this gentleman,' the waiter, unaware that his left eyebrow has risen to form a quivering arch, fixes Pablo with his cold eyes. 'He swiped his card in the lobby, and will provide a pin when you leave.'

I wait until the waiter is beyond the range of my voice before remonstrating with my friend. 'You simply can't pay,' I protest. 'It isn't the done thing.'

'Forget it! I've already paid.'

'But you're our guests. We *invited* you.'

'Even more reason why I wish to pay,' Pablo twists an argument I'm familiar with. 'Occasions like this make life worth living. For a man who understands why Jains see suicide as sacred, you can't imagine how happy your engagement with Maria makes me.'

'Oh no, you don't,' Maite puts her hand across Pablo's mouth. 'We don't want any more of your *to be or not to be.* Nor another word about your precious gift of reading faces. What we want *now,* is to get merry. Isn't that so, Maria?'

'Yes,' Maria replies meekly before swallowing more champagne.

'Right,' Pablo removes his wife's hand to reveal an expansive grin. 'I get the picture.'

'So we're not going to hear about Serbia or dead bodies on the streets of San Salvador?'

'No, of course not,' Pablo responds to his wife's injunctive request. To show he's serious he tells me that Real Madrid are after Harry Kane.'

'They're rich, but *not* that rich,' I laugh, 'but there's no harm in dreaming.'

When the coffee arrives with a platter of cinnamon-flavoured apple tarts, Pablo winks at me, before pulling two cigars out of his shirt pocket. 'Cohibas from Cuba,' he says, handing me a cigar.

'But, surely we can't smoke here?'

'No, not here. But this place has a patio at the back.'

The patio, although walled, isn't particularly private, but overlooked by several windows and balconies belonging to neighbouring houses. 'This is where the staff smoke,' Pablo says conspiratorially, leading me through a tangle of broken chairs and crates of empty wine bottles to a table in a corner shaded by the twisted vines of bougainvillea. Reassuringly, there's an ashtray on the table brimming with cigarette butts.

'So what happened in Serbia?' I ask, after I've clipped and lit my cigar.

'Oh, I took a few risks in Belgrade, but I'm not supposed to talk about Serbia,' Pablo smirks. 'I've been censored by the wife.'

'Then it's between you and me.'

Pablo blows smoke from his cigar into the bougainvillea before he begins his tale. 'It was during the Kosovo war. I went to Belgrade under the aegis of Amnesty International to negotiate the release of a political prisoner, a professor of economics, a conscientious objector. While I was there I stayed with someone I met on my first trip to India, an old friend called Yanis, and his young wife. My friend was a gifted musician, and like the professor, against the war. But his protest was more personal, less public. Every night, when the Nato bombs rained down on his city, unlike his neighbours, who ran to their cellars, Yanis and his wife, and a few like-minded friends, mostly artists and musicians, went to his roof terrace to play their guitars and sing love songs.'

'You went with them.'

'You read faces too,' Pablo smiles weakly. 'Yes, I went with them,' he sighs. 'What else could I do? I couldn't sit under my friend's kitchen table with a bottle of slivovitz while the others were on the roof watching the fireworks of fate. But Maite has never forgiven me. She thinks I had a death wish.'

'Did you?'

'Perhaps. But if I did it was to know the light of life, the spark within that can be snuffed out in a split second.'

I fear the answer, but have to ask: 'Are you still in touch with Yanis?'

'Two days after I crossed the border into Romania, a bomb struck his building. It was a direct hit. There were no survivors.'

'I'm so sorry,' I caress my friend's arm.

'At least it was immediate,' Pablo sighs wearily.

'And the professor?'

'At the prison where he was held I was given an official report that said he had had an *accident* the week before I arrived.'

To say sorry a second time doesn't seem adequate, so I keep my hand on my friend's arm, cast the sadness in my eyes to a discarded tissue stained with lipstick on the tiled floor. For a while, we're both silent, locked in our own thoughts, until Pablo leans across the table to lift my chin. 'I might understand why the Jains turn a suicide into a saint, but I don't actually share their view. Camus thought there was only one philosophical issue in a man's life, to live or to commit suicide. I might've rolled the dice in Belgrade, but I chose light over dark, with Death as my mentor. Death awaits us all, there's no need to jump off a cliff. And in the meantime, I do what I can, I try to help out. It's my way of finding meaning in all this mess. Even in Serbia, there was a scintilla of silver in the mist of man's madness. I didn't get to Romania alone. With the help of AI, and some fake papers, I got the professor's wife and two kids through the check posts and over the border. Today, they're all US citizens, his son a doctor, his daughter studying law.'

'That's *something*,' I respond, rallied by Pablo's spirit, 'that makes the game, like love, worth living.'

'I like to think so,' Pablo smiles.

For several minutes, in companionable silence, we smoke our cigars. It's how our paramours find us when they arrive in the patio twittering like a pair of sparrows in spring. 'You took so long, we thought we'd join you,' Maria says, as she puts a half empty bottle of champagne on the table.

'That's a different champagne,' Pablo remarks, peering at the label on the green bottle.

'That's right, Sherlock,' Maite bursts into giggles.

'Are you drunk?'

'Me!' Maite raises her eyebrows to simulate disbelief. 'I might be,' she flutters her eyelashes at her husband. Refilling her glass until there's bubbles at the brim, she asks Pablo if he'd like a sip.

'It's just that I was wondering how we're getting back to the village.'

'Oh, you worry too much,' Maite dismisses her husband's concern. 'Maria's already reserved us a room in her hotel.'

'Well, then it's time for champagne,' Pablo beams, grabbing the heavy-bottomed bottle by the neck to have a sailor's swig.

I try to follow suit, but Maria grabs the bottle from my hand. 'No, that's not the way', she says, before draining her goblet in one gulp to press her lips to mine to show us how champagne should be drunk.

'*Bravo,*' Pablo claps in delight.

'Aren't they romantic?' Maite slurs her words. 'Just like us when we were their age.'

'We still are, aren't we? Never again as young as this moment.'

'Yes, darling,' Maite responds sarcastically, but when she tries to pass a swallow of champagne to her husband, she belches to spray the Brut all over his shirt. '*Oops!*' she exclaims before flopping into her chair. 'The bubbles made me sneeze.' Maria finds a tissue paper in her bag, titters behind it before offering her friend the chance to blow her nose. 'So what kept you out here so long?' Maite throws the tissue to the floor, her voice sluggish to avoid stumbling over her words. 'I hope you didn't tell Kim the nasty story you told me in the car?'

'*Story?*'

'How you nearly had your head chopped off in the Hindu Kush.'

'No, he didn't,' I intervene on Pablo's behalf. 'We were talking about how love makes a difference. How *we* can make a difference.' I look at Maria. 'How a solitary flower, unseen on a barren mountain, makes the world a better place.'

'That's good,' Maite smiles at her husband.

'And you? Betwixt bottles of champagne, what lofty thoughts did you entertain?'

'Oh, I'm sure nothing as lofty as yours,' she glances kindly in my direction. 'Just small talk. Where and when you plan to wed? What you've been up to since our night in Seville? How you slept in your car one night, and then in a room with a view of the sea the next. How some pensioners talking about England upset you...'

'*Dios mio,*' Pablo cries out in such a strange voice that we all turn to stare at him. 'I completely forgot,' he says, reaching for his wife's handbag, from which he extracts an official-looking brown envelope. 'This came for you the other day, when we were at your house watering your plants,' he hands me the envelope. 'I signed for you, forged your signature with my finger on an electric pad.'

The envelope has a small emblem of a harp on the back, leaving no doubt as to where it's from. I open the envelope to pass the contents to Maria, copies of my mother's birth and wedding certificates, a brand new Irish passport.

'*Felicidades,*' Pablo rises to his feet to hug me, followed by his wife, who kisses first Maria, and then me, on both cheeks. Next, it's the turn of Maria, to offer her congratulations, to tell me she's overjoyed. But there's a question in her beautiful brown eyes that needs to be addressed. I mention a journey for a honeymoon, the valley of Kathmandu, a rooftop restaurant in Durbar square where you can see the Himalayas above the pagodas.

'It's only an idea, but if you want, I'll make it a reality.'

'*Si, quiero,*' Maria whispers, struggling to smile before she bursts into tears.

'*Viva los novios,*' Maite raises her empty glass to bestow longevity on the lovers.

'*Viva,*' Pablo responds, before telling us we need more champagne.

I'm about to seize Pablo's shirt tail, arrest his munificence, insist that the next bottle is on my card, when my phone rings.

'*Kim,*' I recognise alarm in Bill's voice. '*Where the hell are you?*'

'In a restaurant in Granada. Why?'

'*Why!* Because I'm sitting on your doorstep.'

The Author

The author was born in London, where, between bouts of truancy, he was educated, read philosophy and ended up teaching English as a college lecturer. The author's main interests are Indian classical music and travelling. He has spent time in more than one hundred and sixty countries including several years in Spain.

Printed in Great Britain
by Amazon